$ 9 00

D1786992

LOST IN THE CROWD

LOST IN THE CROWD

Jalāl Āl-e Ahmad

Translated by John Green

Introduction by Michael Hillmann

Named Best Translation Accepted for Publication in 1984
by the American Institute of Iranian Studies

First English Language Edition
Three Continents Press
1346 Connecticut Avenue NW
Washington, D.C. 20036

ISBN 0-89410-442-X
0-89410-443-8 (paper)
LC Cataloguing No.: 84-51088

Cover art by Max K. Winkler

Acknowledgments

One of the most interesting translation problems for Āl-e Ahmad's Mecca travel diary is the title itself, *Khasī dar Mīqāt.* No English word has the connotations of the term *Mīqāt*, designating the area containing the shrines at Mecca which are the goal of the Muslim pilgrimage. The term *Khasī* means "a chip of wood" or "a piece of straw." A literal rendition might be "A Chip of Wood Among the Muslim Shrines," but explanation would still be needed for many readers. The translation we have chosen emphasizes Āl-e Ahmad Ahmad's sense of anonymity among the 266,000 pilgrims who were in Mecca when he was. The rest we leave out of the title.

For other translation problems, we are grateful to those who took the time to read the manuscript, to comment, and to answer questions. Among those who did so are Abul Hamid Abumdas, Jamshid Aziz, Michael Hillmann, Ahmad Jabbari, Paridukht Muhtadi, and Gernot Windfuhr. Raymond Stock read the manuscript for stylistic evaluation and gave many useful editorial suggestions. Special thanks for help with the bibliography are due to John Eilts, Michael Hillmann, and Paul Sprachman. We would also like to thank Allin Luther, Ernest McCarus, and Mary Ringia of the University of Michigan's Center for Near Eastern and North African Studies for help in the procurement of text processing resources, and Kari Gluski of the University of Michigan's Computing Center for her friendly and patient assistance with the use of Donald Knuth's TeX, the computer typesetting software used to produce the text of this book.

For those with an interest in transliteration systems, we regret to say that this volume has three: one for Persian, one for Arabic, and another one for Persian terms likely to be searched in libraries. All Arabic terms are transliterated using the the system presented in the American Library Association and Library of Congress Romanization Tables in Cataloging Services Bulletin Number 118 (Summer 1976). Persian terms in the text are transliterated using the system proposed by Naser Sharify in his *Cataloging of Persian Works* (Chicago: American Library Association, 1959). For

Persian terms in the bibliography, the system presented in the American Library Association and Library of Congress Romanization Tables in Cataloging Services Bulletin Number 119 (Fall 1976) is used. The spellings for the names of authors are the ones established by the Library of Congress, and may or may not conform to a particular transliteration system.

John Green

Introduction
by Michael C. Hillmann

Cultural Dilemmas of an Iranian Intellectual*

At the time of his sudden death at forty-six years of age in September 1969, Jalāl Āl-e Ahmad was Iran's best known social critic. During that decade, younger Iranians in the last years of high school and at colleges and universities throughout the country thought of him as the chief spokesperson for non-establishment views, as someone who dared to question Pahlavi government policy to the limits official censors allowed and who served as their conscience with his distinctively direct, forceful, unrelenting criticism of Iranian society in his equally distinctive and much imitated prose style. Among Iranian writers, Āl-e Ahmad was generally acknowledged as the central figure of the day.

In the 1970s, younger Iranians opposed to the Pahlavi monarchy seemed to revere Āl-e Ahmad as a prescient martyr to the cause of intellectual freedom and social revolution. Furthermore, his name was often invoked in 1978 in behalf of the overthrow of the Pahlavi monarchy, a cause many allege he would have wholeheartedly supported. In the early 1980s, the Islamic Republic of Iran approved the naming in Āl-e Ahmad's honor of a section of a new north Tehran boulevard and a high school in the Tajrish neighborhood where he lived from 1953 until his death.

Because of Āl-e Ahmad's accomplishments and influence in a writing career that spanned a quarter of a century and because also of his posthumous reputation, he would seem to deserve attention in any attempt to appreciate contemporary Iran; and no serious inquiry into post-World War II

Iranian intellectual life can be undertaken without considerable attention to him. One important dimension of both such appreciation of contemporary Iran and such analysis of Iranian intellectual life is the subject of this essay: cultural conflicts and dilemmas which thinking Iranians have had to face at least since the Constitutional movement (1906-1911) brought issues of political nationalism, modern secular versus traditional religious values, individual rights of citizens, and the influence of the West in Iranian life, among others, to the center of the Iranian social and political arena. Because in his personality and views Āl-e Ahmad embodied, perhaps uniquely, such conflicts and dilemmas, their description is undertaken here through focus on him as a case study.

The first part of this essay is a thumbnail sketch of Āl-e Ahmad's career as a writer and social critic, which is taken to be more or less typical of Iranian intellectuals in post-World War II Iran. The second part of the essay presents a contrasting biographical sketch of family and personal relationships and experiences which may not be typical per se but which give vivid voice to conflicts and dilemmas common to many Iranian intellectuals. In the essay's third and final section, attention focuses on a single work by Āl-e Ahmad called *Lost in the Crowd*, which seems particularly revealing of cultural conflicts faced by Iranian intellectuals and especially significant today in light of the establishment of the Islamic Republic of Iran in the spring of 1979 and subsequent political developments in Iran. Of course, this whole essay serves specifically as an introduction to the English translation of *Lost in the Crowd.*

1

Al-e Ahmad's career as an intellectual and writer began in the summer of 1943. At that time, as a twenty-year-old Tehran high school graduate, he travelled outside of Iran for the first time, visiting the shrine to Shi'i Moslem Imam Hosayn (d. 680) at Karbala in Iraq. That fall Āl-e Ahmad entered the undergraduate Persian literature program at the Teacher's Training College in Tehran. The following year he joined the Tudeh Party of Iran. Also during the War years Āl-e Ahmad became familiar with the writings of social reformer Ahmad Kasravi, who was assassinated by a member of a Shi'i religious group in 1946, and journalist and social critic Mohammad Mas'ud, who was assassinated in 1947 by a member of the Tudeh Party.

Āl-e Ahmad's first published story was inspired by his 1943 trip. Called "Pilgrimage," it appeared in a spring 1945 issue of *Sokhan*, the best known Iranian literary journal from the war years into the 1970s. Subsequent issues of *Sokhan* featured several other Āl-e Ahmad stories. Then in February 1946, his first book was published, a collection of twelve stories including "Pilgrimage" and these other stories called *The Exchange of Visits.*

The stories in this collection reveal Āl-e Ahmad as especially sensitive to Shi'i Moslem religious customs, laws and superstitions that seemed to him to contribute to the perpetuation of ignorance among the general population and to Iran's helplessness in the face of the Allied Occupation that began in August 1941 and resulted in the deposition and exile of Rezā Shāh Pahlavi (ruled 1925-1941) in favor of his son Mohammad Rezā Shāh Pahlavi (ruled 1941-1979).

Later in 1946, Āl-e Ahmad finished his undergraduate program at the Teacher's College in Tehran. He began his teaching career in 1947 at 24 years of age. Teaching Persian language and literature at the secondary and college levels were to remain Āl-e Ahmad's primary source of income through his whole adult life. He participated in a Ph.D. program in Persian literature at the University of Tehran in the late 1940s, but never submitted his dissertation, which was on the subject of Persian versions of the Thousand and One Nights tales.

By 1946 Jalāl had a reputation as a writer of promise. He participated and received mention in the First Congress of Iranian Writers held at the Iran-USSR Cultural Society in Tehran in the summer of 1946. This reputation led to his becoming an editor of the Tudeh Party's monthly *Mardom* in which capacity he collaborated on fourteen issues. He also spent six months as an editor of the Tudeh Party's publishing house Sho'leh'var. In the latter part of the summer of 1947, after the defeat of the Communists in Azarbayjan, Āl-e Ahmad published a second collection of short stories called *Our Suffering.* If *The Exchange of Visits* shows Āl-e Ahmad as typical of post-World War II writers in emphasizing the value of social commitment in their literary art, the stories in *Our Suffering*, which Āl-e Ahmad later characterized as stories portraying the defeat of leftist movements in Iran with a socialist realist point of view, present an Iranian writer typically subordinating artistic concerns to predetermined messages. Years later, Āl-e Ahmad agreed that these stories were seriously flawed for this reason.

In January 1948, a serious *sécession* took place in the Tudeh Party, with a large group of intellectuals formally breaking with the Party, most prominent among them Khalil Maleki (d. 1969), who subsequently established the Third Force Party (i.e., a force other than America and Russia). These intellectuals later declared that the fact that the party leadership was in the hands of persons following Moscow's directives precipitated the split; whereas their Tudeh Party confreres maintained that the inability of the Maleki faction to achieve control over the party prompted the action. Āl-e Ahmad, who joined Maleki in leaving the Tudeh Party, dedicated a third collection of short stories called *Seh'tar* (1948) to him at a time when Maleki was being vilified in the Tudeh press and on Moscow radio. Āl-e Ahmad viewed this period and Tudeh reaction to the defections as a time of enforced silence. From this period dates a series of translations from French of works by Camus, Dostoevski, Gide, and Sartre to which he was attracted because they seemed relevant to Iranian problems or western concerns with similar problems.

Then, with the oil nationalization issue, the formation of the National Front Movement in which Maleki's Third Force Party was a constituent organization, and the election of Mohammad Mosaddeq to Parliament and his designation as Prime Minister, Āl-e Ahmad again involved himself directly in politics.

In 1950, Āl-e Ahmad married Simin Dāneshvar (b. 1921), then a teacher of art history at the University of Tehran where she remained employed until the mid-1970s. Also a translator and writer of fiction, Dāneshvar authored a novel in 1969 called *The Mourners of Siyāvash* which became perhaps the bestselling Iranian novel ever by the late 1970s. Āl-e Ahmad came to trust Dāneshvar's critical judgment and showed her everything he subsequently wrote before submission to publishers. In addition, because Āl-e Ahmad's anti-establishment views through the 1950s and 1960s often brought official reaction in the form of his temporary suspension from his teaching assignment of the moment, the Āl-e Ahmads needed Dāneshvar's university income.

Āl-e Ahmad's fourth collection of short stories called *The Unwanted Woman* appeared in 1952, featuring a preface by *Sokhan* editor-in-chief Khānlari who had spoken of Āl-e Ahmad's promise as a writer in the 1946 First Congress of Iranian Writers. An expanded edition of *The Unwanted Woman* published in 1964 lacked Khānlari's preface because Āl-e Ahmad disapproved of Khānlari's assumption of important government posts from the mid-1950s onward, a typical reaction of many writers and other intellectuals to those among themselves who chose to work in the upper echelons of the Pahlavi regime.

With the fall of Mosaddeq and his nationalist government in 1953 and the return of Pahlavi monarchical control, Āl-e Ahmad's days of direct political activity ended. Subsequently, he considered writing as a sort of political activity and his pen as a political weapon.

In early 1955, Āl-e Ahmad published his first piece of longer fiction, a "once upon a time" allegory called *Tale of the Beehives* on economic exploitation in general and on the then timely subject of Iranian oil in particular.

Also during the early post-Mosaddeq period, Āl-e Ahmad began to travel a great deal throughout Iran. Other writers shortly followed suit in what seems to have been a Marxist-inspired impulse to get to know the people before trying to influence them to political awareness. In Iran's case, this meant non-urban peoples, over 50% of the population living in more than

65,000 villages. The upshot of Āl-e Ahmad's excursions was the publication of a series of ethnographic articles and monographs on various Iranian locales, among them Yazd, Khorasan, two villages near Qazvin, Khark Island, and the Caspian littoral region of his ancestors called Owrazan. Then in the early 1960s he assumed editorship of a monograph series published by the Institute of Social Studies and Research of the Faculty of Letters of the University of Tehran and supervised five of their publications, among them *Ilkhchi* (1964), a volume on a village in Azarbayjan by Gholāmhosayn Sā'edi (b. 1935), a short story writer and dramatist from Tabriz who was Āl-e Ahmad's most prominent follower and one of his closest friends during the 1960s.

In 1958, Āl-e Ahmad published a second piece of longer fiction called *The School Principal*, a first-person account of most of a school year experienced by a new principal in an elementary school in a newer Tehran neighborhood. As an indictment, however mild, of the Iranian educational system and as a novel concerning middle class life, *The School Principal* was almost unprecedented. Readers saw in it details of their own experience rather than the author's wonted excursions into lower class or village life. With *The School Principal*, Āl-e Ahmad began his most influential years as a writer.

In fiction, Āl-e Ahmad published a second allegory in 1961 called *The Letter 'N' and the Pen*, which was never allowed distribution during the Pahlavi era. It is the story of a religious-political revolution which overthrows a corrupt monarchy, but is ultimately replaced by the return of that monarchy. In the story, which has a pseudo-historical once-upon-a-time setting, Āl-e Ahmad declared he had at least two thematic intents. First, the story is designed to depict the effects historically consequent upon the official linking of the Twelver Shi'i religious establishment and the Iranian monarchical state with the advent of the Safavid Dynasty (1501-1722). The consequence of this, according to Āl-e Ahmad, was the creation of a society no longer willing to suffer for principles and ideals, but preferring to pay lip service to past heroes and martyrs instead. Secondly, Āl-e Ahmad asserts that the novel portrays the course of the defeat of leftist movements in post-World War II Iran.

In the fall of 1962, Āl-e Ahmad clandestinely published a polemic essay called *Weststruckness* which ran through numerous underground printings in subsequent years and became his most popular piece of nonfiction. Actually, the first chapter of *Weststruckness* had appeared in a journal called *Kayhān-e Māh* which began publishing in the spring of 1962. According to Āl-e Ahmad, the journal was banned after two issues because it included the section from *Weststruckness*.

Weststruckness is a forceful, angry polemic secondarily attacking the hollowness and decadence of contemporary western civilization and primarily warning Iranians not to succumb to the disease of adopting western evils. Āl-e Ahmad argues that although Iran and the West have been in conflict for millenia, only in recent centuries has it been an uneven, unequal contest with the dominant West forcing upon Iran treaties, products, educational ideas, and alien cultural values. The essay struck a chord in many Iranian readers who surreptitiously passed around copies of the book, the possession of which in the late 1960s reputedly would earn the owner a certain time in prison. From the vantage point of post-Pahlavi Iran, the special significance of *Weststruckness* lay in Āl-e Ahmad's recognition of two important facts he argues educated urban Iranians were ignoring: first, the role of traditional Shi'i Islamic values as the basic mind set of the vast majority of the Iranian population; and second, Islam's potential as a social and political force in Iran's future.

From the early 1960s onward, Āl-e Ahmad made a number of important trips abroad. Actually his first visit to Europe had been with his wife to Rome in the summer of 1957; but for Āl-e Ahmad it was just sightseeing. In the summer of 1962 he travelled again to Europe, this time sponsored by the Iranian Ministry of Education to study European school textbooks. Then in the spring of 1964, he made the Moslem religious pilgrimage to Mecca called Hajj, the record of which he published in early 1966 with the title *Lost in the Crowd.* This important travel diary is discussed in part three of this essay.

In the summer of 1964 Āl-e Ahmad accepted an invitation to attend the International Congress of Anthropologists in Moscow. Upon his return from the Congress, Āl-e Ahmad presented an oral report to the Iran-USSR Society that was printed later that year in the Society's journal *Payām-e Novin.*

A fourth important trip was his visit to Harvard University during the summer of 1965 to participate in an international writers' conference. In previous summers, his wife Simin and prominent short story writer and novelist Sādeq Chubak (b. 1916) had also participated in the Harvard conference. Āl-e Ahmad prepared a report of this trip as well, which he published a year later in *Jahān-e No* magazine. Then there was a trip to Israel which resulted in a 1967 essay called "Israel: Agent of Imperialism."

All of Āl-e Ahmad's travel reports as well as their nationalist, leftist, somewhat anti-American tone were typical of the non-establishment Iranian writers of the day.

Another important activity of Āl-e Ahmad from the early 1960s onward was his interest in and assistance of younger writers and college students. Typical of a number of prominent literary figures of the day, Āl-e Ahmad attracted and nurtured a following among younger intellectuals some of whom thought of themselves in the Āl-e Ahmad camp as it were. As for his interest in students outside the classroom, Āl-e Ahmad regularly lectured at colleges throughout Iran.

In one important speech Āl-e Ahmad gave to college students in Abadan in 1961, he notes general characteristics of contemporary Persian literature: factionalism, pessimism, humanism, the influence of translations of Western literary works on contemporary Persian literature, the status of Persian literature as an avocation rather than as a profession owing to the limited number of readers, and the inability of writers to support themselves through writing.

In the spring of 1964, Āl-e Ahmad participated in a question-and-answer session with university students in Tabriz, in which among other things he discussed the Iranian tendency to make cultural heroes out of literary figures after their death, but not to hold writers in much respect while they are alive.

In January 1968 at the Faculty of Fine Arts at the University of Tehran, Āl-e Ahmad gave a memorial speech on Nimā Yushij (1895-1960), the "father" of modernist Persian poetry and Āl-e Ahmad's neighbor, stressing Nimā's individualism and perseverance as a pioneer in poetry. Later in 1968, Āl-e Ahmad visited the University of Mashhad where he addressed enthusiastic groups of students. Ne'mat Mirzāzādeh, who organized that visit, recalls Āl-e Ahmad's tirelessness in sitting and talking for hours with students whose own professors generally would not become involved in such informal rap sessions.

The content and flavor of some of Āl-e Ahmad's interactions with students are communicated in chapters of his lengthiest collection of essays, a volume called *Hasty Assessment* (1965) whose publication by a Tabriz press Sā'edi had encouraged. Its eighteen articles also included a number of linguistic and literary critical pieces, as had earlier essay collections *Seven Articles* (1956) and *Three More Articles* (1958). *Hasty Assessment* reveals Āl-e Ahmad as a significant literary critic whose first important critical essay called "The Hedāyat of *The Blind Owl*" appeared shortly after the April 1951 suicide in Paris of Iran's most famous and controversial 20th century author. It was the first of a series of insightful critical testimonials. Among them was "The Old Man Was Our Eyes" on Nimā Yushij, published shortly after the poet's death in January 1960, and "Samad and the Folktale," which appeared in a special Fall 1968 memorial issue of *Ārash* magazine and was a tribute to Samad Behrangi, the Azarbayjani Persian teacher, short story writer, folklorist, and educational reformer who became an Āl-e Ahmad protégé in the mid 1960s and whose elementary Persian textbook designed for speakers of Azarbayjani Turkish Āl-e Ahmad tried unsuccessfully to persuade the Ministry of Education to publish. Altogether, Āl-e Ahmad published some twenty literary and critical essays from the early 1950s onward.

In 1966, Āl-e Ahmad was closely associated with *Jahān-e No* Magazine, that year being edited by Baraheni. Only four issues of the Āl-e Ahmad circle were published. In two of them appeared essays on intellectuals entitled respectively "What and Who Is an Intellectual?" and "Is an Intellectual Native or Foreign?" that later became chapters in Āl-e Ahmad's posthumously published work called *On the Service and Treasonable Activity of Intellectuals* (1978), in which Āl-e Ahmad sketches the history and evaluates the contribution of *rowshanfekr* [intellectual] Iranians to their society. One of the book's most interesting chapters, called "Recent Examples of *Rowshanfekri* [intellectualism]," focuses on the career of and Āl-e Ahmad's association with already cited socialist Khalil Maleki, who had been one of the famous "53 persons" sentenced to prison in 1937 in accordance with terms of a 1931 anti-communist law and became a leading leftist and nationalist theoretician in the 1940s as well as the first signatory to the *sécession* declaration in 1948 from the Tudeh Party, the founder of the Third Force Party, editor of *'Elm va Zendegi* magazine from 1950 until it was banned in 1960, and, according to Āl-e Ahmad, the best possible example of intellectual commitment to social and political progress. Āl-e Ahmad's specific stimulus for focusing on Maleki in this chapter was the early 1966 trial of the latter and several socialist associates accused by the Pahlavi government of seditious activity. Maleki, who had been previously convicted and sentenced to prison several times in post-Mosaddeq Iran, was sentenced this time to three more years in prison. As upsetting as that was for Āl-e Ahmad who saw this 1966 trial as the Pahlavi government's definitive condemnation of socialism and political freedom, what he found more disconcerting about the trial was the reaction of Iranian intellectuals, many of whom were followers of Maleki in the 1940s and 1950s or at least owed him debts as their intellectual mentor. At some trial sessions, Āl-e Ahmad was the only court visitor except for defendants' family members. He wonders why no one else was there to offer at least moral support. The open letters he wrote to *Khāndanihā* magazine asking these and other questions were naturally not published. Āl-e Ahmad's disenchantment at this point with Iranian intellectuals who he assumed had been coopted by the government or were afraid to appear interested in or supportive of Maleki was typical of those writers in the later Pahlavi era who felt that they were firm in their refusal to submit to government inducements or threats.

However, a more serious problem confronted Āl-e Ahmad and other non-establishment writers at this point: a new government censorship system. In 1966, a Pahlavi government directive informed publishers that copies of books in press had thereafter to be approved by a writing bureau at the Ministry of Arts and Culture before the books could be distributed. To register their disapproval of this form of censorship, Āl-e Ahmad, Sā'edi, Baraheni, and several other writers met with Prime Minister Amir 'Abbas

Hovaydā in December 1966. The latter established a committee to investigate the question of censorship with a representative of the writers participating. Regardless, the new censorship system remained in force, which encouraged the writers to think of possible group action.

In late 1967, Āl-e Ahmad spearheaded a drive by anti-establishment writers to boycott a literature symposium planned by the Pahlavi government. Subsequent to their success in having the government's symposium plans aborted and as a means to combat government censorship, they decided to form an organization of writers. In April 1968, the group produced a declaration signed by Āl-e Ahmad, Dāneshvar, leading modernist poets Ahmad Shāmlu (b. 1925) and Nāder Nāderpur (b. 1929), Sā'edi, Baraheni, and some forty-six others. In this fashion, the Association of Writers of Iran came into being for the express purpose of guaranteeing writers' rights against government censorship. But because these writers had no real leverage with the government in the form of broad-based readership or in the form of services of theirs the government might need, the organization did not prove very influential or effective except as a moral rallying force for its members. And, it ceased to function for all intents and purposes when Āl-e Ahmad died in September 1969. In the spring of 1979, after the fall of the Pahlavi monarchy, the organization reemerged and functioned thereafter for a year or more, during which time six issues of its journal called *Nāmeh-ye Kānun-e Nevisandegān-e Irān* appeared, the first of which featured a 50-page memorial section on Āl-e Ahmad. In 1981, the Islamic Republic of Iran suppressed the organization and its publication. Organization member Sa'id Soltānpur, a political activist and minor poet and dramatist, was executed by the Khomayni government in June 1981 for "warring against Allāh." Subsequently an Organization of Writers of Iran in Exile was established in Paris, but without the participation (as of mid-1984) of any significant Iranian literary figures except Sā'edi.

In early 1968 Āl-e Ahmad published his fourth and lengthiest novel called *The Cursing of the Earth*, which like *The School Principal* is a story with a protagonist and incidents that are essentially autobiographical. The action focuses on the Pahlavi land redistribution program of the 1960s, which was the cornerstone of a wide-ranging government program of reform officially termed "The White Revolution." *The Cursing of the Earth* recounts a year in the life of a school teacher in a village where the new Pahlavi agricultural system fails and the villagers lose their traditional roots and sense of identity as well. The novel was unavailable in bookstores until 1978 during the last days of the Pahlavi monarchy, although two chapters of the novel had appeared earlier in *Andisheh va Honar* and *Ārash* magazines. The expression in *The Cursing of the Earth* of a sense of loss of roots taking place during the later Pahlavi era became a commonplace among non-establishment writers.

Equally significant is a comparison of the outcomes of Āl-e Ahmad's four novels, which seem to indicate an increasing sense of pessimism typical of post-Mosaddeq intellectuals. In other words, the protagonists become progressively or ultimately passive as modern individuals vis-à-vis political force and oppression. In *Story of the Beehives* (1955), the bees decide to return to their ancestral home. In *The School Principal* (1958), the title character renounces corrupt society and prefers to preserve innocence by retreating to his individuality. In *The Letter 'N' and the Pen* (1961), 'Abdozzaki goes to India to escape the returned monarchy, and Asadollāh goes to the desert to live a solitary dervish life. The cynical teacher protagonist in *The Cursing of the Earth* (1968) also takes leave of the village once it is in disarray. Anti-establishment intellectuals in general became progressively pessimistic about social progress in Iran during the post-Mosaddeq 1950s and 1960s.

Shortly before his own death at Esalem, a Caspian littoral village on the road between Enzeli and Astara where the Āl-e Ahmads had a summer cottage which he had built himself, Āl-e Ahmad returned to Tehran to attend the funeral of Khalil Maleki, his political leader and ally of twenty years earlier. It was his last relatively public appearance.

On September 8, 1969, according to Dāneshvar, Āl-e Ahmad complained in the morning of severe pain in his neck. Regardless, he busied himself with repairing the chimney in their cottage. He was planning a trip to Tehran the following week and to come back to Esalem with Sā'edi—the two of them were going to spend some time studying Tāti-speakers in the area. He did not have to worry about returning to Tehran for the beginning of the academic year because he knew he was to be suspended once again from teaching duties, this time from the Nārmak Technical School, as a result of his writings and speeches. He took a shower at noontime. After lunch, he took a nap, complaining in mid-afternoon of feeling very cold. Then he went to a friend's house for a half hour or so, stayed outside talking, and returned home pale and complaining of pain from his legs to his chest and from one wrist and arm to the other. He decided to go to bed. Simin went for the doctor. When she returned, Āl-e Ahmad was dead.

The local doctor and the Āl-e Ahmad's family physician determined the cause of death as a heart attack. Simin herself accepted this diagnosis at the time and wrote about it in her 1981 essay called "Jalāl's Dusk." But Jalāl's younger brother Shams, who rushed to Esalem from Tehran when told of Jalāl's death and who investigated its circumstances, became convinced that the Pahlavi government assassinated Jalāl. Other anti-establishment writers and intellectuals shared this view. For example, Baraheni tried to draw attention in the English-speaking world to alleged Pahlavi government crimes through citation of Āl-e Ahmad's death as an example. He announced in a 1976 collection of his verse in English: "This book is dedicated to Jalāl Āl-e Ahmad, *friend, killed*... Then, in his *The Crowned Cannibals: Writings on Repression in Iran* (1976, 1977), Baraheni asserts: "During the Shah's... reign dozens of writers have been liquidated:... Jalāl Āl-e Ahmad, one of the most formidable writers of oppositionist literature in Iran, who was mysteriously killed on the coast of the Caspian Sea... "

Even Dāneshvar in a 1983 interview wavers in her original view, responding as follows to a question about her husband's death: "They tormented Jalāl so much he eventually died of frustration. The harassment by SAVAK and the constant suspensions from teaching were the cause of his premature death. However, as to whether or not they actually killed him I don't know, I'm not certain. If they did, it was so expertly done I was unaware."

The popular attitude about Āl-e Ahmad's death, for which there is no compelling evidence, is the same attitude which anti-establishment Iranians have held with respect to the deaths of wrestling champion and popular hero Gholāmrezā Takhti (1930-1968), Samad Behrangi (1939-1968), and 'Ali Shari'ati (1933-1977), among others. In short, the extent of fear and cynicism many Iranians felt about the Pahlavi government and its security arm SAVAK was such that almost any death of an opposition figure in circumstances other than extreme old age was assumed to be an assassination.

Back in Tehran, several thousand people accompanied Āl-e Ahmad's casket from his family's home to the cemetery. Friend and associate Eslām Kāzemiyeh recalls how upset the mourners were, mostly people who thought they were truly Āl-e Ahmad's friends because he often had that effect on people he met: he listened to whatever was told him, was genuinely curious about others' personal situations and problems, and remembered such facts about people the next time he saw them. On behalf of the Association of Writers of Iran, Nāder Nāderpur presented the eulogy at graveside. The Iranian print media were full of expressions of grief and remembrances. On the evening of the 7th day after his death, at services at Firuzābādi Mosque, Sā'edi and Baraheni spoke.

For the traditional 40th day of mourning, Simin Dāneshvar, Shams Āl-e Ahmad, Gholāmhosayn Sā'edi, Eslām Kāzemiyeh, Manuchehr Hezārkhāni, and several others traveled to Mashhad, where Ne'mat Mirzāzādeh made arrangements for memorial services at both Hāj Mollā Hosayn Mosque and the Faculty of Letters at the University of Mashhad. He recalls not telling the mourning party or anyone else of the location of the first service until shortly before it was to begin out of fear that SAVAK might decide to have it cancelled. Shari'ati was the only university professor to participate in the service at the Faculty of Letters at Mashhad University.

But once the Mashhad services were over, the government refused to give permission for further memorial services. And much less writing on

Āl-e Ahmad appeared from then until the late 1970s than might have been expected, except for annual remembrances on the anniversary of his death. From 1977, when censorship began to relax, through the early years of the Islamic Republic of Iran, a great deal of writing on Āl-e Ahmad appeared.

Of all the eulogies and elegies, remembrances and articles, perhaps the most artful was the 1969 poem by then leading modernist poet Ahmad Shāmlu (b. 1925) called "Anthem for the Bright Man Who Went into the Shadows," presented here in poet Esmā'il Kho'i's translation:

Contentment-like
he was thin:
slim and tall
like a difficult message
in one word

And with eyes
of question
and honey;
and with a face scorched
by truth
and wind.

A man with the whirling of water:
a laconic man
who was his own resumé.
Beetles stare at your corpse with suspicion.

◇ ◇ ◇

Before being turned to ashes
by the wrath of the thunderbolt
he had forced the steer of the tempest
to kneel before his might.

To test
the faiths of old
he had worn out his teeth
on the locks of ancient gates
On the most out-of-the-way paths
he struggled
an unexpected passerby
whose voice every thicket and bridge recognized.

◇ ◇ ◇

Roads remain wakeful with the memory of your steps;

for you were going to welcome the day:
although the dawn
emitted you
before
the cocks heralded morning.

◇ ◇ ◇

A bird bloomed in its wings,
a woman in her breasts,
a garden in its trees.
We bloom in your angry look,
in your haste.
We bloom in your brook,
in defending your smile
that is certitude and faith.

◇ ◇ ◇

The sea envies you
for the drop you have drunk
from the well.

2

The foregoing sketch of Āl-e Ahmad's career as a writer and social critic presents a picture of an active, conscientious intellectual whose concerns were the exact issues that one would in retrospect expect an Iranian intellectual to have addressed during the post-World-War II era, among them: westernization and modernization, Pahlavi regime superficiality, inefficiency and corruption, Iranian identity and national integrity in a modern world, the role of religion in contemporary Iranian life, and the social responsibilities of Iranian writers and other intellectuals.

However, a contrasting side to Āl-e Ahmad emerges in the characterization of personal dimensions of his life as recorded in autobiographical material in his published works and corroborated by the recollections of acquaintances. This other Āl-e Ahmad is full of conflict, contradiction, and dilemmas which seem to be the common lot, to one degree or another, of the majority of Iranian intellectuals of his and subsequent generations. Not that Āl-e Ahmad was especially typical of Iranian intellectuals in general or that other intellectuals of his and subsequent generations agreed with many of his views. Nonetheless, the conflicts particular to his personal life are both typical and singularly revealing of conflicts in Iranian society today.

Sayyed Jalāloddin Sādāt Āl-e Ahmad was born into a religious family from the village of Owrazan in the Caspian province of Gilan. The Āl-e Ahmad family was closely related to prominent Shi'i cleric Āyatollāh Hājj Sayyed Mahmud Tāleqāni (1910-1979), an opposition figure imprisoned several times during the Pahlavi era. Āl-e Ahmad's father, his older brother, two brothers-in-law, and a nephew were all Shi'i clerics. The family referred to themselves as *sayyeds*; that is, they claimed to be direct descendants of the Moslem prophet Mohammad (ca. 570-622). Incidentally, "Jalāl," the first name which Āl-e Ahmad used throughout his adult years, was really a shortened form of "Jalāloddin," [splendor of religion].

Jalāl was born after one brother and seven sisters, only four of the latter living through mature years. His younger brother Shams, actually "Shamsoddin" [sun of religion], also a writer, has been primarily responsible for making Āl-e Ahmad's writings available from the 1970s onward, which he has been able to do because of close ties with the Islamic Republic of Iran.

By Āl-e Ahmad's own account, his early childhood years were spent in the relatively luxurious environment of an important Tehran cleric's home. But when the Ministry of Justice during the reign of Rezā Shāh Pahlavi (1925-1941) began regulating and bureaucratizing registry operations, Jalāl's father refused to participate. He thereafter functioned unofficially as an *āqā-ye mahall* [neighborhood religious elder] responsible for leading the community noon prayer at the local mosque, preaching sermons, and attending to other religious needs of the neighborhood.

Āl-e Ahmad's father was a stern, demanding patriarch who treated his wife and children as his inferiors. He cursed and swore at them when irritated. The whole family, which did its best not to displease him, seems to have thought of this minor religious figure as a man of great importance. In turn, he seems to have had a sense of self-importance. None of his children was apparently ever able to talk intimately with their father whose first wife gave birth to thirteen children altogether. He also married a second wife who died before his first wife died. In addition, he had at least one *sigheh* [temporary wife] as described below.

When Āl-e Ahmad was twelve or thirteen years of age and in the 6th grade, an incident occurred at home that created a lasting impression on him. One day the mailman delivered a printed invitation to "Mr. and Mrs. Āl-e Ahmad" to attend a party commemorating the anniversary of Rezā Shāh Pahlavi's 1936 banning of the chador veil traditionally worn by Iranian women. Āl-e Ahmad's father became angry at receiving such an invitation and told his son to inform the people at the mosque he would not be coming that day because he was not feeling well, and also to tell his uncle to stop by the house. Whan Jalāl's mother interrupted to suggest that he be allowed to eat some lunch before going on the errand, the father replied: "You loudmouth. Are you interfering in my affairs again? Now I've got to take you to a reception, bare-headed and bare-bottomed."

After returning home with his uncle, Jalāl left for school. He always had to get to school before the other boys because of a special problem he faced as a stern cleric's son. The government rule stated that boys had to wear short pants at school. Because Jalāl's father was against the policy, his mother sewed buttons inside his trouser pantlegs so that he could walk to school in long pants and then, before the other boys and the principal reached school, tuck and button the bottom half of his long pants up so they would become short pants.

After school that day, Jalāl had to take firewood to the bath in the Āl-e Ahmads' home, which his father had installed right after Rezā Pahlavi outlawed chadors so that his wife would not have to leave the house without a chador to go to a public bath. Jalāl did not like the chore, which was almost an everyday occurrence since all the family's female relatives had started coming to Jalāl's house to bathe rather than go to a public bath.

That night Jalāl's father again did not go to the mosque. Someone knocked on the courtyard door. Jalāl opened it. There was a military officer and behind him a young woman in high heeled shoes with only a small kerchief on her head. It was the first time a woman had ever entered their house without a chador.

Jalāl heard bits and pieces of the grownups' conversation. The young lady was to become his father's temporary wife for two hours so he could take her to the reception and not have to take his long-time wife without a chador.

A second, more serious experience for Āl-e Ahmad was the death of his older sister at age 35. She was married but childless and thus had to give permission to her husband to marry again and subsequently put up with a rival wife at home. Then she becomes ill, in fact is stricken with breast cancer. Her husband, whom Jalāl never liked, brings her back to her parents' home. She is bedridden, but has refused to submit to a medical examination and treatment by a male physician on the grounds that it would constitute a religious impropriety. Instead, she finally submits to a home remedy. One day Jalāl is sent to the bazaar to bring back a bucket of lead fillings. After he brings them home, not understanding how they are to be used, a local woman expert in folk remedies places them red hot on Jalāl's sister's breasts. She dies.

After Jalāl finished elementary school, his father sent him to work in the bazaar as an apprentice in watch and electrical repair, and leather goods. At night, Jalāl attended Dārolfonun, Tehran's most important secondary school. In 1943, he finished high school, having kept at electrical repair work on the side with one of his brothers-in-law.

Then came the trip to Karbala. Apparently Āl-e Ahmad's father and the other clerics in the family were hoping that Jalāl would be inspired to pursue theological studies and follow in their footsteps. But a misunderstanding between father and son ensued, with Āl-e Ahmad breaking off relations with his father some time after this return to Tehran. Āl-e Ahmad stopped praying and otherwise observing Moslem regulations at this time, during his first years at college. Also connected with this break from religion is the mysterious death of his older brother, the cleric who became Āyatollāh Borujerdi's representative in Mecca for two years and died there. His brother's death stayed on Āl-e Ahmad's mind as much if not more than his sister's.

Such a sequence of events in Āl-e Ahmad's life may imply for some readers that his involvement as a young man in Marxist activities and a secular life-style may have been less the result of reasoned intellectual choices than the need to express his independence and rejection of his father's Shi'i traditionalism. According to his good friend and follower of the 1960s Sā'edi, Āl-e Ahmad was never able to shake his attachment to his traditional religious upbringing despite his efforts, in part inspired by his break with his father, to become a secular intellectual, writer, and social critic. At the same time, however, Sā'edi does not think that Āl-e Ahmad at any time in his adult life was deeply religious, or, for that matter, believed in Allāh, the Shi'i Imams, or heaven and hell. Rather, as a response to increasing Pahlavi control over Iranian life during the 1960s with the manifold threats that Pahlavi westernization posed for Iranian cultural identity, Āl-e Ahmad saw in Shi'i Islam a cultural banner that might be waved as a rallying point, as a means of assuring cultural survival. In the same fashion, according to Sā'edi, Āl-e Ahmad was not an advocate of Ruhollāh Khomayni's political ideas, even though Āl-e Ahmad travelled to Qom in 1963 to see Khomayni and present him with a copy of *Weststruckness* and even though he included the text of Khomayni's famous October 1964 speech (which Āl-e Ahmad asserts was the specific cause of Khomayni's exile) in the *Addenda* to *On the Service and Treasonable Activity of Intellectuals.* Rather, according to Sā'edi, Āl-e Ahmad saw in Khomayni merely the strength of opposition to the Pahlavi regime.

In short, the first dilemma Āl-e Ahmad faced in his life and career was between a possible lack of personal faith in Shi'i Islam and his assertion of its deleterious effects as an institution and traditional force in Iranian society and culture, on the one hand, and the unifying power which Shi'i Islam could represent for the country of Iran as well as religion's potential strength as both a check to absolute monarchical control and a bulwark against the threats the West posed for the future existence of Iranian culture. If Āl-e Ahmad never resolved his personal sense of dilemma in this regard, one can say that the attempts at resolution by Iranian society at large have been equally unsuccessful: i.e., the pendulum swings of Pahlavi secularization and westernization and the Khomayni theocracy.

Critic Baraheni, another Āl-e Ahmad friend and follower during the 1960s, views Āl-e Ahmad's break from his family, his Tudeh Party years, and, for that matter, the other important events of his adult life as a series of attempted escapes on Āl-e Ahmad's part from patriarchal forces: first from his patriarchal religious family, second from the patriarchy of the Central Committee of the Tudeh Party, and third from patriarch Khalil Maleki. But ultimately, according to Baraheni, Āl-e Ahmad himself became in the 1960s that from which he had expended so much energy earlier trying to escape. In Baraheni's words, "I met Jalāl when he was about forty years old, but when he talked with those about him, you'd think he was eighty... he perforce thought of younger writers around him as his own children. The behavior which his father had displayed in the family toward him (commands and prohibitions), and the behavior which the Tudeh Party exhibited toward its members... Āl-e Ahmad transferred to his association with younger writers around him." Baraheni seems thus to be agreeing in his psychological analysis with Sā'edi's view that Āl-e Ahmad remained a prisoner of his background and upbringing. Although both views are interesting in that they come from persons very sympathetic to Āl-e Ahmad, they are no more than speculation in areas in which Āl-e Ahmad has himself discussed his sense of the situation rather straightforwardly, especially in *A Stone on a Grave* and *Lost in the Crowd.* Readers of this essay can let Āl-e Ahmad speak for himself as they read *Lost in the Crowd.*

Next to his distinctive religious upbringing, his falling out with his father, and his inner conflict with his inherited traditions, the most important subsequent event and permanently influential feature of Āl-e Ahmad's intellectual character was Marxism. The list of writers and intellectuals of Āl-e Ahmad's generation to flirt with Marxism or join the Tudeh Party is almost endless, among them: Mehdi Akhavān-e Sāles, Bozorg 'Alavi, M.E. Beh'āzin, Hushang Ebtehāj, Ebrāhim Golestān, Nāder Nāderpur, Siyāvash Kasrā'i, and Ahmad Shāmlu. But if it turned out to be a stage, it nevertheless had lasting effects on such writers as Āl-e Ahmad. Or in other words, they never outgrew it and its clear, black-and-white analysis of issues that rendered their judgments almost invariably simplistic and politically naive in comparison with the real live issues of the day in Iranian society. Moreover, the contradiction between Iranian nationalist aims and pro-Moscow values became evident in the Azarbayjan crisis when many intellectuals abandoned the Moscow alignment then represented by Tudeh Party leadership. Still they seemed not ever to abandon the half-digested philosophy of Marxism which for Iran's heterogeneous agrarian society may never have been an appropriate framework.

In any case, Āl-e Ahmad's youthful experience with Marxism left him with at least two symptoms. He had an almost paranoic fear of material comfort and aversion to people of wealth, as if wealth might somehow corrupt him or render him useless. Ironically, he and his wife were self-conscious about their limited means and referred constantly in print to money problems and in disparaging terms to their home, summer cottage, and other possessions. Throughout the 1960s, Tehran intellectuals remained sensitive to references to their being bourgeois. A second symptom was Āl-e Ahmad's suspicion of things American. As late as 1967, he refused an invitation to speak at Tehran's Iran-America Society precisely because it was American, although he felt no such aversion to speaking at the Russian equivalent in Tehran three years earlier.

A minor writer in the next generation who viewed the figures in Āl-e Ahmad's generation from close-up during the 1960s, Goli Taraqqi (b. 1939), asserts categorically that Āl-e Ahmad and his contemporaries just could not ever get over or rise above either their family origins or Tudeh Party experiences. In her view, they will take both as cultural baggage to their graves.

If his religious upbringing and Marxist reaction to it can be assigned to his youth, Āl-e Ahmad's most important decision as an adult was his marriage at twenty-seven to Simin Dāneshvar, according to whom they were friends, lovers, confidants, and kindred spirits during their nineteen years together. Āl-e Ahmad himself refers to Simin over and over again in his writings as a partner. But he also represents her in other ways in print that seem to belie culture-specific attitudes toward women. For example, in his 1968 autobiographical essay, Āl-e Ahmad matter-of-factly observes on the aftermath of leftist defeats in Iranian politics: "Also during this period I got married. When one comes up short in the big world, you build a smaller one with the four walls of a house. Flight from the paternal home to the society of the Party and from that to one's own home." He intimates that he got married as something one does when one loses in the grand arena: one establishes control or victory in the smaller arena of domestic life; i.e., one gets a wife.

But here too, if one can surmise on the basis of Āl-e Ahmad's own writings, there was a conflict in Āl-e Ahmad of cultural significance. One is struck, for example, at the role played by the title character's wife in the presumably autobiographical novel *The School Principal.* The first person narrator-protagonist describes most of a school year in which he serves as a new school principal in a relatively new elementary school. Home is not part of the narration, and his wife is unmentioned until the crisis of the novel occurs: a rape of a smaller boy by a larger boy. Then the reader sees the protagonist, who has lost control for a moment and badly beaten the sodomizer, going home to a protecting, domestic wife who is there behind the door to offer him a cigarette and solace. One wonders if this traditionally raised Āl-e Ahmad can have thought of any woman as an equal in public.

Another illustration of this conflict in Āl-e Ahmad is offered in his reported disapproval of Iran's most important poetess in history, Forugh Farrokhzād (1935-1967), whose attempt to live an independent life of her own and to reveal her feelings and thoughts in writing in an open, natural way would seem to parallel Āl-e Ahmad's own goals for himself. Only Āl-e Ahmad thought that Farrokhzād was using sexuality in her verse and her sex in life sensationally, that is to gain attention as a poet. Āl-e Ahmad, who thus apparently was unable to accept the same outspokenness and individualistic behavior on the part of a woman that he exhibited in his own personality, seems to exemplify culture-specific male chauvinism and double standards that the poet-critic Mahmud Āzād Tehrani asserts were typical of Tehran intellectuals of the day. Āl-e Ahmad admits an awareness of shortcomings in this regard in the posthumously published essay on the childishness of his marriage called *A Stone On a Grave*. There he asserts that there are really two men in his personality. One is an educated, modern mid-20th century social critic and writer. The other is "an eastern man, full of tradition and history and desires, all of them in accordance with religious and common law. My father was one, and so was my [older] brother. My brothers-in-law are [eastern men] too, and so are my neighbors and my fellow teachers and cabinet ministers and every merchant and villager. Even the Shāh. And all in accordance with religious regulations and common law."

As described in detail in *A Stone On a Grave* (a volume whose publication in 1981 by Shams Āl-e Ahmad surprised Simin Dāneshvar because Jalāl had apparently not intended for it to appear without rewriting which he did not apparently live to undertake), Āl-e Ahmad discovered after two or three years of marriage that his sperm count was too low for Simin to conceive. After attempts at diverse remedies and recourse to experts of all sorts, Āl-e Ahmad learned that he might be able to father a child with a woman other than Simin, or at least the chances of pregnancy would be enhanced in sexual relations with other women, younger women in particular. According to Āl-e Ahmad, at this point, the "eastern man" in him—Mohammad Rezā Shāh Pahlavi took a third wife because his first two were not able to produce a male heir for him—felt that being a father, the father of a male child, took precedence over any considerations (on the part of the modern man in him) of his wife's rights, feelings, or needs. Āl-e Ahmad proceeded to reveal that during his 1962 trip to Europe he had sexual relations with a stewardess in Switzerland, a girl he picked up on a street in Hannover, and a recent divorcée his own age who after a week with Āl-e Ahmad in Amsterdam accompanied him to London for ten days. He told this woman at their parting that he would marry her if she should happen to get pregnant, which she did not.

Baraheni sees the personal revelations in *A Stone On a Grave* and *One Well and Two Pits*, another posthumously published essay describing Āl-e Ahmad's errors in judging people, as an indication that "with respect to himself, Jalāl was more courageous than many other writers. Iranian writers are afraid to admit to their own weaknesses... Jalāl... had the courage to confront the moral problems in his own life." Other Iranian intellectuals, however, have found the revelations in *A Stone On a Grave* foolish, pathetic, or embarrassing. Dāneshvar's judgment is that the book is a valuable account, its ultimate nihilism being particularly remarkable. It proved too controversial for the Islamic Republic of Iran, which finally banned it. In any case, the fact of such cultural conflicts in Āl-e Ahmad is the point to these comments on *A Stone On a Grave*; the conflicts themselves and what Dāneshvar calls Āl-e Ahmad's nihilism in attempting to resolve them are illustrated further in *Lost in the Crowd*, discussed below.

By the late 1950s, Āl-e Ahmad's attention had focused on the modernization and westernization that the Pahlavi monarchy promoted as its basic economic and social program for Iran. The upshot of his thinking on the subject was *Weststruckness*, a monograph that circulated clandestinely throughout Iran from 1962 to the end of the Pahlavi era and was the best known non-fictional work of the age. Aside from important thematic thrusts enumerated earlier, *Weststruckness* sheds special light on several important conflicts and dilemmas in Āl-e Ahmad's thinking and personality that were common to many Iranian intellectuals in the 1960s.

First and foremost is Āl-e Ahmad's conspiratorial view of history and international affairs. For example, he asserts that "Behind the scenes of every riot, coup d'état or uprising in Zanzibar, Syria, or Uruguay, one must look to see what plot by what colonist company or government backing it, lies hidden." For Āl-e Ahmad, the world, especially the third world and its markets, are manipulated by the White House and the Kremlin. He does not share the still popular Iranian view that behind the White House lurks still dominant and insidious British power. Moreover, since Āl-e Ahmad argues in various contexts that the potential political force of Islam in Iran should not be overlooked, he might not have subscribed to a view current among some Iranian professionals and intellectuals that the West engineered the overthrow of the Pahlavi monarchy and the establishment of the Islamic Republic of Iran both because Mohammad Rezā Pahlavi was behaving independently and because an Islamic Republic might serve more dependably as a barrier against Soviet expansionism. In any case, the dilemma for Āl-e Ahmad is that he refuses to suggest that Iran submit to such external power even when he argues that it is almost limitless.

Second, Āl-e Ahmad voices disgust at what he sees as a sense of inferiority on the part of his fellow countrymen vis-à-vis the West. However, in his own representation of fear of machines and his constant recourse to western works and figures for buttressing his arguments, Āl-e Ahmad seems not immune to these same feelings himself.

Third, Āl-e Ahmad exhibits a typical division between Pahlavi era intellectuals or educated people in general who received their education in Iran as opposed to those who received it abroad. As a member of the former group, Āl-e Ahmad is suspicious of the latter group, sensitive about his own limited acquaintance with foreign languages, and xenophobic, as a foreign-trained Iranian might not be, about foreign goods and western machinery. Throughout the 1960s, these two groups were often at odds, not being able to unite in pleas for social reform and progress. Āl-e Ahmad argues, fourthly, that for Iran to emerge from its weststruck situation, it has itself to be a master of machines; but that ironically may lead Iran in his view to the diseased, machine-struck situation in which he feels the West is mired, the situation he argues that Camus is describing allegorically in *The Plague* and Eugène Ionesco in *Rhinocéros*. But he asserts that there is more to the diseased condition of the West than this in concluding *Weststruckness* by drawing parallels between Ingmar Bergman's *The Seventh Seal* and his view that "when the age of faith ends it will usher in a time of punishment. When the age of belief ends there will be an era of experimentation. Experimentation will lead in turn to the atomic bomb." Fifth, Āl-e Ahmad implies that traditional religious values may be the last bastion against Weststruckness, but argues that religion itself has perpetuated superstition, ignorance, and the like.

However, the ultimate dilemma for Āl-e Ahmad in *Weststruckness* is that he does not know what to do or suggest. He asks: "Should we close the doors of our lives to machines and technology and withdraw into the distant past, with national and religious traditions? Or is there a third alternative?" The answer to his rhetorical question is hardly an answer at all; he says: "A third alternative... which cannot be avoided is to put the genie of machines back in his bottle and make him work for us, like a beast of burden... Machines are a means... The aim is to eliminate poverty and to see to the spiritual and material welfare of all of humanity."

Āl-e Ahmad's *Weststruckness* does not stand up well to scholarly scrutiny. One critic in the mid-1960s rightly pointed out that Iranian culture had for 1,400 years been more essentially altered by *'arabzadegi* [Arabstruckness] in the form of religious and linguistic influence than by weststruckness in the 20th century. Historian Faridun Ādamiyat, writing in the late 1970s, demonstrates the tenuousness of many of Āl-e Ahmad's historical arguments. But the fact remains that *Weststruckness* struck a chord in the minds of many educated Iranians—the book warned of real dangers. As for its shortcomings in the context of its value, an interview I had with an Iranian writer in Paris provides the fairest view.

One Saturday morning in June 1984, I was sitting talking with Eslām Kāzemiyeh (b. 1932), a former high school student, follower, and colleague of Āl-e Ahmad's, about the emotional conflicts and contradictions in the latter's personality and writings. There was not a little irony in the facts that Kāzemiyeh was now working for the Amini-Bakhtiyār coalition which began supporting the elder son of Mohammad Rezā Pahlavi as the Shāh of Iran and the wished-for successor to the Islamic Republic of Iran and that we were having our conversation at Deux Magots Café on Boulevard St. Germain in Paris, three tables away from where Jean-Paul Sartre used to sit. Sartre, of course, introduced Āl-e Ahmad to many of his dilemmas: social responsibilities of the writer, non-Moscow aligned communism and socialism, literature and society issues. Kāzemiyeh was saying that Āl-e Ahmad's strident, belligerent, negative voice was actually a life-long cry for help. Then Kāzemiyeh took out a felt-tipped pen and on a napkin drew likenesses of Notre Dame Cathedral, Place de la Concorde, Arc de Triomphe, and the La Defense complex along a single horizontal axis. He talked about there being 400 years between Notre Dame and La Defense, observing that the French people at least had that amount of time to proceed from Notre Dame and what it symbolizes to Place de La Concorde, Arc de Triomphe, and finally to La Defense. He then drew an x on the diagram between Notre Dame and La Defense and a curved line around it. This, he said, was Āl-e Ahmad, reaching for the 21st century, but having had to leap from the 16th century or earlier without the benefit of time and gradual stages in between. As he fell in the abyss, he at least screamed with articulate despair to let those who would follow know what lay in front of them.

Consequently, Āl-e Ahmad may deserve special respect: he set out from the shores of the traditional past when he need not have; and he struggled to reach today while maintaining his Iranianness, which he likewise need not have. Many other intellectuals have avoided such a fall to the depths by renouncing traditions or by in effect abandoning them. The journey Āl-e Ahmad took, one that one can take only alone, so to speak, he describes from his earliest short stories to his latest essays. But nowhere is the description more pointed and the cries more gripping than in *Lost in the Crowd.*

3

The crux of Āl-e Ahmad's cultural conflicts and dilemmas was obviously Twelver Shi'i Islam which, as a result of serving as the basis of the religious state established with the Islamic Republic of Iran in the spring of 1979, is at the cultural vortex for all Iranian intellectuals. In the most simplistic terms, the culturally nationalistic Iranian intellectual is caught in a dilemma. An Iranian religious solution by which fear of mortality and individual insignificance can be assuaged means acceptance of Islam, a religion of 7th century Arab invaders. A secular modern solution, whether stressing the significance of the individual or that of one's society, means acceptance of western orientations toward life, human perfectibility, progress, and the like. As Akhavān-e Sāles implies in "The Ending of the *Shahnāmeh*," Iranians may thus be people after their time who, with their own history and culture weighing heavily on their shoulders, cannot turn to available balms because they may be traitorous to Iranianness.

The politically nationalistic Iranian intellectual faces an equally harsh dilemma, with potentially much greater prices to pay for his or her convictions. The secular nationalist is obliged to make use of western forms of speaking and writing and to hope for some western sophistication in his or her audience in attempting through non-native media to decry the very sources of that media. Then the very concepts involved in secular political nationalism are not only western but little appreciated by the bulk of the Iranian population if popular support of the Islamic Republic of Iran during its first five years is any indication.

Āl-e Ahmad's case, as the foregoing sketch of family and personal relationships and experiences shows, is both especially significant and relevant to post-Pahlavi Iran. For in honoring his memory, the Islamic Republic implicitly imputes anachronistic sympathy for its policies on Āl-e Ahmad's part. At the same time, some anti-Khomayni intellectuals assert that Āl-e Ahmad was somehow instrumental in paving the way for the Islamic Republic of Iran. For example, an October 1982 report in the Paris-based anti-Khomayni weekly *Irān va Jahān* on the subject of attention given in Iranian newspapers to the 13th anniversary of Āl-e Ahmad's death reads in part: "*E'tesām Magazine* writes about Āl-e Ahmad—'He was a Marxist, then [he found] socialism and after that [he was] in the National Front Organization, but ultimately he realized that his lost soul belonged in righteous Islam, period. He tried to become alienated from himself and drown himself in the abyss of intellectualism. With the motivation of the confrontation of his pure Islamic mentality and his authentic Islamic nature he returned to his true self.' Alas that Āl-e Ahmad did not live to see the exaltation of his beloved [Islamic] culture."

Simin Dāneshvar herself has lent credence to speculation about Āl-e Ahmad's hypothetical approval of the Islamic Republic of Iran by asserting that her husband toward the end of his life "turned to religion... [as] the result of his wisdom and insight because he had previously experimented with Marxism, socialism, and, to some extent, existentialism... his relative return to religion and the Hidden Imam was a way toward deliverance from the evil of imperialism and toward the preservation of national identity, a way toward human dignity, compassion, justice, reason, and virtue. Jalāl had need of such a religion." In other words, Āl-e Ahmad may have found a resolution to his cultural conflicts and dilemmas in Shi'i Islam. Perhaps Dāneshvar's view implies something less than such a resolution; but the popular view, held by some admirers and most detractors of Āl-e Ahmad alike, is that he found answers in religion during his last years, answers to personal, cultural, social, and political questions and dilemmas.

The ultimate judgment as to Āl-e Ahmad's religiosity, or better, how Twelver Shi'i Islam may ultimately have figured in any resolution of conflicts and dilemmas described to this point in this essay, ought to be based in large measure on the most directly religious of his writings, *Lost in the Crowd*. One of his last major works, this 1966 essay has been mentioned several times to this point as being particularly significant in several regards.

A record of Āl-e Ahmad's two-week trip to Saudi Arabia in April 1964 as a pilgrim in the Hajj religious pilgrimage, and interestingly a book that even the most critical of Āl-e Ahmad's contemporaries find particularly appealing, *Lost in the Crowd* is particularly significant in literary terms: as a *safarnāmeh* [travel diary], it is the most prominent example of a traditional Persian literary form that goes back at least to Nāser Khosrow (1004—ca. 1088), the important literary figure and Isma'ili propagandist whom Āl-e Ahmad mentions several times in *Lost in the Crowd*. Nāser Khosrow's *Safarnāmeh*, which describes its author's seven-year travels begun in 1045 and including five pilgrimages to Mecca, has served as a model for Persian *safarnāmeh*s for nearly a thousand years. In turn, Āl-e Ahmad's *Lost in the Crowd* has influenced or inspired more recent *safarnāmeh*s, among them volumes by Baraheni and 'Abbās Pahlavān, an Āl-e Ahmad follower and then editor of the important weekly *Ferdowsi*.

A second significance to *Lost in the Crowd* relates to Āl-e Ahmad's perspective on travel in general, which he views as "another way of knowing the self, of evaluating it and coming to grips with its limitations and how narrow, insignificant, and empty it is, in the proving ground of changing climes by means of encounters and human achievements." Such a view of travel may be an implicit impulse behind the many *safarnāmeh*s in Persian literature; but given Āl-e Ahmad's wonted candor and directness in writing, his perspective on travel makes *Lost in the Crowd* almost unprecedented in Persian literature in terms of self-revelation of personal and cultural doubts, misgivings, and dilemmas.

In *Lost in the Crowd*, Āl-e Ahmad presents himself as an almost unwilling Hajj pilgrim, or if not unwilling, at least unlikely. At the outset, he admits that he is unclear as to why he is going. It is a question he repeats again and again through some fifty-seven entries in the diary covering the period from Friday, 10 April 1964 through Sunday, 3 May 1964. Not having prayed for the previous twenty-or-so years, he is self-conscious about performing ritual prayers at the beginning of the pilgrimage. In addition, he reveals in several places his recognition that secular intellectual confrères in Tehran will think his going on the pilgrimage foolish—some diary entries seem self-consciously to have them on Āl-e Ahmad's mind. On the pilgrimage itself, Āl-e Ahmad hardly contemplates or mentions Allāh, sin, heaven, human souls, or the like. His participation in Hajj events is represented as much less spontaneous than that of his fellow pilgrims; he is much more observer than participant, as his taking notes from the very beginning reveals (he presumably planned from before the Hajj to write a book on the experience). Even in his reports of Hajj events and ceremonies, Āl-e Ahmad's focus is far different from that one would expect from most pilgrims; his primary interest seems to lie in presenting ironies and conflicts that the fact of the pilgrimage and its events raise in his mind.

First there is Āl-e Ahmad's urge as a contemporary Iranian to represent Islam as an essentially non-Arab force worthy of respect and adherence in a 20th century world. As a nationalistic Iranian, Āl-e Ahmad seems to need to find in early Islam such Iranian connections as Salmān the Persian, one of Mohammad's earliest followers, and in contemporary Islam an Iranian association with Shi'i Islamic doctrine as opposed to Arab association with Sunni doctrine. Time and again he expresses irritation at Sunni belittling of Shi'i practices and views. More interesting in this regard is Āl-e Ahmad's animus toward the Arabs, a feeling he had expressed in his earliest story, the 1945 piece called "Pilgrimage" which recounted part of his trip in 1943 to Karbala. In his xenophobic view toward the Arabs and feeling of Iranian superiority, Āl-e Ahmad expresses typical 20th century Iranian intellectual feelings. The same holds for Āl-e Ahmad's constant criticism in *Lost in the Crowd* of the Saudi Arabian government for its alleged inefficiency, greed, and other shortcomings, another manifestation of his nationalistic, anti-Arab sentiments (these are the same Arabs with whom Āl-e Ahmad's family in claiming to be *sayyeds* asserted ultimate blood relationships); but his criticism in this regard may have the equally important further dimension of serving as indirect criticism of the Pahlavi regime as well. Āl-e Ahmad criticizes the Saudi Arabian government as a monarchy, attacking the institution there as he was never able openly to do with respect to the Pahlavi monarchy. Readers can judge for themselves if they think Āl-e Ahmad is somehow implying through indirection that eventually monarchy itself must disappear, in Saudi Arabia and in Iran.

Ultimately, Āl-e Ahmad's firm cultural and political nationalism makes it impossible for him to accept the notion of a future in which there might be a world government. But he argues throughout *Lost in the Crowd* for internationalization of control of the Hajj pilgrimage sites and of Islam as a social force. Interestingly, the Islamic Republic of Iran has argued forcefully in recent years for internationalization of the Hajj, asserting that the Arab Sunnis are prejudiced against Iranian Shi'is.

Of course, too much should not be made of anachronistic connections and other similarities between Āl-e Ahmad's views and the position of the Islamic Republic of Iran. Āl-e Ahmad's Iran in mid-1964 when he made the Hajj and wrote *Lost in the Crowd* was a separate age in comparison with post-Pahlavi Iran in the 1980s. Mohammad Rezā Pahlavi was firm on his throne, not to be challenged for another fourteen years following the monarchy's successful suppression of religious uprisings in June 1963 led by a dissident cleric named Ruhollāh Khomayni (b. 1902), who would be exiled in the fall of 1964 to Turkey and then to Iraq. In 1964, the Pahlavi reform program known as the White Revolution, promulgated in early 1963, was in full swing. Iran's economic boom of the late 1960s and early 1970s was just ahead at this time, as was subsequently substantial American business involvement in Iran: a decade later, there would be upwards of 40,000 Americans living and working in Iran; two decades later, no more than a handful of American men would be in the Islamic Republic of Iran.

In short, the mid-1960s' Iranian intellectual perspective from which Āl-e Ahmad speaks in *Lost in the Crowd* was formed in and relates to an age significantly different both from the early and mid-1970s of Pahlavi suzerainty and from the Islamic Republic of Iran that came into existence in early 1979. Nevertheless, in his participation in the Hajj, which has been undertaken annually by tens of thousands of Moslems for over 1,400 years, Āl-e Ahmad perforce speaks from other Iranian perspectives which transcend both the Islamic Republic of Iran and the Pahlavi monarchy before it and which extend back from the Qājār era (1796–1925) and earlier dynastic epochs to the Arab Moslem conquest of the Iranian region in the middle of the 7th century. In other words, Āl-e Ahmad raises both timely and almost timeless Iranian issues in *Lost in the Crowd*, perhaps none more thought-provoking for Iranian intellectuals today than the dilemma of feeling significant and distinctive as individual Iranians while being asked by one's historical religion to be no more than a chip in a wood pile, a Moslem believer lost in the Moslem crowd. Readers of *Lost in the Crowd* will have to judge for themselves whether or not Āl-e Ahmad actually was such a believer. Writers in *Sokhan* (1978), the *International Journal of Middle Eastern Studies* (1983), and elsewhere assert that he was. But I wonder.

* Grants hereby gratefully acknowledged from the Center for Middle Eastern Studies and the Research Institute of the University of Texas at Austin made possible the research and writing of this essay in Paris in May and June of 1984. I am grateful as well to the following individuals whose views on Āl-e Ahmad shared with me in conversation have contributed substantially to my thinking on the subject: Sādeq Chubak, Simin Dāneshvar, Majid Davāmi, Ebrāhim Golestān, Ahmad Karimi-Hakkāk, Eslām Kāzemiyeh, Hosayn Malek, Dāryush Mehrju'i, Shāhrokh Meskub, Ne'mat Mirzāzādeh, Nāder Nāderpur, Hosayn Narāqi, Gholāmhosayn Sā'edi, Ārshāk Tahmāsebi, Goli Taraqqi, and Gholāmhosayn Yusofi. The present essay develops themes suggested in the "Preface" and illustrated by the translations in Jalāl Āl-e Ahmad, *Iranian Society: An Anthology of Writings*, compiled and edited by Michael Hillmann (Lexington, Kentucky: Mazda Publishers, 1982). An expanded version of this essay with full documentation appears in a forthcoming volume of mine called *Iranian Culture: A Persianist's View.*

[redacted]

LOST IN THE CROWD

TRANSLATED BY JOHN GREEN

It is related that Abu Yazid said: "I went to Mecca and saw a house standing apart. I said, 'My pilgrimage is not accepted, for I have seen many stones of this sort.' I went again, and saw the House and also the Lord of the House. I said, 'This is not yet real unification.' I went a third time, and saw only the Lord of the House. A voice in my heart whispered, 'O Bāyazīd, if thou didst not see thyself, thou wouldst not be a polytheist (*mushrik*) though thou sawest the whole universe; and since thou seest thyself, thou art a polytheist though blind to the whole universe.' Thereupon I repented, and once more I repented of my repentance, and yet once more I repented of seeing my own existence."[1]

'Ali ibn 'Usmān Hujwiri
Kashf al-Mahjub p. 134

[1] 'Ali ibn 'Usman Hujwiri, *Kashf al-Mahjub, the Oldest Persian Treatise on Sufism*, translated by R.A. Nicholson (Leyden: E.J. Brill, Imprimerie Oriental, 1911). (tr)

CONTENTS

Introduction:
Cultural Dilemmas of an Iranian Intellectual/vii-xxxiii

Lost in the Crowd/5-124

Translator's Glossary/125-133
Bibliography/135-157

Friday, 21 Farvardin, 1343 [10 April 1964] Jedda

We started at 5 a.m. from Mehrabad airport. We got here at 8:30 (7:30 local time), having had breakfast on the plane without tea or coffee. Bread, a piece of chicken, and an egg, in a box bearing the airline's logo. The "hajjis[2]-to-be," however, were unsure at first. Was it edible or not? Had it been killed according to religious law? I missed whatever it was that removed their doubts. It may have been our *hamlehdār*,[3] who took such an interest in helping the flight attendants distribute the food that one would have thought he was paying for it himself. After the meal we each got an orange, again with the guide's help. Then one of the passengers asked for water. A Lebanese stewardess brought it. I heard a young man who was her colleague tell her "*Commeenc pas si tôt*," exactly like that in French. I laughed, and they saw me. They spoke in Armenian after that. A Lebanese Armenian Arab flight attendant taking pilgrims from Tehran to Jedda! But who am I? I remember praying this morning in the pilgrim's assembly area at the Tehran airport, after who knows how many years. I probably quit praying during my first year at the university. Those were the days! I would do my ablutions and pray. Sometimes I even did *namāz-e*

---

[2] *Hajji* is a title given to a Muslim who has made the pilgrimage to Mecca. (tr)

[3] A *hamlehdār* (hereafter referred to as "guide") acts as a guide for a group of Muslims throughout the pilgrimage, providing them with details on ritual formalities at the shrines themselves as well as obtaining practical information on procedures and arranging for facilities and provisions. (tr)

shab![4] Of course, towards the end I didn't even put a *mohr*[5] under my forehead. This was the beginning of infidelity. Frankly, it isn't the same anymore. I feel like a hypocrite. It just isn't right. If it isn't hypocrisy, neither is it faith. You just do it to blend in with the crowd. But does one go to Mecca without praying?

We were supposed to leave yesterday morning, but we did not. We had gone to the airport at four in the morning, but we went back home at seven with weary looks on our faces; the pilgrim assembly area had been full of people, with sleeping children littering the floor in various postures, curled, stretched, and contorted. There had been a group of Kurds praying, wearing *kalāghīs* on their heads, hands on their chests; their *imam*[6] was wearing a white turban. One of the ones in the prayer line was so tall that he looked like a chess king standing in a row of pawns, while the *imam*, with his white turban, wasn't even the size of a pawn. Such is the Hajj![7] There was consolation in the fact that we slept yesterday afternoon and from the early evening on. We were awakened by a telephone call at 2 a.m. telling us to hurry to the airport. Then farewells, kisses, and such joy for those seeing us off! They imagined the lost lamb returning to the flock. There were two friends with knowing smiles, thinking to themselves, "What is this character trying to pull?" They didn't know it was neither a trick nor a matter of a lamb and the flock. It was something entirely different. The lost sheep had now turned into a mangy goat that simply wished to hide himself in the crowd.

As we waited for the plane at the Hajj assembly point, the young inspectors looked upon us with a mixture of amazement and contempt. All of us. Especially me (was I imagining things, thinking I stood out in the crowd?), thinking yes, "What fools!" No doubt. And themselves? They were top-notch consumers of razor blades, ties, and toothpaste. And the hajjis-to-be? Villagers, merchants, bossy old ladies, stuffy old men, and one or two people like me. And, wonder of wonders, all of them had abandoned their razors and face paint; each was out to gain insight in his own way. One sought the insights of travel, another to discover the Kaaba,[8] another to discover self-discovery. A merchant had gotten out his Mecca compass and was busy discovering Mecca right there behind the door to the ablutions

---

[4] *Namāz-e shab* is an extra, non-obligatory prayer which may be offered between the first light and sunrise. (tr)

[5] A *mohr* is a small rectangle of packed clay from Mecca or Karbala which is placed on the ground by Shi'is when they pray; the forehead touches this remembrance of sacred turf during the prostration. (From Michael M.J. Fischer, *Iran: From Religious Dispute to Revolution*, Harvard University Press, Cambridge, Mass., 1980)

[6] The word *imam* as used here refers to the one who stands in front of the ranks of praying Muslims and leads the prayer. (tr)

[7] *Hajj* is the Persian/Arabic word for the pilgrimage to Mecca. (tr)

[8] An irregular, cube-shaped structure located in the courtyard of the Grand Mosque at Mecca, which, according to legend, was built first by Adam and reconstructed by Abraham after the flood. (tr)

pool. The first experiences of the journey! You'd have thought we were lost in the African desert (now they're sounding the call to prayer over the loud speakers, right on the edge of the Hajj Village, for the evening prayer; it is exactly 20 minutes to 5), even though the Mehrabad airport had a specially constructed area for pilgrims that even had a mosque where one could read the direction to Mecca written above the prayer niche... What was the real meaning of the Hajj assembly area? It was there to separate the lambs from the goats. Those bound for Paris, London, or New York must not be allowed to see these hajjis, each one holding an *āftābeh*,[9] his thermos over his sack of dry bread, homemade yogurt, and other odds and ends. Anyway, these two groups must be separated! Of course the man or the made-up woman headed for Europe must be protected from the sight of these people who have answered the primal call of a desert religion.

We flew above the clouds for a time in the aircraft, a fluffy blanket of them beneath our feet, with the occasional hole. The clouds passed and were replaced by dust, and everything below turned red. Then we were over the desert and there were mountain tops rising up out of the sand, like islands protruding out of the sea. In other places there were bright ochre depressions, places where it had probably just rained. Black, rocky heights. No trace of civilization. Sand, sand, sand. I wearied of it.

Sitting next to me was a swarthy old man submerged in himself, somewhat frightened. It was his first flight. He was snapping at people. I helped him position the little tray so his food could be served. "Yes," he said, "thanks, but I know how this works." We talked a little then. A retired police major. His children had married and he and his wife were alone. Now he was going to go into the presence of God and offer thanks. He was frightened, however. "Is *'Arafāt*[10] as strenuous as they say?" I told him it was my first pilgrimage too. Then the group's preacher got up and started talking through a megaphone:

"Come friends... See Zainab's[11] helplessness. See how she beats herself about the head and breast."

---

[9] A long-spouted water can or ewer used by Muslims to comply with the Prophet Muhammad's injunction that one cleanse oneself with water after answering a call of nature. (tr)

[10] *'Arafāt* is the name of a mountain and the plain surrounding it in the vicinity of Mecca. It is the site of one of the rituals of the Pilgrimage. In order for a pilgrimage to be valid, each pilgrim must be standing on the plain of 'Arafāt on the afternoon of 9 Dhū al-Ḥijjah, Standing Day. This is arduous because it necessitates a full day of walking and exposure to the hot sun. (tr)

[11] Zainab was the sister of the Shi'i Imam Husayn. She witnessed his martyrdom at Karbala, and was said to have been the first to mourn his death. (tr)

There are 85 in our group. Twenty or 30 merchants, about 15 Mazandaranis, five or six *sayyids*,[12] *ākhonds*,[13] *maddāhs*,[14] and preachers, and about 10 villagers from the Arak area who speak only Turkish. There are 20 women. In my group, there is my sister and her husband Javad, another of the husbands of my sisters, Mohaddes, and my father's uncle. We are a little group unto ourselves in this crowd. Our guide is from our area. He was one of my father's[15] followers. I had persuaded the others that we ought to let him take us. He had been a gable builder. This was my reciprocation for the devotion someone once extended to my father. The guide's job belongs to him, along with his son, a cook, and the cook's assistant. I don't think we'll lack anything with this arrangement.

Night. Same day, same place.

This won't work if I have to wear myself out this way every day. I must take it easy. Especially with this water we have to drink. I bought a lot of salt tablets, but I haven't eaten a one of them. That's exactly the sort of thing I wanted to get away from. Water? I must have drunk more than 10 liters of it since this morning. But I must stick to the spirit of this enterprise.

When we deplaned this morning we came directly to this building in the "Hajj Village" beside the airport. It's an enormous structure of three or four corners with squinches, three or four stories high. It has spacious balconies, open windows on all sides, and rooms designed to trap and circulate the wind. You drink water and perspire. There is so much wind in the room you'd think you were right at the peak of Tuchal.[16] Luckily, the morning we arrived I packed my Tehran clothing away in the suitcase. I purchased an Arab *dishdāshah*[17] for eight Saudi rials—one rial = 18 Iranian *qerāns*[18]—and a pair of Javanese elastic slippers for two rials. The shirt was delightful, like a cone of sugar cubes. Yet I split open the two sides of it with a knife so I could sit and stand. But the shoulders are so tight it feels like someone is hugging you all the time. But I'm getting off the track. I was talking about the Hajj Village. It has four floors. We are

[12] A *sayyid* is a descendant of the Prophet Muhammad, as used here; it can also be simply an honorific title, especially in Arabic. (tr)

[13] An *ākhond* is a lesser member of the Shi'i religious leadership. He performs everyday religious functions such as leading the prayers in the smaller mosques, etc.; the term, synonymous with *mulla*, has a pejorative connotation. (tr)

[14] A *maddāh* sings songs and recites poetry about the Imams on special Shi'i anniversaries such as the 9th and 10th of Moharram (when Imam Husayn was martyred), and at funerals. He may be merely a gifted performer, with no religious or scholarly credentials. (tr)

[15] The author's father was a Shi'i clergyman. (tr)

[16] Tuchal is a mountain in the Alborz range of northern Iran. (tr)

[17] The long gown worn by the Arabs of the Arabian peninsula. (tr)

[18] Ten *qerāns* are equal to one toman. (tr)

on the third floor (each side on each floor has six or seven facets. It's an irregular trapezoid). The state owns it. They come here from the airport for a little break until it's time to go to Jedda, en route to Mecca or Medina, depending on whether they arrive early or late in the season. They say the hajjis are sometimes detained for up to three days. I think we'll be leaving tonight, however. In the meantime, I pass the time with this notebook, waiting for our departure.

Maintenance is unspeakably bad in this building. All the privies are clogged (I looked at 10 of them), and there is no water in the sinks and showers. They had water when we got here this morning, but it was all gone by afternoon. Then came the swarm of people, the filth, and fruit peelings strewn everywhere. There were kerosene lanterns in every corner, with samovars, camp stoves, or complete kitchens clogging the building's corridors, rooms, and threshold-like balconies. Piles of Pepsi and Coke cans and traveler's paraphernalia. There were rivulets of water everywhere, and you always wonder if it isn't sewage coming out of a privy with the top opened. This glorious Saudi Arabian government (Peace be upon it)! Evidently preoccupied with guzzling up oil profits. Let all these hajjis burst open because of the filth, but keep those oil wells pumping. I remember stretching out for a little while in the afternoon when two red-haired Europeans in shorts came to look at us. Sort of an inspection. They were with two Saudi Arabian Boy Scouts, complete with insignia, whistles, scarves, and all that nonsense. I asked the Saudi Arabian boys in my broken, halting Arabic, "Are you sure these people are Muslims, that you bring them here?" They either didn't understand what I said or chose not to answer. The word "Muslim," however, is intelligible to any deaf person from the mouth of any mute. There was no time anyway, since they left immediately. They would peek into each room and then hurry on. There were at least 50 hajjis lolling about in every room; there wasn't space for bringing in random guests.

When we changed locations in the morning—from the aircraft to the Hajj Village (and it took two hours to move that 50 steps!)—I dashed outside and grabbed the first taxi (what a lot of new Chevrolets!) and made a deal with him in my terrible Arabic to drive me around the city for 15 Saudi rials. He drove me, but my driver and makeshift guide knew nothing but Arabic. This was enough to enable me to get information from him about prices, however. A litre of gasoline costs 4 of our *qerāns* (an 18-litre can costs 4 Saudi Rials), a taxi costs 2 rials, a bus 4 piastres—and so on. He provided first-hand information: Jedda has a population of 250–300 thousand, Saudi Arabia itself 7–8 million.[19] There are 3 newspapers in

---

[19] Yet the population of Saudi Arabia is 3–4 million at most. I have to question the other information provided by this unsalaried guide of Jedda. In any case, as a patriot (though an Arab), he had the right to show off, put on airs, and so on for a foreign tourist. (A)

the whole country, "*al-Bilād*," "*al-Nadwah*,"[20] and a weekly called "*Umm al-Qurā*." All three are run by the state. The Arabs of the East drink coffee, in the aristocratic style of the Bedouins. The Westerners (the ones from the Hijaz[21]) drink tea, or "*shāy*," as the Arabs say... We passed Eve's grave at this point. High, thick walls, just like the walls of an old ice house, with a short, narrow door in one corner. It had fallen into disrepair and looked worse than the most obscure and forgotten shrine of an Imam's descendant in Abarqu. The grandmother of humanity! Then we passed the Foreign Ministry. Such splendor! Then the Bedouin bazaar, which was still bustling. Then we passed alongside "The Palace of the Great King," with its walls reaching to the sky and its gate guarded by soldiers shouldering machine guns. Then we passed beside a low, crumbling wall, which they had laid around a large tract of land. "The Place of Prayer." The place for Friday prayers. Too bad we got there late. In the middle of it were a number of assembly areas or pulpit-like structures for preachers (no doubt), or for the muezzins. The area is the size of Tupkhāneh Square. An old city shedding its skin, becoming modern, and laying down new streets, the same sort of surgery they're performing on Yazd, Tehran, and Kerman. There is dirt, dust, construction machinery, mud and sludge.

In two or three places they have poured black oil on the graded roadbeds of future streets. Then we're at the seaside, with the smell of salt water in the air and ships at anchor. Then we come to the maritime Hajj Village. (We are staying in what is called the "airport" Hajj Village.) There is an Indian ship docked there with hajjis unloading, the simplest of hajjis, and the least encumbered. They come wrapped in saris, wearing loin cloths, and carrying tea kettles for drinking, steeping tea, and washing. Iranians carry *āftābehs*; Turks have long tubes with bulbous ends that look like tin kerosene lamps. The Lebanese and Syrians have plastic *āftābeh*s that are smaller than ours—and the Indians and Africans carry kettles. These are the most meaningful national emblems, and they aren't found on flags, but in peoples' hands. And how handy they are!

The hajjis in our group seem unhappy about being idle. They have been unpacking and repacking their luggage since this morning. Maybe they're paying the price of their idleness at home, where their wives undoubtedly took care of everything, and with such precision. All the suitcases have covers of canvas and tarpcloth, with straps, locks, and ropes tied around them. They take the prayer mats out one by one and roll them into the suitcases. "No, that's not it. It just doesn't look right." Then they start over. This is the quest of the Hajj, and of the wind-swept plain! Every one

---

[20] Both *al-Nadwah* and *al-Bilād* were founded in 1963, and have circulations of around 10,000. (tr)

[21] The Hijaz is the area of highlands and narrow sea coast in the north-western Arabian peninsula that was the cradle of Islam. It is now a province of contemporary Saudi Arabi which includes Medina, Mecca, and Jedda. (tr)

of these people left his livestock, his cash register, or his desk just yesterday. They're getting an experience, in any event. Even though it takes the plane only 3 hours to bring you to Jedda from Tehran, and you don't get a chance to spend a year getting here by mule or camel from Mazlaqān or Sūleqān, they make up for it by detaining you the same amount of time it would take to make the trip by camel in this Hajj Village, to give you a chance to pack and unpack your bundles. Even more interestingly, they are Turks from Arak. One of them, who had not yet taken off his leather waistcoat (in spite of this humid early evening heat) had just gone out this afternoon and bought a *dishdāshah* to wear over it. His shoulders were held in awkwardly and tightly. Although his Persian was not good, I had joked with him in the afternoon: "I hope you didn't catch cold?" One of our companions from Esfahan said: "Hajji *āqā*, he's sewn his money into his leather coat." We are already practicing calling each other "Hajji *āqā*." More interestingly, it's money he's already converted at the market right here in the courtyard of this Hajj Village. I've seen four people so far asking about the currency conversion rate from our *qerān*s to Saudi rials, fearing they might be cheated. It's obvious that they've never even made a pilgrimage to Qom, and now? They've traded their tomans for rials in Jedda. The money-changers know Persian, Turkish, Urdu, and Javanese, to the extent necessary to do business.

The air is miserably humid. The body stays wet all the time, and the bones will surely ache tonight. If you can sleep, that is, with legs exposed, and an even more exposed chest and neck area. No matter what, one must get used to it for the days of *iḥrām*.[22] And these ceiling fans go continuously. What would we do if they didn't? When the wind stopped at sunset, we ourselves turned on the fans. According to what they say, we will be traveling tonight. I went in the afternoon to visit the other corners and floors of the building. In front of the balconies around the building were clusters of flags of various nations and the names and emblems of this or that guide: Turkish, Persian, Iraqi, Syrian, and Moroccan. Guards continually walked the path going around the building. All of them young, wearing khakis, berets, revolvers, and carrying clubs, watching. A black stood to one side with a small bag of a hand's width and a combination lock over his shoulder, praying and holding his hand over his chest. He didn't curtail the prayer or leave out the *qonut*.[23] A trickle of water passed beneath his feet— that same ubiquitous water—and, interestingly, there were three diagonal scars on each of his cheeks. I have seen a lot of those

[22] The term *iḥrām* refers both to the ritual of purification that pilgrims perform prior to entering the shrine area and to the garments which are worn by one who has completed the rituals during his stay in the shrine area. For men, the garments are two seamless, usually white pieces of toweling or sheeting, one covering the body from waist to ankle, the other thrown over the shoulder. For women it is usually a simple white gown with a headcovering. (tr)

[23] *Qonut* is the second standing phase of the Muslim prayer, done with the upturned palms resting on the chest while reciting a prayer formula. (tr)

scars this morning. The scars on all of their cheeks are just alike. Some of them have plus signs, some multiplication signs, some have vertical lines, and some have two horizontal lines, cut in the same manner... I fell in love with one of them, a black woman 20–25 years old, and stunningly beautiful. Slightly plump. The features of her face didn't have Negro characteristics. There were two vertical scars on each cheek. The flesh within the scars was lighter than her shiny, pitch-black skin. She sat in a corner peddling two or three bolts of cloth woven in Africa. I spoke with her. In French! She was from Cameroon. We haggled over prices, but she herself was much more beautiful than her cloth, and this was not something she was selling or I was buying.

I also visited our caravan's infirmary. It was on the second floor of this Hajj Village, in a large, well-appointed, respectable room, with a proper pharmacy, a doctor, and two officious-looking orderlies. They've been on duty since the beginning of this week. There are 72 on the Iranian health staff. Twenty-two of them are physicians, and some of these are women. Up until the time of my visit they had had 449 patients. The complaints: air sickness, heat stroke, and diarrhea (caused by eating rancid yogurt, according to the doctor). Of this group, there were 30 Nigerians, 3 Afghanis, several Sudanese, Turks, and Yemenis, and an Egyptian. The Infirmary's doors are open to everyone. Some of the physicians' staff are now in Medina, some in Mecca, and they will all assemble in Mecca on *'Ayd-e Qorbān*,[24] following the hajjis step by step. These are things I jotted down which were passed on to me by one of the infirmary's physicians.

And these money changers! This morning I went to the bank to exchange currency, on the first floor of this same Hajj Village. They were open for business, even though it was Friday. They didn't change any money, however. They said to go find a money changer. There were some twenty of them right out in the yard, each one sitting in a corner on a small carpet, with a small, open safe, a quantity of Saudi Arabian currency on a small brass tray, and bills from various countries clipped to a piece of cardboard. There would be a likeness of Napoleon, the face of Ataturk, a bust of Queen Elizabeth, and other heads of state. The rate of exchange is the same everywhere for small change. People were already sitting around the grounds in groups, trading. Buying and selling. The stores in the area were full of Japanese battery-powered lanterns, Italian blankets, flasks of unknown origin, prayer mats, canteens, slippers, and umbrellas, umbrellas, umbrellas. The black women were slightly uncovered around the shoulders, the Turkish women were dressed entirely in white with their faces uncovered,

[24] *'Ayd-e Qorbān*, or the Feast of the Sacrifice, is usually called *'Īd al-Aḍḥā* (Persian *'Ayd-e Azhā*); it is a four-day festival beginning on the 10th day of the month of Dhū al-Ḥijjah, the 12th month of the Muslim lunar calendar, during which ritual animal sacrifices are made. It takes place at Mina for Hajj pilgrims. (tr)

and there were three or four Syrian women without even a *ḥijjāb*.[25] And God save us from these Indonesians, who can't even get along without their president's hat here![26]

Saturday 23 Farvardin 1343 [April 11, 1964], Medina

We arrived here at 8:30 in the morning. The greetings from officials at the gate and the flower gardens in the public squares made a happy welcome for us, for we had been on the bus since 11 p.m. the night before. My feet swelled up from sitting on the seats so long, and they're still swollen. I've never felt such pain in my life. I suspect it's the result of running around with exposed legs. Anyway, the only thing I've got on beneath this *dishdāshah* is a pair of shorts. Fortunately, I thought to buy a blanket in Jedda. If I hadn't, I'd have fallen on my face after the first step. It hurts a lot between my shoulders right now, like colic. I haven't coughed yet, though I have some Ipesandrine. "Oh! Look at you! You've come on the Hajj, and you're this preoccupied with yourself? You really must forget these old traveling pharmacies. And definitely yourself as well."

We waited for the bus last night from 8 o'clock until 10. I wrote by the dim overhead light and the others griped at one another continually about space. We finally did get underway. I think it was even later than 11 o'clock. Such joy! At one point I noticed that we were back in the center of Jedda, in order to pay the highway toll and be counted (no doubt) and this sort of chicanery. Then we went back and got onto the road for Mecca in that same vicinity of the Hajj Village. When was this? At exactly 12:15. I didn't last past 1 o'clock. I wrapped up tightly in my blanket and dozed off. I woke up suddenly at 3 o'clock, because of a mechanical breakdown. I woke up again at 3:30, again because of a mechanical breakdown. We stayed awake then until we reached the village of Badr at 5 a.m. The bus stopped every 10 minutes. Then it would lurch ahead. Each time, the driver would get underneath it and tinker with the motor. Then he would run back up and pump the gas pedal—and he pounded it so hard you'd have thought he was driving nails with it. One slam after another, continuously. He had two or three drivers in our group, and no matter how much they tried to help him, he refused. Arab blockheadedness. The carburetor wasn't drawing fuel. The guy would go suck gas out of the tank with a hose and pour it into the carburetor. Then we would go for 5 minutes and stop again. It was a fiasco. The people became loud and agitated, the women whining and swearing, especially cursing everything Arab. It reached a point where I intervened once or twice, yelling at this one or that one "why have you lost control of yourself this way?" Other

---

[25] *Ḥijjāb* is the Arabic word for the veil worn by many Muslim women. The Iranian version of it is called a chador. (tr)

[26] The Indonesian president in 1964 was Achmed Sukarno, who had become Head of State for Life the previous year. (tr)

passing vehicles stopped occasionally to sympathize or help, but the driver was stubborn, or else unauthorized or in danger of being docked part of his pay. That is, the one who helped would be certain to report that "so-and-so was stalled in the middle of the road, I stopped to help him," and so on... It was 6:30 when we left Badr. We had washed our faces, prayed, drunk *barrād* tea, and eaten American corn bread. The bus had been repaired and we had no further problems. We didn't stop again until we got to Medina. My uncle kept on complaining, however; the old fellow couldn't handle it.

During the time we sat in the bus waiting to leave Jedda, we saw what a lot of porters there are, and how many poor people in the villages along the road, and most of them blind and paralyzed! But God save us from Jedda and its porters! It appears that the brunt of the weight of the Hajj rites is carried on the shoulders of the porters. Porters who have no straps or harnesses, only their empty hands. So pointless! They used their teeth to untie the brand-new spools the driver had given them for tying up loads; they placed the section to be cut on the asphalt and spent a full ten minutes severing it with a piece of rock. They didn't even have a pocket knife. The driver stood there and watched, but help or a cutting tool? Never. There were three or four porters working—all bare-handed—with tightly-braided hemp rope that was so stiff it wouldn't even bend. The best example of the relationship between being a manufacturer and a consumer. The more precise the machine, the more backward the consumer, and the more primitive. It is true that the task of transporting 800,000 foreigners in less than a month is not a simple one for a country whose population is only 5 or 6 times that number. Nonetheless, it's obvious that no facilities are prepared beforehand for the Hajj. They have left the matter of the Hajj to the most backward, primitive, untutored, and poverty-stricken layers of society. The only evidence of facilities is that the busses are all of the same type and the same color, belonging to two companies, Al-Tawfiq, and one other. The main shareholder for both of them is undoubtedly the Great King! It's just over 400 kilometers from Jedda to Medina, yet there isn't a telephone line along the road. They have dug drainage ditches alongside the road and the retainer walls have only recently been repaired. The asphalt strip, however, is so narrow that two busses must go onto the shoulder in order to pass, and, being seated over the tire, I could see how they passed each other. It is quite normal to wait in line three or four hours for everything. Wilted hajjis are everywhere in groups of 20 to 30. I am talking about Jedda. Fortunately for us, our guide was experienced. He told us he had paid bribes and inflicted enough indebtedness for us that we moved ahead by 14 turns... Enough of that.

When we stopped at Rabigh, one of our Mazandarani companions asked Mohaddes, "Is this Arabia?"

Mohaddes said yes.

"Is that so," said the man, who began searching the sky for corroboration of this claim. The stars shone brilliantly and the sky was incredibly high. The retired police major, however, exhausted and holding his teacup, stared in amazement at a pack of intricately marked black dogs following a bitch around in the dirt and grime. At that hour of the night! One of them's thing was protruding bright red. This Rabigh is at the halfway point. It didn't even have electricity, however, or if it had it it was turned off. The kerosene lanterns sputtered. The tea was too sweet, and oversteeped. The town of Badr also lacked electricity. Some five or ten kilometers outside Medina, however, telephone poles—short and slender—began to file past us.

It is now past noon. There is no word yet, however, from the other travelers in our group, and no word of my sister who is with her husband on the next bus. Our guide says that Saudi officials do not allow any bus to venture out into the sun after 9 in the morning. They must wait until sunset—and this is further evidence of an orderly system—but it is mostly on account of the busses, which would overheat in the sun and cause company losses. The house where we are staying is of recent construction, outside the city, near the date gardens, in a neighborhood called *Ḍarb al-Janā'iz.* You can look into the middle of *Baqī'* Cemetery[27] from the northern window. They bring our water in a tanker. Every half cubic meter costs one Saudi rial.

Same day. Same Place.

There was a fat, robust sayyid in our vehicle whose beard had two or three colors. Its base was white, its middle was red, and the end of it was black (and it was overdue for more henna). In the middle of that restless journey, this gentleman began to assail his fellow passengers with advice and admonitions against evil, such as: "Don't carry your *mohr* with you when you visit the holy shrines, and don't call attention to your differences with the others. Don't be kissing the doors and walls all the time," and so on. It was beautiful.

While in Jedda we saw the word "Peugeot" on a storefront, "Bijou" another place. The sign "Ministry of Pilgrimage Affairs and Religious Endowments" also caught the eye. And all this disorganization! What would happen if there were no ministry? The villages and streets are much wider here in order to make room for neon lights. Right at nightfall the coffee houses along the road looked like oil refineries in the distance, with all the

[27] The Baqī' Cemetery, located to the east of the city of Medina, is a major religious shrine and historic landmark. It is the final resting place of most of the companions of the Prophet Muhammad, as well as a number of his other important contemporaries. (tr)

neon lights above the doorways and on signposts. (Evidently they turn off the power after midnight. I have to be careful going back.)

In the Jedda Hajj Village at the airport, and here as well, you sometimes see notices on the wall that say "Drink a large glass of water every hour and use your umbrella." I have drunk water so far without help from this announcement, but I lack the motivation to carry a lot of baggage. This bag I have over my shoulder, with my cigarettes, a little money, and my little notebook inside, is enough. I ought to buy a stocking cap too. Our traveling companion from Arak with the sheepskin jacket went and bought one with a tassel. An umbrella, that is. A reversible one. Green on the inside, black on the outside. He's so attached to it you'd think it was Moses' cane. As for myself, near Gabriel's Gate I bought a canvas water bottle that resembles the style of the leather ones. It makes one feel more primitive. My stomach can't handle ice water anyway. At this point an itinerant coffee vendor came up, coffee pot in hand, with a pail slung over his shoulder containing the implements of his trade. I drank two cups of coffee; it was terribly sweet, too aromatic, and too watery, a low-grade aroma. Two cups for 4 piastres. The fellow had a striking way of pleading; he was more of a beggar than a coffee-seller. He said his work was fully dedicated to God, he was from Gaza, and so on. Frankly, these Gaza Arabs who've fled Palestine are an embarrassment to Islam. How many years since that happened? It must be 10 years now. These gentlemen have been installed in their tents as beggars with no responsibility, and they are the basis for the dispute between Israel and Egypt. They have no jobs, no homes, no way to return to Israel, and they aren't allowed to enter Egypt. I saw another of them at sunset, at the mosque alongside the Hajj Village. He was begging the same way, without even making the pretext of selling something. After he said "hello," however, the prayer line broke up so fast he didn't even get a chance to ask a question. The prayer there was without the *qonut*, with the hands on the chest. In my row, however, four or five people's hands were at their sides. The mat on the mosque floor was cool, beautifully designed, and long. Its design designated rows of people praying, and it was very tightly woven. Most of the hajjis took off their shoes and brought them inside under their arms. It was really interesting when they assumed the *tashahhod*[28] position. Most of them put their right feet beneath their rumps, as if preparing to run, toes on the floor, the sole of the foot extending vertically above the toes, and visible from behind. Their heels were cracked. They looked as if they were ready to begin a race. The blacks were more picturesque, however. They sprawled out so much for *tashahhod* that one would have thought them incapable of sitting on their knees. It looked like they couldn't position their calves under their thighs. That's what I thought. I realized at that prayer that the

[28] *Tashahhod* is the concluding segment of the Muslim prayer, done in a kneeling position while reciting a final ritual formula. (tr)

custom of kneeling is an ancient one that comes from Asia, from Islam, India, Buddhism, Japan, China, and other parts of that area. Neither the Europeans nor the Africans have mastered it. In any case, all the blacks in the file took at least twice the space of a kneeling person.

When I left the mosque I went into a coffee house, again near the Hajj Village in Jedda, so I could practice my Arabic. I smelled *shāmi* kabob from the shop next door as I ordered one of those cola drinks. I asked what it was called; the name was *choghortmeh.*[29] I asked them to bring me some. There were chunks of meat pressed together and impaled vertically on a stick before a glowing electric coil. What a smell! I don't know how many years it's been since my stomach was excited. I chatted with the person next to me, waiting for it to be prepared. The Bedouins wear red headbands, the city dwellers white ones. The Hajj season doubles the population of Jedda. The demand for sacrificial meat put the herdsmen and drovers in motion six months ago. They drove the animals on foot towards Mina. Most of the meat comes from Africa, from northern Ethiopia. He didn't know, however, whether the animals had eaten *sana* grass or not, and the Iranian hajjis were very skeptical of it. The fellow I was talking to was young. His shirt and headcloth were very white, and he wore no headband. He had thrown the headcloth over his head like a scarf. He told me his profession, but I didn't understand him, and I was embarrassed to repeat the question. What he had to say was more interesting than who he was. When he realized I could speak a bit of *Engrish* he became quite enthusiastic. Now it was his turn for language practice. I drew him into a discussion about politics. He was violently opposed to the current situation, and basically opposed to the Hajj. He called it a disgrace, and said it was one of the causes of backwardness in the country. It doesn't let us do anything. It has taught us to be idlers, and so on... I chewed my *choghortmeh* with relish. I saw that everywhere the worm comes from the tree itself. I was about to start talking about the matter of his oil and the special relationship between raw materials and manufactured goods, and this kind of nonsense, when I realized it was getting late. I said goodbye and left Jedda with this memory.

---

[29] *Choghortmeh* is a Turkish form of shish kabob, for which the meat is fried in oil rather than roasted or broiled on a spit. It appears that the author has either been given the wrong name for the food he is describing or the "glowing coil" he mentions is being used to keep the meat warm, rather than to cook it. (tr)

Evening. Same day.

Medina

Early evening in the Prophet's Mosque. I took a walk after the sunset prayer. The people were talking in groups or saying *zekr*[30] and reading the Qur'ān individually. After the prayer rank had been formed two or three people passed back and forth and fanned the crowd. One of them didn't have a fan. He opened his headcloth and waved that, in a whip-cracking motion. The ceremonial water distributors[31] began their work at the conclusion of the prayer. Each one carried a cup or a pitcher. And such pitchers! I took a gulp from each one, whether white or yellow. Most of them were made in India or Pakistan. So cool. At the mosque entryway there were small groups of people listening to preachers. A Pakistani was preaching in Urdu, which I didn't understand. Three were speaking in Arabic. I stood between the groups assembled around two of them. One spoke fluently and eloquently on the virtues of the Prophet, saying "Taha. We have not sent down the Qur'ān to thee to be (an occasion) for thy distress."[32] As I left, I heard: "'Ā'ishah[33] awoke in the night, saw her husband making a prostration, and thought him dead..." Another one, who looked like an Indian, speaking in relatively clear Arabic, surprised me by talking about the same nonsense that was in *Weststruckness!* The concept is so commonplace that even the preachers in Medina discuss it, probably every day! And in such epic language. His upper teeth were pushed forward and his lips were parted; yet he spoke of faith, of Islam, and of the great danger to the Western world in the event of Islamic unity. (The power has now been cut off. I'm scrawling by the light of Javad's flashlight. A moth that looks like a mature silkworm has flown up from the lamp base and is now flying around the face of the flashlight. He's fuzzy! The fuzz is short and shaggy, and it flies loose when you blow on it. Now he's landed on my notebook. I put him out through the window and return.) The guy understood the relationship between manufacturer and consumer and was explaining it to the people. I don't know why, but there was something about it I didn't like. I remembered Sayyid Jamal al-Din Asadabadi[34]... And I left. The people gathered around the Prophet's grave, touching and kissing it. The Saudi police put a stop to that and dispersed them. There was no violence or bad language involved, however.

---

30 *Zekr* is the repetitive utterance of Muslim litanies. (tr)

31 Also called *Zamzamī*, after the Zamzam well, these are members of a guild in the shrine area who provide water from the holy well to all who ask for it. This is done the year around, but is especially important during the Hajj. (tr)

32 The Holy Qur'ān, Surah 20, v.1,2. (Yusuf 'Ali translation). (tr)

33 'Ā'ishah (ca 614 - 678) was the daughter of the first Muslim caliph Abu Bakr, and the child bride and "favorite wife" of the Prophet Muhammad. (tr)

34 Better known as Afghani (1838-1897), Sayyid Jamal al-Din was a controversial 19th century thinker. An Iranian by birth, Afghani usually said he was from Afghanistan. He was an influential pioneer in the development of secular political thought in the Middle East, and helped organize the tobacco rebellion of 1892 in Iran. (tr)

On my way someone placed his *mohr* on the ground and did a prostration. Then when he lifted his head the *mohr* was clasped in his hand.

In the afternoon I went to the post office. The postal clerk gave me an 11-piastre stamp for an envelope and a 12-piastre stamp for a postcard. (I haven't yet determined whether a rial is 20 or 21 piastres.) As I was coming out of the post office they were giving the afternoon call to prayer and by the time I began to move [to get a place] the alley and the street were clogged with files of people praying. This happened in a flash. The shop keepers continued doing business, however. I stood barefoot next to a woman in the middle of the street. I touched my brow to my shoulder bag on the ground as I did my prostrations. The woman had a daughter who was playing in front of her. She herself wore a white mantle and didn't look Arab. When the prayer ended (no one left out anything, or at least I didn't see it), I went looking for a map. From this store to that store. There were five stores identified as hardware stores. I visited five stationery stores and bookstores before I finally found a map of *Madinat al-Salām*, printed God knows when, based on designs produced during the Ottoman occupation, about two palms wide. The "Zahra Date Tree" was shown planted just as it is now in a corner of the Prophet's Mosque. They've repaired the Prophet's Mosque two or three times since then. They had expanded it and knocked down the date trees and other odds and ends, but the map still depicted the situation as it was 50 or 60 years ago.

As for this village of Badr we passed on the way, I realized when I got to Medina that it is the same Badr that was the site of that battle and that victory.[35] It's a village full of date trees and gardens. There are several coffee houses along the road, and there's a large square full of stores that sell oil and gasoline and do repairs. The town has now been conquered by machines! Just like every village everywhere else in the world located between two large cities. There was a small locally-made crane (coarse pieces of iron very clumsily welded together) beside the coffee house. There was a sparrow sitting on it. It was relieving itself as the sun came up. With every dropping it hopped ahead, just like Big Bertha during the bombardment of London.[36] A local black-skinned Arab—a coffee house attendant—had two extra scars on his two cheeks. An African custom imported to Saudi Arabia? The kid was fat, too, with puffed-out cheeks. The scar-marks on his cheeks were darker than the rest of his face, and of

---

35 On the 15th of March, 624 A.D., at the Village of al-Badr, the Prophet Muhammad and a small force of volunteers from Medina intercepted and captured a wealthy caravan returning from Gaza to Mecca. Although the Muslims were outnumbered by the force that was escorting the caravan, they won decisively. About a dozen of Mecca's most important leaders were killed, and a number of others killed and captured. (tr)

36 Big Bertha was a nickname given to a class of World War I German long-range cannons with a range of up to 76 miles. They were used to bombard Paris, but never London. (tr)

course they were grooved. Just like the groove you make with a knife on black bread dough before putting it in the oven, so it will rise.

I should also mention that during the trip I learned what the *moghilān* thorn bush is. I saw it. It's a type of shade tree found in desert areas that is plentiful in the dry river beds in the high valley towards the end of the road to Medina, like a forest, a sure sign that there has been a recent prohibition on cutting them. In any case, it produces a type of oil people burn in place of wood. Something resembling foothills begins to appear about a hundred kilometers before you reach Medina. They're a little like the foothills of Manjil, and later they start looking like the Bajgah foothills to the north of Shiraz. Then, as we speed ahead in the bus, the Medina skyline appears. The ground is covered with porous black rocks. They resemble pumice (the remnants of a volcanic eruption...?). From a distance they look like the dark-green foliage of date trees. They were rocks, however. In the city and the vicinity around it a great many buildings were made from them. On the fringes of the city there was no outer covering of plaster, cement, or lime. Most of the buildings in the center of the city, however, were finished on the outside. If this were not the case one might have said that Medina is black city, just as Jerusalem is cream-colored, Rome is ochre, and so on.

A final observation for tonight is the amazing way they carry on business in the vicinity of the Prophet's Mosque. Bazaar after bazaar after bazaar. Non-local businesses, established traders, itinerant traders, one by one, in groups, trading by barter, local people and visitors, all together. Was the *'Ukāẓ*[37] [market] also here? Or did it come later? Do business and worship really belong in the same place at all? Or is one of them a misbegotten child of the other? Or one of its amusing by-products? Which is which? Before and after the 5 rituals of prayer, everyone buys or sells something. A fellow will spread his prayer rug out in the street to reserve a place to pray, but after the prayer is over he will lay his merchandise out on it. What does he have to display? A handful of agates, turquoise, prayer beads, perfume, handkerchiefs, or tamarisk[38] toothbrushes. They are lined up shoulder to shoulder like this. Automobiles are forbidden in the streets around the Prophet's Mosque. Just during the Hajj season, no doubt.

---

[37] The *Ukāẓ* market was held in pre-Islamic times during the lunar month of Dhu al-Qa'dah in an area between the cities of Ta'if and Nakhla. It later became a customary stop for Arabs making the pilgrimage to Mecca. (tr)

[38] A toothbrush can be made by fraying and wetting the end of a twig from the tamarisk tree. (tr)

Sunday 23 Farvardin 1343 [April 12, 1964]

The obligations of *'Ayd* will become clear tonight. They will announce whether they saw the moon or not. It was announced in *al-Nadwah* that whoever sees the moon should notify the *shar'* court[39] judge. There will be, according to me, one day, and according to another person a two-day interval between the announcement by these Saudi gentlemen and the appearance of the new moon according to the Shi'i calendar. It's quite clear, however, that *'Ayd* must be observed according to the celestial position of this location. A guy who comes from Indonesia by way of Turkey will surely have a different lunar calendar, but the rites of the Hajj must be enacted here. I don't see why the Hajj couldn't be kept in one season of the year—in the solar calendar. Wasn't it this way originally, so the hajjis from northern countries wouldn't defer their journey to some year when *'Ayd-e Qorbān* occurred during the winter? I realized that the Hajj, with this lunar calendar, has confined Islam to the equatorial regions.

Today I didn't set foot outside the house. I slept from 8 to 11 in the morning, in order to compensate for the lack of sleep these two or three days. I was in such a state that at night I didn't hear what anyone said. I couldn't focus my attention. The day before that I couldn't focus my memory, that is I couldn't find words. I'm trying to drink less water. The heat is such, however, that you perspire away whatever you drink. It's such a pleasure, this perspiring after drinking one's fill, and the kidneys are amazingly comfortable! (Again I'm preoccupied with myself!) Last night I no sooner laid my head down when it was four in the morning and a new group of hajjis came in and made a commotion in the house. They turned on the lights and everyone got up. Then we cleansed ourselves and went to the Prophet's Mosque. The greatest damage from these years of not praying was the loss of the mornings, with their delicate coolness, and the energetic activity of the people. If you get up before sunrise it's like getting up before creation, every day witnessing anew this daily transformation from darkness to light, from sleep to wakefulness, from stillness to motion. I was feeling so good this morning that I said hello to everyone, didn't feel like a hypocrite when I prayed, nor that I was doing my ablutions out of imitation. Yesterday and the day before I still couldn't believe this was me performing a religious rite just like everyone else. I remember all the prayers and the short and long verses from the Qur'ān I memorized as a child. Arabic words, however, weigh heavily on my mind and tongue, excessively so. I can't pronounce them quickly. In those days I could read them off like a litany with no problems. I realized this morning, however, that Arabic has become a heavy burden on my conscience. In the morning when I said "peace be upon you, O Prophet," I had a sudden start. I

39 *Shar'* courts deal with matters under the jurisdiction of Islamic law, as opposed to secular law, which is handled by the *'urf* courts

could see the Prophet's grave and the people circumambulating. They were climbing all over one another to kiss the shrine. The police were continually scrambling to prevent forbidden behavior... I started crying and abruptly fled the mosque...

This house we have is newly built, made of cement bricks. They are a little larger than red earthenware bricks, and they used them to fill the foundation. Only the lower level has been completed and finished. What remains is the second floor and half the third floor, where the bricks are visible, the wiring is hanging out of the walls, and there is no running water. Again, there is a bit of water in the pipes in the morning and the evening. Yesterday when I was taking a shower there was an uproar from my traveling companions. Water was seeping out of the shower room under their belongings. I had to interrupt my shower. There is a corridor running the length of every floor between the rows of rooms. The shower and the toilet are on opposite sides of the hallway, the toilet at the mid point and the shower at the end. The toilets, however, are not yet clogged, and that's something to be thankful for. There are three identical housing complexes. They belong to a man named Sayyid ʻUmar the Abyssinian (but he isn't black). Two of them have been rented by two Iranian guides at 700 rials apiece for the duration of the Hajj. The third one is vacant. The yard, which is shared, is in the hands of a group of people from Buhrah, who are living out in the open air, grouped together by families. They bathe with a bowl of water by the garden and stay at home all the time. They appear to be neither pilgrims, followers of the rites, nor observers. They're just a group of people squatting on the land baking bread in an open pan or husking rice and bulgur, for lunch and then for dinner. And they eat a lot of bread and dates in this heat. There are really a lot of sweets and halvah in the bazaar, and there is a great deal of perfume being bought and sold! I saw some thick stalks of aloe yesterday in the bazaar for the first time. There are so many blacks, and they have the most interesting faces of the Hajj. Especially when they are wearing the white *iḥrām*. The whiteness of the *iḥrām* and the blackness of their skin are poetically beautiful. I saw two of them in Badr wearing *iḥrām*s on their way back from Medina. They had gotten out of their hot bus, which needed repair, on order to sit in a corner in the shade. I was worried that they would sit in the dirt and soil their white garments. Then they stretched out, as if they didn't know how to sit. Either they stood up, stretched out, or slouched on the ground, leaning on their elbows, like old men who need a cane to stand up.

This guide of ours is a real penny-pincher, especially when it comes to buying water. He prepares segregated meals for us. The women are in one room and the others are assembled in peer groupings. My relatives and I, the 5 of us, share the smallest of the rooms, even though another person was added to the group today. She's an old woman who made her daughter's girl Javad's temporary wife so she would be *mahram*[40] and be under supervision. Now she not only thinks she's *mahram*, but also that she's everyone's stepsister. She's a small woman, quick and sneaky like a mouse. She goes gossipping from this room to that one. We've created a domestic scene in very short order. The old retired police major has also given up in very short order. His roommates are at their wits' end, seeking advice from everyone. Today I went to see him at lunch. He was in a daze. He seemed to have given up. He had withdrawn into himself in a bad way. A lifetime of military service with rank, tassels, and marching in step, and now he was just like everyone else, but in worse condition. I don't think he will make it to the end.

Same day. Same place.

I went and walked around the Baqī' Cemetery in the afternoon. The west side of it faced on the city, and the east side looked out on the date groves. Its walls were high and thick, just like prison walls. After going all the way around it I found myself at the gate. Entry was impossible, however. The police were chasing the hajjis out, and with brutality and force. The end of visiting hours? No doubt. Then I went for a walk around the city. First I went north, then west, then to the center. At the northern gate there was a mosque called Abazar. I went inside. It was totally empty. I prayed on the tightly woven, exquisite, but filthy prayer carpet on the mosque floor. Then I opened the Qur'ān at random. I read "Indeed the righteous believers will inherit the earth," surely the answer to this morning's sermon in the Prophet's Mosque. There was an intersection in front of the mosque with a concrete traffic control kiosk. The policeman was blowing his whistle, automobiles were blowing their horns, and in the two little gardens in front of the mosque there were tree seedlings about the size of irises, or something on the order of Khark's *leyl* trees, with broad, cork-like leaves. Then I visited the Abu Bakr Mosque, where I made two more prostrations and opened the Qur'ān at random once again. The Tubah Surah came up. I didn't say "In the name of God." In my heart I said "What does it all mean?" And I went out. A mosque of Ottoman vintage, perhaps older. It has a bulbous dome and a single minaret, with a date tree alongside competing for height, fresh and lush. Then I dropped in on al-Ghamamah Mosque, with its cluster of domes, large and small, huddling together. I sat next to the *minbar*.[41] The afternoon prayer had just ended, and the imam was preaching, sitting on the *mihrāb*.[42] I was in an introspective mood,

[40] A woman who is *mahram* in relation to a particular man is permitted to see him unveiled, but prohibited under Islamic law from marrying him. The term is usually applied to relatives, and may be used to describe a man or a woman. (tr)

[41] A *minbar* is the "pulpit" used in a mosque. It is actually a portable staircase with a small platform at the top on which the preacher or teacher sits. (tr)

[42] A *mihrāb* is a niche in a mosque that indicates the direction of the Kaaba. (tr)

thinking of what had crossed my mind in the Abu Bakr Mosque: "In any case he was an old man who undoubtedly corrected their youthful rashness and extremism. Who knows what happened in the cave,[43] and before it and after it, that he came to be known as the Sincere Friend. And what controversies? What advisements? It can be seen that he added the Hajj rite to Islam, which he derived from the customs of the Quraysh[44] tribe. He was a man in any case, the image of his daughter 'Ā'ishah. She must have been an interesting woman. She is said to have married the Prophet when he was old and she was very, very young, even a child. Wouldn't it seem that Abu Bakr had sacrificed his own daughter in this way? What are you saying?"

In any case I realized that in accepting the position of "Mother of the Faithful" as a child she can be seen as the cause of so many events, including the Battle of the Camel[45] incident... I don't know anything about the rest of it. "Why haven't you studied the life of this woman before now?" It's interesting that not even the Shi'is are critical of her. They merely cite her as a "special" kind of woman who at least had the attribute of cleverness and a knack for getting into everything. Let's drop it. That's enough.

At the northern gate of the city in the middle of a broad—but filthy—plot of land, tents had been erected. It was a camp for Turkish hajjis. Just like the desert of Karbala.[46] Such dust, and tremendous traffic. In the middle of that dust there was a man in his store down on his hands and knees mindlessly sprinkling water around him, with a plastic hose, without moving from his position. When I stopped a few steps farther along to write something down, someone ran into me from behind. Apologies on both sides, laughter, and farewell. I was about to go on when I saw that same shopkeeper standing naked in the same place holding the same hose

---

43 The leaders of the Quraysh, and others, were jealous and suspicious of the Prophet Muhammad's teachings in the early stages of his career as a prophet. In September of 622, his enemies plotted to murder him; being forewarned of the plan, Muhammad left his bed with 'Ali ibn Abi Talib, his first cousin, later son-in-law, and the first convert to Islam according to legend, sleeping in his place. He then fled to a nearby mountain cave, accompanied by Abu Bakr. Two nights later, on September 24, he arrived in Medina, then known as Yathrib. It is this flight which has come to be known as the *Hijrah*, or Hegira. (tr)

44 The Quraysh were a major tribe in the time of the Prophet Muhammad, to which he belonged. He was a member of the clan of Hashim in that tribe. (tr)

45 The Battle of the Camel (Arabic *Jamal*) took place in 656 A.D. During the battle around 70 men were killed defending 'Ā'ishah as she rode a camel inside a covered pavilion. It was fought against 'Ali ibn Abi Talib and his followers by a contingency, including 'Ā'ishah, which demanded punishment for the assassination of the Caliph 'Uthman and 'Ali's resignation as caliph. (tr)

46 The desert of Karbala is a symbol of oppression and misery for Shi'i Muslims. Besides being in a hot, dry Iraqi desert, it is the site of a bloody battle in which Husayn, the son of 'Ali and the rightful successor to the Islamic caliphate, was killed along with 70 of his followers in a bloody massacre by the "usurper" Yazid and his army. This took place on the 10th of Moharram, a day that is still observed with mourning and religious passion in Iran. For many Iranians, however, the events at Karbala are a potent metaphor for suffering and injustice the year around. (tr)

above his head, bathing. He was so quick to pull off his *dishdāshah* and pour water over his head!

All the busses the Turks had brought bore emblems, the names of companies. I wrote down those names: Seljuk, Tourism, Siyahat, Jet Kabnak, and Ulusavi, all written in the Latin alphabet... All their hoods were raised, the drivers busy making modifications and repairs. It was obvious that the local Hajj companies had picked up the Turks at their doorsteps and brought them here by way of Syria or Iraq, all with their own vehicles. The Iranian hajji, however, is obliged to come to Jedda by air, and after that confusion, and after all that waiting, and then this feeling of being imprisoned, the prisoner of monopolists.

At the western gate of the city I visited the firewood dealers' lot. They had big bundles of thornwood [*moghilān*] bushes (Mohaddes calls them mother *ghilān* or mother *ghulān* [monsters' mother]. He gripes continually these days. Why did we come with this guide and not the other one? He isn't a happy traveler. He's very accustomed to his house and his library.) which had been piled up for tomorrow morning's market. The smell of the camel's thorn bush is in the air, rising from its leaves. Don't tell me the camel's thorn and *moghilān* are from the same family? They smell the same in any event, mingled with a trace of frankincense. It causes a pleasant irritation at the base of the throat. Beyond the field was Mount Sal', behind which was dug the famous *Khandaq*[47] [trench]. At every point along it there are the remains of a mosque or tower and two or three cannons. A bit farther in that direction, to the right of the road coming into the city, there are the remains of an Ottoman fortress, which has been deliberately destroyed. It's magnificent, even in ruins. I greeted a young man sitting in a corner, and we exchanged pleasantries. I asked him a few questions for Arabic practice. He was in his fourth year of high school, and had trouble understanding me. The cannons were aimed away from the city; the young fellow said they still fire them ceremonially and on holidays. While visiting the other Ottoman fortress, I thought that we and the people here are part of a single piece of canvas, they at the bottom end and we at the top. Or vice-versa. Why shouldn't a fortress like this be preserved? All through the Muslim world we trample the remnants of those who've gone before, and wipe their traces off the face of the earth, so we can blossom ourselves. The only aspect of others that interests us is their graves and buried artifacts. It must be this way. With all your contempt, you flourish in the act of trampling someone else's glory, and this very contempt is gratified as you weep over the bones of this very other person. The date groves I saw to the east of the graveyard weren't in very good condition. There were some

[47] This trench, designed by the Iranian Muslim convert Salmān Pārsi was dug in March of 627. Its purpose was to defend the city of Medina from an impending attack by a superior force of pagan Meccans who sought to break the Prophet Muhammad's power. The trench effectively thwarted the invasion. (tr)

summer crops being cultivated on their fringes. The irrigation ditches for the date trees weren't full of water like those around the Karun, Tigris, and Euphrates rivers. Rather, the dates were cultivated on irregular patches of land, within a fine network of small ditches, and everything was covered with dust, with the sound of the pumps resembling, with quicker pulsations, the sound of the ringdove in the air. *Haq haq haq haq*. Just like that. There were Arabs going to and fro with radios that played songs in Arabic. One or two had shovels on their shoulders with the tails of their *dishdāshah*s pulled up, fastened to their waistbands. They said "Good day, hajji," and "Peace be upon you..." I went out in the direction of the city.

Mimosa saplings (or something between a willow and a mimosa—some kind of tropical shade tree) had been planted alongside the canals flanking the road. Each one had a protective iron rail around it—just like prison bars. The bars were crooked and flat, and if the sapling was small you couldn't see it at all. Perhaps these were shields to protect against the burning heat of the sun. Despite all the pains that had been taken, most of them were damaged and dried up. I looked at the largest ones. They were very fresh and hopeful, promising to bring beauty and greenness to the city. At one point I slouched onto a bench in a coffee house, the bench where these pages were written. It was high and knotty, like the boards we put over a *howz*[48] to make a platform. The woven straw seat was caved in. I ordered coffee, which they didn't have. I settled for tea. He called out "Christian tea!" I understood the second part, but the first? You've gone to all this trouble to be like everyone else and now you're "Christian?" When they brought the tea, however, I had reason to doubt my understanding of Arabic, because there was no doubt of the tea's being tea or of its ordinary character. It was the same old sweet tea, but served in a teapot. The sugar had been mixed into the tea in the pot, and there were two handled teacups beside it. It was extremely hot, and there was also a bottle of ice water beside it. He charged 12 piastres. I bought two books of matches from the cigarette stand next door for two piastres and got up to leave. I had brought some *Oshno* cigarettes,[49] and it was a good thing. They have no locally-made cigarettes here. As much as you like, however, there are Camels, King Size, Stuyvesant, Pall Mall, and so on, various American brands. And so expensive, too. Our traveling companions from the villages are really overdoing it. They try a new brand every day, and cough "*kuheh, kuheh*," just like an old pack horse. And is it possible to get any sleep? You can hear the sound of the dry bronchial coughing of one of them in the room on the end. Tonight I must remember to give him some Ipesandrine, in case it isn't caused by switching brands.

---

[48] *Howz* is the Persian name for the Iranian courtyard pond. (tr)

[49] A very cheap and strong brand of Iranian cigarettes. (tr)

This morning a young black man, a member of the Nakhāwalah clan[50] (according to Mohaddes they are date growers), came to see our guide. He had known my brother, who died here in Medina 13 years ago. He was the late Borujerdi's[51] representative here... The young man was looking for a job as someone's surrogate on the Hajj. I didn't know what this meant. I asked. Our guide said it was a hajji hired in this locality on behalf of someone's father, mother, or relative, to make the trip from Medina to Mecca to observe the rituals. What was his price? He said "They pay up to 500, but if 250 is satisfactory, that's alright." He was talking about Saudi rials. I remembered that last night our group's preacher had spoken favorably about this at the close of his sermon, saying,

"If your father and mother are remiss [with respect to their religious obligations] and etc... There are people here who will act on their behalf for a small price to release them from this great obligation..."

Last night I had thought he was making suggestions in order to fill his own belly. Now it seems that this is a business for the Nakhāwalahs, a Medina Shi'i minority. My brother had been an agent for them. He continued this for no more than two years. They buried him in that same graveyard. I'm going to find his grave tomorrow. This preacher in our group is originally from Hamadan. He's been forbidden to preach [in Iran] for political reasons. I know him from the Tuesday night *rowzeh*s[52] in my father's house.

---

50 The Nakhāwalah are a Shi'i sect found in Medina and Jedda. They are holdovers from the days when the Shi'is contributed to the conquest of western Arabia. Most of the other early Shi'is have since converted to the Shāfi'i school of Islam; the Nakhāwalah, who did not, became a despised group which was compelled to follow the lowest of trades. (tr)

51 Ayatollah Mohammad Hoseyn Borujerdi, the Iranian scholar and clergyman, who had become the leading religious dignitary of the Shi'i world by the time of his death in 1961. (tr)

52 *Rowzehs* are impassioned verse accounts of the tragedy at Karbala. They are often used to excite the emotions of listeners by preachers prior to a sermon. (tr)

Monday 24 Farvardin [April 13]

Medina

I went to the Baqī' Cemetery this morning, looking in the dirt for traces of tradition in the hot sun, and above all, for traces of my brother. There were none, however. When the graves of four Shi'i imams, that of 'Uthman,[53] and the Prophet's wives and children are unmarked, who is my brother? Now, he's an unmarked particle of dust on top of these layers of tradition. All over the graveyard are mounds of earth—very soft earth—and clusters of black stone markers sunk into the ground here and there, or the corpse of a piece of marble with a corner of the *kāf*[54] in Kufic script knocked off, marking a grave whose marker stone they've smashed to dust. The work of the Wahhabis[55] of 40 years ago when they came to power in Saudi Arabia. Did they do all this simply out of Wahhabi prejudice? At one time every grave had a dome and a courtyard. Now there is justice and equality in death such as I've never seen! Or perhaps the presence of the graves of men from various Islamic sects in one place is comparable to the shahs who could sleep together on one carpet but could not rule together?[56] Or perhaps they wanted to keep other graves from standing out too prominently near the Prophet's grave? After all, the distance between the graveyard and the Prophet's Mosque is less than 200 meters. No... One cannot expect to find that much intelligence—especially back then—among these Saudis. Someone who knows these expressions and explanations will conclude in his mind that they ought to put up a monument in the middle of the graveyard instead of individual graves for all these great people, with all their names and the dates of their births carved on a stone. One must conclude that the Saudis aren't capable of managing these shrines. Medina and Mecca must be set free from the disgrace of these gentlemen and be declared two international Islamic cities. I was thinking these thoughts, walking, and remembering my brother and all the heartache he endured just to put stone borders around the graves of four imams; I thought about the photographs he took of what was happening, how he soiled his hands, how unexpected was the news of his death, how I swore at my father that day, and what infidel thoughts I had which I kept to myself... I removed my shoes with the others, and opened the soft earth of this ancient graveyard. I realized that 14 centuries of Islamic tradition in such soil—now lead to nothing. They are a people, after all, with their beliefs, and suppose they do worship the dead. Suppose I'm stupid and you Saudis are extremely wise! What right

---

53 'Uthman ibn 'Affan was the third Muslim Caliph. He was in power from 644 to 656 A.D. (tr)

54 *Kāf* is the name of the letter "k" in the Arabic alphabet. (tr)

55 "Wahhabi" is a term applied to those who follow the Hanbalite teachings of Shaykh Muhammad ibn 'Abd al-Wahhab, whose 18th century religious movement provided the moral basis for the unification of most of the Arabian Peninsula under the House of Sa'ud. (tr)

56 The author is referring to a story from Sa'di's *Golestan*. (tr)

have we to reduce to dust shrines which are a part of Muslim daily life? The one who has fled the baseness of his daily life and come here wants to see the grandeur of eternity manifested in the beauty of a court, with his physical eye. To you this is idolatry, but what do you do with mythology? Haven't you read that even Moses went into retreat to contact God? To see him with his physical eye... Now you're collecting a toll from him too. From this very idolatrous Shi'i, Hanafi, Zaydi, or Bohara[57] who has come on a pilgrimage. Are you inquisitors for the Judgment? The Quraysh, who were the door keepers of that House of God, placed their faith in Islam by contributing to the Hajj rites, and you're now gathering the spoils of their good works. If these oil wells ran dry, which are your only means of rising above life in tents to a government of prejudice, don't you see that you would still need these pilgrims? I ask you, which will dry up first, the oil, or these annual Hajj rites? You certainly know the answer to this. But don't you see what seeds are sown each year for acquiring worldly wisdom, for abandoning baseness, and forgetting the parts within the whole? (Oh ho! I seem to be following up on *Gharbzadegi*.)

Same day in the afternoon.

Today we went to Uhud.[58] Five people riding in a passenger-car taxi for 10 Saudi rials, round trip. Just two steps down the road. I must walk there some time. All the graves were covered with sand. The walls were whitewashed. There were neat, broad steps in the entryway, and the grilled enclosures around the former graves were like fences atop walls. The graves of Hamzah and Mus'ab,[59] in the center of the graveyard, were surrounded by a wall of people. They were vaults covered with dirt. Coins had been tossed into the earth and sand. Bedouin and Berber women came and pushed themselves closer through the crowd. When they saw that the police were a little ways away they would snatch a fistful of dirt from the grave and run, the police swearing in hot pursuit, brandishing their headbands like whips in their hands. Javad was upset very much by this. At one point he finally took one of them by the collar and said in Arabic "You're a dog! You're a Jew!" I didn't think he had it in him. The base

---

[57] Hanafis are followers of the Sunni school of Islamic law founded by the Muslim jurist Abū Ḥanīfah (d. 767). Theirs is the only major Muslim sect that permits prayers in languages other than Arabic. The Zaydis are followers of Zayd al-Shahīd, who rebelled in 737 A.D. against the Umayyad caliph Hishām 'Abd al-Malik. They regard him as the fifth Imam in the Household of the Prophet. The Boharas are an Indian branch of the Ismā'īlī sect. It was probably originally formed in the 11th century by converts from Hinduism under the influence of Ismā'īlī propagandists who were active in India during that period. (tr)

[58] Uhud is the site of the first battle fought by Muslims against non-believers, and the burial ground of the first martyrs of Islam. (tr)

[59] Hamzah was an uncle of the Prophet Muhammad, said to be the first one killed at the battle of Uhud. Mus'ab ibn al-Zubayr was the brother of 'Abd Allāh ibn al-Zubayr, a rival of the Umayyad caliph 'Abd al-Malik (685 - 705). He was killed in 691 in a battle against 'Abd al-Malik. (tr)

of the graveyard was right in a big pit with no grave markers. It looked like a freshly-dug reservoir, but it was the common grave of the martyrs of Uhud. There were also coins and even bills everywhere at the bottom of the depression. Two groups of Iranian hajjis sat on either side, wailing mournfully with great excitement in the *shūr*[60] mode, in a way that would have melted the hardest heart, crying and beating themselves about the head and chest. All this was taking place at the foot of Mount Uhud, north of the city of Medina, with the village of Uhud on the fringes. There was a group of hajjis praying in a corner of the cemetery, lined up front to back in the narrow shadow of the wall. I thought they were trying to get out of the sun. Others, however, stood and prayed in the middle of the cemetery, and two or three young Arabs came to prohibit evil, saying "Forbidden! Forbidden! Do not make a mosque of the graves of your fathers," repeating the surah[61] and rotating passionately. No one paid any attention, however. There was little protest from the police against all of Javad's remonstrations. As it turns out the Saudis are not as praetorian this year. Mother's brother struggled along behind us in a terrible state. Mohaddes moaned stridently. I've never seen the like of it. Then we went out and had tea together at a coffee house in the village and watched the people while waiting for the taxi. There were a great many Turkish hajjis, but in their own busses, as before. There were legions of beggars. The drivers were lazy. The coffee house proprietor fried eggs for the customers on the counter grill in a deep copper pot.

Returning, Javad and I went looking for the Garden of Purity, the one the hajjis talk so much about. They went garden, garden, garden so much I expected to find something like the Erām Garden of Shiraz, or maybe the Garden of Eden itself; but it was nothing but a decrepit old date orchard, with water from a pump house above it pouring into a pool. The people were right in the pool soaping themselves down and washing clothing. The water looked like whitewash. There were pipes carrying water to the date orchard from this pool, with a faucet at every corner. People were spread out among the date trees in the cultivated area with their belongings. They had made canopies of whatever was available and tied them to the trunks of the date trees. Men and women, young and old were lolling about side by side in the midst of bedrolls, primus stoves, samovars, blankets, bowls of salad, and kabob braziers. The irrigation canals served as a kind of sewer. People from the same cities were grouped together. In one place I passed the Esfahani accent; in another the Yazdi; and in another, the Khorasani. These people are all hajjis who manage their own disbursements. They've paid only a small amount to a guide for supervision in religious matters. Every night they pay 1 Saudi rial to rent space in the garden; in return

---

60 *Shūr* is the name of a scale in classical Iranian music. (tr)

61 Although the Arabic in the text resembles the style of a Qur'ānic verse, it is not actually in the Qur'ān. (tr)

there's no charge for bathing in the pool. I also visited the public toilet. The Shah Mosque was 100 times cleaner 20 years ago![62] And such dirt, heat, and filth! Just like *sizdahbedar*[63] at an *Emāmzādeh Dāvud* in a Sousa date orchard. Yet these good people are so happy they've come here and set up housekeeping in the date orchard! The owner of the garden is himself a Yazdi or an Esfahani who's become a permanent resident here. He's grossly fat and very charming. Like Shamshiri in his kabob stand. In addition to the garden, he also owns an ice factory. Ice costs 2 Saudi rials per kilo, post cards are 1 rial each. Writing materials are unbelievably expensive. I've been unable to buy a ball point pen, but I bought a pocket-size notebook for 1.5 Saudi rials.

I got the urge to go barefoot today. My feet aren't comfortable in these rubber slippers. They've blistered. The asphalt was too hot, however, and the sand around it was hotter still. It was burning hot. Obviously, the soles of the feet and the top of the head must be carefully protected from the primitive life.

Same day. Afternoon.

There's no alternative but to internationalize these shrines, Mecca, Medina, ʿArafāt, and Mina, to place them under the management of a joint council of Muslim nations, and to remove them from Saudi Arab control. The revenues must come from income generated by the Hajj. Instead of Saudi Arabian police there must be guides from every nation. Legitimacy must be granted to the special customs of each sect. Road tolls must be lifted, and gardens, courtyards, houses, and dwelling places must be constructed for every group. Especially since most of the Medina businessmen are foreigners. Iraqis, Iranians, Pakistanis, and even Javanese, who have come and settled permanently. They pay exorbitant fees for key money and tolls, and they barely survive.

But this heat! It's so intense that I carefully poured three bowls of water over my head today—so it wouldn't seep under the walls of the shower stall and run under the belongings of my fellow travelers—and it felt like the best cold water shower I'd ever had. My God, what will it be like here in the summer? This itself could explain why my poor brother died in this city.

---

62 The Shah Mosque of Tehran was renowned for its filthy toilet in Āl-e Ahmad's day, but conditions there are said to have been even worse during previous periods. (tr)

63 Literally meaning "thirteenth outside," *sizdahbedar* comes on the thirteenth day of the Iranian year, and is an important part of the Iranian *Noruz*, or new year's, celebrations. On this day people vacate their homes for the use of denizens of the spirit world, who will then presumably leave them in peace for the rest of the year. The traditional thing to do is to have a picnic in some beautiful part of the springtime countryside. *Emāmzādehs* are often lovely places for such outings, but the image given here of an *emāmzādeh* in a date orchard in the hot deserts of the Sousa region is sarcastic. (tr)

The buildings of recent construction are designed to catch the wind. They've made the windows so large, however—the idiots!—that you'd think this was the Norwegian coast. And these flies! I've never seen the like in my life, not even in Khorramshahr, not even in Sagzabad before the advent of DDT—to mention only a few places. Yes. There is no alternative to international Islamic control over these rites.

Evening. Same day.

Late this afternoon I met three young freshman and sophomore high school students at an ice cream stand on 'Ayinah street, across from *Bāb al-Salām* [The Gate of Peace]. They were from 'Ur'ur "in northern Saudi Arabia," near where the Iraqi oil pipeline passes on its way to Syria and Lebanon. Theirs is the only secondary school in a city of 12,000 people. They closed the 8th grade class and brought it to Medina. The freshman class went to Dammam (20 kilometers south of Dhahran) because the Egyptian teachers had left, and even the newly-arrived Syrians and Lebanese couldn't take their places. There is no sign of the Egyptians at this year's Hajj. "This year we wouldn't even accept a shroud for the Kaaba from the Egyptians," they said. "We made it ourselves." They were so happy. They didn't know, however, that the dispute between Egypt and Saudi Arabia was over Yemen. The young men were eating their ice cream—and myself as well—when an Iranian Sayyid came up with a loose, drooping turban, trying to raise money from his supporters for the construction of the Bahar Mosque. I don't know in which city. He had an Esfahani accent, however. The discussion became jocular and there was bazaar-style bargaining. The young Saudis, half in jest and half seriously, kept telling him that it was near sunset, the call to prayer had been given, why didn't he go, and so on... I got it across to them that our lawful sunset for religious purposes doesn't come until after the natural sunset and that there was still plenty of time for prayer. I said it in "Engrish," because I'd heard them exchange a few words in broken English when they were making fun of the other gentlemen. This started a discussion. According to them, the country is violently opposed to "The Great King," wants a republic, and worships Nasser. They were young people, infatuated with Arab nationalism and the power it will have. They were showing off the pictures under their arms in illustrated, Westernized Egyptian magazines showing naked women, fashions, toasts to the health in Cairo and Beirut parties, and Egyptian tanks... When they were writing down their addresses, they took pains to spell their names in the Latin alphabet. "Why don't you write in Arabic," I asked them. They were surprised, and they handed me their magazines to see if I could read Arabic. Later, when I really got going, I started showing off, just as if I were teaching a class. They realized that I know some "Franch," and stubbornly insisted on hearing a sentence in it, so I wrote this for them next to a picture of an Egyptian tank: /*comme vous êtes innocents, mes chers enfants perdus sous la reigne d'un governement primitif...!*/[64]

Then they wanted to know what it meant. They didn't understand it in *Engrish* and I couldn't say it in Arabic. I certainly won't write it in Persian. When we left the ice cream stand—with good-byes—I was thinking that you can't blame the Saudis for having more homosexuality than any other place in the world. There probably haven't been more than one or two unveiled women since I left Tehran, and even fewer who were pretty. Those three young men were quite handsome, with beautiful smiles. One of them spoke with a womanly suggestiveness. Only one had a deep male voice. All were fervent admirers of Nasser. Are all Saudi Arabians like this? Or only these educated ones, from classes that were taught by Egyptians until the year before last? It's interesting, however, that none of them knew his own religious sect! When I asked if they were Hanafi, Māliki,[65] or what else, they were stumped at first. Then they thought about it and one of them said Hanbali.[66] He was obviously talking nonsense. The contagion of irreligion is everywhere. How disappointed they were when the Egyptian teachers left! They had such a desire for the American teachers the Aramco company[67] [Arabian American Oil Company] had promised to send to their schools to teach English. They were certain that within 3 years Nasser would swallow up Israel, and dump the Israelis into the sea.

---

64 The sentence in French (between slashes) was censored in some earlier editions of the book. (tr)

65 Mālikis are followers of the Sunni school of Islamic law named after the Muslim jurist Mālik ibn Anas (d. 793). This sect is noted for its emphasis on the importance of *Hadith* (the Traditions of the Prophet) in resolving religious and legal questions not specifically covered in the Qur'ān. (tr)

66 Hanbalis are followers of the Sunni school of Islamic law founded by the Muslim jurist Aḥmad ibn Ḥanbal (d. 855). Ḥanbal had been a student of Muhammad ibn Idris al-Shāfī, the founder of another of the four orthodox Sunni sects, but led a "back to the Qur'ān" movement that rejected many of Shāfī's teachings, including the validity of religious law formulated by boards of religious scholars. Hanbalis are the majority sect in Saudi Arabia today. (tr)

67 The Aramco company was originally formed in 1933 as a subsidiary of the Standard Oil Company of California, whose purpose was to act on Standard's behalf in a concession agreement signed that year with Saudi Arabia. At the time *Lost in the Crowd* was written, Aramco was owned jointly by Standard Oil Company of California, Texaco Inc., Standard Oil Company (New Jersey) and Socony Mobil Oil Company. (tr)

Tuesday 25 Farvardin 1343 [April 14, 1964]

Medina

It's only for the Iranians that both directions of the Hajj pilgrimage are under an air transportation monopoly. The problem is that when they return they can't even go to Iraq. If someone wants to visit Karbala and Najaf[68] also, or Damascus, he must forget about buying a round-trip ticket and purchase another ticket later for Baghdad or Damascus, and with a thousand delays at Jedda thrown in for good measure; in such a season, priority goes to those who have prepaid tickets. Other hajjis of the world, however, have the option of coming by whatever means they wish. Another market is sewn up by the air transportation monopoly. So much the better. Monopoly of the *muṭawwifs*,[69] the Sahrahs, the Shajrahs, and so on. Those are their names. They are companies that supply hajjis with busses, who set up tents at 'Arafāt and Mina, and this sort of thing. Their names are officially listed in every Hajj directory. The first thing they asked us at the Jedda airport was "who is your *muṭawwif?*" Ours was the Sahrah agency, the name of which was whispered several times in each of our ears before we deplaned. Then this second monopoly clears the way for a third, which is associated with our own *hamlehdār*s. A *hamlehdār* is someone who takes one, two, or three hundred people with him on the pilgrimage. Each of them makes up to a thousand tomans. These guides collaborate and work with the other monopolies from the first step, and, depending on the amount of money they receive from the hajjis, they procure food and necessities en route and at stopping places, and make arrangements for housing and shelter. What can one hajji do on his own against all these monopolies? I saw four of my former classmates in Medina who had come on the Hajj in a vehicle with massive amounts of baggage—tents, beds, cooking equipment, ice box—who were pooling their resources. When they got off the ship at Jedda, however, they learned that they had to become a part of some guide's party, or at least become associated with an agency, because they were Iranian. Not Turks, Egyptians, or Syrians. They were thus detained for a week. They paid a fixed toll, attached the name "Sahrah" to their vehicle, and then received permission to enter. I do not yet know what the situation is at 'Arafāt and Mina, or what new problems will be created by living two to three days in a tent.

In any case, something can certainly be done so that the hajji will not be such a prisoner to so many monopolies, each of which milks him in some

---

[68] Najaf is a city of about 25,000 in Iraq which has become one of the most important centers of Shi'i religious scholarship, and the home of some of the most prominent leaders of the Shi'i community. Najaf is also a shrine city where Imam 'Ali is buried. It is thus frequently the goal of religious pilgrimages as well. (tr)

[69] *Muṭawwif* is the Arabic term for a guide whose function is to provide pilgrims with guidance on how to properly perform the rituals of the Hajj. He also sees to their material needs in some cases, performing essentially the same function as a *hamlehdār*. (tr)

way, controls him, and destroys his freedom. The Hajj has thus become a device for making millionaires of the "National Airline," its local shareholders, and "The Great King," with Sahrah, Shajrah, and so forth...in Saudi Arabia.

The stupefaction of our retired police major has now turned to terror. He is a morose man with no conception of a good disposition. He's done so much running around in the sun the last few days that he's losing his senses. No matter how much we try to get him to take off his city clothing and loosen his tie, to put on a *dishdāshah* or a mantle and a night cap... In any case, it would make no difference if he did as those around him do. He has kept up a stiff demeanor right along, as if he were at his administrative post, and he's always bringing up 'Arafāt and Medina and the terror of living in a tent. A man who's spent his life protecting the high walls of houses and prisons is now going to live in a tent? With no walls or doors? I spent an hour last night consoling him and so on. One of his roommates told us that according to a woman in his family, his wife in Tehran had told him that if any problem or any reason to do so should arise he must drop the whole thing at once and go home. It appears that we must expect new developments.

Among those 4 or 5 preachers, *rowzeh'khāns*,[70] and mullas, there is a sayyid in our group from Borujerd; he's hot to find supporters for some mosque they're building in Tehran; I don't know the name of it. He has acquired a following of four or five merchants, and every day they pray together in their room. They have asked us indirectly two or three times why we don't join their prayer. Mohaddes, who follows no one. Uncle, who is not up to it. And Javad, who's strung out all over the place. By process of elimination, I'm the last one left in our family. He is one of those who think that 5 extra minutes of prostrations will take him 5 kilometers closer to the throne of God. Worse than that, he insists that I go listen to his talk to the villagers following the *maqhreb* prayer. I finally went last night. Up on the roof. He did such a job of spoiling the delicate air with the same old nonsense about *shakkiyāt* [uncertainties], *ghusl* [cleansing], *tathir* [purification], and *nejāsat* [uncleanness] that it made me sick at my stomach. These things ought not to be said even to the dummies of Mazandaran. Anyway, how long must religion be tied to the handle of an *āftābeh*, and be confined to the realm of "cleansing uncleanness?" Or be a menace to an old fool like me? Do these people bear the highest responsibility of religion? The guy doesn't even have the decency to refrain from immediately raising the subject of the unallowability of a moustache the minute you come near him. Worse than him is the hired mourner in our group, who's evidently deranged. He is in the habit of asking, "Why don't you beat yourself about the head and shoulders?" That's like saying "Why don't you jump off the

[70] A *rowzeh'khān* specializes in the recitation of *rowzehs*. (tr)

roof" when I talk about the tragedy. Praise be unto the preacher in our group, who speaks in terms of history and *hadith*,[71] and reasonably. He has begun a discussion of the historical period in which the Kaaba was built and the customs of the Hajj were established. For the villagers. It is useful in any case, if his sermon finally gets around to the Karbala desert situation. He brings tears to the people's eyes, but not with images of tragedy and martyrdom. His words are warm. His own heart has broken. I have explained why.

Tuesday 25 Farvardin 1343 [April 14, 1964]

We set out for Uhud early in the morning. Afoot. It isn't far—three or 4 kilometers, across from the recently built Senegalese billets, which are 3 or 4 stories high and built recently. There was a tall black man there who was carrying on playfully. I didn't understand at first. He was wearing pilgrim's garb. But I realized suddenly that it was an African dance. I went on. The sun, which had just arisen, was a big brass tub behind a veil of dust. It was around 6 o'clock, and you could look right at it. It was so huge, and pale orange. There was a beautiful young woman begging, wearing a cloth mask over her nose and mouth. As she approached I saw a glint in her eye that ought not to be seen during the Hajj season. And such eyes! Just like the eyes of a deer, of which you have read in so much poetry. But as they say, you had to be there. Her black gown was very thin, and beneath it she wore a long tattered shirt. She must have been cold. Her small, erect breasts did not move beneath her shirt. I was cold myself. I was wearing nothing but a long shirt, thinking I was in Saudi Arabia, where it is warm. Too early in the morning face to face with a woman like that... I walked on quickly. Last night on the roof (our family sleeps on the roof with another group of Esfahanis who travel with us. The rest sleep inside the room with their belongings, for fear of theft and the like) I got cold with one blanket. The problem is that we sit up and talk every night on the roof until at least 10. By the time you eat and get to sleep it's midnight, and we get up at 4:30 in the morning, or even earlier. Meals and sleep are most irregular. Food is not important, but I'm behind on sleep. It could incapacitate me. I must be careful.

---

[71] Also called a "tradition," a *hadith* is an accepted account of something said or done by the Prophet Muhammad, his companions, or one of the Imams. *Hadith*s have the status of scripture in the determination of precedent in Islamic law. (tr)

I passed a school on the way, at the northern gate of Medina, "The Teacher's Training Institute," founded in 1952/53 by the Ministry of Education. When I returned I saw the students clustered in the doorway. They were youths like those three I had met at the ice cream stand. I had an urge to go inside and find out about their studies, training, books, and teachers, but it was time to go back, I was tired, the blisters on my feet had broken, they burned, and when I came to the city I realized I could go no farther. So I sat in a corner and made sketches and notes of everything to keep myself busy. A bus passed right then. It was full of ripe young girls in smocks. "Girls' School" was written on it. I set out again after I felt rested, and passed in front of the "Maternity and Womens' Hospital." Then I went looking for the Mosques of Ali and Abu Bakr, and other places. This all happened on the way back; I'll discuss the trip there first.

Near Uhud there was a white school beside the road. It was clean and attractive on the outside, and children were hanging around in front of it. The door of the school was locked. It was only kept up on the outside. On the inside, however, it was a mess, just like our own schools. I looked through the windows. That its door was white instead of green[72] was an ominous sign to appear just before reaching the garden of Uhud, also built in the year 1372 of the Muslim lunar calendar. There must have been something afoot in Saudi Arabia that year. Either someone with an interest in culture had come to power, or etc... It took 50 minutes to go from the door of the house to the Shrine of Uhud, with long strides and without stopping. On the way I passed vegetable plots, gardens, and winter houses. Pollen—like date pollen—was blowing over the field. The sun was not yet warm, and there was little traffic. Today, however, they did not allow women inside the shrine. Police stood at the gate to stop them, no doubt because of yesterday's thefts of holy soil at the grave. The women were forced to stand outside the entryways in little groups. The professional eulogists were drilling them: "Oh friends! Oh martyrs! Oh departed loved ones!" It was empty inside the mosque, and tidy. The police kept the people away from the grave in a large circle. There was no sign of bills and coins on the graves.

On the way back I ordered coffee and fried eggs at yesterday's coffee house. "*Burrād wa khubz ma' bayḍīn.*" He did understand my Arabic. The eggs, which he took out of the copper pot on the fire, were the same kind. I asked for vegetables too. He went and brought 5 sprigs of mint. The yellow and white of the eggs, the honeyed color of the tea, the toasted whiteness of the bread, and the jade-green mint. The most beautiful plate in my memory. But on a tin tray bearing the Aramco trademark! And sitting cross-legged on the same straw benches with the pain of the feet's blisters being relieved

---

[72] Green, representing purity, is considered the proper color for a garden gate in Iranian culture. (tr)

by the warmth of the opposite leg; such pleasure! An old blind Arab passed, with a cane as thin as a finger, undoubtedly made of bamboo. Another old Arab who wanted a ride accosted a driver. The driver hit him in the chest so hard that the food in my mouth turned to rock. They're so very violent. I saw something even worse in the Prophet's Sanctuary: A young man and his wife were walking along holding onto each other. The crowd separated the woman from her husband for a moment. The man went back and hit a white-skinned (Syrian or Lebanese) woman who was between him and his wife in the back hard with the palm of his hand. He snatched his wife's wrist so violently with the other hand that I was sure her hand had come loose. They are dangerously violent. They talk much too loudly. And how their drivers blare their horns! With absolutely no need of it. And that driver that brought us from Jedda to Medina! Lord have mercy.

Uhud is a winter retreat like Medina. It has plenty of water and facilities. Date trees everywhere of all ages preserve examples of the plant's entire cycle. It is a village in the middle of a valley, with the graves of martyrs on its slopes and running up the side of the mountain. There are many functioning and abandoned wells, and the *haq haq haq haq* of the motor pumps comes from every direction. Long and slow beats. I looked one of them over. It was shallow and broad like the cattle troughs of Gorgan. A donkey driver followed his donkey saying *eeshshsh.* Another time he said *hooshsh.* Just like our own donkey drivers. When I reached the white school on the way back a fat black woman was leaning against the wall selling treats to the children. It was something that had been cooked. I didn't recognize it. The door of the school was still locked. It was still a long while before 8 a.m. The children were more numerous, boys and girls together. So many vehicles! Busses, trucks, and dump trucks. Most of them had been painted with designs, and they had baggage hanging out the doors and sides. There was one huge truck full of Bedouin Arabs, with the women sitting pressed together in its bed. Right over their heads was a wooden ceiling; the men sat on it, squatting squeezed together, watching the sights. Hanging over the sides were leather flasks for water and oil, tents and tent posts. The most interesting sort of truck to be seen on this journey.

The trees planted along the Uhud road were catalpa, Indian fig trees, camel's thorn, mimosa, and another tree I didn't recognize. The Indian figs were green, the new leaves at the branch ends like dark red buds opening. The leaves in front were flat, oily, and the color of myrtle. All the trees are young and tropical. What a blessing each is in a desert like Saudi Arabia. Even the Saudis know the value of trees.

When I got to the city I turned toward the bazaar, to the west of the Prophet's Mosque. Bedouin women sat waiting for customers with chickens or colored chicks (evidently done by machine) in elegant cages made of date wood, or holding out 4 eggs in the palm of a hand extended from beneath a cloak. Most of them were wearing veils like masks, resembling those I have seen on Khark Island. There was oil in small and large bottles, even bottles made of sheepskin. An Iranian in the middle of the market had spread out 2 small carpets from Qom. He was doing business in broken Turkish with an attractive woman dressed in white. I overheard that each one was priced at 400 rials. Then I passed a row of people selling the heads and feet of animals. Their ovens were hot, and heads of sheep and cows were heaped together in a single cauldron. I then retreated to the ice cream stand I knew.

A red-faced man there was exchanging money with two or three people. We chatted, half in Persian, half in Arabic. He was an Iraqi guide. He had been a tailor originally, from a family of Iranians that had moved to Karbala. He told me the ice cream stand owner was Javanese; the spice-seller next door was Indian, the bookseller next to him was Iraqi, and so on... He knew every merchant. Then the talk turned to ['Abd al-Salām] 'Ārif,[73] whom he did not like; then to ['Abd al-Karim] Qasim and Dr. [Mohammad] Mosaddeq,[74] who were just alike (in his view). Where is Mosaddeq, he asked. I said he was in a better place than Qasim. And there were regrets and expressions of remorse. He then said that this year Iraqi teachers had made a group agreement with the Saudi embassy in Baghdad so they could come on the Hajj without visas or tolls. Was this because of the great Saudi need for teachers? Even that tailor guide knew that the Saudis are short of teachers.

Then I went to the Prophet's Mosque. I usually enter it through the Door of Peace. It is larger and easier to go in and out of. I walked around the portico. I hung around among the pigeons, and walked on the sand strewn at the edges of the courtyard. The grains of sand and wheat blended so well the pigeons could hardly tell them apart. All around the courtyard, above the arched doorways, were written the names of the great men of the golden age of Islam. Even the 12 Shi'i Imams,[75] the companions of the Prophet, and the leaders. An old black woman with tiny features distributed ritual servings of water. I took a cup from her. The backs of her hands were covered with moles all the way to the fingernails; her face was also covered with them, from below the eyes to below the chin, even on her throat. All the moles were flower-like and tiny. I remember seeing another mole-covered woman a few days ago, with a snake design under her throat. The

[73] 'Abd al-Salām Muhammad 'Ārif was President of Iraq from 1963 to 1966.(tr)

[74] 'Abd al-Karim Qasim was Premier of Iraq from 1958 to 1963. Mohammad Mosaddeq was Premier of Iran from 1951 - 1953. (tr)

[75] For Ja'farī ("Twelver") Shi'is, there are 12 legitimate leaders of the Muslim community, or Imams. In all but matters of actual prophecy, they are considered successors to the Prophet Muhammad. All are blood descendants of 'Ali ibn Abi Talib, the Prophet's son-in-law. The term *īmām* is also used in Arabic to refer to a learned man in Islamic sciences. (tr)

snake's head was in the dimple of her chin, and the tail went down to the middle of her chest and disappeared. They must be Berbers. They sit in groups at the base of the mosque's columns with rectangular stainless steel trays full of empty cups large enough for one gulp. Grandiosely written in Arabic on the tray was: "Endowment of the Ministry of Pilgrimage Affairs and Religious Trusts." In any case, supplied in lieu of the 10 or 20 electric water coolers which are in every government office, it too is another example of how Hajj affairs are organized, and of the Saudi government's attentiveness and concern for the condition of the hajjis. They were totally negligent in the Prophet's Mosque. Architecturally it is half Andalusian, half Ottoman, with a veneer of cement slabs in three or four colors. They have laid huge slabs of red, cream, and black concrete alongside one another and stacked them to the top. Covering the roof were larger, continuous pieces, no doubt supported by iron rods embedded in the cement, instead of all these beautiful black stones that surround Medina and which they could have easily shaped and laid over the building. But perhaps they didn't want the Prophet's Mosque to be black? Excepting the foundations of the mosque, which are marble on the inside and granite on the outside, the exterior of the rest of this glorious mosque is all concrete slabs, even the minaret tops, which are so high. The walkways and the porches are also marble. Black and white. I really wanted to know who the architect was so I could collar him and say, "Sir! The supernatural magnificence of a building like this must be expressed with the simplest natural materials. It must be achieved with stone, not these molded concrete slabs. If there was a time when the Ottomans made these irregular incisions into ceiling arches, or when the Andalusians decorated the floors and walls of buildings with 8-color mosaics, they lived in another part of the world, in another time. You, who were responsible for the construction of such grandeur in Medina, did it not occur to you to seek assistance from engineers and architects from all Muslim countries? Or consultation on the various kinds of vaulted arches that were brought to Andalusia from India?" I'll drop this subject.

I also circumambulated the grave. The place was relatively empty. Everyone did what he was there to do in peace. The police didn't bother people. At the corners and sides of the sanctuary, the people had taken places in a file awaiting the prayer; they were intensely protective of the spaces they had claimed. How possessive people can be, even on a trip like this. I wasn't aware of this until my foot turned back the corner of a prayer carpet. The fellow hit the back of my foot so hard I didn't know how to react. I just looked at him. He was an old man, evidently not an Arab. He was turning a rosary and saying *zekr*; but there was a predatory look in his eye. I was embarrassed... A lot of people were lying down sleeping under the part of the mosque that had a low ceiling. It is a well-ventilated, cool area where the wind circulates. Definitely the coolest place in the city, and the quietest and most beautiful as well. A man was rattling the silver grill work around Sultan Salim's grave so hard (the Imam's tomb is raised above floor level) that I thought he was going to shake it loose. He was asking for something. Sometimes, therefore, the police are justified in what they do. (That woman who shares our room—the 6th member of the family, related by marriage—is here now, delighted and happy, saying she bought some souvenirs for the people at home. These women can't pass up anything in the bazaar. She purchased some thin muslin for a head scarf, with repeating playing-card designs, clubs, diamonds, and aces... undoubtedly made in Japan or somewhere in the east. A fine souvenir of Medina! I didn't say anything to her; I told my sister to reason with her, however).

Afternoon of the same day.

The retired police major is not doing well. We put an ice pack on his head and forced him to lie down. I think he is one of those who are accustomed to solitude; he doesn't know what to do with himself now in the midst of a group. This trip is such that if you are overly concerned with etiquette you'll have a very difficult time. And we just got the old fellow's thick winter coat off him today! I don't think he will make it to the end of the trip. Besides him, our own uncle's blood pressure has gone up; it has reached 200 mm. I still don't understand those numbers. His nephew, who is also Javad's brother, is a member of our own infirmary staff. He came today to take him to the infirmary, and he asked him "Why did you come?" Now he is quite uncomfortable. He won't even consider food. He can't walk, but we can't be slowing down for him all the time. Right now there is quite a row taking place in the women's room. There are curses flying everywhere. It seems that my sister finally convinced that old woman who lives with us that such a piece of cloth is inappropriate for a visitor to the house of God. She went and tried to pawn the cloth off on another of the women, who raised the same objection, and made fun of her. Now just look at the fuss! I told my sister to get the old woman out of there and calm the others down. Our guide came in as well, saying "You ought to be ashamed of yourselves, hajji ladies!" He yelled so loudly I thought our major would go into a frenzy.

Javad sold two of his carpets today for 370 Saudi rials. He was delighted. He says he made a 150-toman profit. They were coarsely woven carpets made for everyday use. When I figure things I realize I seem to be one of the poorest in this group. I saved one month's salary from the spoils of one or two of these silly books, and set out with 4 or 5 thousand tomans for the Hajj. That's very inexpensive.

Our situation is such in this house that you wouldn't think we had come for a journey, or at least not for a special kind of journey. We have a common room for prayers and *rowzeh*s in this house, which bears a striking resemblance to the most ordinary hotel on Naseriyeh[76] Street—but in Bushehr—and so on... We have a room for the ladies for arguing and chattering, which goes on constantly. We also have a sick room. I went to ask about the condition of the retired major; I saw there were also two other people sleeping on the opposite side of the room. One had diarrhea, the other a cold. My sister said he was afflicted by the heat. I found some "vitamin C" among my belongings and took it to him. When I gave it to him he said he thought he had some of his own, and he did. We agreed that he should suck two of them before nightfall so he would feel better. But then I'm feeling pretty bad myself. I've had a headache since noon. Is it possible to remain isolated in the midst of the crowd until the end of the journey? We have been content within the nobility of our own family until now. But later... (My condition is clearly not good). It's easy to be among the people and not be a part of them. I have followed in the shadow of the group up to this very moment. They are all rich and capable! Yet they're so poor it's frightening. They've lived in such poverty that they can't stand any change in routine. I try to get them motivated, but I know it's useless. One's sense of loneliness becomes more acute in a group like this. Not even Javad believes that I've only spent 73 Saudi rials so far. I have entrusted my money to him. Like the others, he has a money pouch on his belt, and other baggage. He's come fully equipped for a major expedition. He's brought all the necessary implements. I get money from him now and then. What have I spent? Shirt, 8 rials. Stocking cap, 1 rial. Slippers, 2 or 3 (I forget)—writing materials and envelopes, 15 rials—postage stamps and cards, 10 rials—car fare to Uhud, 10—what else? Oh yes, I bought a blanket for 22. This makes 69 or 68. The rest went for fruit juice or was spent at the Uhud coffee house, etc. I ought to stop playing clerk.

Among the African blacks there is a group of half-naked women. They customarily wear low-cut dresses. Their décolleté begins four fingers below the shoulder, and above that they are bare. There is another group of them that wears prissy, inappropriate blouses in the European style with lace collars. Perhaps they were hand-me-downs from the Europeans who lived in—or had fled from—their countries in Africa. You see less of the influence of European customs among their men, however. There is only the occasional French or English word that you hear in their speech and you know they've come from areas that are still under European influence, or from newly independent countries. Their currency notes still bear portraits of Napoleon, the Queen of England, or the King of Belgium. Yesterday was something. An African woman stood in front of *Bāb al-Nisā'* [Women's Gate] with a large bundle opened in front of her, full of colorful blouses. They were second-hand European ones, however, with the same silly frills, with petticoat attached, a gaily-patterned décolleté, and

[76] Naseriyeh Street is in one of Tehran's older, shabbier neighborhoods. (tr)

you name it! There were no takers, however. They were just like the old clothes rich Americans give to the Red Cross as charity. Now they are being bought and sold by hajjis in Medina, the wealthy of the Muslim world, so they can take them back to their own countries and say "I have brought you a souvenir of doings in the city of Islam." I was looking at this very display when I saw my sister's husband for the first time in a long while. He was the husband of my sister who died of cancer. His second wife was with him. He stood to one side and we nodded to each other from a distance. Then we exchanged information about health and fortune. Finally, he said, "If you have any money, buy liras. They're very cheap here." I said "Don't you know that money here is pegged to Aramco dollars?" He didn't know what Aramco was. I explained it to him. "I wish I had seen you in Tehran," he said. "Why?" I said. "I brought liras with me from Tehran," he said, "thinking they would be high here, but now I know they are lower."

Wednesday 26 Farvardin [April 15]

It is now clear that the Saudis have set Tuesday as the first day of the Hajj month. Next Wednesday is therefore *'Ayd*, one day away from the Shi'i day. This very thing is the subject of unbelievable controversy. They all reinforce each other in the belief that one must follow a practice, that individualism has no meaning on the Hajj. But can you be a Shi'i, after all, and stand aside without complaining among the Sunnis?[77] Our entire gathering last night was taken up with this matter. Our *ākhonds* ascended the pulpit one after another to address it. Then our *maddāh* [panegyrist] started in. He has a good voice, when he doesn't shout. He also recited a lovely poem. Our preacher discussed the *symbolique* quality of the Hajj rituals (using that very European term. I must convince him that he has no business altering his language just because of a few educated people) saying that the *sa'y*[78] between Safā and Marveh[79] represents Hagar's[80] effort to

[77] Sunnis are followers of the majority "orthodox" sect of Islam, the sect of "the way and customs of Muhammad." They all subscribe to one of the four Sunni schools, the Māliki, the Shāfi'i, the Hanbali, or the Hanafi. (tr)

[78] *Sa'y* is the Arabic name for the ritual run performed by pilgrims in commemoration of Hagar's search for water. See glossary. (tr)

[79] Safā [al-Safā] and Marveh [al-Marwah] are two small hills about 400 yards apart now enclosed within the Grand Mosque, between which Hagar is said to have run in search of water for her son. (tr)

[80] Hagar was one of the wives of Abraham [Ebrāhim], and the mother of Ismā'īl. There is a story that Abraham's wife Sarah was jealous of Hagar and her son and persuaded Abraham to abandon them in the desert. Abraham did so reluctantly,

find water for Ismā'īl, and that the *iḥrām*, the attire of submission, is an unadorned form of clothing, and the clothing of the next life. He did not know, however, that the construction of the Kaaba and its attribution to Ebrāhim Khalil represent the settlement of a tribe in an area, and is a mark of urbanization. I will tell him this also. He is a good man. Now how does this go? Ebrāhim Khalil is an architect and the builder of the Kaaba. The prophet Noah is a carpenter and a ship builder. David is a player of pandean pipes and a poet. Our prophet is a merchant, or a liaison between cities. (Wasn't this why he ordered the trading practices at Ukaz to be aligned with the Hajj?) Thus, each of them was engaged in an urban occupation. Buy why are Moses and Jesus shepherds? I think this can be explained by the fact that under the Pharaonic rule of Egypt and that of Caesar's Rome there was probably no alternative but to flee the city, to go out into the wilderness and get close to the soil and to nature. The others, who are connected with the early settlement of the Semitic tribes, all take up trades. We have the same feature in our own mythology. Keyumars,[81] who was a demon catcher, learned the culinary arts and tent-making, and so on...

I also visited the Coral Garden this morning, a copy of the Garden of Purity. The same pool, the same system of pipes to the irrigation canals, the same shade canopies, and the same hajji infatuation with life in a garden. Most of the people there were from Abadan, sitting among the old tree trunks beneath the wide, patchy shadows of the date fronds. Three young Nakhāwalah girls were sitting at the entrance. (All the Nakhāwalahs are black, and self-proclaimed descendants of the Abyssinian Bilāl.[82]) They were singing a song together which I couldn't understand. The repeating chorus was "*al-Ḥajj ḥaji...*" I must listen to it carefully one day. The people gave them money. Later, as I was returning, I saw written on a bus belonging to Turkish hajjis: "*Haci Kurup.*" Meaning "group of hajjis?" Then I saw a beautiful black woman, one of whose eyes had no pupil at all. In such a lovely face, the whiteness was unpleasantly prominent. She obviously had no husband. God help you when you are desperate for a man and obliged to view the world through one eye as well.

---

but only after determining that the place of abandonment was the site of the Kaaba, where no harm could come to them. After being abandoned, Hagar ran after a water mirage until she reached the top of al-Safā, then ran to the top of al-Marwah chasing another one. After running back and forth several times, she returned to Ismā'īl and found the Zamzam well miraculously flowing in the place where she had left him. (tr)

81 Keyumars was a monarch in Firdawsi's *Shah Namah*, or "Book of Kings." He introduced the ceremonial of throne and crown, ruled the world for 30 years, and commanded the allegiance of all living creatures, wild or tame. He enlisted the aid of leopards, lions, wolves, and tigers in his campaign to defeat his arch enemy, the Black Demon. (tr)

82 Ibn Rubāḥ Ḥabashī Bilāl was one of the Prophet Muhammad's slaves, a close companion of his, and the first muezzin in Islam. Stories about him are often told by Muslims to demonstrate that in the eyes of the Prophet Muhammad, the measure of a man's worth was neither nationality, wealth, nor social status, but piety. (tr)

Later I asked about telegraph prices at the post office. Ten words cost 12 Saudi rials. Why? Because the telegraph doesn't run directly to the other Islamic countries. They still use the same ocean cable from the Persian Gulf to the Suez Canal, no doubt. Corpse washers! Telegrams from hajjis of the Muslim world must go to Jedda from Medina and then to Paris, London, or Geneva, and be distributed from there. And this they call a perfect example of national management![83] Yet the Americans working for Aramco at Dhahran and Riadh get their new year's turkey hot from Los Angeles without fail!

The building's temperature is tolerable only until 10 a.m., although I am now perspiring as I write. I'm using a Bic pen, and have to press hard. The wind blows coolly from then until 3 in the afternoon through the northern and southern windows. It's too bad that the wind scatters grit from half-finished buildings everywhere, and one's eyes and face are unprotected indoors. Until 5 in the afternoon, when we go out or on the roof, the air is so humid that one can barely breathe. The nights are pleasant, however.

I couldn't run around today because of the blisters on my feet. (But what nonsense I'm writing! I must be brief—my pad is almost full.) I flipped through the pages of the newspapers I had bought. Some statistics from *Al-Bilād* of 7 Dhū al-Ḥijjah, 1383 [April 19, 1964]: "There are 510 doctors in all of Saudi Arabia. There are 263 treatment centers and infirmaries, 135 of which were added last year, and the total will reach 800 within 5 years. There are 45 hospitals with 4,823 beds. In addition, it must be added that there are 800 beds maintained at the temporary hospitals in 'Arafāt and Mina during the Hajj season only." And so on... This is for 4 million people, and with all the income generated by the Hajj and 100 million tons of oil every year! Here's to the health of these ignorant Arabs that rule this corner of the world in the name of Islam.

Wednesday night

It seems that we'll be leaving for Mecca on Friday, wearing the *iḥrām.* Today Ahmad ibn Wa'il came looking for us. He had been my brother's agent, or his local guide. He had been with him until the moment of his burial. He's black, tall and powerful, 50 years old, and a clown. He didn't know what had been the cause of my brother's death. He had been out visiting one night, and the next morning his wife told him to get himself over there, but by that time it was too late. He said the Nakhāwalah number 5 thousand, engaged in farming, butchering, buying and selling, and this sort of thing. He is one of them himself. My nephew had sent a

[83] The postal service is even worse than this. An airmail letter from Medina to Tehran takes 15 days! No exaggeration. Two or three of my letters to Simin came to me personally in Tehran. (A)

letter to him through Javad, who found it this morning and took it over. He brought him to lunch at noon. When we started eating I saw that he was not. I asked why. He said he wouldn't touch anything until we promised to come for lunch tomorrow. Arab custom. We promised. His purpose in coming, however, had been more to find clients for his services as a surrogate hajji than to seek out old acquaintances, thinking we would praise and recommend him to our guide or our fellow travelers. Javad said he would be happy with 300 tomans. A good price for the dead relatives of the gentlefolk who are with us. He said the population of Medina is 60,000. It has three ice companies, two of them in the same gardens I visited. (On the roof next door, the travelers are practicing saying formulas of praise and surahs, in a trial run for the prayer during the circumambulation at *Nisā'*. The *mullas* have put the idea in their heads that if they don't say *wa lā aḍ-ḍ-a-a-a-lin* correctly their wives will be forbidden to them for the rest of their lives. It's no joke. The most effective form of blackmail, right at the gates to heaven.) Javad spoke of a man at lunch who stood for prayer at the Prophet's Mosque with one foot on a step of the *mihrāb* and the other on the floor, for lack of space. Then someone found a place for him and called him. He said the man found three different places, but the other man kept the same position the whole time.[84] I didn't ask Javad where his own concentration had been. Then Ahmad Ibn Wa'il told us about a Sudanese man who farted right before praying and then stood up to pray. The usual Shi'i humor and mockery at the expense of the Sunnis.

I went looking for one of the gardens in the Medina area—to the East of where we are staying—to bathe at the water pumps. I knocked on the door, holding a one-rial bill. A young man came, wearing shorts and holding an *āftābeh*.

"Hello. I came to bathe."

He smiled. Then, "Come in."

I held out the bill. He didn't take it. "Why not?" I said. I realized that he was Shi'i. "Are you Nakhāwalah?" I asked. He said yes. He was not black, however. He knew a bit of Persian. Like all those living in the shrine area, he knew a few words of all the foreign languages. I then discovered that he had known my brother. He asked about his son. He was of the age that they might have been playmates. His name was Abbas. Then he guided me to the fixtures that brought water from the well. They were four inches across, and beneath the spray of water there was a shallow little cement pool. I got his permission to use soap and washed my entire body thoroughly. The date trees in the garden were young. Rue and sweet basil were planted beneath them. The soapy water drained through a gutter

[84] In Muslim ritual, if the prayer position is broken during a prayer it is necessary to begin the prayer anew. (tr)

behind a wall that separated one part of the garden from another. Even as I delighted in the cool water I felt sorry for the date trees which will be injured by the nitrous, soapy water. Also for the pomegranates, lush, blooming, and short, growing in clusters below the date palms or in the middle of the plots, giving wonderful coloration to the lifeless, monotonous green of the date palms.

The pump worked constantly, the water came up continuously, and I squatted. Under four inches of water, it was as though I had dived into the ocean. After I came out I hung around in the gardens until the sunset call to prayer arose from the tops of the minarets in the Prophet's Mosque.

Mohaddes had brought a couple of books along with him. One was *Hedāyat al-Sabil*, a travel diary by Hāj Farhād Mīrzā Qājār. I think the same one whose *Safarnāmah-'i Baluchistān va Kirmān* [Baluchestan and Kerman Travel Diary] was recently published. I spent some time flipping through the pages. It isn't bad. The prose isn't irritating, but pomposity is another matter. He knows something about everything and rambles a lot. (This wind really blows the sand and grit in the building in your eyes. There is no table here. For the page to be legible one must lie down on one's belly to write.) He also wrote *qasidehs*,[85] and he sent letters in Arabic to some Ottoman ruler. He recounted some history as well... and so on. He also explained the rituals of the Hajj from A to Z, just like a Hajj ceremonial manual. With all this, it is worth something. I will read all of it on the way.

Today at the Prophet's Mosque I saw an interesting sort of combination pilgrimage and sightseeing event. Three or four Turks were standing in a ring around two sundials where the Zahra garden and date orchard once were. One of the sundials had a brass indicator, slender and conical with a sharp point, standing vertically on the flat dial. The gentlemen came up to it one by one and felt the indicator from top to bottom and from bottom to top. A form of gratification? You will excuse me.

[85] In Persian and Arabic poetry, the *qasideh* is a poem in which each pair of verses ends with the same rhyme. The first line is a closed couplet, followed by open couplets, all monorhyme. (tr)

Thursday 27 Farvardin [April 16]

Medina

I set out at 6:30 a.m. The blisters on my feet finally got better. I ate a few bites of twice-sifted bread and drank some tea in the doorway to the tea room on the floor below. Our guide came and sat next to me, confiding that the fellow had gone mad. He was talking about the retired police major. Yesterday he had personally seen him playing with himself when he had come upon him unobserved. It turns out that they had confined him yesterday in one of the lower rooms, which is a storeroom, when this happened. That night he had gone looking for the "supervisor" of the hajjis and asked to be sent back. I thought he wanted my opinion. He didn't wait, however. Continuing, he said "Yes, when he returned it was learned that he had broken dishes, scattered the rice, urinated on the door and walls of the room, and other things." The others had swarmed in on him, tied up his hands and feet, rolled him in the dirt, and reported him to the police that night. The police had come and put him in a temporary prison. (We had heard a commotion from the roof where we sleep, but had paid no attention to it.) He had gone to get him out of prison himself and sent him to Jedda the same night to be sent back to Tehran. He boasted that he had gotten a taxi to Jedda for 250 Saudi rials and had sent one of his employees along with him also. I said it seemed that they had been very hasty and harsh, and certainly, before that, very nosy about his affairs. In any case, however, what choice was there?

"The Hajj is just like the Plain of Judgment," he said. "No one thinks of anyone else." He couldn't let a lunatic like that run loose all day among our women. And so on. I said it was over now. I gave him a cigarette and headed for *Khandaq*.

On the way I saw a black man (probably African) on al-Ayinah street with a heap of old European clothes piled in front of him. He called out something. A crowd formed around him immediately. One piece of clothing was in the hand of a customer who was examining it, top to bottom. It looked like a bridal gown, with an extended train and attached petticoat, decorated with ornamentation and lace. I went on.

In the *Bāb al-Miṣrī* [Egyptian Gate] neighborhood there was an alfalfa market, and the sweet smell of its blossoms was in the air. There were stacks of large bundles of alfalfa tied together with the plant's long stalks. Everyone bought a bundle and carried it off, probably for goats, or for sheep to be sacrificed. I thought of Farhad Mirza, who had taken pity on the goats and bought a bundle of alfalfa for them in fulfillment of a prayer covenant. Dirt- and paper-chewing goats, scavengers with long teats and short hair, that look like dogs at a distance. In the row of food concessions there were heads, livers, hearts, and kidneys sitting on a counter on a tray.

Their oil-burning ovens, sitting on the ground, were flaming up. And such a crowd! Blacks, Arabs, Turks, and Iranians all together. Mostly blacks. They were sort of taking turns. I went on.

To the West of Medina, Mt. Sala' seemed to be blocking the city. As I passed its wide slope on which there were dwellings and streets in every corner, there was a carpet of plastic hoses, each one a different color, green, yellow, red, and blue, carrying water from one side of the street to the other, from this house to that house. They were very long, up to 50 meters, like translucent colored snakes, showing the passage of water and bubbles inside. If the hoses crossed a street used by carts, for two or three meters they turned into iron pipes, and then became plastic again. The city's water circulation system obviously leaves something to be desired. The hoses run to spigots which come out of the ground at every intersection, each hose leading to a house. Beside each spigot there were three or four hoses waiting for a turn, with only the small orifice of one of them drawing water. As I went down to the West the traffic diminished. I now passed another city full of trees, date palms, and pomegranates. All the date palms were young. All were situated behind the mountain, cut off from Medina, but a part of the city.

A young man passed me on a bicycle on the narrow road at the base of the Western side of the mountain, far from the roads used by automobiles, where no dirt flew into my mouth. I stepped aside as he passed. Hello! I asked if this was the road to the Fath Mosque, also to practice my Arabic. He said "yeah" and went on. Several steps ahead, however, he halted, dismounted, and waited for me to reach him. Then he began a long discourse about the Hajj and its merits.

"You must have come walking to the Fath Mosque in order to secure a reward in the hereafter, but what is this moustache?" And so on...

"What school of Islam do you follow?" I asked. He was Maliki. "Do you recognize several of the Islamic schools?" I asked.

"Four of them," he said.

"They recognize 72 of them in our country," I said, "and I belong to one of them."

He frowned and left.

Yesterday or the day before, I forget which, I was sitting in the Prophet's Mosque, thinking, when someone came up and said hello.

"Sir, what sect do you follow?" he asked in Persian. I looked at him and realized he was referring to my moustache.

"Son," I said, "it would be better for our mouths to be locked shut than for us to argue about this sort of thing. Beards and wool grow by themselves.

We simply don't have the ambition to trim them," and so on. He was a man of 50 years, and very ill-tempered. He got up and left. If he had stayed I would have reminded him that Nakir and Monkar[86] are to come after a man the first night he is in the grave, but it is impossible to talk to these Arabs. Try to say two words and you will get into a thousand difficulties. They don't understand most of your Arabic. Even that Iranian fellow who was wanting to know what sect I follow was simply looking for someone to talk to, to find a peer for a moment in the midst of the strangeness of this journey. This young Arab, however, was a resident of the shrine area, and he was just trying to show off his own superiority. Just like the French in the Parisian shrine areas, and their behavior towards foreigners, or just like the people of Mashhad. My wife once asked one of them for directions, right near shrine. She asked a woman wearing a chador, who looked at her and said [in the dialect of Mashhad] "I know but I ain't gonna say."

The Fath Mosque is situated on a height, overlooking the flood channel dug out by Salmān [Pārsi]. The water running down from Uhud winds behind Mt. Sala', and goes to the west of Medina. There the ground is hollowed out like a flood channel. Alongside this flood channel the historic mosques of that time are close together. After the Fath Mosque is the Salman Mosque. After that one is Abu Bakr's, then 'Umar's, 'Ali's, and also the Zahra Mosque. The largest of them is the Abu Bakr Mosque, with three domes and a portico. The others—with the exception of the Salman Mosque—have short, thick foundations, arches, and porticos. Their architecture has been preserved by primitive will power. The Zahra mosque has none of these things, just a platform beneath the sky, with hand rails around it. On one side there is a small *mihrāb* showing you the direction of *qebleh.*[87]

I saw another young man on the way back, again riding a bicycle. Straining up the hill, he aided his pedal strokes with rhythmic, staccato verse. I didn't feel like practicing Arabic anymore, however.

The young man was badly parched and discolored by the sun, and his eyes were wonderfully large. The Arabs here have much healthier eyes than those I saw in Iraq in 1943. Is this due to the difference in locale? Or the result of medical care, and the better hygiene that has been practiced in the last 20 years in this part of the world? Whatever it is, eye ailments have been eliminated. The old people are still blind or with poor eyesight, most of them. Adolescents and younger, however, have large, black, shining eyes.

---

86 Nakir and Monkar are the names of two angels who, according to Shi'i popular belief, interrogate the departed in their tombs on the first night after burial. According to legend, they will be asked questions about their belief in God, the Prophet Muhammad, the first Imam ('Ali) and Shi'i doctrine. If unable to respond properly, the subject of the inquisition will be struck on the head by a burning bludgeon and sent directly to hell. (tr)

87 A Muslim must face in the direction of the Kaaba in Mecca when offering prayers; this direction is called *qebleh.* (tr)

I also saw some older school girls. They had cape-like mantles over their shoulders, tucked around the neck and open in the front, with their colored or white blouses visible beneath them. Sometimes when they opened or fastened the opening in front of the cape or shook hands, the young buds on their chests were visible. They wore scarves on their heads, made of black muslin, just like big hats. Their socks and shoes were both white. The truth is that the first thing that caught my eye was the color of their shoes, and then my gaze moved higher. They stood in groups of two or three along a street in a village on Mt. Sala'. Young men stood at a distance hoping for a chance to move in, some smoking cigarettes to show their manhood, winking and making gestures. Then the "Girl's School" bus came, took them aboard a few at a time, and left. It was around 8 in the morning.

The sweet smell of alfalfa stopped me when I reached The Egyptian Gate. As I walked among the bundles of it, a barbershop caught my eye. I went inside. I had them bring me a pot of tea from the coffee house next door. My turn came as I was sipping the second cup. I drank tea for half an hour while he cut my hair, talking the whole time. He shaved my beard. He wanted to cut my moustache too, but I stopped him. "That's my profession!" And I got up. I gave him a 10-rial note and he gave back 5 rials. I had not shaved my beard since Tehran, and it itched.

Then I went to the post office. It was closed. It was a quarter to 9 by my watch. I asked a young merchant with a shop next to the post office, "why is it closed?"

"It will be open at 3 o'clock," he said.

"Three o'clock?"

He showed me his watch. It was a quarter to three. Strange! They must stop the clocks at sunset. Then I bought several Egyptian and Lebanese magazines. One of them was *Akhbār al-Usbu'*, or *Usbu' al-Mahdi*, from Egypt. The censor had cut out a square with the name of the magazine on it. The rest of it was intact. It was full of the usual pictures, Westernized material, calls for Islamic unity, curses on Israel, quotations from Gustave Le Bon, and other nonsense. Then I went to the public libraries. Two of them side by side on a street to the south of the Prophet's Mosque. Of recent construction and unfinished, the first was called *Maktabat al-Madīnat al-Munuwrat al-'Āmah* [Public Library of Luminous Medina], and was a cylindrical building with three floors. The reading room was in the middle, and the upper level was like a circular portico on the inside. The stacks had shelves that had books in some corners and were empty elsewhere. There were books in boxes in other corners. Two or three people slowly entered and left. It takes a lot of time to make a library a library. I went out. Ten steps away was the *Maktabah Shaykh al-Islām 'Ārif*

Ḥikmat [Library of Shaykh al-Islam 'Ārif Hikmat]. There was an entrance and then a cool courtyard, with a pool and a little garden. Hajjis in *iḥrāms* were lounging on benches at the edge of the courtyard. The courtyard's ceiling was like scaffolding, covered with various kinds of vines, perhaps grapevines. I didn't notice. The courtyard was very cool, however, and relaxing. Then there was a place for taking off shoes, followed by a domed chamber, like the chamber of an *emāmzādeh*,[88] but without a grave in the middle. All along the sides, however, were bookshelves reaching to the rim of the dome. Below were cushions behind low bench-like tables, and there was a small alcove across from the entrance.

A bespectacled man sat beneath a window that opened on the Prophet's Mosque, wearing a very white *dishdāshah* and an even whiter headband. He sat on a cushion behind a table, engrossed in what he was doing. I said hello and sat beside him. I told him I was an Iranian and a man of books. I asked him many questions, and he was at a loss. He was director of the library, but he couldn't understand broken Arabic. He had to call his assistant, who was lurking nearby moving books around. He was a dwarf-like man with a round face. As soon as he said hello I knew he was Afghani. He was from Kabul. His name was 'Abd al-Vahab. He had moved here 20 years ago. His salary was 300 Saudi rials. The director's was 700. The library budget was only 2000 rials per month. On a normal day the number of patrons was between 10 and 20 people, and on Hajj days it increased to 200. It had 7,000 books. Five of them were manuscripts, the rest published volumes. History, poetry collections, religious doctrine, the Qur'ān, commentary on the Qur'ān, and biography. He said there were four libraries in the entire city. The third one is *Maktabat al-Sultan Maḥmūd al-'Uthmānī* [Library of Sultan Maḥmūd al-'Uthmānī] and the fourth... One thing led to another and I have forgotten. Then I made a brief tour of various parts of the library. There were two or three manuscripts under glass, in a bookcase on a low table with cashmere lining, and two battered, dusty globes positioned on the east side of the library, sitting on tripods. The list of the library's books was in six large leather-bound folders, each containing a single sheet. He said "We have recently decided to modernize the library and install a microfiche system, just as you saw in the building next door," and so on. He said that almost all the libraries in Saudi Arabia are still run with antiquated methods. The books are stacked on their sides on the shelves, their spines facing out, some with leather covers. None standing on end, in any event. I was reminded of the days of the caliphs–the Abbassid[89] caliphs. It was very cool beneath the dome of the library. They ordered tea for me, which was served in a narrow-waisted cup with

---

[88] An *emāmzādeh* is a shrine where a descendant or a relative of an Imam is buried. The term literally means "born of an Imam," and can also apply to the descendant himself. (tr)

[89] The Abbassid caliphs ruled the Muslim world from their capital in Baghdad from 750-1258 A.D. (tr)

a painted design, along with sugar cubes. I didn't want to get up. I finally did, however, after turning through several books from the *Hadith* shelf. Many thanks, hoping to meet again. I must remember to tell Mohaddes that there is such a library.

As I came out into the courtyard from the library I noticed a two-story stone building, made of that same black stone native to Medina. Very beautiful, in the Ottoman style. It was written above the door that it belonged to *awqāf*, with the number of the *vaqf*[90] register. It looked like an inn. There was a crowd of blacks coming in and going out, and three or four people sitting on the two stone benches outside. Such a strong latrine smell, mixed with disinfectant, came out the door that I didn't feel like looking around or asking questions. I hastily left.

Same day. Thursday.

We were guests in the home of Ali ibn Wa'il for lunch. It was an old house in the Nakhāwalah district, made entirely of clay in the traditional manner. The only modern(!) implements in that house were a ceiling fan, a long tube light, and a plastic fruit dish holding grapes, bananas and apples. As we went through the single-panel door, there was a dark, cool foyer. They turned on the light, and there was a platform on the left like an alcove, one meter above the floor, and a guest room, but no sign of my brother. After going through the foyer you came to a covered area. On one side of it was the kitchen, and on the other were the inner rooms, and a well-house, a bath house and a privy in a corner, side by side. The platform was covered with *misk* carpets and carpets made locally. The walls were covered with linoleum up to a meter's height from the floor. Cushions were laid out all around. There were three or four Italian machine-made carpets with Ottoman scenes hanging on the wall. He laid out lunch himself. When we offered to help he insisted fiercely that we had no right to do so. The food consisted of chicken and rice with *qeymeh-ye torki*,[91] *memsā-ye bādemjān*,[92] and an abundance of fruit. There were oranges, bananas, apples, and cucumbers, all fresh. (A smelly, charcoal-burning samovar sat boiling on one side; I promised him that when he came to Tehran I would buy him one that burns oil.) There was a strawberry drink served in a large pitcher tasting something like *Limulax*,[93] and fresh cucumbers from Mecca. Just like the cucumbers in Ahvaz. The apples and oranges were from Lebanon, wrapped in fruit tissue with the fruit company's label. He had gone to a

---

90 *Vaqf* [Arabic *waqf*] is the Persian term for a pious Muslim endowment, or mortmain, permanently allocated for some religious purpose, such as the building of a mosque. The plural, *awqāf*, is the same in both Arabic and Persian. (tr)

91 *Qeymeh-ye torki* is a Turkish dish made with diced meat, beans, and spices. (tr)

92 An Iranian dish in which eggplant is the principal ingredient. (tr)

93 A laxative sold in Iran. (tr)

great deal of trouble and expense. He had a mature daughter wearing a mantle who served us. She gave us sidelong glances with her large eyes, either to size us up or out of curiosity. Javad was moved to say "We should have stipulated that he give us his daughter as a condition of accepting the invitation." His son was 7 or 8, and very glib. I would not have imagined that there could have been such a smooth-talking young Arabic speaker. He called an electric meter *'addād*, which I thought a fine translation.

We learned that within three years the hajjis would be taken from Medina to Mecca in trucks. Now they use busses with the roofs removed,[94] and passengers sit comfortably in seats. We took a nap after eating lunch and then left. We went together to visit the Qoba Mosque, south of Medina, closer than Uhud. The mosque is said to have been built on a foundation of piety.[95] It is a large, wide mosque with one minaret. There is a colonnade [*shabestān*] on the side facing the *qebleh*, and the other three sides have porticos; there is also a wide courtyard. We passed new construction everywhere along the road south of the Prophet's Mosque (city expansion is blocked on the West by Mt. Sala', and on the east by the graveyard, and also on the north in the direction of Uhud, which is still a shrine area), or new gardens. And such pomegranates, with their blossoms, and minarets, atop newly-built mosques with modern designs, all in cement—but white. The city is under construction, with new streets, trenches for pipes, street lights, and half-finished structures.

Evening of the same day.

In the afternoon I visited *Bāb al-Awāli*, to the East of Medina, south of the graveyard. I found a colored box in a gully beside the road at the spot where the asphalt ends in the desert, a container for "Eau de Cologne Bourgeois," made in Paris. No doubt a present purchased for the people at home by a hajji who decided it would be a shame not to use it himself.

There were the sounds of various kinds of motorized water pumps: *burup burup. Jik jik jik. Hak hak hak. Hap hap hap.* A complete musical scale. The date palms were showing their first green fruit pods, the size of lentils, with little green nodes clinging to the yellow stems. There was the sadness of the sunset, and for the first time I felt homesick. Again I asked myself, what did I come on this journey to do? Visit shrines?

---

94 One of the ritual dress requirements for the performance of the Hajj rituals is that nothing be worn on the head. Some pilgrims therefore refuse to ride in vehicles with covered tops. (tr)

95 The Qoba Mosque, located about three miles southeast of Medina at the site of the Prophet Muhammad's first stopping place after completing the Hijrah, is mentioned in the Tawbah Surah of the Qur'ān, verses 8 and 9. (tr)

Worship? Observe? Go sight-seeing? Make discoveries? I returned to the city. In front of the entrance to the graveyard where hajjis were coming out there was a pile of empty cola bottles in wooden boxes stacked up to the top of the wall. I wondered what was the source of this legendary Saudi Arabian security, and whether the stories one hears are true. Hajjis have no need to steal. They are usually rich, and have come to visit shrines or worship. But what about the local people? There is an abundance of beggars and poor people, and porters, porters, porters. No one, however, has said anything as yet about theft. There are no soldiers in sight. Police, however, patrol everywhere, even inside the Prophet's Mosque, and their presence is somewhat irritating. They function as doormen. Just footmen with silver canes, cloaks, turbans, courtesy, and this sort of thing.

The sunset prayer had been completed some time ago. The people were sitting together in groups, and again there were the usual preachers. One of them was a non-Arab who preached in literary Arabic. I was strongly reminded of Sa'di. Another sat on his knees and held a microphone in his hand. The speaker was standing next to him. Only his unamplified voice could be heard, however; there had evidently been a power failure. He spoke of the quarrel between Islam and the West. The same nonsense that was in *Weststruckness*. Another was a young man whose beard was still forming, speaking in a hoarse voice (he had shouted so much), and calling for Islamic unity. Another was a tall black Arab with a white turban tied in the Damascan style, with his mantle folded into a narrow strip and thrown over his shoulder. His speech was so eloquent and penetrating that he seemed to be a born orator. He spoke of the reasons for the Hegira, of the justness of the first caliph, and the plot to kill Muhammad and Abu Bakr by libertine infidels, continuously inserting verses from the Qur'ān into his smooth, rhetorical speech. It is interesting that he also gave *rowzeh*s. I had never seen a Sunni do this. It was about the difficulties endured by those two friends on that journey. He even cried once himself. At the peak of excitement his voice broke and he covered his face. The assembly began shouting. At this point someone put a hand on my shoulder. I turned around, and there was a fair-skinned man smiling and saying something in Turkish. I convinced him that I did not speak Turkish. He was surprised and wanted to know why, and I told him why. (People take me for a Turk all the time. The barber next to the alfalfa market thought I was a Turk too.) He was a tailor from Maltiyah. He insisted on exchanging addresses. I went on my way. A woman laid her child at her side and prayed. The child was lying face up. Its large eyes were closed, but heavily coated with indigo dye [woad]. It was no more than a year old. Its eyes were like the silver eyes they give to the *emāmzādeh*s. I went out then towards home. I try to get there as late as possible, because of this Sayyid Borujerdi and his nightly meetings on the roof. He's surprised that I pray with the Sunnis, and not behind him.

"My dear sir," I once said to him, "We came here to lose ourselves in the crowd. We didn't come here to reinforce our personalities and our isolation."

I don't think he got the point, however. This devotee of God has dropped everything in his name except the word Borujerdi, imagining that all that is round is a walnut. His words are uninspired and he preaches with a thick provincial accent about doubts and omissions. Even worse is another fellow who's begun imitating his arrogance. And now—I saw this tonight—he's practicing panegyrics. As if there weren't enough *rowzeh khwāns*, preachers, and panegyrists in our group, now we're taking this newly-created one back home with us as a souvenir. (I don't really know whether Medina has a cinema or not. I haven't seen any in the shrine area. I went through the new city in the south today by auto, and didn't see any there.) What did this gentleman say in the pulpit? He talked about Qur'ānic stories in imitation of our preacher, saying that God tested Abraham and Solomon, and that we would be tested as well. I knew about Abraham's trial, but had never heard of Solomon's. Oh yes. Solomon had 100 wives, and from all of them he had only one child. He was afraid of jinn, however, and he entrusted the child to the care of the angels. Then the child died in bed. The point being, take the hint and entrust your children to God from now on. A commentary on the verse: "We placed on his throne a body (without life): but he [Solomon] did turn (to Us in true devotion)."[96]

Friday 28 Farvardin [April 17]

Still at Medina.

I was incapacitated today. I've had diarrhea since last night. Six times as of morning. I can't do anything now. Always drinking water, ice water at that, on a sort of orange and apple juice diet. My sister says I've burned my stomach raw. Probably from eating at that gathering yesterday in 'Ali ibn Wa'il's home. I also vomited once this morning, frightening my sister. I saw her. Our guide came saying "I told you not to go walking around so much," and this sort of talk. They finally took me to the doctor at noon. I don't feel like exploring and investigating with such a stomach ache. The doctor gave me carbo-guancydine. I asked Javad myself to buy Entero-Vioform, which they didn't have at the infirmary because it's expensive, the management budget is small, and so on... even though they collected

[96] The Holy Qur'ān, Surah 38, verse 34 (Yusuf 'Ali translation). (tr)

50 tomans from every hajji for this sort of medicine. I've been taking medicine regularly, but my stomach still hurts, and I'm still secluded in a corner of the privy. The problem is we have to leave for Mecca tonight, 400 kilometers on the road in a topless vehicle dressed in *iḥrām.* They're loading the vehicle, which is parked by the door, right now. Everyone is bustling about, but I'm laid out flat in an empty room where they've taken up the carpets. My bed is a blanket spread out on the floor over empty cement sacks. I think I've caught a cold as well... I had an inkling of it last night... I don't feel like writing anymore. It is 3:30 in the afternoon.

Saturday 29 Farvardin [April 18]

Mecca

We got to Mecca at 4:30 in the morning. We left Medina last night at 8:30. Our vehicle was a bus—one of those red ones—whose top had been removed. The passengers took their places in the bus at 5 in the afternoon. Then there was a very long wait, until 8 o'clock, when Javad came and called me. I got stuck with a bad seat, on the third row, next to my uncle. I was the third person in a two-person seat. The driver was a good man. His bus was in good condition, and our guide was claiming he had greased his palm. And so we came directly here, with only one stop in Rabigh, and another one at the beginning of the trip at the Haflah Mosque, where we made ourselves *muḥrim.*[97] In the dark of the night, with no water and no privy. We performed the ritual purifications in the light of the bus's headlights. We had already put on the *iḥrām* garments in Medina, followed by the mosque rituals, getting back on the bus, and riding on and on and on. The sky and stars overhead were very low, the sky was amazingly close, Scorpio was right in front of us, and the wind blew in our faces constantly (some 80-100 kilometers per hour). We were huddling all the time. Then there was the job of looking after my uncle, an old man who was continually nodding off and in danger of hitting his head on the back of the seat in front of him. Never have I spent a night so awake, and so mindful of nothingness. Under the cover of that sky and that infinity, I recited every poem I'd ever memorized—mumbling to myself—and looked into myself as carefully as I could until dawn. I saw that I was just a "piece of straw" that had come

[97] The term *muḥrim* is applied to someone who is in the state of ritual purity required for entry into the Mecca shrine areas for the Hajj. (tr)

to the "*Miqāt*,"[98] not a "person" coming to a "rendezvous." I saw that "time" is an "infinity," an ocean of time, and that "*Miqāt*" exists always and everywhere, and with the self alone. A "rendezvous" is a place where you meet someone, but the "*Miqāt*" of time is just such a meeting with the "self." I realized how beautifully that other atheist, Mayhaneh'i, or Bastāmi, had put it when he told that hajji bound for the House of God at the gates of Nishapur, "put your sack of money down, circumambulate *me*, and go back home." I realized that traveling is another way of knowing the self, of evaluating it and coming to grips with its limitations and how narrow, insignificant, and empty it is, in the proving ground of changing climes by means of encounters and human assessments.

Same day. At Bayt al-Ḥarām[99]

It appears that even the Kaaba will have been rebuilt with steel reinforced concrete by next year, just like the Prophet's Mosque. Not only has the *mas'ā*[100] between *Safā* and *Marveh* been transformed to a huge two-level cement passageway, they are already busy putting in a new rectangular two-story outer colonnade, thereby destroying the one built by the Ottomans. They've already taken out one side of the old outer colonnade, the one facing the *mas'ā*, and will undoubtedly destroy its other parts within a year or two. It's true that the space available for circumambulation will be wider and that a larger crowd—three or four times the size of the current one—will be able to circumambulate the Kaaba, but the problem is that they will still be using these cement slabs attached to reinforced concrete pillars, and building upward with them... With beautiful hard rock close at hand, they still use this cement and these cement forms. Apparently, the only thing left of the old outer colonnade will be two or three minarets. They've covered the circumambulation track around the Kaaba with marble, and those in the covered colonnades as well. There were more people doing the run between *Safā* and *Marveh* than there were making the circumambulation. As soon as the sun gets hot the circumambulation virtually ceases. (I'm now sitting on the upper level of the outer colonnade, writing.) From up here the Kaaba is just half the size I had imagined. That individual who was architect of this new outer colonnade was evidently unaware that when you destroy proportion you change architecture. The Kaaba is still the same size, but they've made the outer corridor twice as wide, and twice as high. How about destroying the Kaaba itself and making it higher and

98 The term *Miqāt* can designate either the area containing the Muslim shrines in Mecca, or the entry stations surrounding the shrine area where the purification rites are performed in order to enter into the required state of *iḥrām*. (tr)

99 *Bayt al-Ḥarām*, or "The Sacred House," is the Arabic term for the Grand Mosque in Mecca, the goal of the Hajj. (tr)

100 The *mas'ā* is the long covered runway where the *sa'y* is performed between *Safā* and *Marveh*. (tr)

larger? Out of reinforced concrete, no doubt? (A tall, fat, swarthy man carrying an umbrella just passed, saying "Hajji sir, mention me in your journal too—Qandahāri of Mashhad."

"Sit down," I said, although there was a hint of mockery in his voice. It seems that this sort of activity is distastefully ostentatious in this setting, although so far I myself have seen two or three others writing on paper, note pads, or what-have-you. I must be more careful after this. Out in public and writing?)

Afternoon. Same day.

Mecca.

The house our guide procured for us is in the Sulaymaniyah district, in northern Mecca at the foot of Mount Hindi. It's really a three-story house with three large rooms. The women are packed on the first floor, the men on the other two. The owner of the house himself and his wife and children are temporarily living on the roof. Our guide says the guy works in the Mecca treasury offices. Money managers are the same the world over. Yes indeed. That gentleman Sayyid Borujerdi and his followers, who've now become a tight little group, have gone to the upper floor, and we constantly hear their calls to prayer, the *rowzeh*s, and their mournful eulogizing. The rest of us, who are less fanatical, and do not think ourselves in need of *ākhond*s and mullas, are here on the middle floor. My sister has gone to be with the women. There are four of us left in my family with several people from our neighborhood back home, 8 or 10 Mazandaranis, and a villager from Sagzabad who insists on saying he's from Tehran. He's always trying to hide his accent. Worse yet, he's always trying out foreign cigarettes, and thus coughs all the time. The house has a bath house, which was immediately converted to a pantry. There's also a shower on every floor, with a privy. Our floor also has a small room with a sash window of colored glass, which was taken by the Esfahani family. Our roommates have deprived us here in Mecca of the privileged status we had in Medina. They are three women and three men, all of them young. On both sides of our room at the base of the wall are high, interfacing wooden trunks that line up in bench-like fashion. We let the old people and those who are spoiled sleep on those. The rest of us roll up in blankets on the floor. We all eat from the same undivided *sofreh.*

The old Mazandarani man, who looks just like Nima [Yushij], and has his picky eating habits, behaves for all his years just like a child. For whatever reason, he left his fellow Mazandaranis in a huff at lunch, taking his plate to a corner of the room. After lunch, he said, "You educated people! What would you say is the difference between a round prayer and a linear prayer?" (The words seemed to slosh in his mouth as he spoke) and of course we didn't know. Then he explained that a round prayer is the one offered by the people assembled around the Kaaba, and a linear prayer is the one they offer at his village mosque. It turns out that on his first encounter he became deeply involved in the Kaaba experience. After him the others began telling stories, recalling Hajj incidents and exchanging friendly banter. Everyone obviously feels rested now.

Mecca has more mountains around it than Jerusalem, and the city is largely made of stone. So much granite! No wonder the pre-Islamic Arabs had crammed so many statues into the "House!" *Bayt al-Ḥarām* sits in a depression right at the bottom of the drainage area between the mountains. The water of *Zamzam*[101] is a kind of reservoir for the rainwater that runs off these granite mountains and collects in that channel. The streets go up and down, mostly following the valleys, with homes on both sides, going up the sides of the mountains, and you find another flank of the mountain in every corner, with another neighborhood and another street. The streets have neon lighting, and there are multi-colored mini-skyscrapers along the streets, with garish colors in the new windows, such as bright green and burgundy... Very primitive, and it badly defaces the city. There are enough garages and motels to satisfy anyone, and then shops, shops, and more shops. They've torn down everything all around *Bayt al-Ḥarām* in order to build a square which is not yet completed, and dirt is piled up all around in heaps and pits. Hajjis come and go in the midst of the remaining construction equipment. To build something in this city, there's no need to dig and pour a foundation. No matter how high a building is to be, it may be laid right on a natural stone base and raised from there, except in the depression in the city's center where *Bayt al-Ḥarām* is located. It's really in the middle of a big bowl that has a flat layer of sand on the bottom. They've dug a thick foundation there for the new colonnade, and the reinforced concrete forms are still in place. The entire Eastern side of *Bayt al-Ḥarām* is joined to the city by a continuous network of wood and iron construction scaffolding.

The first thing in the morning when we reached the gates of Mecca we were welcomed by a kaleidoscopic fountain that sprayed water 3 to 4 meters into the air in the center of the square at the gate. I wished Maham[102] could be there to see it, and have the happiness of knowing that they're using the colors he likes all over the world. Neon fills the streets everywhere. It's even on top of the House's minarets and the Kaaba itself. When it pleased God to have a house built on the surface of this land, he should have realized that

---

101 The Zamzam well, located just outside the Grand Mosque, is said to have appeared miraculously when Hagar, the wife of Abraham and mother of Ismā'īl, had been abandoned in the desert. Legend has it that Hagar was chasing mirages looking for water when the young Ismā'īl inadvertently dug into the water source. The well was also revered in pre-Islamic times. (tr)

102 Maham was mayor of Tehran in the early 1960s. He was often ridiculed for his obsession with building fountains as a part of his program to beautify Tehran. (tr)

land would one day fall into the hands of the Saudi government, and that its doors and walls would be covered with neon because of the exigencies of oil exportation. I'm not advocating replacing the neon with kerosene, but, for the sake of dignity, why shouldn't they order specially designed lamps from these companies that would be worthy of such grandeur, and not have even the House of God become a common consumer for Pennsylvania? Doing things this way means tainting even the world of the unseen for company profits.

I also visited the infirmary this morning. It was quite crowded. There was a lot of sunstroke and diarrhea. The bald head of one of our Esfahani traveling companions was so blistered it frightened me. I got some Sulfaguanidine and left. I'm still on a restricted diet. Tea and canned fruit. My gripes and stomach pains subsided before we left Medina, with the help of several Bladons pills. I showered in the afternoon, in the shower above the sump in the privy. I ran the water over my head. Two or three of my fellow travelers saw me, and looked at me with unspeakable disgust, with looks that said "you'll be ritually unclean," and so on. They said nothing, however. After all, an important concern on such a journey is the enjoinment and prohibition of others, of good and evil...

At lunch—served on a common spread (I think we are now about 20 more than we were)—we had watermelon, *pāludeh*,[103] and bread and cheese. I opened the compote, and put a bit of lemon juice on it so I could eat it. I can't stand sweets. I also abruptly stopped drinking water today. Tea, tea, tea.

Same day. Saturday.

Mecca.

This *sa'y* between *Safā* and *Marveh* stupefies a man. It takes you right back to 1400 years ago, to 10,000 years ago (it isn't hopping, it's simply going fast) with its *harvaleh* [jogging], the loud mumbling, being jostled by the others, the self-abandon of the people, the lost slippers—that will get you trampled underfoot if you go back for one moment to recover them—the glazed stares of the crowd, chained together in little groups in a state not unlike a trance, the wheelchairs bearing the old people, the litters borne by two people, one in front and one behind, and this great engulfing of the individual in the crowd. Is this the final goal of this assembly? And this journey? Perhaps 10,000 people, perhaps 20,000 people, performing the same act in a single instant. Can you keep your wits in the midst

[103] *Pāludeh* can be either a sweet beverage made of water, flour, and honey, or a sweet frozen dessert resembling ice cream made from starch, lemon juice, and syrup. In this context it is likely to be the former. (tr)

of such vast self-abandon? And act as an individual? The pressure of the crowd drives you on. Have you ever been caught in the midst of a terrified crowd fleeing from something? Read "self-abandon" for terrified, and substitute "wandering aimlessly" and "seeking shelter" for fleeing. One is utterly helpless in the midst of such a multitude. Which one is really an "individual?" And what is the difference between 2,000 and 10,000?

Each of the Yemenis, filthy, with tangled hair, sunken eyes, and a rope tied around the waist, looks like another John the Baptist risen from the grave. The blacks, heavy, tall, and intense, froth on the lips, moving with all the muscles of their bodies. A woman with her shoes under her arm runs crying like someone lost in the desert. Whatever they are, they don't seem to be human beings to whom one may turn for help. A strong, smiling young man collides with someone and moves on, like a fool in a frenzied bazaar. An old man, panting, is unable to continue, but he is swept on by colliding bodies. I realized I could not watch him be trampled by the people. I took his hand and guided it to the rail in the middle of the runway that separates those coming from those going back. A group of women (there were 12-15 of them) wearing the white *iḥrām* garments, had marked the backs of their necks with violet flower designs, and each held onto another's *iḥrām* by the waistband. They were moving in one line towards the circumambulation.

You see the ultimate extent of this self-abandon at the two ends of the *mas'ā*, which are a bit elevated, and at which you must turn around and go back. The Yemenis jump and spin every time they get there, say *salām* to the Kaaba then start again. I realized I couldn't do it. I began to cry and fled. I realized what a mistake that infidel Mayhaneh'i or Bastāmi made by not coming to throw himself at the feet of such a crowd, or at least his selfishness... Even the circumambulation fails to create such a state. In the circumambulation around the House, you go in one direction shoulder to shoulder with the others, and you go around one thing individually and collectively. That is, there's an objective and a system. You're a particle in a ray of being going around a center. You are thus integrated, not released. More importantly, there are no encounters. You're shoulder to shoulder with the others, not face to face. You see selflessness only in the rapid movement of the bodies of people, or in what you hear them saying. In the *sa'y*, however, you go and come, in Hagar's same wandering manner. There's no aim to what is being done. In this going and coming, what's really disturbing is the continual eye contact. A hajji performing the *sa'y* is a pair of legs running or walking rapidly, and two eyes without a "self," or that have leaped out of the "self," or been released from it. These eyes aren't really eyes, but naked consciousnesses, or consciousnesses sitting at the edge of the eye sockets waiting for the order to flee. Can you look at these eyes for more than an instant? Before today, I thought it was only the sun that could not be regarded with the naked eye, but I realized today that neither can one look at this sea of eyes. . .and fled, after only two laps. You can easily see what an infinity you create in that multitude from such nothingness, and this is when you are optimistic, and have just begun. If not, in the presence of such infinity you see you are less than nothing. Like a particle of rubbish on the ocean, no, on an ocean of people, or perhaps a bit of dust in the air. To put it more clearly, I realized I was going crazy. I had an urge to break my head open against the first concrete pillar. Unless you do the *sa'y* blind.

When you leave the *mas'ā* there is a bazaar, with people packed tightly together. I sat in a corner with my back against the wall of the *mas'ā*. I was quenching my thirst with one of these "colas" and thinking of something I'd read by a European on the question of the "individual" and society, and that the greater the society that envelops the "self," the nearer the "self" comes to being nothing. I realized that the Eastern "ego" that forgets itself and its troubles in such a state of equality in the presence of the world of the unseen is the same one that, in the ultimate individualism of seclusion, claims to be divine. Just like that infidel, Mayhaneh'i, or Bastāmi, and others. The Joks of India as well. I realized that this "ego" is sacrificed in isolation just as much as it "sacrifices itself" in society. At its highest levels of satisfaction, what is the ultimate attainment in yoga if not this? To give peace of mind over to asceticism, for if one is nothing in the manifest world of action outside the self, one can at least impose the design of one's will on one's body! Therefore, what is the difference between existentialism and socialism? In the *sa'y* we escape our confinement, and we do something that is to "our" benefit, whether in the mind or in reality. In yoga, we remain in "self" confinement, which is to say that since we have no power to act outside the body, we settle for the small, weak domain of our bodies. In the *sa'y*, we accept society's domination, but only in the presence of the world of the unseen. If you came and took the "world of the unseen" out of this multitude, what would be left? In our system, neither the individual nor society has priority. Priority goes to the world of the unseen, which is connected to the bazaar, and has come under the control of companies. The individual and society are two transient phenomena contrasted with something that signifies eternity: but they are two sides of the same coin. It is only in such a domain that "Sign of God"[104] and "Shadow of God"[105] have meaning. Both individually and as a society, we have closed the door to the manifest world of action. When a meaning is found for the relationship between the individual and society, whether by the individual or by society, you move in the direction of manifestation and action, or

[104] *Āyat Allāh* (Ayatollah), the Arabic-Persian term the author has used here, can refer to verses from the Qur'ān as well as to high-ranking Shi'i clergymen. (tr)

[105] *Zell Allāh*, or "Shadow of God," was originally applied to the Muslim caliphs, emphasizing the religious sanctity of their authority. It was later adopted by secular monarchs, such as the Shah of Iran. (tr)

society does. Just like that evangelist Qobādiyāni.[106] Otherwise, we've been doing the *sa'y* for 1400 years, and for 1000 years we've had isolation, seclusion, and martyrdom, but not for the sake of manifesting anything. This is the opposite of self-sacrifice. This self, if it doesn't exist as a particle working to build a society, is not even a "self." It is absolutely nothing. It is a piece of rubbish or particle of dust, except (and 1000 exceptions) when it exists in the context of a great faith, or a great fear. Then it becomes the builder of everything from pyramids to the Great Wall of China, and even China itself. This goes for the entire Orient, from the Fall of man until today.

With these futile ideas in my head and my thirst for a "cola" purged, I went looking for the Zamzam well. They had positioned the mouth of the well below the surface, right beside the "House." There are wide steps in the middle of the square taking you down. Then there is a corridor with pipes along the walls on both sides and a spigot every two steps. At every spigot three or four people are holding pails, pans, and canteens, waiting for a turn. Then you come to a door leading to the mouth of the well, through which women are not allowed. And what could be better? Such commotion! Like a men's bathhouse, all of them soaked in water and sweat, the well in the center with a tall, thick, cylindrical mouth and three pulleys above it attached to the ceiling, each one dangling a rope into the well and buckets being raised and lowered in turn. Is it possible, however, to distribute the water without wasting it? The pails the hajjis have brought for bearing the water have lids, and on each lid is a narrow screw-on cap, so they can take the well water back home uncontaminated. In all that crowding, rushing, and scuffling, how can one pour a narrow stream of water from the big well buckets into such little holes? I waded *slop slop* through the water, made one round with difficulty, and came out. *Iḥrām*s were clinging to everyone, and there was a kind of good-natured quarreling going on among all of them, as they reached ahead of one another to take the water buckets and empty them into their souvenir buckets. God save us from the police, who are everywhere, with their hats, badges, and pistols. One of them stood at the mouth of the well just watching the operation of the pulleys. His clothes clung to his body and water dripped all over him. He held his pistol to his side with one hand and fanned himself with the other. There were two or three aggressive hajjis standing at the mouth of the well drawing up water and pouring it on the other people. Just like a bathhouse. What would it be like if you didn't see these trademarks, emblems, and weapons at the mouth of the Zamzam well and you forgot

---

[106] Qobādiyāni Marvazi, 1004-88 A.D., better known in the West as Nāṣir-i Khusraw, was a famous Iranian poet and writer who became a convert to the Ismā'īlī (Seveners) sect in Egypt under Fatimid rule. He returned to Khorasan to propagate his beliefs, but met with opposition from the authorities. He is especially well remembered for his *Safarnāmah* [*Travelogue*], and may have been one of Āl-e Ahmad's sources of inspiration for the present work. (tr)

that there too you're under government control? Even on the Hajj there's not a moment's opportunity to evade this ugly, unavoidable reality. Oh yes. Unless the Hajj rites were to be brought under international Islamic control, and so on.

It's quite a spectacle when the people are poising themselves outside the Kaaba or beneath a portico for the circumambulation. The *muṭawwif* gives instructions and the others, who have already made arrangements among themselves, listen attentively. Holding onto one another's hands, chadors or *iḥrāms*, they start out, walking in place at first, then swarming ahead. I'm certain, however, that they become dispersed and scattered at the very outset. Each one in the multitude goes in a different direction, and each loses his way going home and spends half a day wandering around aimlessly. The women are really just spectators in these rites. They're not admitted to the graveyard, nor to the shrines of Uhud and Zamzam. Tonight, on the second floor above the *mas'ā* between *Safā* and *Marveh*, there were a number of them in front—at the edge of the room—having taken places for the prayer. They were quite happy, watching the "House" and the circumambulation around it, when two or three Turks came up insisting that the women ought to be behind the men. And the women yielded.

Then there are these huge cloths they spread out underfoot! First they soak them with water from the Zamzam well, then they spread them out beneath the hajjis' feet, end to end, over the House of God's marble carpet and over the hot sand (the marble carpet over the mosque floor is not yet completed) both to prevent the hajjis from burning their feet and to bless the cloth as a commodity for the next life. Apart from the *iḥrām*, which each keeps, the hajji's greatest souvenir is his burial shroud.

I then went up on the Eastern roof and kneeled to pray in a place at the roof's edge overlooking the entire House and the surrounding area. The call to prayer came at 6:20, later than the usual Medina time. As the call arose, the crowd circumambulating the Kaaba, moving to the center from the edges, began to quiet down and form circular ranks. By the time the words *Allahu akbar* [God is great] were heard the entire mosque population was in concentric files. The last circumambulators lined up instantly, but there was still a flurry of activity in that corner where the Black Stone[107] sits in one of the Kaaba's walls as I began my prostrations. By the time I raised my head again the entire mosque population was lined up, from one end of the porticos and rooftops to the other. The greatest number of human beings anywhere who are gathered in one place in response to

[107] The Black Stone is mounted about 5 feet above the ground in the eastern corner of the Kaaba, surrounded by a stone ring and held in place by a silver band. It has no direct relationship to Islam, but is kissed and touched by pilgrims in emulation of a similar gesture of respect made to the Stone by the Prophet Muhammad on his last pilgrimage to Mecca. (tr)

a command. This assembly must have some meaning! A meaning higher than this dealing, marketing, tourism, discharge of obligation and ritual enactment, economy, government, and a thousand other inevitable things! When the prayer reached the second *salām*, from that corner in front of the Stone there was a sudden explosion of people rushing to kiss it. Then the prayer ranks broke and the circumambulating began anew. At first the ranks nearest the Kaaba arose and began circling, then those behind them followed in a stately rippling motion moving away from the center. The gentlemen who built these new arched porticos were aware of the grandeur of their task, but it's a pity. And God save us from all these molded reinforced concrete structures. Despite this, when finished it will be the largest uncovered temple on earth, with two new monstrous minarets competing for height.

As I descended the steps I suddenly realized my foot was burning painfully. I withdrew into a corner and bent over to find the cause of the burning, and saw that there were new blisters. Then I looked at my shins and saw that they were covered with strange red blemishes, which continued higher up. I hiked up my *iḥrām*. It was on my chest and belly too, as well as my arms. Because of my bad liver and this hot sun. As I straightened up to leave, I caught a woman lifting her eyes, looking me over.

Sunday 30 Farvardin [April 19]

Mecca

This morning I went to see Abu Talib's grave above Sha'b Amir, which is a continuation of the new Mecca graveyard, in the bottom of a northern valley. They have deliberately destroyed and broken everything in that other graveyard and in this one as well. Carved and inscribed marble headstones have been scattered and strewn everywhere. Nothing is recognizable anywhere without the help of a guide. This is how tradition has assured the survival of a number of people who specialize in the dead past. The destruction of a grave in this part of the world (where they burn libraries) is the equivalent of burning a book. Every grave is a closed book, the headstone its cover, or the other way around. These people have even covered the cover. Why do we bury the dead? Why don't we burn them? In the traditions of nations that have graves, and burials and shrouds, respect for the dead precedes respect for the living. What does this really mean? Aren't those nations with no burial practices (the Indians and others) always cut off from their traditions? What ordinary man's grave lasts longer than 30 years? It is the graves of famous people which are shrines, refuges, shelters, courtyards.. Enough of this.

There was a pillar-like marble stone (broken and scattered, of course) bearing the name of some Ottoman commander. Another stone had the remnants of a name "Shmu'il, Sultān of Dāghestān" (or something like that). The stones standing above the graves were designed like the carved and truncated ends of prayer carpets. I walked among these remnants from the carpet of tradition, curses on my lips, when a young man approached, a friendly smile of recognition on his lips. We greeted one another. He was a Shi'i from Lhasa, the same place to which Nāṣir-i Khusraw had traveled in the 11th century in order to see its semi-socialistic life. He was 23 or 24 years old, feeling sympathy for the graves and their occupants. I said, "Let's sit down somewhere for coffee and talk." We went. There was no coffee, so we settled for mango juice. He knew a little *Engrish*, his more broken than mine. He said he was a white-collar employee of the Aramco Oil Company, with a monthly salary of 650 rials. (I think he was exaggerating.) We talked for an hour, trying to recall the splendor of the dawn of Islam, and other matters. He said that in all of Aramco there are 7,000 Arab workers and 3,000 Americans. The three main oil centers are Dhahran, Abqaiq (Abquq?) [Abqaiq], and Ra's al-Nurah (Ra's al-Tanurah?) [Ras Tannūrah]. In the third location there is only a refinery. Daily Saudi oil production is 2,000,000 barrels. I didn't know how much that was, and he didn't know the amount that represented in tons. He said each of those three locations has a manager, and the general manager lives in Dhahran. Each of them gets 10,000 to 12,000 rials per month salary, and the general manager gets 30,000. The highest salary for a Saudi Arab, however, is 3,000 rials per month.

I then asked him about 'Abdullah Tariqi, who had one day made an issue of the Gulf oil situation and the amount of it plundered by foreigners. He said he is now in exile, either in America or Lebanon. It seems he is teaching. He had studied in America. He was one of the young people sent to study in America at Aramco's expense. Right away when he returned he had begun doing things to support the local white- and blue-collar workers, and since he was making trouble they got rid of him. He said that in Hofuf, Qatif, and Ahsa', most of the people are Shi'i, 80 percent of them. I was reminded again of that Qobādiyāni. I told him a few things about the Qarmatians, the story of the place of the Black Stone,[108] and similar

[108] The Qarmatian [also Carmathian and Ḳarmaṭian] movement of the 9th to the 12th centuries was a Shi'i insurrection against the Baghdad caliphate aimed at social reform and equality. The name may be derived from that of the movement's first leader, Ḥamdān Qarmaṭ, who revolted early in the latter half of the 9th century. The movement later spread into what are now Egypt, Saudi Arabia, eastern Iran, and India. On Jan 12, 930, a successor to Qarmaṭ, Abū Ṭāhir Sulaymān, carried a Qarmatian military campaign into Mecca and seized the Black Stone, which he carried to al-Ahsa. (tr)

speculations. He knew nothing of history, however. Totally cut off from tradition. He was very interested in Tehran and was aware of the events of the 15th of Khordād,[109] asking about their outcome. He said the Shi'is in Saudi Arabia have only been allowed to teach for two years. Then he boasted that it had been arranged for Ayatollah Hakim[110] to come for the Hajj this year, but he did not come, because the Saudi government did not accept all of his conditions. And the conditions? To be allowed to repair the grave structures in the Baqī' Cemetery, to construct a Shi'i *mihrāb* in the *Bayt al-Ḥarām* (but I saw that there was only one Imam's grave there, not four), and finally, authorization to announce officially the appearance of the moon. He said the Saudis had accepted the first two, but not the final one. The same sort of outrageous claims the Shi'is always make. I then asked him about the bus companies that transport the hajjis. He knew more about this than I did. He said there are three companies: *Ba Khashb,* owned by a man of that name, *Shirkat al-'Arabi,* owned by a man named Tamimi, and *Shirkah al-Tawfiq,* owned by a man named Sharbat Li. Saudi millionaires, and of course the Great King has a share in each one of them. The busses are all American: Fords, Chevrolets, and Dodges.

He asked me, "What is your religious school?" I told him I wanted to be of the same school as the Muslims at the dawn of Islam. He was surprised. "Why did you come to Mecca, then?"

"I don't know."

"Is it true what they say about the Iranians...?" But he stopped. After a moment he added, "It's better if you choose one of the 72 religious schools, because you'll be confused if you don't."

"I'm confused by this very choice."

There was an argument at breakfast (bread, cheese, tea) between Mohaddes and that Sayyid with the colorful beard (white, black, and brown) over a grammatical point. The Sayyid was calm, but behaving like a mulla and a buffoon. Mohaddes was agitated and shouting, swearing by the House of God. I went to his aid, telling the Sayyid not to imagine he was talking to an ignoramus. Moreover, Mohaddes was right. The Sayyid did not want, by his turban, to back down in front of a group that was asking him about

---

109 On the 15th of Khordad [June 5, 1963] a general religious uprising began in Iran. It started in Qom as a response to the arrest and imprisonment of Ayatollah Musavi Ruhollah Khomeini for his outspoken criticism of the government, and spread quickly to Shiraz, Varamin, Kashan, and Mashhad. It took the government 6 days to repress the disturbances, using extreme force and violence and causing heavy loss of life. (tr)

110 Ayatollah Shaykh Mohsen al-Hakim was an Arab Shi'i jurist living in Najaf, Iraq. At the time *Lost in the Crowd* was written, Hakim was attempting to enlarge his following and to become the sole *marja'-e taqlid* [source of emulation] for the world's Shi'i community. He was never able to attract more than a small following within Iran, however. (tr)

doubts and omission and to reveal that he knew less. But he did know less. Mohaddes was unaware of this. In any case, they were right on the verge of exchanging blows. I am just beginning to understand Mohaddes. He is the same argumentative student he was 25 years ago.

The local Arabic newspapers were full of boastful pride today because the Kaaba's shroud was made by the Saudis themselves this year, and they did not accept one from the Egyptians. They had washed the Kaaba in the morning in order to change the shroud. Each one of our fellow travelers returning from circumambulation was full of talk about having seen the changing of the Kaaba's shroud. There was an unspeakable uproar. One of their feet was black and blue from being stepped on so much. Another had lost his shoe. Another had stood guard with three others so a fourth one could pray at *Maqām-e Ebrāhim.*[111] They had taken turns. As for myself, my side hurt. The run between *Safā* and *Marveh* is a long one, and tiresome, even though I was never able to do more than two laps without stopping. I get exhausted and stop. The circumambulation is easier. But why does my side hurt? Aha. These Yemenis are very rough. In order to clear a path for themselves they elbow the hajjis in the side, pushing on both sides. I saw this two or three times. I can't recall if they did this to me or not. They surely must have, however. If they hadn't I'd be able to walk now.

Yesterday at sunset I cut my hair[112] like the others, in order to remove the *iḥrām*. That is, I cut my moustache. At the two ends of the runway on the heights of *Safā* and *Marveh*, a group of people stood holding scissors and mirrors in order to cut the hajjis' hair. They were clipping hair from heads, beards, and moustaches, and taking money. The hilltops of *Safā* and *Marveh* were like the floor of a barbershop, just from the single finger's width of hair they cut from the hajjis' beards and fuzz. I took the scissors and mirror from a fellow and trimmed my own moustache. I gave him half a rial and went on.

This Meccan mountain sun is dangerous; it brought back my dry cough. Every day I take a drop of Ipesandrine. So many of the Iranian hajjis are bald! The old men, of course. Especially the villagers. One of them is a very quiet old man who hides his baldness beneath a stocking cap, and avoids the others like an ailing fowl. He lives in the corridor night and day. I paid him no heed in Medina, but here I can't help it. Yesterday, when I went to get a drink from my canvas water bottle which I hang in

---

111 According to legend, when Ebrāhim [Abraham] was rebuilding the Kaaba, he had to stand on a large stone after the height of the building had risen above his reach; the stone now called *Maqām-e Ebrāhim* is said to be the one he used. It is enclosed in a kiosk near the Kaaba. (tr)

112 This haircut, called *taḥallul* in Arabic, is one of the desacralization procedures which are carried out before leaving the shrine area. When the haircut is completed, a pilgrim is no longer subject to the restraints of *iḥrām*, with the exception of the prohibition on sexual intercourse. (tr)

the window that opens on the corridor, I saw him. We were all having lunch. He, however, had placed a bowl of ice water in front of himself and sat alone, arms around his knees, smoking a cigarette, like a scolded child. You would think he came on the Hajj to mourn. I sat beside him and told him these things. It turned out he was from Tafresh, alone, with no friends in the group and no one from his province. Worst of all, he had diarrhea. I called among the women to my sister to see if anyone had some mild food for him. Then I said to him "Hajji dear, everyone gets diarrhea. The climate is bad. I am still on a restricted diet myself; diarrhea isn't contagious," and this sort of nonsense. Now he has come and joined the group. Really, the incident with that police major has made me apprehensive. At least this Tafreshi knows he is bald and protects his head from this fiendish sun. The others don't know this much. Their heads are blistered, just like the effects of erysipelas. I saw another one at the infirmary with a swollen head. Instead of a bandage, they had wrapped a turban around it and sent him back. The sun shines and the wind blows on all these heads. I have now gradually become a full-time doctor and secretary for our group, dispensing salt tablets, vitamin C, Ipesandrine, and the like, and most often, bandages. Every time the good people return from circumambulation and *sa'y* it is as if they have just returned from the battle of Khaybar[113]—some part of them is injured. They all know I have bandages. So much skin had peeled off a Mazandarani's big toe that I put three Band-Aids on it. Today I wrote my second letter as group secretary, for that fussy Mazandarani who looks like Nima. He has an interesting name as well, Haj Ba'uch. What does that mean? He did not know. His letter consisted of two lines of news of the journey and then two pages of greetings to about 50 people. One of them was Mashhadi Manuchehr!

Other prices I have recently obtained: yogurt in cups is 1/2 rial (and it is very tart). A bag made from lamb or kid guts[114] is 3 rials. A barrel of water, which cannot be taken to high remote alleyways by any means except a donkey, is 1/2 rial. One donkey carries 8 barrels. There are small slings on his back with 4 barrels hanging on each side. People carry water as well. They put a pole on their shoulders with a barrel hanging at each end of the pole. The price is the same, however. The donkeys climb the stairs easily, zigzagging and ascending, like mules on a mountain. On very high streets, stairs have been carved from stone all the way to the top. The donkeys have designs on their rumps and necks, and their skin is like a carpet. It looks like they have been decorated with a branding iron. They probably apply the design first and then burn it in with a branding iron.

[113] Actually a siege for the most part, this battle was fought in May-June of 628 at a Jewish oasis by the same name, located about 100 miles north of Medina. In winning this engagement the Prophet Muhammad effectively destroyed all remaining Jewish political opposition to the Islamic movement. (tr)

[114] Such bags are used to store yogurt and butter. (tr)

The designed areas are white and hairless, or dyed. All the donkeys are the *bandari*[115] breed, very frisky.

The city of Mecca is expanding dramatically, like every other city. "Development" has caught on even in the vicinity of the holy shrines. Upon approaching every shrine, you see that there is no "sanctity" in its exterior. It is in you, in your mind. Or it was. The symbolism of every shrine is hidden within its inner sanctuaries, in the spaces. Without the sanctuaries, it is just a thing, a person, or a process. Of course, if the city of Medina is stretched out and flat, here the town is rising, going up. The heights of both the buildings and the streets are increasing on the sides of the mountains around the city. In the true meaning of the word, the city of Mecca is "growing." There is reinforced concrete everywhere being buttressed by stone supports, without a trace of the beautiful woodwork of old. There are only these huge steel and glass windows, and the same disastrous consumption of foreign products, beneath this fearsome sun.

Three times so far I have seen young men holding the hands of their brides—almost embracing them—during circumambulation. A Hajj "honeymoon"? I say they were brides because of their beautiful, intricately designed, flowered or silver embroidered veils, or because of their jealously protective men. I also saw pregnant women two or three times, almost due, doing the circumambulation the same as the others, without any precaution or fear. The hajjis, however, are extremely solicitous.

On this Ghaza Street (the largest street in Mecca) there is a mosque called Mosque of the Jinn.

Same day. Same place.

In the evening when it was cool I came out of the house to go for a walk. I had thrown an Arab head cloth over my head like a scarf, with Javad's mantle on my shoulders, like the others. There is no alternative. It was so dusty! And so sunny! I went to the north as far as *al-Mu'ābidah* Square. The sunlight was reflected on the upper side of the mountain. There was beautiful landscaping in the middle of the square with benches amidst little flower gardens. The tropical trees are still young and without a shadow, except for one or two eucalyptus trees that cast shadows and were covered with a lot of dust. Here and there were zinnias and verberas around the garden, on a little patch of lawn. I made a circuit once or twice and sat down beside a tall young man who was reading some photocopied pages to prepare a lesson. I said "hello" in my limited Arabic and asked to sit down; he stopped reading to talk. It seems that he was an officer just returned from al-Khamis on leave. (The days of *'Ayd-e Qorbān* are an

115 These donkeys originated in Cyprus. (tr)

annual, official holiday for the Saudi government, something on the order of our New Year's.) Al-Khamis is at the border between Yemen and Saudi Arabia, and he was in charge of I don't know how many soldiers, protecting the border from Sallal[116] and providing a kind of shield for al-Badr.[117] His monthly salary was 750 rials, with one wife and a child. He was himself an Anizah Arab. I never thought an Anizah could be just like a human being, and so neat. He recited some of their poems in praise of Wahhabi power and their government. He really wanted to know if I was *muwaṭin ṣāliḥ* or not. I didn't understand what he meant. I resorted to English, which he knew a little. "Do you mean 'good citizen'?" I asked. He didn't understand. I had to explain to him that if he was talking about a world state, I was not in favor of such a thing.

"Why not?" he asked.

"Although a human being is not a stone to be laid on a foundation and held in place," I said, "everyone is subject to the limitations of his language, culture, and traditions," and this kind of thing. I had to hear something from him, however, so I cut it short and gave him my attention. The book he was reading was a history of World Wars I and II in Arabic, a translation of an American text. He said he was a communist, a "revolutionary." He mentioned Machiavelli, Marx, and Hegel, talked about "tempered steel," and *ra's māliyah* (which I realized was a literal translation of our word for capitalism). Some time ago he had gone to Egypt for three months for some kind of military training, and he had brought back all these books and names. From the names he mentioned and his reliance on Harold [Joseph] Laski,[118] I realized that he was about where we were 20 years ago. He also knew a bit of Hebrew, which they had taught him in the military school, so they would not be at a loss to manage Israel after they captured it! We inevitably turned to the subject of Israel. I used the example of the hand and the heart (which I also remember explaining to the young men of 'Ur'ur at the ice cream stand), saying that one must disable the heart in order to stop the hand, and the dangerous heart in the East is foreign capitalism, and Aramco and the other oil companies are its hands. Israel is one of them also. He didn't accept this, however. I tried to find the word for "demagoguery" in Arabic (he didn't understand it in English) in order to describe Nasser's behavior towards Israel for him. The words didn't

---

[116] Marshal Abdullah Sallal was a Yemeni army officer and politician. In 1962 he became Commander-in-Chief of the Republican forces fighting in the Yemeni civil war, after serving as Chief of Staff to Imam Muhammad al-Badr, his future foe, earlier the same year. (tr)

[117] Imam Muhammad al-Badr was Imam of Yemen (head of the Zaydi sect and chief of state). He first came to power in 1962 after the death of his father, but was soon overthrown by a military coup d'etat. He then organized a number of tribes in the northern mountains of Yemen in a counter rebellion against forces led by Marshal Abdullah Sallal that succeeded in retaking parts of the country. This struggle was in progress during Āl-e Ahmad's pilgrimage to Mecca. (tr)

[118] Harold Joseph Laski, 1893-1950. (tr)

come to hand, however, or to my tongue. He was aware of the danger of capitalism, but didn't understand that the Arabs ought to be united against the oil companies instead of Israel.

He later became alarmed that I was taking notes, especially when I wrote down the command of the Great King of Saudi Arabia, who said "Don't teach your young or they will eat you." He said they would seize a man in a second and take him away (or something like that). I wanted to know where the Saudi prisons were located. He looked around and then quickly mentioned a name—or perhaps two—which I didn't understand. He knew I wanted to write it down, so he wouldn't repeat it.

"Where is it?" I asked.

"In the Empty Quarter," he said. Then he said he was not alone. There are many like him in the army. Then he leaned over and said into my ear, "Israel must first be killed in the palaces of the Arab kings, and afterwards in Palestine itself." Then he deplored such things as poverty and the lack of medical care... I forgot to ask his rank. Judging from his youth, however, he must have been a first or second lieutenant.

After I left him I was thinking that the West has really used Israel as a cover for its own misdeeds, or as a way of hiding them. They have planted Israel in the heart of the Arab lands so that the Arabs would forget the real troublemakers in the midst of Israel's trouble-making, and not realize that the water and the fertilizer for the tree of Israel comes from the Christian West, the French and American capitalists. Then there was the support which the Pope of Rome gave them, in lifting the curse of Christ from them, I think by a decree from Pope John 22. Then I was thinking that if Nasser became famous overnight it was because he took a stand against the West—without having any underground oil reserves—and that channel of water, the Suez Canal, was not worth a lot of trouble. When we opposed them we had such oil deposits, and this is one of the reasons we failed /with Dr. Mosaddeq and the events of his time—not because of outsiders, but because of internal problems. Of course the West penetrated, because something was rotten on the inside/.[119] If the West is pushing the wagon of Christianity with its neocolonialism, why have we in our area allowed the cart of Islam to become so rusty and abandoned it? I asked myself, wouldn't these Hajj rituals themselves be a good launching pad for taking a stand against the West? (Oh ho! I'm back to *Weststruckness* again...)

[119] The section between slashes was censored in earlier editions of the book. (tr)

Same day.

I've been on a restricted diet ever since leaving Medina. Tea, compote, and yogurt. I adopted the latter in Mecca, but it's too bad it's so sour. The compote I had for lunch was from Japan, something like peaches or apricots. The mango juice was from India. Everything is from somewhere. They bring food here from all over the world. It's no joke. All these people, and such a market! Perhaps one may say that the Hajj rites provide an occasion to liquidate surplus for all the factories in the world. The good people traveling with us are all busy buying things. Now they are inspecting their purchases, comparing prices and exchanging information on what is available where and which merchants have bargains and which don't. Tea, tamarind, cloth, red rubies, snake skins (for the well-to-do), robes, black chadors, perfume, *mumenā'i* (which is pure pitch from oil wells), watches, men's shirts, socks, shoes, and a lot of other things... All of them from some corner of the world.

The neighborhood dogs, goats, and cats are having a tremendous feast behind the walls of our building. There is food for a flock of them, the leftovers from the hajjis, who are not eating much because of the warm climate. They are all so peaceful, the dogs and cats together. The cats quarrel with one another, but not with the dogs. Their dinner: rice, bread, meat, and chicken...whatever they want.

Among our traveling companions is an old bespectacled man. He is very dignified. He is a retired school principal from the Sari area. He has just come in, cross and complaining. He had collided with someone during the circumambulation, and his glasses fell underfoot and were broken. He is quite helpless. He said he had been working his way here ever since the *maghreb* [sunset] prayer. Feeling his way, saying nothing, he had lost the way and was about to die by the time we got to him. We all pitched in and fed him tea, water, *khākshir-yakhmāl*[120] and dinner. I promised I would go to a local doctor with him tomorrow so he could get new glasses. I asked him his prescription. He said 10. His glasses, however, are really not that thick.

In the afternoon the local children (whose schools are closed for vacation) were watching the chickens thrash as they were beheaded. We had chicken with rice [*morgh polow*] tonight. Among the guide's employees is an Arab who has learned a few words of Persian. He was joking with one of our traveling companions who deals in rice flour in the Mo'ayyer market.[121]

[120] *Khākshir*, or *khākshir-e shīrīn*, is the Persian name for a tiny red seed obtained from the pods of one member of a family of plants known as *cruciferae* (Latin *sisymbrium sophia*), which includes the mustard plant. The seeds, 1 mm. in length, are used for medicinal purposes, and are considered aphrosidiac. They are sometimes drunk with lemonade or sweetened water with ice. In the latter case the beverage itself is also known as *khākshir*, or *khākshir-yakhmāl*. (tr)

[121] A large market in Tehran. (tr)

His head is quite bald. He said to the fellow "*tow mokh nadārī*" [you have no brain] and everyone laughed hysterically. This happened over and over. A hundred times a day when he saw the man he'd say "*mokh nist*" [no brain] and everyone would laugh.

People have now begun to carry flags, a precaution against getting lost at Mina and 'Arafāt. Every group carries the flag of its country with the name and emblem of its guide, and so on... above it. That employee of our guide's who went to Jedda from Medina with the retired police major has not yet returned, and we are still short-handed.

Monday 31 Farvardin [April 20]

Mecca

This morning I began buying things too. A market like this gets a person into the mood to buy things. I think most of the things people buy as souvenirs are bought in this very manner, as a reaction to the frenzy of the bazaar. Then when they return to their own country they label each purchase as a souvenir for some family member, relative, friend, or acquaintance. I bought two Arab head scarves, three bamboo canes, several bundles of aloe branches, and four ball-point pens. "What did you buy?" asked my good fellow travelers. They liked the pens, and several people went to buy some of them. They didn't like the bamboo, however. No one said anything, but the reason was understandable. After all, the lance that struck 'Ali Asghar's[122] throat was made of bamboo. Can one write a Mecca travel diary and not go into the events at Karbala?

The movement towards Mina began today. The streets are unbelievably crowded. And how these drivers honk their horns!

122 'Ali Asghar was the infant son of Imam Husayn, who was killed along with his father at Karbala. (tr)

Same day. Same place.

I was writing when my uncle asked to have a letter written. A scribe all his life, his hand now shakes and he can't write. I have just finished his letter. He wanted to sign it himself. He took the pen in his fist and put it to the paper, like a knife you take and stick into the top of a table vertically, and with the same difficulty. He scrawled a "Muhammad" the size of a one toman coin[123] in a large hand. He was truly afflicted with old age (perhaps you don't have this problem) and infirmity. When I think about it I realize I have absolutely no ambition nor the good health necessary to reach such an age. Eighty years! The age of Noah. Unlike the villagers (this is the twelfth letter I have written for my fellow travelers) he thought about his words first and then spoke them, with everything carefully reckoned and in the right place. A lifetime as a notary public has taught him the financial and legal value of words, but he is a terribly feeble old man. His foot had swollen yesterday, not from walking a lot, but because of the fear of getting lost. Today he went and got an injection, and now he thinks he is better. He did the circumambulation and *sa'y* in a wheelchair, at a total cost of 40 Saudi rials. On returning, however, Javad never came for him, although he waited and waited. I found him at the door of the Grand Mosque. He was perspiring, and his eyes were darting back and forth so much I thought he was going to fall over. But he didn't. I consoled him a bit and we slowly returned. Moreover, his ankle has swollen.

This hajji Ba'uch was telling a story or making a point this morning at breakfast, when one of those from his province said mischievously, "Hajji, speak properly!" The old man argued with him and left in anger again. Not only was the original point forgotten, but he also neglected to drink his tea, as if he did not want to talk a lot, and he's the type of man who's forthright and fearless, and talking easily.

The retired school principal went to the doctor today with his son. He got temporary glasses until his permanent ones are ready. The borrowed glasses look like a gas mask on his face.

---

[123] About the size of a U.S. silver dollar. (tr)

Same day. Mecca.

We are to leave for 'Arafāt at 6 or 7. Right now there is an unspeakable uproar in the room. Everyone is bustling about, pushing, hurrying, and closing and opening luggage. One of them forgot to pack his *iḥrām*, for example. They teach each other how to wear belts and wallets so they remain hidden. There is a lot of uncertainty among them about whether to take all of their money with them or to leave part of it here, since most of the hajjis' luggage will remain here, and we have only a small quantity of necessities with us for two or three days at Mina and 'Arafāt.

Most important of all, the water is cut off again, just when we need it to wash *iḥrāms* and this kind of thing. Precisely when water is necessary, there is no sign of water. Just like the jinn and *bismillāh* [in the name of God]. There is plumbing in the house, for example, but what can all these people do in that one place with four spigots? Moreover, the owner of the house is constantly coming and going saying do this, don't do that. There is an air conditioner in the house that he regards as a treasure from the Taj Mahal. He's like an effete Tehran intellectual telling you how to treat his car. Just like him. He is always coming in and going out to make sure no one touches the controls and makes it go faster or slower. I wish it weren't here at all and we didn't breathe all this artificial air, with all its irritating whirring that doesn't let us sleep. The good people have learned his weak points and are always fiddling with it. Just like children. For my part, I am delighted that we will be freed from the aggravation of this air conditioner for 2 or 3 days in 'Arafāt and Mina.

There is a quarrel taking place now among my fellow travelers, over shoes. All the slippers are alike, but each pair is a different color, and they are different sizes. One of them has lost his shoes. Another's have been mismatched. This kind of thing... In the middle of this commotion, a worthy gentleman (I'm referring to our preacher, who has pleaded with me two or three times to speak to the others on his behalf–and please do it now.) is in fine form today. I didn't get what the occasion was for telling the story of the frogs, but he says they once complained to Solomon about the cold and asked for *qabās*[124] to wear. Solomon promised, but didn't live long enough to keep the promise. This is why frogs always say *qabā qabā*. Then he told approvingly of a demonstration last night in the House of God after the sunset prayer. A political one. Two people got up and spoke. One spoke of Israel, another of Syria. I didn't get the reason for the second one. The shoe argument rages on. Other things have also been lost: two rings, a glazed bowl, three bottles of lemon juice (Mohaddes bought one of them yesterday, with a Glasgow-Aberdeen trademark, for 2 1/2 rials). Such swearing, such altercations over these things—and from whose

[124] An outer garment with full-length sleeves. (tr)

mouths? From the mouths of the respected hajjis to the Holy Sanctuary of God. The well-to-do of the Muslim nation of Iran.

Night. Same day.

'Arafāt.

We started out in a truck at 9 p.m., and we got there at 11 p.m., although we had been waiting to leave since 5 p.m. This "mechanized" primitivity is something else. Leaving Mecca and reaching the Plain of 'Arafāt was a supreme effort in every way. A person learns the meaning of religious expressions here. Waiting, waiting, waiting, as in the past. The saving grace is that in such a situation I immerse myself in this little notebook, sequestering myself behind its paper doors—no matter what happens. Then we left and traveled 21 or 22 kilometers in 3 hours. The truck was constantly braking, with the hajjis continually falling all over one another and shouting. (Javad called me to get on top of the truck over the driver's cab, so I did. I didn't know why at first. The wind blew under my *iḥrām* garments and I was badly chilled.) We would take off suddenly at full throttle, and two steps later, the blaring of horns, the squealing of brakes, and then the angry shouts of hajjis falling all over one another. The women had been seated in front of the truck, the men behind. When the brakes were applied everyone was dumped together, and such pandemonium. Then we reached a desert, one *farsakh* by two *farsakh*s. There were tents erected everywhere, ropes crisscrossing, and a crossroads in the middle. There was a mosque on one street, on another stores, bakeries, and butcher shops. The entire plain was without electrical power. In the light of kerosene lanterns large and small, hanging and setting, meat carcasses hung on large tripods in front of stores and tents, and there were coffee houses open for business. A store owner was asleep on the counter, bakery ovens were still wet on the outside, and the Bedouins were asleep right alongside the main road among their goats and sheep, which had blue feet and henna-dyed backs and necks.

There were tents, tents, tents. Here, even the police and the armed soldiers were dressed in *iḥrām*, but they patrol with rifles on their shoulders. Only the traffic police are allowed to wear their uniforms, guiding the Bedouin drivers with motions of their nightsticks. There are also boy scouts helping people locate their tents. We are relatively comfortable, and we are now in our tent. Everyone is worried about his place, about the carpet, about dinner, and everything else. It turns out we are at the foot of a mountain. It is cold, and everyone is talking about Mount Rahmah, which we saw at a distance as we were arriving, with the moving flickers of hand lanterns on its flanks and peak. Too bad it's so cold, and my fatigue and cough won't let me; otherwise I would go out and spend an hour mingling with the crowd. The devil take this *bronchite*, which by now is tracheitis. For tonight I will note that they call the place 'Arafāt[125] because Adam and Eve found each other and got acquainted on that mountain after their expulsion from Paradise.

Tuesday 1 Ordibehesht '43 (9 Dhū al-Ḥijjah) [April 21]

I awoke to this song in the morning:

> *Yā 'Umm ul-Ḥajj, Ḥaji*
> *Allāh qabbal lak, Ḥaji*
> *Hayy bilriyāl, Ḥaji*
> *Siwā' siwā', Ḥaji*
> *Yā bu tarbush, Ḥaji*[126]
> *Tarbush ḥumrā, Ḥaji*[127]

and so on, with the rhythm: *rim bam bam bam - bam bam.* The chorus of the song, which was *ḥaji* (with short instead of long *a* and doubled *j*) was chanted by a seven-year-old girl, who also made movements as she spoke. She would bend her knees suddenly and become shorter, which is to say she backed away, and a mature young girl with a good figure and a beautiful face sang the rest of the song. Such a warm voice. I think this is the same song I had heard being sung at the entrance to the Garden of Purity by two or three *Nakhāwalah* children.

We woke up once at 5 to pray and then went back to sleep, we were so tired, and slept until 7:30, when the song woke us up. There was breakfast with twice-sifted bread. Last night we had cold rice and lentils, which had been cooked in Mecca and brought to 'Arafāt. (Now we are having a *rowzeh. Rowzeh, rowzeh, rowzeh.* I'm fed up with it. A fellow has come for the Hajj and made a pilgrimage to the very House of God itself, but all the same he constantly whines that he wants to visit Karbala... And as if we didn't have enough preachers and eulogists, today two Karbala preachers turned up, with Arabic accents.) After that there were two people who sang eulogies, took a collection, and left. A woman came wearing a scarf over her face, a child under her arm, with eyes and eyebrows like a deer's.

---

125 The name 'Arafāt is from the Arabic root *'Arafa*, "to know." (tr)

126 *Tarbush* means hat. The rest is evident. A red hat is perhaps a reference to the red fez worn by the Ottomans and Egyptians. The song itself may therefore have been written in that time. (A)

127 The Arabic children's song translates: Oh, Uncle Hajji, May God accept [your pilgrimage], Give us a rial, Hajji, Anything at all, Hajji, Oh wearer of the *tarbush*, Hajji, Your *tarbush* is red, Hajji. (tr)

She sang religious anthems as well, took up a collection, and left. The lyrics of her anthem were difficult—I couldn't write them down. Her face, however, was more beautiful than her voice. We are the only group on this side of the plain that is putting on a *rowzeh*, and the gathering has become very crowded. It is no longer our place. I must go for a walk to have a look around 'Arafāt.

Last night when we got here my sister lost her watch. Now she is quarreling with her husband. She also lost her ring when she was in Medina. I don't know why she got scatterbrained.

The *voquf* at 'Arafāt is the most important pillar of the Hajj, where one stays awake and conscious from noon to sunset (*zekr* - *tazakkor* - *motazakker*).[128]

Same day. 'Arafāt.

When we got here last night we were spreading out our lightweight bedding when I saw a large insect walking on the blanket. It resembled a beetle. I killed the poor thing, and all at once I realized I shouldn't have. Killing God's creatures dressed in *iḥrām!* But it was too late. Mohaddes, who took one end of the blanket so we could shake him off, said that it was dangerous. May it rest in peace, God willing! Then we ate dinner and went to sleep. And such a cold night! I wrapped the towel of my *iḥrām* around my body beneath the blanket and lay down, coughing, with the help of 15 drops of Ipesandrine.

As for this 'Arafāt, it is a desert, like a plain surrounded on three sides by mountains, on the road to Ta'if. An elevated plain, with a concave surface and cooler than the surrounding area, to some extent a grassland, especially at the base of the mountains. It is to the east of Mecca. The bottom of the concave surface is covered with fine sand, resembling that of the sea, with seashell fragments, or something bright, shiny, and cream colored. Even at the top of the heights and between the rocks on the mountains. When we got here last night a cool breeze began to blow. I saw a bush resembling heather today on top of the rise. Then the sheep and goats were grazing on the heights of the area in groups, in addition to the livestock that was lingering with the people among the tents. It seemed as if they wanted to let the sheep feed on grass once more before sacrificing them. (Yesterday—8 Dhū al-Ḥijjah—was *Yawm al-tarwiyah*, or the Day of

[128] *Zekr* is the subdued, repetitive utterance of Muslim litanies, often done while turning a rosary. *Tazakkor* is the verbal noun meaning "saying *zekr*"; *motazakker* is the active participle meaning "sayer of *zekr*". (tr)

Washing.)[129] I saw this business of coming to 'Arafāt in a throng as being originally a kind of *sizdahbedar*, like a "picnic." The side we are on is at the base of a mountain, and the tents of all the Iranians and Shi'is are over on this side, grouped together. A worthy gentleman said in a sermon that it would be better if the *voquf*[130] at 'Arafāt be done at the top of a mountain, or on its side. He thought of the mountains of Iran at this point and said, "The Hejaz mountains are more alive than the mountains of Iran." Then he added: "I say this for your benefit, sir," addressing himself to me. He was right. Both mountains and deserts in this area are barer and purer. They are inevitably more striking. There are no obstacles between you as a human being and each element of nature. The sun is in its place, full, clear, and hot, like a blacksmith's forge. The desert is just that, dry as a bone and full of mirages. The mountains are big chunks of rock piled up to the sky, with no plants. This is why they used to come to 'Arafāt searching for a bit of pasture.

I walked around for an hour this morning. The condition of the toilets is the most disgraceful thing imaginable. For every 100-person tent, there is a small cloth booth over a sump dug right in the sand, with room for only one person. When you squat down your knees come together, and you are right next to the other hajjis. It is true that they have called the people to a primeval state for the Hajj, and to life in the desert, and in tents, but when jets and Chevrolets are used by hajjis instead of camels, some attention ought to be paid to the privies too. Permanent, large concrete privies could be built for each group, in good working order and with running water, so that the hajjis would not have to stand in such long lines, and then be so exposed while attending to their private functions.

God save us from this bickering over water that started up first thing in the morning. For every 5 or 6 tents, there's one spigot mounted in a concrete platform, and above it is a lot of boasting and propaganda concerning the fact that it's a gift from the Great King! Yet this is the very water of Zubaydah, wife of Harun al-Rashid,[131] and in any case this very handful of spigots is entirely at the behest of the water sellers. And such quarreling! They assault one another at the slightest provocation with twisted and soaked bath towels, using them like whips. *Sharq shurq!* "Son of a dog!" And so on.

---

129 On the Day of Washing, a white shroud which was draped over the Kaaba just before the beginning of the Hajj is removed, and the Kaaba is given a ceremonial washing. Then a new black and gold embroidered shroud, called a *kiswah*, is draped over it. (tr)

130 *Voquf* [Arabic *wuqūf*], literally "standing," is an obligatory vigil at 'Arafāt. It begins at noon and ends after sunset on 9 Dhū al-Ḥijjah. (tr)

131 Harun al-Rashid (ruled 786–309) was the 5th and most famous caliph of the Abbassid dynasty. His wife Zubaydah had a 16-kilometer canal to Mecca dug to provide water for the city. (tr)

First thing in the morning they, mostly Bedouins and Yemenis, began slaughtering animals. Carcasses being skinned or gutted are hanging by their tents on frames, with little piles of sheep guts, intestines, and skin and a pungent smell in the air. I don't know what we would do if this sun weren't so hot that it dries anything in half an hour.

On the rocks of the mountain are displays of Arab and Persian products. The sesame seed halvah merchants are extremely active. The ground is covered with banana and orange peels, empty Kent cigarette packs, human and animal feces, and half-burned camel's thorn branches. They've even set up tents on the heights surrounding the Plain of 'Arafāt. These are privately-owned tents, of course, belonging to those who aren't in the clutches of the pilgrim guides and can move freely. Families and local residents mostly. On this entire plain and the surrounding area only Mt. Rahmah has no tents. Apart from the main mountain arch, it is a rocky hump rising up behind the plain with a fat minaret on its peak, and wide stair steps carved in stone on its eastern slope, the work of Jamal al-Din Javad, Minister to Atabak Zangi.[132] The people have swarmed over it like ants and locusts, reciting prayers or reading the Qur'ān. Most of them are standing in the sun, some holding umbrellas over their heads. Even now, past 11 o'clock, the commotion of the multitude is audible at a distance. A mirage appears, a frayed image, and heat waves shimmer upward.

And God save us from the beggars. Women, children, old and young. Not only the blind, paralyzed, and the crippled, but healthy ones too. In a one-hour walk, all the pocket change I had disappeared. I saw someone distributing one-rial notes. So many poor people flocked around him that he lost his *iḥrām*. Someone was making popcorn in another place on a tin tray over a camel's thorn fire, selling it in bags. The way they do for *sizdahbedar*. As I walked I passed several temporary kitchens. There were tantalizing pots of rice, soup, and *khoresh* on the stove. Their smoke was reminiscent of the pre-dawn meals of Ramazān.[133] A large black man rushed by, shielding himself from the sun with a small spatula. An Arab man was bending over kissing the hand of a woman dressed in black, through the window of an automobile. The automobile was stalled in the crowd and couldn't even move in second gear. I think they were Syrians. Behaving like the French bourgeoisie right on the Plain of 'Arafāt! A half hour earlier they had come into our tent and taken a picture of the group after the *rowzeh* was over, with our guide standing in the middle. Our preachers were there too, standing stiff and puffed out.

I put out a cigarette in the sand the way one does at the seaside. It has become very hot, and I have taken the towel from my shoulder and

---

[132] 'Imād al-Dīn Zangī b. Aq Sonqur, governor of Iraq, Mosul, and Aleppo from 1127 to 1146 and founder of the Zangid dynasty. (tr)

[133] *Ramazān* is the ninth month of the Muslim lunar calendar, during which Muslims must fast from dawn until sunset. (tr)

replaced it with a white cambric shawl. Last night there were perhaps 500,000 kerosene lanterns burning in the desert. Only a few official health facilities and the mosque had electricity. The four main streets are asphalt, 3 or 4 kilometers. The rest of the roads are dirt, meaning sand. It turns out that one simply cannot leave the tent in the afternoon. I thought I would read the Qur'ān awhile. Now I am at the end of the Surah of the Cow. I was making notes on my problems in the margins of the Qur'ān's pages when I saw that my companions couldn't stand to see it.[134] It seems that I ought to stop it. Some restrictions must be preserved in any case.

Wednesday 2 Ordibehesht, 1343 ('Ayd-e Qorbān) [April 22]

Mina

Yesterday afternoon at 4 o'clock the people began leaving for Mina, beginning with those on foot, the Bedouins, the nimble-footed, and those with no baggage. We stayed until 9 p.m. We ate dinner on a carpet of sand, outside the tents, beneath the sky, when our belongings were in the truck, the other people had gone, and the feeling of this one day of Bedouin life in the open spaces was coming alive. The tents—now that the people aren't here to separate you from the environment with their trampling—are quite beautiful. They erect the tents for the 'Arafāt rites 2 or 3 days beforehand in anticipation of the arrival of the hajjis, and then after the pilgrims leave they remain up for 2 or 3 more days until they come and collect them. I walked among them. They are like capsized ships, the guy lines their oars, and they are in sand instead of water. (Thus it was not for nothing that Manūchihrī[135] became the "Poet of the Desert.") The remains of this Bedouin picnic consisted of campfire ashes, the remains of carcasses, and little piles of bones. There is no sign of a dog or a cat. What would happen if we stayed here 1 or 2 more days?

Last night was the most difficult we have had on this journey. We rode on top of the same truck from 9 until 10:30, dressed the same way in *iḥrām* garments, in the same cold. We went back by the same route until we reached a pass that was full of busses, automobiles, and trucks. Scattered

---

134 The author's companions probably viewed his note-taking in a copy of the Qur'an as a sacrilege. (tr)

135 Abu-n-Najm Aḥmad b. Qūs Manūchihrī (d. 1040-1041) was a Persian court poet of the Ghaznavid era. He was a connoisseur and admirer of pre-Islamic Bedouin Arabic poetry, and often emulated its descriptions of deserts, adventures in the wilderness, the heavens, the vegetation of the plains, camels, horses, and other characteristic themes. (tr)

campfires flickered in the darkness; there was the smell of livestock, and the sound of the herd's footsteps, like a continuous thumping sound behind a wall at a dark meeting where you are sitting and waiting, along the edge of the pass. We slept on rocky ground. The women stayed in the truck, the men on the ground at the foot of the mountain. The four of us had one travel carpet which we spread out beneath ourselves, and we stretched out in pairs, each sharing half the blankets, which we pulled up to our shoulders. My back was up against a thorn bush, and there beside me were my uncle, Mohaddes, and Javad, in that order. Our traveling companions searched for small rocks in the darkness or by lamplight, for use in tomorrow's stoning of Satan. From time to time a flock passed below us, without a sound, as if they were all asleep, with only the striking of their hooves to indicate that they are alive. Sometimes there was the clop of a camel's hoof passing among the flock. Until morning there was the *hee haw* of the shepherds and the tossing and turning of the other travelers, the cold that came into the unprotected *iḥrām*s, my coughing, and my uncle's complaining. My thoughts concerned the conditions for perpetuating the ecstasy of a tradition. I know that on such a night one must try to perceive the significance of the coming dawn. One thinks and then it becomes clear, just when the world becomes clear; it is like the experience of that old woman who waited and swept for 40 days in her home expecting a visit from Khizr,[136] and on the final day didn't see him. At the last moment, fatigue, the cold, and sleeplessness had so overwhelmed me that I didn't even want to get up, even to look inside myself in the darkness of the last of the night. Self and other were quite intermingled, and the borders unclear. In that dark pass of *Mash'ār al-Ḥarām*,[137] even the distinctions between human and animal were blurred. I asked myself as I lay there "Wasn't this the goal of the call? Isn't this also the thing you said *labbayk*[138] to? What does it mean to get beyond self?"

The pleasant aroma of coffee assailed my nostrils. Several steps away from us a "Bedouin" family was making coffee on its morning campfire. Such an aroma arose from it into the dark air that you might have thought it was a smell that could lift you into heaven. Javad got up. I heard him saying hello and exchanging courtesies in his broken Arabic, and the sound of cups and boiling coffee. I was in such bad shape, however, that I couldn't even get up and take part in that coffee banquet. I thought that for the one who

---

136 Khizr, or al-Khadhir, "the Green One," is a famous figure in Arab folklore. He is said to have discovered and partaken of the fountain of youth, and thereby become immortal. Legends say that he wanders about in a green cloak, carrying out God's commandments and protecting people from misfortune. (tr)

137 Meaning literally "the Sacred Grove," the Mash'ār al-Ḥarām is a roofless mosque located in Muzdalifah, a small town about four miles from 'Arafāt. Pilgrims are required to remain there until after midnight on 10 Dhū al-Ḥijjah, after which they are to proceed to Mina. (tr)

138 *Labbayk:* A ritual word said in response to a religious call, meaning "Here I am!; I am ready!" (tr)

has been reared and trained for this life, and who knows all its ways, there is even poetry about nights in such a desert, and hot coffee at its dawn. This is not only a renewer of strength for himself, but there is also even a share for me in its aroma, and God knows why I came from that side of the world on this journey.

Same day. Same place.

We left *Mash'ār al-Ḥarām* at 5 a.m. We came two kilometers until the road was blocked. This took two hours. No exaggeration. We had to go through another narrow pass. Everyone was in a hurry. If one meter's space appeared among the vehicles they gave it full throttle, then a sudden braking, and the 90 people in the truck were so piled together I couldn't stand the sight of it. I jumped down off the top of the truck and began walking among the multitude of pedestrians. I knew the direction of the Shi'i tent area. I had directions. Now I was one among the many. We gradually moved ahead of the line of vehicles where hajjis were packed together waiting. Waiting, waiting, waiting, for the road to open, for the commotion to die down, for the heat of the sun to subside, for there to be water in the faucets, for the privy to be empty, for food to be ready, and a thousand other "fors." On this journey you continually go from one rendezvous to the next. But time is so meaningless that it has no structure.

I'm not suggesting that with all this waiting to obtain the most minimal of daily necessities there is no longer room for the world of the unseen and its expectations. I'm saying that every year a million people take part in these rites, and that if there were order, facilities, procedures, and creativity, there could be great power. After all, the Muslim people of today don't have to accept pre-Islamic Arab life or Arab ignorance in order to partake of such primitiveness! In any case, if Hajj rites are to continue and not be consigned to the oblivion of the pre-Islamic age like the slave trade, something must be done to save them. And how? I have high expectations. Through placing the shrine cities and their administration under international Islamic control. Just as Islam became Islam by reaching Baghdad, Rey, Damascus, Cairo, Bokhara, and Andalusia, now all of these places must hasten to the aid of this "mechanized" primitivity.

I first passed behind a high cement wall, a slaughterhouse. Then I collapsed on a straw mat at the first temporary coffee house along the road, beneath a thatch awning. I had a bit of bread with *borrād* tea and continued. At the base of the mountain I passed a water tower under construction and turned onto one of the streets passing among the tents. The crowd of pilgrims was intermingling in groups, with the leaders bearing emblems to show the way. They passed swarming among the tents with the kind of fear and urgency

I used to see as a child in the Tehran bazaar on *'Āshurā.*[139] Everyone was saying *labbayk*, and wearing white. For the first time today I realized how many varieties there are even of the color white. Dirty white, cream, blue-white, milk white, shiny white, dark white, and so on. The people were making a huge uproar, and there was a lot of extra activity generated by the fear of getting lost! As we went I felt that we were climbing. The road became narrower, and I said to myself that surely we were approaching the *rajm*[140] area. There were residential dwellings here and there, built on naked boulders, with walls, balconies, doors, and water faucets. People stood watching on the rooftops. Or pilgrims? As we were climbing the road suddenly ended, and it became apparent that an unguided group had come to a dead end. I was terrified for a moment by the pressure of the crowd. Alone in an unfamiliar crowd, everyone speaking a different language. The Tower of Babel fallen into a tiny cobblestone street. I climbed up on a carved stone wall; from a half-meter above the heads of the crowd, I called out to every Iranian pilgrim that this street was a dead end, that they must go back, and to help pass the word to the back of the crowd. They began doing this. Then in Arabic: "*Awqifu. mā bishāri'!*" Several times.

The crowd crushed an old man so hard against the cobblestones of the wall that he passed out. We lifted him up to the top of the wall where the local people brought water to bring him around. Fear of getting lost, fear of unfamiliar places, the desire to see things, and the desire to participate in the acts and rituals of the Hajj make a strange, totally unfamiliar amalgamation of every hajji. Totally agitated and without "self," a particle in a flood. All the preliminaries are there for you to forget your will. My own *iḥrām* came open three times. Not only the towel over my shoulders, even my *izār.*[141] I understood then why pilgrims bring so much baggage with them, plus wallets, iceboxes, and so on. I lost my field notebook with the pencil inside it during all this. On the way back from *rajm* I looked everywhere in the temporary stores, but couldn't find a note pad. I bought a pencil, however, for 6 piastres.

Let me now say something about Mina itself. It is a valley between formidable mountains, with other runoffs and branches going through other valleys in the region. There are a few buildings on both sides of the main street, then stores, and then the Khayf Mosque. At the end of the valley, at the mouth of a pass leading to Mecca, is the final stoning pillar. Behind the buildings alongside some streets in the tent area. The first stoning pillar

---

[139] *'Āshurā* is the 10th day of the lunar month of Moharram, the day when Imam Husayn and his followers were martyred at Karbala in the year 61 A.H. (tr)

[140] *Rajm*, or "pelting with stones," is another important ritual during the Hajj. Each pilgrim must throw seven stones at the first stoning pillar, *Jamrat al-'Aqabah*, the first day; on each of the following two days, all three pillars are stoned seven times each. (tr)

[141] The *izār* is the lower half of the *iḥrām*, covering the body from the navel to the knees. (tr)

was right beside a police traffic-control kiosk, at a kind of intersection. The devil and all this right together! All the stoning pillars are made of stone, one and one-half times or twice the height of a man, light-blue in color. The pillar is enclosed within a low, circular wall, and there is a space where gravel and rocks collect so as not to be scattered. From two or three steps to twenty steps away there was a raining of rocks. If you were near the pillar you had to watch your head, because they threw odd shoes as well. In all the Hajj rites, what remains on the field to document the frenzy of a crowd is odd shoes lying about. Odd light-weight elastic slippers made in Java. They used them here to revile Satan, and they are the physical evidence of vows kept to slap him.

The guides' banners were something to see, carried by leaders, *muṭawwif*s, and guides. One was a bedding cover attached to a pole (they must have been from Qom). Another was a large cardboard box. Another was an inverted tin *āftābeh* on the end of a pole. Another was a Kurdish turban on a placard attached to a pole, and so on. The official national flags and the names and emblems of the guides were painted on them. The main street was crowded, the side streets were more crowded, and parked automobiles, busses, and trucks—the means for transporting pilgrims—flanked the side streets, making them narrow. People were coming and going in all directions, people pushing carts, and with great difficulty. Then there were porters, porters, porters, moving with great difficulty. In one place where the road was blocked, the crush of the crowd was so concentrated that you were terrified by it. In the midst of such pandemonium stood a little stand in a corner of the street with a four-by-four-meter glowing neon sign above it. It said "*al-barq wa al-bārid*," meaning post office. I pressed into the line, and sent two post cards to Tehran. After that I realized that my energy was spent. It takes energy to go walking and sightseeing. Just going and coming back to the stoning pillar tired me so much you would have thought I'd returned from a holy war with the Devil himself. I walked a little while, continually passing remnants of the slaughter, the crowd so dense you couldn't see the ground at all. Suddenly, however, I felt something soft underfoot, probably a skin, a stomach, or part of a carcass that had been discarded. I came to the end, and walked slowly for a time among the maze of tent ropes, until the "Sahrah" headquarters appeared, but there was no sign of our guide, or of our group. I was so tired that I laid right down on the bare ground inside the first empty tent. I think I went to sleep, because suddenly I saw that the tent was full of commotion, people coming and going and Arab legs stepping over my body. It was a Lebanese Shi'i group. Their guide explained to me that the Sahrah camp was in another location. I went walking again, until I found our own group.

What's more tiresome than anything else about walking in this crowd is the roughness of the blacks and Arabs. It seems that the blacks have learned, like the Yemenis, to elbow people in the side in order to clear a path. My fellow travelers, having just returned, were tired, stupefied, and disoriented; they had lost their luggage, each one was in an extremely foul mood, and the heat of the day was beating down on them too. Lunch was diluted yogurt and cucumbers. Then it was time to go make animal sacrifices.

A word about this slaughterhouse. It's a huge area surrounded by a wall with two entrances. There are large pits dug and prepared in groups, with mounds of earth scooped out of the pits and piled up higher than the walls, visible from the outside. All the ground is covered with carcasses, goats, sheep, and camels; there are no cattle to be seen. The muscles quiver on freshly-killed carcasses. Children, knives in hand, play with their remains. One's feet are constantly stepping in blood and entrails, and I held up the hem of my *iḥrām* as I walked. One individual wearing the *iḥrām* was making a film with a 16 millimeter camera. Two or three employees of the "Office of Health and Security" were with him.[142] Everyone was standing around holding dull knives. They decapitated a goat and threw the head to one side. A young boy came and drove the point of a knife into the goat's throat, and the goat went into violent convulsions as the blood spurted out of its throat. It was clear that the boy was experienced and knew what to do to make the carcass dance. I don't know where he thrust the knife to make the convulsions greater. In any case he knew something that I did not know. A camel lying on the ground jerked twice—from one end to the other—by the time I got to him, and that was all. The blood coming out of a hand's-width gash in his neck was frothy, looking like fluffy light purple soapsuds on the ground. Such a huge carcass! A man had thrust a dagger into its neck above the sternum right where it stood, in the tuft of hair at the base of the neck. He made a hand's-width slash downward, and when the animal tried to turn its head he struck it in the nose with his fist. The animal roared and tried to run, but its legs were hobbled. If fell on the ground. It tried to get up, but the blood spurted out, it couldn't, and it slowly, slowly collapsed. It lowered its neck gradually until its head touched the ground. When I got there it was gasping; this stopped. a moment later. Then two jerks, and that was the end. This is the most terrifying facet of this motorized primitivity. I almost passed out two or three times. I remembered the first time I visited the anatomy hall at the medical school. I had stopped to look with blind, adolescent courage. I rationalized to myself that this day of killing—and of animals—was perhaps originally a way to prevent the killing of people. If we go back to Abraham's sacrifice of his son...this is true. It can be rationalized, in any case, but a slaughterhouse of this type is a scandal. Seeing it once is the best possible advertisement for vegetarianism. If they had had just one scene from this

[142] I heard that the same year a group of Indonesians made a film of the Hajj rituals, as well as a French group. The French film was shown on French television. My brother saw it in Paris and told me about it. (A)

slaughterhouse in the film *Mondo Cane*, they would have made a fortune.

All the streets end at a slaughterhouse, covered with mutilated carcasses. They quickly cut away the choice pieces of meat and abandon the rest, especially the goat and sheep heads, which have been crushed under cars. Then comes the grave digger for this entire huge wasted sacrifice, a red bulldozer, which is continually digging pits in the corners and sides of the slaughterhouse, filling this one and going on to another. This huge wasted sacrifice! In any case, what would happen if they got ten refrigerator trucks and took all these carcasses to Jedda in an hour (it's less than 100 kilometers from Mina to Jedda), put them all in a two- or three-thousand-ton ship for cooking and preserving, freezing and salting, and sent them as gifts to the poor people of the world? Why doesn't the Red Cross see this barbaric waste, when two-thirds of the people don't even eat meat once a year? Why don't they pack this meat in containers identifying it as sacrificial meat from the slaughterhouses of Mina, to be used as a spiritually powerful gift for all the afflicted Muslims of the world, or for all those who are dying of malnutrition? Enough of this. The Saudis are too busy to think about these things. These things can only be resolved through Islamic internationalization, and if you want to take the narrow, calculated point of view of the Europeans, let me tell you that all the administrative expenses of Medina and Mecca could be met just through the proceeds from the sale of this meat. During these rites, a million pilgrims have made animal sacrifices, each one at least once.[143] Let's suppose that each one of them kills a skinny sheep or goat. Every carcass would have 20 to 30 kilograms of meat. Let's forget about the camels. This would be about 20,000 tons of meat, apart from the skin and entrails. . .such wealth! And thrown on the ground! Such a stench! So sickening! Who provides these corpses? According to what I have heard, most of the animals come from Sudan and Ethiopia, and a few from Yemen, Syria, and Iraq. Is it possible to develop a system for breeding special sacrificial stock according to the number of pilgrims in each nation and also with a view to their easy shipment and thereby return the wealth of the Muslim nations back to them? You see there are many questions. Enough of this.

The slaughterhouse ground and the surrounding streets are covered with blood, entrails, skin, bowels, meat, bones, and finally, black and muddy earth. Everyone is carrying a knife. They are either paid butchers, trimming carcasses to get next year's meat supply, or carrying entire carcasses

---

[143] According to the newspaper *Al-Madīnah*, dated 16 Dhū al-Ḥijjah 1383 [April 28, 1964], "The total number of pilgrims is 800,000 persons; 266,555 of these are foreigners and non-Saudis. The rest are Saudis. Of the foreigners, in descending order, there are 26,093 Pakistani pilgrims, 22,381 Turks, 21,416 Indians, 20,501 Iranians, 17,743 Egyptians, 16,937 Syrians, 15,207 Indonesians, 14,445 Sudanese, 13,889 Iraqis, 12,322 Yemenis, 8,301 Algerians, 6,339 Palestinians from various countries, 6,809 Moroccans, 6,359 Jordanians, 5,229 Malaysians, 3,177 Afghanis, 1,790 Thais, 423 Phillipinos, 913 Ghanians. . . ." and so on. (A)

on their shoulders. They don't even skin the carcasses. I had heard that the Saudi government takes the skin and intestines, but I saw that they were cutting off the heads and those making the sacrifices took whatever meat they wanted, even with the skin. The rest they laid aside and left. People were bringing a white-haired sheep out of the slaughterhouse when they were stopped by the police. They were told to remove the skin and keep the meat. Was the government going to take these hides?

I saw three blacks—a woman, a man, and a child—who had claimed a camel. They were cutting the red flesh away from the bones piece by piece. The animal's large white ribs were just like long stalks of rhubarb.

In another place a young man holding a knife stood up from inside the rib cage of a fallen, half-stripped camel so suddenly that I was stopped in my tracks. It startled me. Groups of live sheep and goats stood waiting in the midst of this filth, with the occasional huge camel. The goats were chewing their cuds, the sheep napping. Only the goats sensed what was happening; they were very upset and kept bleating. The police at the slaughterhouse entrance would not allow new groups to enter before the others already inside had been killed.

As I see it, they satisfy two or three primitive human urges with this huge sacrifice. One was mentioned previously: sacrificing animals instead of human beings. Sheep instead of Ismā'īl. Kill animals, in order to refrain from killing human beings. It is also the best possible practice in the use of knives, in shedding blood, seeing blood. Women, men, and children, knives in hand, take such delight in carcasses, for procuring provisions, or simply for the thrill of it. Several times I saw people cutting up carcasses just for fun, and such a gleam of delight in their eyes. You'd think they were all studying anatomy, or exulting in victory after some heroic deed. Finally, this is itself a form of exercise. Standing and bending, skinning the carcasses, dallying with them, and so on. We get no other exercise on the Hajj except walking and pelting the pillars. This primeval picnic needs two or three vigorous activities in any case, and this is the third and last of them.

In all of Mina there are perhaps 20 or 30 trees. The rest of it is the valley itself, surrounded by rocky mountains. Under the eternal blackness of the scorched rocks is the body and flesh of a white mountain that looks green, or bluish. Zubaydah's water is truly a blessing here. For years now they've been moving oil from Dhahran to Syria by pipeline, but after 1000 years they still haven't been able to install a proper water pipe for the Hajj rites. Of course, during the Saudi period they have made some improvements on these same ancient water wells, with plaques above every faucet that say "*al-sabil al-malik* [for the King's sake]," and "*Zubaydat al-'azizat al-Sa'udiyah* [dear Zubaydah the Saudi]."

As for electricity, Mina has it. They've even wired the tents. They brought a long cable in the afternoon with a socket and bulb and hung it on the tent post. It is now well-lit. Tents have been pitched the whole way from east to west, usually in pairs, with the sun constantly circling above them. I heard that the United Nations assumed the task of providing water and power for the Hajj, but can this be true, and in the kingdom of Saudi Arabia yet? Never!

The poor people that thrive parasitically on the Hajj and its pilgrims, and serve as its porters, are so beneficial to the antiquated Saudi system, and such a well-established institution, that I don't think they'll take steps to eliminate their poverty so soon.

It's clear that for years and years to come the Hajj rites will continue, because they provide visits to shrines, tourism, business, entertainment, and experience for every villager who leaves his farm and has no other opportunity to see the world and have the experiences of a journey. If, however, we were able to make this pilgrimage suitable, not for a man of the 20th century, but for a man of the 14th century, one could hope that the Hajj would be a stage of development and an experience in the lives of the people of the Muslim nations. If not, as it stands now the Hajj is mechanized barbarism. That's all. My hand is aching.

Thursday 3 Ordibehesht 1343 [April 23]

Mina.

I forgot to write that on *'Ayd-e Qorbān* (yesterday) they fired cannons in Mina (which we heard in *Mash'ār al-Ḥarām*) both in the morning and at noon instead of the call to prayer. Three shots. That is, *'Ayd-e Azhā*. The Saudi government has placed a sword on the green field of its flag and written above it "There is no God but God," and now to announce *'Ayd-e Qorbān* they fire cannons. I am unable to say what this means. By putting a sword beneath "There is no God but God," do you want to say that Islam conquered the world with the sword? The Europeans put these words in your mouth. Anyway, when Islam conquered the world with the sword, you were nothing, sir! A Wahhabi tribe owning lands rich with oil, and now keepers of the *Kaaba!* You drove the Hashemites out with help from the Aramco company. Now you're just a keeper of pipes. Nothing else.

Haj Ba'uch blew his top yesterday morning, after all his silence and reticence, and attacked that gentleman, our guide. He gave him what he deserved. It's a pity he isn't more articulate. Most of his swearing was in Mazandarani, which I didn't understand, but he evened the score. All the Mazandaranis in our group were relieved.

"Why are you so stingy," he said, and "Why did you send that major back, don't you know there's a thief among us, why do you extort so much of our money, why have you made us miserable with so many *rowzeh*s," and other complaints. This outburst came in the interval between our morning prayers and breakfast. Our guide kept quiet, because he will be collecting gratuities after the Mina rites for his employees. After breakfast a number of the Mazandaranis went to the slaughterhouse. When they came back, each had a piece of meat, or a whole thigh, and so fat! I haven't seen so much good meat since we left Tehran, and I've been eager to have some, although my appetite has been poor. They were looking around for kabob implements, to the chagrin of our guide, who hissed disapprovingly and got rid of them with the help of one or two merchants.

"You ought not to eat meat," he said, "we won't be responsible if you're sick later," and so on.

"It is religiously recommended to eat sacrificial meats," said the Mazandaranis, and so on.

Later I heard from the Mazandaranis themselves that they had surreptitiously collected a few skewers and some charcoal and eaten to their heart's content. It's interesting that most of the villagers and Mazandaranis in our group made their sacrifices with their own hands. They had pooled their money to buy a good knife and taken turns making their sacrifices. And such meat! It was mouth-watering to hear them describe it. Our guide's menu, however, calls for as little meat and as much diluted and undiluted yogurt as possible.

My sister and her husband reported today when they came back from the stoning pillars that Saudi employees have collected the meat, hides, and manure strewn in the streets, disinfecting them with hand pumps. Yesterday there was a veritable carpet of meat covering the entire surface of this tent encampment, especially on the road that leads from the slaughterhouse entrance to the main pilgrim encampment. Nigerians were living on both sides of that street. Right beside the street yesterday afternoon I sat in a black's barbershop to have my head shaved, for 2 rials. The man was a black but said he lived in Ta'if, and had been a pilgrim's barber for 30 years. And such bragging. He was tall and slouching, like the slaves of the old days. His razor was really dull, just like our own knives from Najafabad.

Javad said that this morning an Arab was squatting beside one of the stoning pillars (I forget which one) relieving himself in the middle of the milling crowd. An Esfahani in our group said "This hajji gentleman must have been rockless, and had to dump some manure to throw at Satan." Another said the man must really hate Satan... and this sort of clowning around.

I haven't left the tent yet today. It's too hot, and I'm coughing excessively. The view is not all that attractive either, to prompt a yearning to go out. The women in the caravan adjacent to us—who are Iranian—have a green emblem on their chadors. They've sewn a green leaf above their foreheads. Our guide has designed a monogrammed seal with his own name and emblem, which he has put on the backs of the women's heads, on their chadors, and it's very poorly designed as well! Even so, 5 or 6 people get lost every day. Our hide-wearing villager is still wearing his sheepskin vest. Definitely he's hidden his money in the lining. Himself, he swears by the Qur'ān that his back hurts, and so on... But is this to be believed?

Today's shaved heads are an interesting sight. They look just like melons. The bald people are delighted that they are now exactly the same as everyone else, with no feelings of inferiority and so on... There are three-lobed heads, melon-shaped heads, round ones, heads with flat backs, and many variations and kinds. The most interesting ones are the Mazandarani heads, which look just like the ones from Qazvin, with the back of the skull flattened. As if the backs of their heads grew into the shape of a hookah, the way a gourd does growing on the vine. I myself have difficulty removing my cloth hat. The stubs of hair penetrate the cloth like porcupine quills and snag it.

Then there are these itinerant merchants, who circulate among the tents in little groups. And all kinds of beggars, beggars, beggars. I don't have the energy to describe them one by one. Only one of them was interesting, an Arab woman with a long written Arabic explanation of her problems that said she was eligible to receive both *khoms* and *zakāt*[144] and with the signature and seal of some Arab religious magistrate. Some had shoes, some did not, and the ones without them were filthier than those with. There were ice vendors, cigarette merchants, orange sellers, beggars, sellers of games, beggars, beggars, and beggars. All claiming to be working for God. The toilet here is also disgraceful. It's a cement pit, with five positions separated by partitions and a half-open wooden door. There's a line at the door from morning until night. And such a stench in the air! Five privies for five 100-person groups!

[144] Literally "one fifth," *khoms* is a religious tax to support indigent descendants of the Prophet Muhammad. *Zakāt* is a "purification tax," levied on the property of Muslims as commanded in the Qur'ān, Surah 9, v. 60. It is sometimes translated as "alms," since it may be paid to the needy at the discretion of the individual Muslim and is normally a voluntary religious duty today. In the days of the early caliphates it was collected by the government. (tr)

Same day. Mina

It was so hot that I didn't go out until 5 in the afternoon. Once in the morning I slept for 2 hours, and once in the afternoon. I don't feel very good. Javad's brother brought a bottle of solocamphor for my cough, which I am drinking, and the cough has diminished. All this time I was sitting and reading Haj Farhad Mirza's travel diary, or making notes or watching the vendors and beggars. Then the *rowzeh* began. Again. First our eulogists began (I am writing during our preacher's final pulpit prayer) and then a Pakistani came, took the microphone, and began a *rowzeh* in Urdu. I had never heard this. In order to prove that he was a Shi'i and not an impostor, he began at first by naming martyrs, and then he listed the names of the 12 Imams. This was the only thing he said that the Iranians, Turks, and Arabs all understood. As for the rest...? Then Javad got up and took a collection for him. The Mazandaranis complained and Javad paid no attention to them. He said (I just asked him) he collected 42 Saudi rials for him. At the same time a Pakistani was giving a *rowzeh* in our tent a group of Lebanese youths were playing cards in the tent next door, in public view, with no shame whatsoever. In the tent on the right, which houses the women with the green emblems on their foreheads, there were self-flagellations taking place that night, cries of "Husayn, Husayn,"[145] and such ardor! People were going back and forth between this tent and that tent, there was tea, and so on... At the same time, from the Lebanese tent where they had been playing cards in the morning with the sides of their tent rolled up, there came the sound of music being played on the radio from between the slits in the tent, which was now closed up. A woman on the fringes of our gathering got up (my sister said she was from Karbala) and began enjoining the good and prohibiting evil with them through the slit in their tent, in Arabic of course. This Arabic is certainly a good language for enjoining and prohibiting. After the sound of the music subsided, the younger ones came out to watch the *rowzeh* at our meeting and the flagellations next door.

Yesterday afternoon quantities of hair were added to all the manure in this great aggregation of tents. It's amazing that you don't see more flies, no doubt because of the intense heat in the day and the intense cold at night. I recall only one fly; it sat on my foot in the slaughterhouse and wouldn't go away.

When I went out in the afternoon there were a lot of carts and cleaning implements moving about, mechanized, manual, and so on... There are still

[145] Imam Husayn was the third Shi'i Imam. He was killed in a battle against Yazid (son of Mu'āwiyyah, founder of the 'Umayyad dynasty) in which he was attempting to gain control of the caliphate. This took place in Karbala, Iraq, in 680 A.D. Husayn is regarded as the greatest of the Shi'i martyrs; the circumstances surrounding his death have become, for Shi'is, the archetypal symbol of resistance to tyranny and oppression. (tr)

carcasses underfoot, however. The bad thing is that the pilgrims themselves aren't concerned about cleanliness. They did their slaughtering anywhere and everywhere. In the middle of the road, at intersections, in the tents, in the gutters along the roads, and so on...

When I was lying down in the afternoon it was so hot that I was reminded of the summer of 1322 [1943] in Iraq. It was as if the tent was not even there between us and the sun. The wind had stopped, and the side of my body that was facing the sun seemed directly exposed. It was so hot it burned, like your hand does on an oven. Yet the Hamadani pilgrim still wears his sheepskin vest.

Kabob smoke has been in the air since yesterday. This afternoon when I went out and looked at the Mina valley for half an hour from the top of the mountains that overlook the Khayf Mosque, columns of smoke rose into the air from caravan campfires. Instead of carcasses on the ground, you now see piles of bones here and there, and partially chewed bits of meat. I saw a camel shoulder lying in one place, with the white part of the hide visible and bits of red meat still clinging to its edges. It was a perfect parchment for writing, like a tablet, large and flat, with handles as well. From atop the mountain I counted the buildings in the valley: the Ministry of Pilgrimage Affairs and Religious Endowments, the Khayf Mosque, Public Security, Capital Security, and the Pilgrims' Guidance Building. There was surely another building for the Great King, although I didn't see it, and also a police headquarters. On top of each building was a large neon display, so that even from up there you could recognize the trademark of stupidity. Every road marker for pilgrims was written in 5 or 6 languages: Arabic, Turkish, Urdu, Javanese, Persian, and *Engrish.* I saw 10 postal stations in the valley, and 10 public toilets. In Urdu they were identified as *paikhāneh* [foot-rest house], just like *chaikhāneh* [tea shop]. Such a nice building, too, so that at first I thought it was a tea house until the smell told me otherwise.

In the doorway of the Pilgrims' Guidance Building, which had a kitchen, tents, and also residential rooms, 10 or 12 guides waited with flags of various countries. Saudi Arabian Boy Scouts in shorts, holding maps and wearing whistles, helped lost pilgrims find their group encampments. "Where can these maps be bought?" I asked one of them. He said they couldn't be bought, that his had been given to him by the Ministry of Pilgrimage Affairs and Religious Endowments. I took a look at it. It was a detailed map, I imagine on a scale of 1/5000, which included all the valleys, hills, streets, and numbered sections. Every tent area, Iranian, Iraqi, Syrian, and Egyptian, was designated, even the numbers of the tents. This is another sign of orderliness, but it's like a drop in a bucket.

The Pakistanis are interesting. They are quite unable to distinguish among the various Muslim nations. Like a stranger coming into a gypsy camp and wanting to find a place for himself. They give water regularly in the name of God, with huge tank trucks, each one with a thousand emblems and announcements. They had an ample first aid station (I didn't go into it, however) and it had an even bigger sign.

As I walked on top of the mountain, I saw another valley in one corner of our valley, very small, in a cleft in the mountain, containing a graveyard. A gathering was being held there. I went down. An old Turk had died and they were burying him. I said the *Fātiḥah*,[146] nodded, and wished his fellow caravan members well. The graves had been prepared beforehand. They had been dug in the earth and a cement niche had been poured for the body. There have been seven deaths during these two or three days, according to a mortuary employee.

Thirteen-hundred tomans were collected tonight for our guide's employees, as a gift, or a final gratuity for the Hajj. Javad gave 40 Saudi rials on behalf of the four of us. Didn't they collect anything from the women? Or was it just my sister who didn't give? I didn't get it.

On the southern side of the Mina valley (I could see all of it from the top of the mountain) there is another valley, just like the first one, with slight differences in the cut of the mountains. Its floor is white, and the mountains are the usual black, with flint boulders piled on top of one another, as if by hand. There's a stream in the middle of the valley with structures on either side, and one huge barracks-like building. I thought it was an extra Mina, so that in case the first one became dirty or overcrowded, tents could be set up in this second one, and so on...with a mountain between them. Perhaps there would be a tunnel through the mountain to give access to the stoning pillars, and so on...

The only bird I saw in Mina and 'Arafāt was there on top of the mountain, a little sparrow with black wings and a grey body, hopping among the thorns. It seems that what I have been calling heather up until now is actually camel's thorn. I looked at it closely. Later when I was sitting on a high point resting and smoking a cigarette, three Arabs came up and said hello. They were Yemenis. As the sun set behind us and lights were coming on one by one on the valley floor at the foot of the mountain, we talked politics. They were supporters of Imam [Muhammad] al-Badr, opponents of Nasser and Sallal, and in agreement with the Saudis. One of them, who spoke for all three, claimed that they were secure from armed attack. No matter how I tried to learn from them where the "Imam" and his front line were, they couldn't comprehend maps and weren't even literate. I drew maps on rocks hoping they could give me an idea of their location, but it was useless. Or were they hiding things from me? They said they would be returning to Ta'izz in three days. It turned out they weren't Zaydis,

---

[146] The opening surah of the Qur'ān, traditionally read at funerals. (tr)

but Shāfi'is.[147] It appears that these Yemenis are the poorest of all the pilgrims in the world. They're all ragged and excessively thin from poor nutrition. These people are the ones who've been having a real feast the last two or three days in the vicinity of the slaughterhouse. As I came down from the mountain I passed among the belongings of the pilgrims, each of whom had spent the entire day hiding from the sun behind a rock and was now coming out into the open. In the moonlight and in the dim light that came up from the valley I saw a wrist watch on a rock along my way. I involuntarily bent over and picked it up. I went two steps, and remembered where I was and who I am. I went back and replaced the watch.

Tonight I realized why the lunar calendar is the official one here instead of the solar calendar, throughout this region, from ancient Babylon to Egypt. The solar calendar can have no meaning in these parts. The winter here is like the fall, and both of them are like summer. They have had to rely on the moon to light the cold nights. For this reason religious rites are usually held during the first half of the month: 10 Dhū al-Ḥijjah, 15 Sha'ban, 3 Rajab, 10 [Muḥarram] *'Āshurā*, and so on. Religious rites, celebrations, and days of mourning usually take place on days when the moon is full and high, or is on the rise, so that the desert, with its cool nights, will be well-lit for religious ceremony.

Mina's electric power is weak and insufficient, despite the lavish illumination of the official buildings and their rooftops, but it is evident that year after year the facilities, electricity, and water are improving. It is also evident that after the conclusion of the Hajj rites, life also goes on here in Mina; it's just a little village the rest of the year.

Our *rowzeh khwān*s and preacher—and every Iranian group I've visited is the same—are very insistent everywhere that the Imam of the Age is present at the Hajj, and that he comes on the pilgrimage every year. They seem to want to convince all the pilgrims that every ordinary man at the Hajj could be the Imam of the Age, lest you show disrespect to others, and so on...and this, of course, is very good.

You see, however, how simply these pilgrims can live, even though they aren't wealthy, meaning they aren't slaves to consumerism, but they're so eager for Western industrial products! Everything they use during the ceremonies is either Western or Japanese. The only thing used during the rites that is not machine-made by companies is the sacrificial animals, which they waste the way they do. If you look at things through Western eyes, "civilization" means "consuming" (and greater need). Thus, all these pilgrims are "backward," and in the process of developing. When will they

[147] Shāfi'is are followers of the Sunni school of Islamic jurisprudence founded by Muhammad ibn Idris al-Shāfi'i (d. 820). The movement arose from the Māliki school, and introduced the notion that local traditions and authorities could be appealed to for resolution of religious and legal questions, without referring to the theologians in Medina. (tr)

be "developed"? No doubt when they "consume" as many "Western products" as possible. The point is precisely that this closed cycle (the export of raw materials, the importation of finished products, then consumption and the need of money or credit for this consumption so you can buy Western products. Where does this money and credit come from? From the export of raw materials, and it starts anew) must be opened somewhere. Gandhi gave the Indians the spinning wheel in order to break this cycle, and Mosaddeq cut off the flow of oil... I will leave this.

A print shop manager in the group next to us reported that he had seen a Sudanese black being led away to prison in chains by the police. The man was crying and begging for forgiveness, and so on...was he a thief? Javad's brother said we have no deaths among the Iranian pilgrims so far.

The stench is high tonight (it is 10:30 now). There is no wind, the air is warm, the moon is high, and the stench of feces and meat crushed underfoot mingles with the smell of toilets. If the pilgrims can survive this night in good health they will have no other worries.

Friday, 4 Ordibehesht, 1343 [April 24]

Still in Mina

They woke us up at 4 a.m. this morning. Mohaddes's "*wa lā aḍ-ḍ-a-a-a-lin*" woke me. I realized that they were praying before the morning call to prayer again. With the light from the streets and the buildings in the center of the valley, which is right on the west side of our tents, they think it's dawn, and start praying. This has already happened two or three times. One of them can't sleep and gets up, probably for a night prayer. Another one thinks it's morning, and they all get up and start praying. I got up as they were going back to sleep, complaining that this is what you get for traveling with the riff-raff. I splashed water on my face and set out for the Khayf Mosque to participate in the morning prayer, which was not due to begin for another half an hour.

There were three pretty girls walking on the road with their father. "Get up at dawn"[148] ... and so on. All three were the same size and shape, like three teapots. They had delicate faces with closely-set features, small round red lips, wheat-colored skin, and tall figures. I realized that the pilgrimage can also provide a means of finding a husband for one's daughter. The father

[148] A reference to a line from Firdawsi: "Get up at dawn and be rewarded with what you desire." (tr)

walked in front, the daughters behind. We smiled and passed. I saw some crab apples later in a shop, and so early in the morning. I didn't think they had day and night stores too during these ceremonies. I saw these apples in Mecca as well. Or did I just imagine that? The size of a green plum. Then I smelled the henna they were rubbing on themselves. In any event, today is *'Ayd*, the ceremonies have ended, and one must pay a final visit to the House of God well-washed and made up. So much henna is sold on this journey! The best souvenir. Along the way there are long lines behind the wooden doors of all the toilets. In addition, a man or a woman was sitting in every corner, with an *āftābeh* or a kettle at one side, for use in answering the call of nature, as well as for pre-prayer ablutions. If you could only see what great things the Africans and Indians can do with a little water!

Later I saw a sign that said "*Ba'thah Ummdarmān Sudāni*," which probably means Sudanese Health Team. Does *Ummdarmān* mean *Umm* [Arabic for "mother"] of *darmān* [Persian for "treatment"]?. Meaning that Persian has somehow traveled so far? I saw this other sign above a water spigot: "*Men jāneb-e Pādeshāh-e Sa'ud. Sabil Allāh. Pa'i Moft. Nahr-e Zubaydah. Irsu chu mari sabilkun. Avaliyyeh bekandarjā Sa'ud. 'Ayn-e Zubaydah.*" (or something like that). Arabic, Urdu, and Turkish all mixed together. It was interesting that they had also written the same thing in English, like this: "King Soud Drinking Water Supply." And what did the entire apparatus consist of? A two-meter pipe with four faucets at the top, and all empty as well. I tried them. In addition to the fact that at that time in the morning you can't find a single faucet without a long line. A water tanker, however, was parked beside these very faucets, with people climbing all over it getting water from its spigot or from the opening on top of it, chattering in Urdu. You have to go on a pilgrimage to understand the meaning of "Gardens beneath which rivers flow."[149] There was also another sign, "*Mu'allim* Hassan Shir Muhammad Panjabi." *Mu'allim*[150] probably means *muṭawwif.* This afternoon we must quit this tent life and return to Mecca.

---

[149] The Holy Qur'ān, Surah II, verse 25. (tr)
[150] Literally "instructor". (tr)

Same day. Friday.

Mecca

Again today we were ready to leave by 1 in the afternoon, for Mecca from Mina. All the baggage was collected and ready. A number of people left early, either on foot or by automobile. We stayed until 4:30, however, when we left, and we got there at 6:30. It isn't far at all from Mina to Mecca, but this congestion on the roads is aggravating, and nothing can be done about it, except to widen the road, and the Saudis have no such ambition. The entire road to Mecca was one-way. Pedestrians carried loads on their heads and shoulders, or on the two ends of poles on their shoulders, or with packs, with men and women all together. The road was absolutely packed. The remnants of the Mina tent camp, bloated sacrificial carcasses which looked like leather water bottles with feet sticking straight up into the air, were lying about on the fringes, and the air was putrid. There were no dogs, not even a vulture or a crow, just a stench in the air. Looking at the carcasses, Uncle said "So where are the cats...?"

As may be seen in Medina, the pilgrimage sacrifices of the Muslim world are the most ill-fated sacrifices in the world. After all, a sacrifice ought either to be eaten, burned, or fed to someone else, not thrown on the ground and added to the stench of the world in this way. As we left the polluted Mina environment, growling bulldozers were scooping out pits.

It was interesting the way the poor people dried and strung the meat. They had cut the meat in finger-width strands the length of a hand, and strung them over a line, the way we string thin red peppers, right there in Mina near the slaughtering yard. There were also strings of meat at all the houses on the eastern side of Mecca as we entered, and sometimes pieces of meat had been laid on rocks around the houses to dry. Two truckloads of Bedouin Arabs passed. They had hung two sacrificial thighs alongside their water bottles. With all this, there were still herds of skinny sheep and goats returning from Mina. They were the main cause of roadblocks and route obstruction, the ones who had survived this pointless sacrifice. To keep these four-footed creatures two more days would mean feeding them two more days, and in this confusion who thinks about feeding animals? As that question came to mind, I realized they pay 20 to 80 Saudi rials for an animal to sacrifice. That Sayyid with the multi-colored beard paid the highest price. A 20-rial goat (36 tomans), however, can be such a scrawny sacrifice! Skin and bones. All of them ought to be buried. I sacrificed one for 40 rials.

On the way back, at one point I passed the water channel for Zubaydah's water. It comes out of the side of the mountain from a covered stone channel like a *qanāt* going to Mecca. They bring it from Ta'if. It went along the road for three or four kilometers and then disappeared, running on high stone supports resting on the mountainside...

Near the city on a stone platform apart from the mountain a home was built surrounded by a rock garden. The rocks had been arranged by hand on the ground, and I saw that each stone had been positioned in place of a tree.

When we got to the city, a sign on a repair shop said "*mustashfat al-sayyārāt*," meaning automobile hospital. Two barrels of water had been placed by the door of a house. The owner of the house stood in the doorway calling out "Cold water, for the sake of God!" A few pedestrians drank the water and went on, water dripping from their faces and onto their clothes. It gave me a chill.

They really decorate these trucks! Just like the paraphernalia that our young construction workers put on their motorcycles. Lights, mirrors, horns, and glitter. This going to Mina and 'Arafāt and returning makes an enormous procession, and it would be much better if no vehicles were used. An appropriate hour at the end of the day ought to be chosen for everyone to leave on foot. It would be magnificent. The old and the infirm could be sent last in vehicles so they wouldn't obstruct things. It isn't a long way, and the walk would do everyone good. Vehicles ought to be excluded from this religious procession, and they can be. Again, the solution is international Islamicization...

Haj Ba'uch bought a new shirt yesterday at the Mina bazaar. His collar had been torn during that argument he had with our guide, and badly. The shirt was ripped all the way to the bottom, such as I haven't seen in a long time. Now he is left with this ridiculous blue shirt with four tails. He's like the skinny bloated goats who have been sacrificed and thrown aside, although he's still on his feet. Our reclusive fellow traveler from Tafresh claimed this morning that they had cut off his money pouch and stolen some 3,000 tomans... Had he been keeping to himself for fear of losing his money?

One is sorely deprived of beauty on this journey, both from the standpoint of art and that of the human figure. The rocks, the desert, and the sky are all wonderful, and one little camel's thorn bush in the desert is a long story in itself. When you live in the desert, you find the necessity for prophecy in the air, and you feel it in the earth. Can one say that the harshness of enjoining and prohibiting, necessary for every religion, has its origins in that natural severity? In any case, the simplicity of the harshness of primitivity (or the primitivity of harshness) still dominates everything. You can see that Abraham, who was an idol-smasher, also destroyed art, and wasn't it he who built this "house of ancient tradition?" Did the Wahhabis thus follow in his footsteps...? The mosques are unusually white. The houses are ochre, black, and sometimes the newer ones are garish blue or green. The older ones, which have cream-colored walls, are completely covered with a wood veneer in its original color, especially in Mecca. These are the most interesting buildings I've seen here. When a man wants to build a 7-story house in Mecca, he simply puts up 7 or 8 vertical supports, and what is left exposed to the air where the doors and windows would be, meaning the space between the supports, he covers with boards, with sliding double doors of slats or sash. Around the roof and on the edges of the building, and just like the minaret tops, there are lights. The House of God has 14 or 15 floodlights.

In any event, these are the days of *'Ayd.* They've covered *Maqām-e Ebrāhim* at the old entrance to the Kaaba with so much gaudy glitter that it's unspeakable. The good thing about it is that the Kaaba itself is made of large chunks of granite. Its very simplicity has such grandeur that it cannot be compared with the decorations on ordinary doors and walls, which change every day. The middle of the "Stone of Ismā'īl" has a raised area.

It seems that when the new portico is completed and the old one demolished, they ought to think about the condition of *Maqām-e Ebrāhim* and the entrance, and do something with them so they won't interfere with the circumambulation, like the *minbar* and the Zamzam well, the first of which they moved away from the House and the second of which they moved underground. I was thinking yesterday that it seems that this Kaaba on this soil is the only shrine in the open air. Other shrines are graves, statues, idols, or places where flames are kept, which are all covered for protection from the wind, the rain, and the sun. Even the Jews have a tent meeting place. Here, however, the main shrine is a four-walled structure, a "house," which ought to be exposed to the wind and rain to be a "house." More interesting is the sameness of all the circumambulating worshippers. There aren't any signs of rank or nobility, and no reserved arches or alcoves.

When we arrived yesterday afternoon, I bathed and went towards the House of God. I circumambulated, prayed, and did the *sa'y*. Then I sat down to watch. The groups of circumambulators clung very tightly to one another, each concerned about the other. You'd have thought the gathering was some kind of quicksand that might to swallow you. Two or three people were carrying their aged mothers and fathers on their shoulders and making the circumambulation. The excitement of the crowd imparts a great sense of urgency to the circumambulator.

I smelled some very pleasant fragrances as six or seven black women passed beside me, two or three kinds of perfume combined. This was the first time I've smelled perfume on black women, although I've never smelled a bad odor from them. Then a very picturesque group came. A group of men had joined hands to form a circle within which their women walked, and they were circumambulating. Then two porters carrying an empty litter on their shoulders got into an argument with a man, right there within four steps of the Kaaba. Such yelling and screaming! I heard the word "madman" through the din of the circumambulation from the mouth of one of them, and then the circumambulating crowd swallowed up both them and their voices. Several circumambulating Arabs had put their hands into their rope sandals. The soles of the sandals were on the backs of their hands as they circumambulated. Then a beggar came asking for donations. Blind and pale, he held a pouch above his head as a sunshade. He had a bamboo cane in his left hand, and the silver chain of his watch in his vest pocket hung on a button. As the people put money in his right hand, he separated the money with the same hand and put each coin in one of his four vest pockets.

When I returned, a black substance caught my eye in an apothecary shop; a pharmacist was removing it from a tin container with a little piece of wood, wrapping it in foil, and laying it out on a woven tray for sale in individual portions. I asked what it was called. He said "*jarāk*," and said it was for smoking. Did it come in bottles? Another man passing by who noticed my curiosity stopped to explain. So far as I could understand his Arabic, he said it was something you smoked to counter the effects of overeating. I asked if it was an opiate or a form of hashish, and it wasn't. It had a fragrant smell which I didn't recognize. It was somewhat acrid, black and oily, resembling a light tar, with the blackness of eye shadow, but it was neither of these things. I finally left without having understood. I haven't had many of these frustrated curiosities. This is the Hajj, anyway. I recognized an Afghani buying henna, which distracted me. We set out talking and walking. He said the Afghani government is controlled by 100 royal families. I said to him that here it is in the hands of 5000 members of the Saudi family, and in our country at one time it was held by 1000 families. And now...?

Saturday 5 Ordibehesht 1343 [April 25, 1964]

Mecca

Haj Ba'uch still shuns the others. It has now become his habit to eat apart from the others. Or is that normal for him? He watches everything carefully, however, and also complains all the time. It's too bad he slurs his words, and in Mazandarani besides. These Mazandaranis in our group are a sect unto themselves, with their own language, subjects of discussion, and regional accent. One of them, named Eslāmi—from Chālus—said that a certain Mazandarani overcome by the difficulties of the pilgrimage ceremonies had cried out one day, "Oh, Imam Husayn! Come and save me from the evils of God!" He said this the day following an evening when we had been so packed together on the side of the mountain at *Mash'ār al-Ḥarām* that we had no room to move around each other. He's a lively man. After this joke I understood why the people living near the House of God cry the way they do at *rowzeh*s for Husayn, the Prince of the Martyrs, and yearn to go to Karbala. Is this a longing for the city in the loins of primitivity?

While we were in Mina I saw two policemen holding whips standing beside the Jamrat al-'Aqabah.[151] I don't know why. I asked the people. It was lunch time. I don't remember whom I asked. One, who was on his second pilgrimage, said that it was because, as he had himself witnessed last year, someone had gone to the stoning pillar and struck Satan with an odd shoe. A bald Esfahani in our group added "Hajji sir, they're standing there guarding the pillar because they don't want Satan to get tired of being stoned and escape." Others said that people had been hitting the pillars with tin cans. I saw them myself doing it with shoes.

I don't feel like doing anything today, except sitting and watching my fellow travelers. A retired colonel, three or four Mazandaranis, a dentist, two or three Esfahanis, that villager who claims to be from Tehran, and several others. Each of them is sitting in his place picking, fussing, and managing very important and detailed matters pertaining to the journey and his baggage, oblivious to the others... (Do you have to do this? Why do you meddle so much in people's lives? Get up, shave your beard, and go outside.) Actually, the day I got my head shaved in Mina, I sat down and shaved my beard when I got back to the tent. In front of everyone. (Was I trying to make a point?) Everyone looked at me with such disapproval you'd have thought I was committing sabotage, although most of those who had stared shaved off their own beards the next morning.

[151] There are three *Jamrahs*, or stoning pillars, in Mina, representing *shaytāns*, or satans. They are al-Jamrat al-'Aqabah, al-Jamrat al-Wusṭā, and al-Jamrat al-'Ūlā. (tr)

Sunday 6 Ordibehesht [April 26]

Mecca

We still have no word on when we will be leaving, although we have done everything we came here to do. We are waiting for permission to leave from the Saudi government. Rumor has it that it was the practice in previous years to let the Egyptians leave first. I've seen no sign of any Egyptians so far, however. I think we'll be here until *'Ayd-e Ghadir.*[152]

The city of Mecca has a "Hello central" telephone system. The flower gardens of its houses are in tin flowerpots, on the rooftops. Its aforementioned *bandari* asses, with the carpet-like designs on their backs, hitched to carts, look just like horses when they run. Yesterday an itinerant merchant was selling tea leaves in large date-leaf baskets. There were three kinds, in as many baskets. He had spread out his display right next to the street. As I passed a mortician's doorway in the same Sulaymāniyyah district, a number of Turkish pilgrims were standing there. They were praying towards a corpse that lay on the bench before them under a shroud. Last night, near the west entrance to Mecca, I finally got some coffee at a very crowded coffee house. There were tea and hookahs, and most of the customers were Turkish pilgrims. The coffee cost two piastres, served in a small coffee pot the size of a coffee cup. It contained chunks of coffee big enough to chew. It tasted bitter. I asked the Turk beside me how many Turkish pilgrims there were. He said something I didn't understand. I gave him a piece of paper and he wrote in the Latin alphabet that there were 60,000, 10,000 of whom had come by air, or *vapeur*, i.e., steamship. Like everyone, he exaggerated. Then a Saudi Arabian Red Cross vehicle passed, with "*Tabarru'* Aramco" written on it, meaning a gift from the company. Before I got to the coffee house, I passed a large square beside a stream, surrounded by a wall. I asked about it, and learned that this was also a graveyard. It was as clean as the palm of a hand, and empty. What was it called? *Harat al-Bāb*, the burial place of a long list of famous people. Then I came to a money changer who had 23 kinds of bills pinned to his display, and still none of our bills. I changed some money with him. He gave 54 Saudi rials for 100 tomans. They paid 56 in Jedda, and it had dropped to 53 in Medina. I had told Javad that he ought to change his money in Jedda when we were there, but he didn't listen. Last night I took the rest of my money from Javad and cleared my account with him. I now have 350 tomans of my own money and 25 Saudi rials. I've spent the remaining 1,000 tomans, a month's salary. How did I do this? I don't know. Last night I bought several scarves, 10 for 15 rials, of the type that have pictures of Mecca and Medina on them. As I was sitting there in the coffee house, I could hear

[152] *'Ayd-e Ghadir* fell on April 30 the year of Āl-e Ahmad's pilgrimage. It is celebrated on 18 Dhū al-Ḥijjah by Shi'is, for whom it marks the day that the Prophet Muhammad appointed 'Ali ibn Abi Talib as his successor. (tr)

the honking and whistling of rapidly passing vehicles. An Arab sheikh, one of the royal top dogs, was passing with his entourage, including police on motorcycles in front saying officiously "*Atrāḥ! Atrāḥ!*," meaning "Get back, don't look," just like in medieval times.

Same day. Mecca.

My ambition has begun to fade. The weather is hot, and one cannot go out during the day. I stayed home until 5 in the afternoon reading *Hidāyat al-Sabil* by Farhad Mirza. The fellow writes the letter "N" backwards, and yet he claims to know European culture. He also explains a nautical chart for the ship's captain. He gives a lump of stamped clay to be thrown in the sea during a storm in order to calm it. He's a real character, although he isn't always confused. Despite all his wealth and leisure, however, and all his knowledge of science and culture, sometimes he's absurdly ignorant. People like him were the men of learning in our country 100 years ago, and they caused things to turn out the way they did in this country.

In the afternoon I had the job of carrying my old uncle's things during a shopping trip to the bazaar. He didn't buy anything. He went from one store to another, always dickering, always complaining, until he got tired. He felt better, however. I took him back and went myself in the direction of Mt. Abu Qabis, and its mosque. It was a charming, small mosque on a platform overlooking Mecca, at the same spot where they say the moon was split... And the blacks, who spend their money so freely, were all nodding their heads to the young guide who was showing them a cleft in a rock—behind the mosque! But there was such filth in the high streets that led to the Abu Qabis Mosque. The real Mecca must be seen in this quarter, and in these streets. The road itself is a sewer, and there is filth and trash in every corner. In the midst of this setting sat a 14- to 15-year-old girl on the balcony of her house opening and closing her gown, showing her white thighs and calves. The opportunity to see women is truly rare here.

The local women don't carry children in their arms or on their backs. They sit them above their hips at the back or on the side. They themselves lean in the opposite direction, and the child looks like he's riding a camel, one foot on the mother's stomach, the other on her back.

Beside Mt. Safā—outside the House of God—they've built a large underground toilet. Recently. I went to look at it. Such stench, and such a crowd, and not one bit of ventilation, not even one window. They could easily put in a fan, but who thinks about these things? Of importance is the fact that I don't know where the Mecca sewage disposal plant is located. In this city of stone, one cannot dig a well. I don't think they have sewage pipes, either. What do they do, then? Isn't this the basic reason for the city's filth?

We still have no word on when we'll be leaving. God knows we will spend several more days here and in Jedda with nothing to do. This Muslim *qebleh* is a pitiful thing. No one cares about the sanitary conditions in the area around it. If we were to adhere to Meccan standards of cleanliness—especially during the Hajj season (what do I know about how it is the rest of the year?)—for the Muslim world, it would be most unworthy of the Muslims. One must see Mecca and the Bedouin Arab-turned-urbanite's life without water in order to understand what it means to have ablutions five times a day. All these religious precepts concerning cleanness and uncleanness are to control the filth you see in those streets. But how long will this go on, anyway? After 1,400 years, and with all these modernizing facilities for pipelines, sewage, and sanitation, if you look at old Mecca it's still like the Jewish quarter of Esfahan. The trouble is that if two days in Mina were enough that by the end of the first day the stench of sacrifices was already present, here, where we must remain for a week, the stench has also begun to circulate beginning with the first day. Enough talk about this terrible scandal. It's worse than ancient Dezful, with those toilets on the rooftops. When you climb up the steps on those Meccan streets you can see how and why that rabble threw trash at the Prophet.

Monday 7 Ordibehesht [April 27]

Mecca

They didn't let us sleep at all last night. One of them went in the evening and came back at midnight. Another said the *komeyl*[153] prayer until morning. Another stayed up all night praying and making prostrations. There is also a group of hypocrites who go to the House of God at midnight and come back in the morning. And calls to prayer, hymns, and so on... After all, these are the final days and nights of the journey. One must make the most of them, like the night before a test in school. It seems that nothing happened on the other nights. Everything had to be put off until the last minute. Every night it's the same.

This fellow who owns the house, who puts on European airs, pours chlorine right on the steps, the brown, thick liquid itself. He can't mix it with water to make a milky consistency so the smell will disappear more quickly. There is such a powerful odor of chlorine in the air that you can't sleep at night.

[153] The *komeyl* is a formulaic prayer named after Komeyl ibn Ziyād al-Nakh'i, a close associate of 'Ali ibn Abi Talib, the first Shi'i Imam. (tr)

It's like living in a toilet all the time. And we have this toilet nearby in the corridor that broadcasts the smallest sound!

This hajji from Sagzabad coughed so much last night that everyone got after him, but I knew what he was going through. This wretched bronchitis is killing. And this is in addition to the various brands of cigarettes he's always smoking (I still have *Oshnos*). This poor hajji doesn't even know how to cough, however. He coughs in a loud three-stroke rattle with all the breath he has, just the way he lies, face up, just like a rhinoceros with a cold. *Pu—ha—uh!* And so grating. I'm quite concerned about his lungs.

In this room there are 2 ceiling fans, 4 electric lights, 5 windows, and an air conditioner. Every one is of vital importance. Someone turns one of them on. Another turns it off. Someone opens one of them. Another closes it. And there are endless quarrels. Anyway, everyone has his own tastes. And then the adjustments on this air conditioner are another story!

It's interesting that the Sayyid with the multi-colored beard hennaed it this morning. The red areas turned black, the white parts green, and the green right next to his red skin now looks grey from a distance. This Sayyid is really a sight. His beard now looks fake. He's very strict religiously too, and he's always deploring it when other people shave their beards. The owner of the house, besides trying to act like a European, is also a man of refined taste. He's always wanting *khākshir*, and demands a cup of it in return for every service he renders for the pilgrims. I don't know what it does for him.

This morning I visited the narrow stairstep alley that goes up beside our house. Ours is the only one that has a sewer pipe running into a pit beside the door. Today the son of the owner of the house took off the cover in order to open up the hole. I looked at it. It goes into a sump that they've dug underneath the house for the privy, and they clean it out once a year. Do other houses have these also? The drainage pipe for every home empties into an open gutter they've made of cement that runs along the stairsteps of the alley. It serves to collect residue, and always has slime coming out from under it. The houses at the beginning of the alley have sewer pipes that empty directly into the alley, no doubt to keep their privy sumps from filling up too quickly. The water-circulation pipe system is something to see. In the beginning I noticed that every day an electric pump comes on. I thought there was a water reservoir. I asked about it, and it turned out that the pumps were used to draw water from the city's pipe system into the house tank. Perhaps I'm mistaken, however. The matter was explained in Arabic, and I couldn't understand it. I'm reporting what was said by our guide.

Same day. Monday night.

Mecca.

Today I went to Mount Hara. *Jabal al-Nur* [The Mountain of Light], the first place of inspiration. I set out at 5 p.m. and I was at the top of the mountain by 7. By the time I got back it was a quarter to 9. It is a very harsh and steep mountain. It somewhat resembles a natural ziggurat.[154] I was really out of breath, especially since the road was dark on returning; I couldn't see underfoot, these sandals got caught in the rocks, and my feet were wounded in two or three places.

They had dug out a cavity at the top of the mountain—like a pool—to catch rain water. It was empty. I was so thirsty that I got water from a woman who was going back with her child, who had a small water bag on her shoulder. I took two gulps from her water bag. It was delicious. Beyond the pool, there was a building on the highest point of the mountain, with no roof, and the remains of the base only a meter high. In the middle of it was a split in the rock of the mountain, pointing to the *qebleh*, or Mecca, like the *shaq al-qamar*. In more than one place? According to Farhad Mirza, it is "a split in the mountain and the rock," instead of a split in the moon. On the way I passed the Mecca flood channel, the history of the construction of which this same Farhad Mirza gave. On the side of Jabal al-Nur [The Mountain of Light] there were two or three tent-dwelling families, whose dogs were extremely hostile as I returned. All the area's valleys are visible from the top of the mountain. I stayed there until dark. Even the dusk had faded and the city of Mecca was like a kaleidoscopic carpet of lights, which began shining in the afternoon.

Two Sudanese blacks and a group of four young Syrians—apart from that woman and her child—were seeing the mountain as travelers and visitors the entire time I was there. You would think they could restore this place, put in water, build a road, put up road markers, and install some lights. The foremost place of inspiration in the world of Islam, the Prophet's place of refuge during the Hijrah...and now it's in this condition! I was looking at the mountain and the valleys around it when it got dark, and I decided not to visit the cave. The mountains and deserts in these provinces are quite beautiful, each one the equal of the other. I was strongly reminded of the Mountains of *Otādā*. At the site of every revelation, one at least wants to find the reasons for the revelation.

The road was quite empty when I returned. The streets, alleys, and districts in the direction of Hayy al-Mu'abidah. The people from the Hijaz themselves have left, and now the rest of the pilgrims are gradually departing. It is still crowded around the *Ḥarām*, however, and the bazaar

---

[154] A ziggurat is a pyramid-shaped, stepped temple tower, always made of brick and having no inner chambers, usually square or rectangular. This type of structure was built in the major cities of Mesopotamia from about 2200 to 500 B.C. (tr)

continues to function. The retired manager who had broken his glasses during the circumambulation finally got new ones today for 130 tomans. One doctor does this in all of Mecca, and one optician, and with all this delay as well. He said his name but I don't remember it. Is it really this way?

Today's paper wrote that 1,066,555 people participated in this year's Hajj. I have already given an earlier figure.

I went to the post office. I was addressing envelopes when two or three people gathered around me. One of them was an Algerian pilgrim. He had a telegraph he wanted me to write for him in the Latin alphabet. Here you are. Another one was a Syrian with six envelopes and six stamps. He wanted me to stick them on for him. "You can do that yourself," I say.

"*Māwa'rif,*" he says, meaning "I don't know how."

Our fellow travelers discussed self-flagellation with knives today after lunch, and whether or not it is religiously permitted. Our witty, bald Esfahani fellow traveler defended it indirectly, and mostly in order to aggravate the pious among us, who were adamantly opposed to it. They brought verses from the Qur'ān and the traditions of the Prophet to illustrate the "harm" of it. They didn't let us sleep, in any case. I got up and went to the bathhouse near our house. When I got back I saw that the people were discarding surplus items. *Khākeshir*, dry bread, lemon juice, homemade yogurt, dried mint leaves, and rock sugar. The owner of the house was delighted, grabbing up everything, except a large sack of dried bread belonging to that hide-wearing Hamadani pilgrim, and two bags of yogurt, which they took and poured out behind the wall. The Hamadani pilgrim had ground up some flat bread (he probably had his wife do this in the village), reconverted it to flour, and brought it along in a big sack the size of a 15-kilo sack of rice. He had eaten no more than a third of it. The yogurt had dried up. It was stiff, brittle, and moldy. And what a smell! They discarded these many provisions with much regret. They spent some time consulting, deliberating, and discarding until they were finally resigned to the situation.

Tuesday 8 Ordibehesht [April 28]

Mecca

There is talk of getting underway. They've given the word that we'll be ready to go at 2 a.m. The time remaining until morning when we will be uprooted is still valuable. Our guide is congratulating himself on how clever he has been, how he paid bribes so we could leave sooner, and so on... Taking a walk last night to Mount Hara was a stupid thing to do. I drank so much water that I stopped eating, and I was so thirsty. When I came back I went into the first coffee house and drank down a whole pot of tea and a bottle of water, and again at dinner, water, water, water. I still have no appetite for food or anything else.

I took a nap this afternoon (it's too hot to go out before sundown). The other travelers were talking about a concoction called "*samanqur*," (?) advertised above the doorway of a shop, and its powers as an aphrodisiac. They said the concoction is taken from a fish that jumps out of the sand in the shifting dunes of the desert. Those hunting the fish take blankets with them to stop the fish from going back into the sand after jumping (or some such thing). This was related by the Tehran rice flour merchant pilgrim. He is the only rice flour merchant who still uses a manually-operated grinding mill and has not adopted the use of an electric one. He is proud of this. He's also bald. He's the same one who became known as "*Mokh nadāri*"—in the words of an Arab employed by our guide. Then they related that the day before yesterday a woman was trampled while doing the circumambulation. I jumped up and began asking for details...which of them had seen this? None of them had seen it. Just like *samanqur*.

It says in Farhad Mirza's travel diary that his interpreter in Tiflis was Fath'ali Akhundzadeh;[155] along with his usual talk of wondrous and strange things characteristic of that time, he proposed new alphabets, and so forth...both at the time of his going and the time of his return. He saw him twice. He must have known about some of his ideas on social democracy and other things, but you would never know it. He's just the same man with closed eyes, supporting the Qajars, and content to live a life of comfort and public prestige.

I'm gradually losing the inclination and the energy to write notes. The novelty of the trip has worn off, and not eating also contributes to this listlessness. I've been sitting regularly, finishing this journal of Farhad

---

[155] Mirza Fath'ali Akhundzadeh (1812 - 1878) held the position of translator of Oriental languages in the service of the viceroy of the Caucasus in Tiflis. He was also a professed atheist who devoted much of his time seeking to reform Islamic practice as it existed in Iran at that time. Ethnically a Turk and a resident of Russia for most of his life, Akhundzadeh nonetheless considered Iran his homeland. He was a prolific writer of essays and plays and is considered one of the early pioneers of contemporary Iranian secular intellectualism. (tr)

Mirza's, and, inevitably, comparing and comparing! And always cursing every manifestation of ignorance.

Wednesday 9 Ordibehesht [April 29]
Mecca

My good health has collapsed again. I went out with difficulty and bought some Entero-Vioform. It was obvious what was going to happen that night. I went walking and got so thirsty and drank so much water, and with these Lebanese oranges that make me nauseous. When I went to buy medicine I also stopped at the auction market. Radios, watches, carpets, bicycles, sewing machines, motorcycles, rifles, cameras, cloaks, flat-woven rugs (*jājims*), daggers, and so on. These were the things being bought and sold. A pretty girl and her mother—they looked like Syrians—were walking, white-skinned from head to toe. Then she stopped to dicker with an itinerant merchant over a small silk carpet of the *boteh jeqeh'i* type. They didn't buy anything. A crowd formed in the middle of the bazaar, however, to see the silk carpet, and blocked traffic. I looked it over because of this, or vice-versa.

The city is gradually becoming deserted. The owner of the house went to work at his office today. He's not here to inspect his air conditioner all the time, but his son has come to take his place, or to take care of the household furniture. He isn't bossy, however; he's come to sell toys. The pilgrims' buying and selling frenzy has affected him too. He has brought the things he had during his childhood to sell, or he may also have gotten them at the bazaar. The other travelers are dickering with him, and they also sometimes play with his toys. A doll, a train, an armored truck, a see-saw, an airplane...and all made in Japan.

Uncle made the circumambulations last night on his own two legs. Two people held him up by the armpits and helped him make the circumambulation during the uncrowded period in the late evening. He was ecstatic. He didn't even complain at breakfast this morning, contrary to habit. He's now sleeping comfortably.

This Mecca bazaar is one of the most prosperous bazaars anywhere. It's full of activity, with a small time remaining to operate. It's a repeat of the Ukāẓ market. The pilgrimage itself is an outgrowth of business, or vice-versa. The space between *Safā* and *Marveh* was originally a bazaar, and the *sa'y* between them was virtually a *sa'y* for bargaining, going from this shop to that shop. Now that they've built a runway and separated it from the bazaar, they've installed 5 or 6 large entrances opening on the adjacent bazaar, each entrance opening upon one. When you're tired you can go buy something, do some bargaining, amuse yourself, or cool off. The most earnest matters of humanity and divinity have been built on the faith of the people, and their transactions must be dealt with in these ways, or their ignorances. Three or four shops have sold out completely, and are now being washed and swept. Are they cleaning up for next year? No. It is for the pilgrims of the *'umrah*, those who come on the pilgrimage in the off-season.

I passed the entrance to a record store; it sold "al-Rahman," "Yasin," and "Hijrat" records along with "Om Kolsum," " 'Abd al-Wahhab," "Jili," and American jazz. A recording of the Qur'ān was 25 Saudi rials, the other records 10-15 rials. I didn't buy any. What was the point, I thought. Are you responding to the buying frenzy again? Or do you want to get a souvenir of this trip? Isn't this notebook itself an adequate souvenir?

Noise dominates the scene here to an incredible extent: The sound of horns (*al-buri*), which you hear more of in half an hour here than in 8 hours of driving in Tehran, the yelling and screaming of commercial activities, and the bazaar and its bargaining. Fortunately, we are a long ways from the street in our Mecca house, but now our fellow travelers are honking the owner's son's toys in the same way. One of them bought an armored train. Uncle goes on sleeping just the same. Coming to Mecca it's better to be deaf like him.

Same day. Wednesday.

Still Mecca

This afternoon I went to the House of God for a final visit. "Visit?" No. Goodbye. "Goodbye?" And to God? Or to his house? When you don't put words in the right place this is the way it goes... In any case, the caretakers were sweeping. Blacks in white with green belts. I asked myself why they hadn't made the new colonnade round, since only the first prayer rank next to the House is rectangular; beyond the Stone of Ismā'īl they are all circular. Wasn't this bow-shaped retainer around the Stone of Ismā'īl made expressly to give a circular shape to the prayer ranks? They don't allow anyone to stand on the stone for prayer, and when you are circumambulating you aren't allowed to enter its area. The new shroud is not so much better than the one the year before last. It's brownish-black, or deep jasper in color. The calligraphy is also irregular. Evidently it will be a long time before the Saudis become masters in their own brocading shops.

I saw the Pakistani fellow I'd seen preaching something along the lines of *Weststruckness* in the Medina Mosque, sitting here beneath the portico at the side of the Stone of Ismā'īl, writing something, apparently notes. Some Pakistanis came, probably to ask about religious problems. He was extremely busy, like an executive; it was a long time before he raised his head to see what they wanted. This very manner of his prevented me from approaching him (I didn't know what language to use—but was it clear to the others?).

On the stairs leading to the Zamzam well, the police were hoisting up buckets of water with a lot of commotion and emptying them, of course for the water sellers, who come early to draw the liquid, store it, and sell it to the pilgrims, with swearing and scandalous language in Arabic, which I couldn't understand. Probably they were telling them not to do business right next to the House of God. Christ raised the same issue, but to no avail. Pilgrimage and business are twins. These remonstrations conceal nothing. And why anyway? The Zamzam water spigots were as crowded as ever. An old woman stood by the stairs while her son went down into the well itself and brought water back by the cupful (with those same one-gulp cups distributed by the Ministry of Pilgrimage Affairs and Religious Endowments), pouring it over her head and shoulders. Then over her body, right on her *iḥrām.* The old woman splashed it on her breasts, her head lifted to the sky, and then prayed until her son came with the next cupful. I enjoyed the experience vicariously. She had no teeth, and though she prayed softly in a language I could neither hear nor understand, I knew she was praying for the entire world. Then I continued on my way. As I walked a pair of pretty Indian eyes and eyebrows passed, on the face of a 17- to 18-year-old girl whose *iḥrām* was just like a sari. Is the *iḥrām* itself basically anything other than a sari? The pause at *Mash'ār al-Ḥarām* has its origins in Buddhism.

An officer wearing a revolver was escorting several women as they circumambulated, definitely the children of his wife. So many pregnant women were circumambulating. The circumambulation and the *sa'y* are less crowded, and pregnant women are more protected. I counted four of them. A crippled man with a crutch under his arm came and sat on the cool sand in the House, that is he first pushed the hot sand aside and then sat on the exposed cool layer underneath. At first I thought he was one of those who had his foot amputated for theft according to Saudi custom (it seems that they still administer punishments of this type) but when he sat down I saw it was inherited. He had a deformed and shriveled foot. One was normal, the other congenitally defective.

Again the women must go behind the men at the time of prayer. In the row where I sat, however, for *tashahhod*, a woman dressed in black, her child behind her, took long strides between the men in the direction of the stone so she could greet it to her full satisfaction. The House was full, with no room to insert a pin, row after row, but the woman seemed to be working through stone obstacles in a desert. She had neither fear of the House nor respect for the praying ranks of men. I realized that she is the master of her own house. I don't know why I thought of that evangelist Qobādiyāni, that great brother who came here from the seat of the caliph's power in Baghdad to seek traces of the Fatimids and the Ismā'īlīs[156]—and then returned to plant the seeds of rebellion in a corner of that seat of power, and to undermine the lower echelons of its hierarchy, at least in Khorasan. Then I thought of that other brother, who was my own. I saw just as little of him—who had come here to the seat of Wahhabi power to keep the remnants of Shi'ism alive—as of the other. Now the only memory of him is in you, and as for you, the youngest brother, why have you come here? To seek traces of a tradition in the seat of Aramco's power? What is the point of all this, anyway—pretense? Didn't you see that the master of this House was that woman? Why had she come here, really, to so fearlessly move her womanly presence next to the Stone? I realized that it is worthwhile that the Kaaba has served for centuries and centuries as a refuge for every weary person, for this forsaken humanity, confounded by poverty, oppression, and anomie, like a wailing wall, if it answers even one of this woman's prayers (a complaint against a rival wife in her harem, a wish for the happiness of a child, a request for a cure for sickness, and so on...).

I bought 5 Parker pens on the way back—souvenirs—for 22 piastres each, at a store belonging to a man on Ghaza Street, who is both blind and dumb, yet can hear. It is delightful to see the way he deals with his customers.

[156] Ismā'īlīs were followers of Ismā'īl, the son of the 6th Shi'i Imam, Ja'far al-Ṣādiq. They believed that he was the legitimate seventh Imam, and are hence known as "Seveners." (tr)

Thursday 10 Ordibehesht 1343 [April 30, 1964]

Jedda

The devil take these pilgrim's guides, with their corporate procedures. We got up at 10 o'clock last night to come to Jedda, began loading and packing, and finally set out at a quarter to two in the morning. Again the road was blocked every 10 steps, to get authorization to pass, and the like. They act like jailers. It wasn't this way when we came. Now that you're returning, however, you'd think every pilgrim was a highway robber making his escape. Later we stopped to drink tea, and finally got to Jedda at 4:30 a.m. How far is the whole trip? Twelve *farsakhs.* Now, like thousands of other pilgrims, we've spread our blankets on the ground and are sitting beside our luggage in the middle of a field by the airport waiting for our turn to get a flight. The sun hasn't come up yet, and already I'm dripping with perspiration. God help us after sunrise, although unloading baggage did tire me and cause me to perspire. There isn't even room in the Hajj Village, it's so crowded. Everyone is in a hurry to leave. Everyone left Mecca as soon as they could and came to Jedda. Now they're awaiting their turns.

Most of the people in our group came in a faster bus. Six or seven of us were left with another bus, which was almost full of Syrians. Mohaddes and I ended up at the back of the bus, next to two of them. One was a Damascus bookseller, the other a blacksmith from the same city. We exchanged courtesies, hellos, and addresses. The bookseller spoke classical Arabic, which I haven't heard before now except from the director of the Medina Library. His friend the blacksmith claimed to know French, but he didn't—he stuttered so much I gave up on him. We spoke Arabic. He said that in the evening prayer last night at the Grand Mosque, the Imam read the surah beginning with "By the sky, (displaying) the Zodiac Signs."[157] Now he interpreted the surah. He told Mohaddes and me about the predictions it contains, and Mohaddes is himself an expert on these matters. Then his friend the blacksmith talked about the grandeur and the splendor of Zaynab's grave in Damascus, and finally offered to take us there himself in his automobile if we came to Damascus. And so on... It was interesting that he pronounced his j's "zh."

When we got off the bus in the morning I bought two *āftābeh*s of water at a milk stand in the field beside the airport for 1 rial. We needed them for pre-prayer ablutions. Then I went and got 3 cups of milk from him. We each took a swallow to hold us until our group's breakfast was ready. The milk was powdered, with water added; it was too sweet. One cup was 12 piastres.

---

[157] Surah 85, verse 1, Yusuf 'Ali translation. (tr)

In the magazine *al-Buldān*, published in Damascus or Beirut (I don't remember. I left all of them in Mecca) one of the articles dealing with other Arabic publications was about this so-called science(!) of orientalism, which said that it was the progenitor of the monster, colonialism, and that the two of them are horses pulling the same cart, etc... The 17 Dhū al-Hijjah issue of *al-Bilād* had a story translated from Persian resembling the stories of Hamid Musta'ān[158]—with the names Ladan and Susan. The same themes of romance, the same melodramatic cheesecake.

The bread we had for dinner last night was just like leather, made from American cornmeal, the original corn of which I had seen sold in the Mecca bazaar. A reddish-gold color, some of them split open with the whiteness of the starchy center visible on the outside. The charcoal here is interesting. It must be made from camel's thorn. It is dense, strong, and long-burning. The opium smokers should have been there to use it, although there are enough Arab surrogate pilgrim hookah smokers to take their places. Now an itinerant barber has come so that if anyone wants a final trim and manicure before returning there will be an opportunity. The final offering of Arab hospitality.

9 a.m. Same day. Thursday.

Jedda

We've changed position three times so far this morning, trying to get away from the sun. We're now beneath a canopy made of leaves in the middle of a garden in front of the airport. We spread out the blankets, each group sprawled out in a bunch. A cat is sleeping on the canopy's trellis in the shadow of the leaves. It's a female, its teats dangling. She has probably fled from her litter.

After breakfast, when I went to the bazaar to convert the last of my money for a few purchases and another walk around the city to the port, again I saw a fat young black woman with a scarred face, this time with two horizontal stripes on each cheek. She was beautiful as well. She ate milk and bread, mixed together like *tirid.*[159] Then I took a taxi to the bazaar. I walked awhile in the al-Badu Market, a few of whose shops were open. The itinerant produce vendors, the milk sellers, and the dealers in draft animals opened at lunchtime. I was looking for an ankle ring for Daryush's

---

158 Hamid Musta'ān was a writer of popular fiction during the Reza Shah period, whose work the author has characterized elsewhere as "commonplace stories," typical of the kind of commercial writing that flourished in Iran in that time of heavy censorship. See Jalāl Āl-e Ahmad, "Hedāyat-e *Buf-e Kur*," *'Elm va Zendagi*, no. 1 (1951), p. 24, and its English translation "The Hedāyat of *The Blind Owl*," translated by Ali A. Eftekhary in "Hedāyat's *The Blind Owl* Forty Years After," compiled and edited by Michael C. Hillmann (Austin, Tex.: Center For Middle Eastern Studies, 1978), p. 27. (tr)

159 *Tirid* is a Persian term meaning soup with bread added. (tr)

child, which I did not find. On the way, however, I passed by a store where a number of people were squatting around the entrance. The proprietor of the shop was behind them bleeding them. There was a sign above the door that read "Salim ibn Muhammad Basayf, Bleeding Doctor. Number 1." I stood watching. Each patient was a spindly, bloodless black, and each one had two or three long, thin bleeding cups attached to his back, which the proprietor removed one after the other; he cut the raised place left behind, then replaced the cup. It is just like the bowl of a hookah, but longer and as wide as a tea cup, made of tin. The top had a pyramid-shaped lid. The bottom, which was open, was placed on their backs. In the middle of the cup was a slender tube mounted at an angle, through which the air inside the cup was sucked out. Afterwards something like a nipple was placed over the tube to keep the air out. I watched for awhile, making the man suspicious. I wanted to ask something, such as the name of the implement he was using. He thought I was an agent from the Ministry of Health, since we had put on city clothing after leaving Mecca. He explained later when his mind was at ease. He called the suction cup a "*hajjām*," and the razor a "*mubarriz.*" The blade was one centimeter wide, had a handle, and was inflexible. The blade was round and sharp. I asked what he charged, and he said 5 rials, but the price was really 1. When I started to leave, an Arab on a bicycle who had been observing me and my curiosity turned to the man and said "do you want to cheat this pilgrim out of 4 rials?"

Then I went looking for the fabric merchants, who were opening for business a few at a time. One of them, a young man with a beard, good-looking and charming, was quite courteous. I went inside. He was a Yemeni Zaydi. The way he put it, he was *Ḥusayni.* For 21 rials I bought enough cloth for two shirts. I was about to leave when he offered tea. We sat down to talk—his *Engrish* was worse than my Arabic—and we talked politics. He said there are now 20,000 Egyptian soldiers in Yemen helping Sallal and the Republic, and the number had reached 40,000 at one time. America was paying their bills. He said America was spending $250,000 a day on this enterprise—an exaggeration. He was opposed to contention between two Muslim brothers. He believed that Sallal was working for Nasser and that al-Badr was working for Saudi Arabia. He sympathized with al-Badr in any case, who was a Sayyid, a descendant of the Prophet, and so on... Gradually customers began coming in and we said goodbye.

They are rebuilding Jedda from the ground up, even in the old neighborhoods, where their buildings are lying beside the streets in a rubble alongside the new streets. Construction materials for buildings in the old days were rocks a bit like the ones they've used to build Bushehr, metamorphic sand and riverbed limestone. The same thing they bring to Bushehr from Bahmani. Here and there are gardens, boulevards, and parks with trees. It will be an attractive port in 4 or 5 years.

As I returned I saw that the Bedouin bazaar no longer showed any sign of primitivity. The itinerant vendors had gone and the shops opened, full of European, American, and Japanese goods, just like a bazaar in any other part of the East. Only a few vendors and shopkeepers wore the Arab headdress.

I returned to the airport on the bus from the bazaar entrance—for 4 rials—with travelers, teachers, businessmen, schoolchildren, and women going shopping or returning.

11 a.m. Same day. Thursday.

Jedda

We've just returned from a walk beside the sea. And what a walk! I went with my uncle and sister. That is, I was about to go out alone again when uncle said "What are you doing going for a walk and leaving us here?" At first we took a taxi to a disgraceful beach—full of trash and filth in the water—with an entrance fee of 2 Saudi rials. I realized that this would not do. I got another taxi to take us to a place where one might swim in the water. We settled on 10 rials. He took us to the ships' docks; we were stopped twice by customs agents for inspections. He explained that we pilgrims had come to look, and so on... Later he stopped within two steps of a huge Swiss ship and I jumped into the water. The water was clean, deep, and crystal-green. You have to have been in such a desert to understand what an ocean is. I washed my body, standing on the rocks and pebbles, a hand in the water by the dock, shifting my feet, which were being nibbled by little fish surrounding them. I felt my foot burning, and told myself it was probably a protrusion from new coral, and jumped into the water again. I splashed my way to the back of the ship and then returned, and then again, on my back. I felt my foot really burning, went to the edge and looked, and yes...it was cut, on the ball of my left foot, by glass—and it was no shallow cut. The blood spurted out, staining the water. I came out hobbling on my heel. The taxi driver had opened his door and was saying "Let me give you some motor oil to rub on your wound." I covered the foot with a handkerchief, however, and got dressed. My sister acted squeamish because of the ritual impurity of blood. I asked the driver to take us to a doctor, and he said there was a hospital right there at customs. What could be better, I said. So we went there. The sign of the Saudi Arabian Red Cross was over the door of a room called the Customs Health Service. A man there washed the foot with alcohol, put *Teint d'iode* on it, sprinkled sulfonamide over it, and then bandaged it. With care. I gave him a pack of *Oshno* cigarettes as a gift. We exchanged names and addresses and I came out. Now the foot is throbbing. God knows when we'll be leaving. Flight 23 has just left and we're scheduled for flight 30. It will probably be night—or midnight. Look at what I've done to myself. I can't walk and I can't do all of my sightseeing by taxi. So I must sit in this public thoroughfare until night...

Two o'clock in the afternoon. Same day.

Jedda

These last few hours are the worst ones, especially since my foot is aching severely, and so far they've only reached flight 28, and they've said nothing about flight 27. I don't know why. The loudspeakers around the airport and around the Hajj Village are always talking. This Jedda airport is certainly crowded these days. The loudspeakers only talk in Persian, meaning that today they're only flying out Iranian pilgrims. Since this morning I've heard Arabic only once or twice, or imperfect *Engrish.* How can all these travelers' luggage get through customs? It makes me quiver when I think of it.

An Arab came and went as I was lying down on a blanket under the lifeless shadow of the canopy. He tied a rope around the neck of a primus stove, and went off swinging it, like a water bottle or a piece of crockery. Even Western industrial products can be adapted to primitive consumption. Beside me they've placed a broken chair over a stack of empty soda and cola bottles. Then there is a cupboard full of white bread. Left over and dried out, the remnants of the hospitality and nighttime provisions of an airport cafeteria. I haven't been able to tell whether you can get wine here or not—there's no sign of the empty bottles. There's also a man in a little shop with canned goods, sardines, juice, soda, and fried chicken. They wanted to collect 1 rial from every pilgrim as rent for this spot, which the guides cleverly did not pay. We lunched on bread, cheese, and watermelon, our guide's last outlay, our last group meal, and the simplest.

The nonsense written to here was done in order to forget the pain in my foot. When I put the foot on the ground and try to stand on it, the blood pumps into the veins and hurts so much I can't stand it. You'd think it was a sabre slash! I've never been such a crybaby. I can still be thankful for my summer sandals, which I wear with a handkerchief.

Four-thirty in the afternoon. Same day.

We're still at loose ends in Jedda. The heat has diminished. A cool wind is blowing that continually keeps the airport's directional wind sock filled and erect. In the worry and anxiety at the dock this morning I lost one of my socks. I bought another one and put it on. Take off preparations for flight 28 are now being announced, saying "Please report to the aircraft for boarding." Passengers for flight 29 are also submitting their luggage to customs. They aren't being very strict. Only the baggage handling remains, and one thing here in abundance is porters.

I had wanted to write down the daily temperatures in the different cities, though I haven't so far. I will draw from memory for help: The temperature now is between 37 and 39 degrees centigrade, the humidity is 80 to 90 percent. Medina was a little less, and Mecca... I don't recall. Why didn't I make note of these at the time?

Now a new group brought by bus—Iranian pilgrims—has come and taken a place beside us. Such worry and fretting over getting a better place, a soft, comfortable place, something to lean on, and so on... And what a funny caravanserai! One of them is a woman who is very flashy. Her chador hangs loosely on her head, she talks very sweetly, she is kind to her neighbors, and so on... In the afternoon another family spread out a blanket beside us. An overly neglected girl was looking me over while she read the Qur'ān. I, who have been the one to observe others throughout this journey, am now the one observed in Jedda. And lame. The throbbing of my foot still hasn't stopped.

6:15 p.m.

We've turned our luggage over to customs and are waiting. Waiting means feeling that there is nothing to do, that all is futility, that you have no way to justify the existence of your living and being. I don't even feel like writing. I will leave it.

9 p.m. Same day.

At the Airport Gate

For exactly three-quarters of an hour now these one-hundred and twenty passengers for our aircraft have been crabbing and quarreling with one another behind the closed gate to the airport, over which of them will be closest to the door, with intervention by the police and airport officials, swearing, and abusive language. Especially when we were joined by a group of 40 strangers from Natanz, and that area. I sat to one side and watched the wandering of a searchlight in the humid, hot Jedda sky. I can't stand up. People have reverted to their true colors, showing themselves as they really are. Selfish and petty, intolerant of one another, deserving of whatever they have.

10:15 p.m.

We're now next to the aircraft, and the same abusive quarreling has begun anew. Airport officials continually make the pilgrims line up in some semblance of order, but as soon as they turn their heads the passengers jumble like a flock of sheep; it's something to see. In any case, the boarding process is taking so long that it's possible to write.

11 p.m.—aboard the aircraft B.U.P. (?)

Now that we've boarded, it's a four-engine propeller-driven craft. They claimed we'd return by "jet." There was no place for myself and three or four other people who came aboard last. They had to bring us into a little compartment behind the cockpit used as a resting place for the crew. There is a table in the middle with two long benches on each side. It was hard to get in. Its disadvantage is the sound of the motor right in your ear. You can't sleep, neither can you do anything while awake. I must again take refuge in this notebook. What would have happened on this trip if I hadn't had the companionship of this notebook? We will be airborne three hours and 35 minutes, they announced. The aircraft vibrates a lot. The nuts and bolts of the seats were loose. I tightened two of them with the screwdriver in my pocketknife. They tore my clothes. An *Engrish* woman in her 40s is the crew chief, and two Armenian Lebanese women are her assistants. The tall young Lebanese man who came with us and rebuked his assistants for giving the passengers so much water is also here. I think he must hold a high position in this Lebanese company, which is collaborating with Iran Air in its monopoly over the Hajj season. He's a handsome young man who gives orders easily. He engaged one of the passengers to help distribute water, and another to distribute bread. He also got one to tell passengers over the aircraft's public address system not to smoke, to fasten their seat belts, how long we would be en route, and this sort of thing. He knows a little Persian. The evening meal consisted of a piece of Holland cheese—which again aroused doubt as to its religious admissibility or inadmissibility—a banana, a pear, two small pieces of white bread, egg, and four biscuits. I don't know what they did in the main cabin, but here they watched each other constantly to see if they would eat the cheese or not, including me, but I wasn't hungry and settled for just the banana and the pear. Now I've turned to my notebook, to see whether I can write something worth reading.

The way I see it, I've come on this trip mostly out of curiosity, the same way I poke my nose into everything, to look without expectations. Now I've seen it, and this notebook is the result. This was an experience too, in any case—or perhaps a very simple event. Every one of these experiences and events was simple and "uneventful." Although it was quite ordinary, it was the basis of a kind of awakening, and if not an awakening—at least a skepticism. In this way I am smashing the steps of the world of certainty one by one with the pressure of experience, beneath my feet. And what is the result of a lifetime? That you come to doubt the truth, solidity, and reality of the primary axioms that bring certainty, give cause for reflection, or incite action, give them up one by one, and change each of them to a question mark. At one time I thought my eyes saw through all the world's illusions. Now that I belong to one corner of the world, if I fill my eyes with images from all other corners of the world, I will become a man of the entire world. I think it was Paul Nizan who wrote in *Aden-Arabie* that "A man is not merely a pair of eyes. If, in your travels, you cannot change your position in history just as you change your geographical position, what you have done is futile."[160] Along the same lines I realized that a man is an aggregation of life and culture mixed together, with certain capabilities and circumscribed ties. In any case, a man is not merely a mirror, but a mirror in which specific things are reflected, even that Hamadani pilgrim who's still wearing his sheepskin vest. But then, a mirror has no language, and you want to have only a language. Is this not what separates the eye in the head from the eye of the heart? When I assess the matter I can see that with the eye of my heart I don't even know myself and the familiar life of Tehran, Shemirān, and Pāchinār.[161] So what image have I given in the mirror of this notebook? Wouldn't it have been better if I had done the same thing a million other people did this year who came on the Hajj? And those millions of millions of other people who've visited the Kaaba during these 1,400 or so years and had things to say about it, but said nothing and took the results of the experience with them selfishly to the grave? Or simply discussed it with their sisters, mothers, children, and families for four days and then nothing? Isn't it really better if we let the experience of every event rot like a seed in the center of its fruit? Instead of eating the fruit and planting the seed? Obviously, with this notebook I have given a negative answer to this sincere question. And why? Because Iranian intellectuals spurn these events, and walk among them gingerly and with distaste. "The Hajj?" they say. "Don't you have anywhere else to go?" Ignoring the fact that this is a tradition that calls a million people to a single place every year and prevails upon them to engage in a single ritual. Anyway, it was necessary to see, to be there, to go, and to witness,

---

[160] (Paris: F. Maspero, 1960). (tr)

[161] Shemirān is an upper class district in north Tehran. Pāchinār is an old district in south Tehran. (tr)

to see what changes there have or have not been since the time of Nāṣir-i Khusraw.

In any event, whether it be a confession, a protest, heresy, or whatever, I mainly came on this trip looking for my brother—and all those other brothers—rather than to search for God. And God is everywhere for those who believe in him.

Sunday 13 Ordibehesht 1343 [May 3, 1964]

Tajrish

It seems that it was 3 a.m. on Friday when we came into the Tehran airport. I was home by five, frayed, coughing, and exhausted. I haven't yet gone out, not even to the bathhouse, out of concern for the injury on my foot and for fear of catching cold again. It is still cold, and it still smells like Winter. I either sleep or greet guests. Simin says "You really burned your feet!"

Translators' Glossary

Abbassids, The caliphs who ruled the Muslim world from their capital in Baghdad from 750-1258 A.D.

Abu Bakr, The first Muslim Caliph, in power from 632-634 A.D.

Āftābeh, A special water can or ewer with a long spout used by Muslims to comply with the Prophet Muhammad's command that Muslims cleanse themselves after answering a call of nature. Usually kept near the toilet.

'Ā'ishah (ca 614 - 678), the daughter of the first Muslim caliph Abu Bakr, child bride and "favorite wife" of the Prophet Muhammad.

Ākhond, A lesser member of the Shi'i religious leadership. He performs everyday religious functions such as leading the prayers in the smaller mosques, etc.; the term, often used pejoratively, is synonymous with *mulla.*

'Arafāt, The name of a dry plain and a mountain located near Mecca, and the site of *voquf*, or Standing Day, a required ritual of the pilgrimage that takes place on 9 Dhū al-Ḥijjah. The ritual is strenuous because it requires a day of walking and exposure to the hot sun.

Aramco, The Arabian American Oil Company. Joint owners in 1964: Standard Oil Company of California, Texaco Inc., Standard Oil Company (New Jersey) and Socony Mobil Oil Company.

'Āshurā, The 10th day of the month of Moharram, when Imam Husayn and his followers were martyred at Karbala.

Awqāf, Plural of *vaqf.*

Āyat Allāh, Lit. "sign of God" (Ayatollah), an Arabic-Persian term that can refer to verses from the Qur'ān or to leading Shi'i clergymen.

'Ayd-e Qorbān, The Feast of the Sacrifice, Arabic *'Īd al-Aḍḥā*; it is a four-day festival beginning on the 10th day of the month of Dhū al-Ḥijjah in the Muslim lunar calendar, during which ritual animal sacrifices are made. It takes place at Mina for Hajj pilgrims, is one of two official national religious holidays in Saudi Arabia. In Āl-e Ahmad's day, as in the era of the Islamic Republic, it has been an official Iranian holiday as well.

al-Badr, Imam Muhammad, Imam of Yemen (head of the Zaydi sect and ruler of the state) beginning in 1962. He was involved in a military struggle for control of the country against forces led by Marshal Abdullah Sallal at the time of Āl-e Ahmad's pilgrimage.

Badr, Battle of, A desert battle at the village of al-Badr. It was fought on the 15th of March, 624, between a small Muslim force led by the Prophet Muhammad and a wealthy, heavily guarded caravan returning to Mecca from Gaza. The Muslims won decisively, and severely weakened the power of the Meccans as commercial leaders of the peninsula by killing about a dozen of Mecca's most important leaders.

Bandari Asses, A breed of ass originating in Cyprus.

Baqī', The name of an important cemetery located to the east of the city of Medina, in which are buried most of the companions of the Prophet Muhammad as well as a number of other dignitaries who were his contemporaries.

Balāl, One of the Prophet Muhammad's slaves.

Bayt al-Ḥarām, Literally "Sacred House," the Arabic term for the Grand Mosque in Mecca, the goal of the Hajj.

Camel, (Arabic *Jamal*), the name of a famous battle in about 656 A.D. Around 70 men were killed defending 'Ā'ishah as she rode a camel inside a covered pavilion. The battle was fought against the followers of 'Ali ibn Abi Talib by a contingency, including 'Ā'ishah, which demanded punishment for the assassination of the Caliph Uthman.

Circumambulation (Arabic *Ṭawāf*), the ritual performed at the Kaaba upon arriving in Mecca after conclusion of the feast of the sacrifice. It consists of circling the structure on foot seven times, reciting a prayer during each circuit.

Dhū al-Ḥijjah, The 12th month of the Muslim lunar calendar, during which every Muslim is to make the pilgrimage (Hajj) to Mecca at least once in his life if physically and financially able.

Dishdāshah, The long gown worn by the Arabs of the Arabian peninsula.

Emāmzādeh, A shrine dedicated to a descendant of an Imam. Literally, "born of an Imam," the term also applies to relatives and descendants of the 12 Imams.

Farsakh, 6.24 kilometers.

Gharbzadegi, Literally "Weststruckness," a term Āl-e Ahmad popularized in Iran in a polemic essay (1962) by the same name.

Hadīth, An accepted account of something the Prophet Muhammad, one of his companions, or one of the Imams said or did. Also called "traditions," *hadith*s have the weight of scripture in the determination of precedent in Islamic law.

Hagar, One of the wives of Abraham [Ebrāhim] and the mother of Ismā'īl. Her run between al-Safā and al-Marwah in search of water for her son at the site of Kaaba is now commemorated by the Sa'y ritual.

Hajj, The Arabic-Persian term for the pilgrimage to Mecca.

Hajji, A title given to any Muslim who has made the pilgrimage to Mecca.

Hamlehdār, Someone who acts as a guide for a group of Muslims throughout the pilgrimage, providing them with details on ritual formalities at the shrines themselves as well as practical information on travel facilities and procedures.

Hamzah, An uncle of the Prophet Mohammad, said to have been the first one killed at the battle of Uhud.

Hanafi, A follower of the Sunni school of Islamic law named after Abū Ḥanīfah, a Muslim jurist (d. 776). Its adherents depend strongly on analogy in the interpretation of the Qur'ān, and it is the only major sect of Islam that permits prayers to be said in languages other than Arabic.

Hanbali, A follower of the Sunni school of Islamic law named after the Muslim jurist Aḥmad ibn Ḥanbal (d. 855), who had been a student of Muhammad ibn Idris al-Shāfi, the founder of another orthodox sect that bears his name (see Shāfi'i). Ḥanbal led a "back to the Qur'ān" movement that rejected many of Shāfi's teachings, including the validity of law formulated by boards of religious scholars. Hanbalis are the majority sect in Saudi Arabia today.

Ḥijjāb, The Arabic term for the veil worn by many Muslim women. The Iranian version of it is called a chador.

Hijrah, The Arabic name for the Prophet Mohammad's departure from Mecca to Medina on July 16, 622. This is the first day of the Muslim calendar. The term also has the general meaning of "emigration" in Arabic, but with emphasis in the meaning on separation from one's own people and attachment to others.

Howz, The Persian name for the Iranian courtyard pond.

Husayn, The son of Imam 'Ali, martyred at Karbala.

'Īd al-Aḍḥa, See 'Ayd-e Qorbān

Iḥrām, The Arabic name for the purification ritual pilgrims must complete before entering the Mecca shrine area to perform the Hajj. The term also refers to the clothing worn by one who has completed the ritual, usually two seamless, white pieces of toweling or sheeting, one covering the body from waist to ankle, the other thrown over the shoulder. Once clothed in the *Iḥrām*, pilgrims are considered to be in a state of grace and purity; they may not wear jewelry or other adornments, nor engage in disputes or sexual activities.

Imam, The one who stands in front of the ranks of praying Muslims and leads the prayer; for Ja'farī and Ismā'īlī Shi'is, an Imam is also one of 12 hereditary successors to the Prophet for leadership of the Muslim community, all of whom are considered divinely guided, infallible, and sinless political and religious leaders. In Arabic and among the Sunnis, the term is used to refer to a man learned in the Islamic sciences.

Imam Husayn, The third Shi'i Imam, killed by Yazid (son of Mu'āwiyyah, founder of the 'Umayyad dynasty) at Karbala, Iraq, in A.H. 61 [680 A.D.], while fighting for control of the caliphate. He is regarded by Shi'is as the greatest martyr of Islam and the quintessential symbol of resistance to tyranny and oppression.

Ismā'īlīs, The followers of this Shi'i sect, known as "Seveners," believed that Ismā'īl, the oldest son of the 6th Shi'i Imam, Ja'far al-Ṣādiq, was the legitimate seventh Imam.

Izār, The lower half of the *iḥrām* attire, covering the body from the navel to the knees.

Jamrah, The Arabic name for any of the three stoning pillars located in Mina, representing *shaytāns*, or satans. They are al-Jamrat al-'Aqabah, al-Jamrat al-Wusṭā, and al-Jamrat al-'Ūlā.

Kaaba, An irregular, cube-shaped structure located in the courtyard of the Grand Mosque at Mecca, which, according to legend, was built first by Adam and reconstructed by Abraham after the flood.

Kāf, The name of the letter "k" in the Arabic alphabet.

Karbala, The desert site of the bloody massacre in which Imam Husayn, the son of Imam 'Ali, was killed along with 70 of his followers while trying to seize the Islamic caliphate from Yazid ibn Mu'āwiyyah on the 10th of Muharram, A.H. 61 [680 A.D.].

Khākshir, Also *khākshir-yakhmāl*, the Persian name for a beverage made with a cold drink such as lemonade and a tiny red seed about 1 mm. in length found in Iran. The seed is taken from one of several members of a family of plants known as *cruciferae* (Latin *sisymbrium sophia*), which includes the mustard plant. It is considered aphrodisiac, and is used for both for medicinal purposes and refreshment. The term *khākshir*, or *khākshir-e shīrīn*, can also refer to the seeds themselves.

Khandaq, The name of a trench to the north of the city of Medina which was dug in March of 627. Designed by the Iranian Muslim convert Salmān Pārsi, the trench was ordered by the Prophet Muhammad as a defense against an impending invasion by a force of some 10,000 pagans from Mecca who sought to break his power. The trench effectively thwarted the assault.

Khoms, Literally "one fifth," a religious tax to support indigent descendants of the Prophet Muhammad.

Labbayk, A ritual word said in response to a religious call, meaning "Here I am!; I am ready!"

Maddāh, Someone who sings songs and recites poetry about the Imams on special Shi'i anniversaries such as the 9th and 10th of Muharram (when Imam Husayn was captured and martyred). He may be merely a gifted performer, with no religious or scholarly credentials.

Māliki, A follower of the Sunni school of Islamic law named after the Muslim jurist Mālik ibn Anas (d. 793). A notable feature of Māliki belief is the special emphasis that is placed on the importance of the Traditions of the Prophet (see *hadith*) in the resolution of religious and legal questions not specifically covered in the Qur'ān.

Maqām-e Ebrāhim, The boulder upon which Abraham is said to have stood while rebuilding the Kaaba after the height of the structure rose above his reach.

Marveh, See Safā.

Mas'ā, The long covered runway where the *sa'y* is performed between Safā and Marveh.

Mash'ār al-Ḥarām, Literally "The Sacred Grove," a mosque located in the town of Muzdalifah, about four miles from 'Arafāt; all pilgrims go to Muzdalifah after sunset on Standing Day en route to Mina.

Mihrāb, The niche in a mosque indicating the direction of the Kaaba.

Mina, The site of the observance of *'Ayd-e Qorbān* during the Hajj, Mina is a small town between Mecca and Arafat. It is also the home of the three *jamrahs*, or stoning pillars.

Minbar, The "pulpit" in a mosque. Physically, it is a portable staircase with a small platform at the top on which the preacher or teacher sits.

Mīqāt, This term can designate either the area containing the Muslim shrines in Mecca, or the stations surrounding the shrine area where the purification rites are performed in order to enter into the required state of *iḥrām* before entry.

Mohr, A small rectangle of packed clay from Mecca or Karbala which is placed on the ground by Shi'is when they pray; the forehead touches this sample of sacred soil during the prostration.

Mollā, A term used generically to refer to clergymen; also synonymous with *ākhond.*

Mosaddeq, Mohammad, Iranian Prime Minister from 1951 to 1953.

Muṭawwif, The Arabic-Persian term for a guide whose function is to counsel pilgrims on the proper ways to perform the rituals of the Hajj.

Muḥrim, A term applied to someone who is in the state of ritual purity required for entry into the Mecca shrine areas to perform the Hajj.

Muzdalifah, The next stop on the pilgrimage route after 'Arafat, to which pilgrims proceed en masse immediately after sunset on the ninth of the month of *Dhu al-Hijjah.* Pilgrims traditionally gather at this spot, located several miles between 'Arafat and Mina, to worship and sleep under the stars.

Nakhāwalah, The name of a Shi'i sect in Medina and Jedda. They are holdovers from the days when the Shi'is contributed to the conquest of western Arabia. Most of the other early Shi'is have since converted to the Shāfi'i school of Islam; the Nakhāwalah, who did not, became a despised group which was compelled to follow the lowest of trades.

Nāṣir-i Khusraw, (Qobādiyāni Marvazi, 1004-88 A.D.) A famous Iranian poet and writer who converted to the Ismā'īlī branch of Islam (Seveners) in Egypt under Fatimid rule. He tried to propagate his beliefs later in Khorasan, but met with official opposition. He is remembered for his *Safarnāmah* [travelogue].

Oshno, A very cheap and strong brand of cigarettes marketed in Iran.

Pāchinār, An old district in south Tehran.

Prophet's Mosque, The most important religious site in the city of Medina and one of the three principal shrines in the world for Sunni Muslims.

Qebleh, The orientation for the Muslim prayer, always facing in the direction of the Kaaba in Mecca.

Qerān, An Iranian coin equal to 1/10 of a toman.

Qobādiyāni, See Nāṣir-i Khusraw

Qonut, The second standing phase of the Muslim prayer, done with the upturned palms resting on the chest while reciting a prayer formula.

Quraysh, A major Meccan tribe, in the time of the Prophet Muhammad. The Prophet was a member of the clan of Hashim within that tribe by virtue of his mother Āminah, who was a daughter of the Quraysh.

Rajm, Literally "pelting with stones," a Hajj ritual performed at Mina, in which a series of three stone pillars representing Satan are hit with stones seven times each on each of two successive days. The first pillar, Jamrat al-'Aqabah, is stoned an extra time one day before the above.

Ramazān, The Persian name (Arabic *Ramaḍān*) for the ninth month of the Muslim lunar calendar, during which Muslims are to fast from dawn to sunset.

Rowzeh, An impassioned verse account of the tragedy at Karbala, given on special occasions and prior to sermons. The verses are taken from the work of Ḥusayn Vā'iẓ Kāshifī (d. 1504-1505) entitled *Rawḍat al-Shuhadā* (Garden of the Martyrs).

Rowzeh'khān, One who specializes in the recitation of *rowzeh*s.

Sa'y, The Arabic name for the ritual run performed by pilgrims in commemoration of Hagar's search for water: "The sa'y begins at al-Safā. Men are required to climb the steps to the top of both elevations, but women, especially when the mas'ā is crowded with hajjis, may do the rite below. After facing the Kaaba (obstructed from view by the walls of the Haram Mosque) and repeating a prayer of intention, the hajji begins his seven trips. At each elevation he repeats a small prayer with hands outstretched toward the Kaaba. During each trip male hajjis must jog (ramal, sometimes also called harwal) between two markers about 250 feet apart. This is after the example of Muhammad. Ironically, although the sa'y is said to commemorate Hagar's running in search for water, women need not run." From David E. Long, *The Hajj Today: A Survey of the Contemporary Makkah Pilgrimage* (New York: State University of New York Press, 1979).

Safā and Marveh, (Arabic *al-Safā and al-Marwah*) Two small hills about 400 yards apart now enclosed within the Grand Mosque, between which Hagar is said to have run in search of water for her son.

Sallal, Marshall Abdullah, Yemeni army officer and politician who was Imam Muhammad al-Badr's Chief of Staff, and then Commander-in-Chief of the Republican forces fighting against him during the Yemeni civil war of 1962.

Salmān Pārsi, A legendary companion of the Prophet Muhammad, Pārsi was an Iranian convert to Islam who helped design the Khandaq trench, dug in March of 627 to defend the city of Medina from invading Meccan pagans. See Khandaq.

Sayyid, A descendant of the Prophet Mohammad.

Shāfi'i, A follower of the Sunni school of Islam named after the Muslim jurist Muhammad ibn Idris al-Shāfi'i (d. 820). The movement arose out of the Māliki school, and is noted for having introduced the notion that local authorities and traditions could be appealed to for resolution of religious and legal questions, and not only those in Medina.

Shar' Courts, Courts dealing with matters under the jurisdiction of Islamic law.

Shemirān, The name of an upper class neighborhood in north Tehran.

Shi'i, The general name for a large and diverse group of Muslim sects, all sharing the belief that 'Ali ibn Abi Talib was the legitimate caliph after the death of the Prophet Muhammad, and that succession to the caliphate should be hereditary. The term is sometimes translated "Partisans of 'Ali." Āl-e Ahmad and most of his associates were members of the majority Shi'i group in Iran, the "Twelver" or "Ja'fari" Shi'is, who believe that there were 12 imams, beginning with 'Ali and ending with Mahdi, the Hidden Imam.

Sizdahbedar, Literally "thirteenth outside," this is one of the festive days of the Iranian new year's celebrations which occurs on the thirteenth day of the new year. On this day, Iranian families leave their houses for the entire day and go to the country or a park for a picnic. There is a myth that if the people go away for the day, spirits will occupy their homes on this day and then leave them alone for the rest of the year.

Shur, The name of a musical scale used in Iranian traditional music.

Sunni, A follower of the majority "orthodox" sect of Islam, "based on the way and customs of Muhammad." In particular, one who accepts one of the four schools of Islam, i.e., either the the Māliki, Shāfi'i, Hanafi, or Hanbali school. Sunnis are distinguished from Shi'is by their belief that the Caliphate is an elective, rather than a hereditary office.

Tashahhod, The concluding segment of the Muslim prayer, done in a kneeling position while reciting a final ritual formula.

Tirid, Soup mixed with bread.

Toman, The basic unit of Iranian currency, equal to 10 *qerāns* or 10 rials.

Tuchal, The name of a mountain in the Alborz range of northern Iran.

Uhud, The site of the first battle fought by Muslims against non-believers, and the burial ground of the first martyrs of Islam.

Ukāẓ, A market established in pre-Islamic times, held during the lunar month of Dhū al-Qa'dah. It later became a customary preliminary stop for those making the pilgrimage to Mecca.

Vaqf, A pious endowment, or mortmain, permanently allocated for some religious purpose, such as the building of a mosque.

Voquf, The Persian term (Arabic *wuqūf*) for the vigil of Standing Day at 'Arafāt which begins at noon and ends after sunset on 9 Dhū al-Ḥijjah.

Wahhabi, A follower of the Hanbalite teachings of Shaykh Muhammad ibn 'Abd al-Wahhab (1703 or 4-1792), whose religious movement became the basis for the unification of most of the Arabian peninsula under the House of Sa'ud.

Zainab, The sister of the Shi'i Imam Husayn. She witnessed his martyrdom at Karbala, and was said to have been the first to mourn his death.

Zakāt, A "purification tax" paid by Muslims to help the poor; sometimes translated as "alms," since the particular poor person to whom the tax is paid, if qualified, may be chosen by the individual Muslim. The payment of *zakāt* is normally a voluntary religious duty today, but it was collected by the government in the days of the early caliphate.

Zamzam, A sacred well in Mecca just outside the Grand Mosque. According to legend it was miraculously found by Hagar beside her son Ismā'īl after she had been abandoned in the desert without water by her husband Abraham. The well was also revered in pre-Islamic times.

Zaydism, The Zaydis are followers of Zayd al-Shaḥid, who rebelled in 737 A.D. against the Umayyad caliph Hishām 'Abd al-Malik. They regard him as the fifth hereditary Imam in the Household of the Prophet.

Zell Allāh, Literally "shadow of God," was originally applied to the Muslim caliphs, emphasizing the religious sanctity of their authority. It was later adopted by secular monarchs, such as the Shah of Iran.

Zubaydah, Wife of the 5th Abbassid Caliph, Harun al-Rashid, remembered for having dug a canal that now provides water for Mecca.

Bibliography

Compiled and Annotated
by John Green

This bibliography attempts to list, according to date of first publication (or probable completion, if the first publication date is posthumous or unknown) all of Āl Aḥmad's articles and books, with comparative listings for variants and reprintings. Some issues of journals to which he is known to have contributed could not be examined prior to publication of this volume, however. A full listing of his translations and translations of his work into English is also provided. The sections on critical works contain the major studies on Āl Aḥmad's life and work, but are by no means complete. The same is true of the section on Hajj literature. Those familiar with Persian will notice that the transliteration system used here emphasizes orthography, rather than phonetic information. It is a close approximation of the Library of Congress system, and we trust that those who may object to its manner of representing the language will appreciate the time its use saves in misguided searching among the public card files.

I. A List of Jalāl Āl Aḥmad's Works

A. Contributions to Journals

1945 (1324) "Ziyārat" ("The Pilgrimage"). *Sukhan* 2:4 (Farvardīn 1945/1324): 283–91.

1945 (1324) "Ay Lā Mas, sabā!" ("Oh Heathens!"). *Sukhan* 2:6 (Khurdād 1324/1945): 452-59.

1945 (1324) "Dīd va Bāzdīd-i 'Īd" ("A Holiday Exchange of Visits"). *Sukhan* 2:9 (Mihr 1324/1945): 697–705.

1945 (1324) "Daw Murdah" ("Two Corpses"). *Sukhan* 2:11 (Day 1324/1945): 885–86.

1946 (1325) "Vidā'" ("Farewell"). *Sukhan* 3:4 (Mihr 1946/1325): 272–75.

1946 (1324) "Lāk-i Ṣūratī" ("Pink Nailpolish"). *Mardum* 5:1 (Mihr 1325/1946): 37–46.

1947 (1326) "Muḥīṭ-i Tang" ("A Tight Spot"). *Mardum* 5:9 (Khurdād 1326/1947): 65–80.

1947 (1326) "I'tirāf" ("Confession"). *Mardum* 5:13 (Mihr 1326/1947): 41–44.

1947 (1326) "Jaryān-i Jashn-i Āghāz-i Duvvumīn Sāl-i Intishār-i Majallah va Guzārish-i Umūr-i Idārī-yi Majallah dar Sāl-i Guẕashtah" ("Events of the Celebration of the Beginning of the Magazine's Second Year of Publication and a Report on the Magazine's Administrative Affairs for the Previous Year"). *Mardum* 5:13 (Mihr 1326/1947): 91–96.

1947 (1326) "Zindagī kih Gurīkht" ("The Life that Fled"). *Mardum* 5:15 (Āẕar 1326/1947): 5–8.

1951 (1330) "Hidāyat-i *Būf-i Kūr*" ("The Hedāyat of *The Blind Owl*"). *'Ilm va Zindagī* 1:1 (Day 1330/1951): 65–78.

1951 (1330) "Ṣifr va Bīnihāyat yā *Ẕulmat-i Nīmrūz*" ("Zero and Infinity, or *Darkness at Noon*," a review of Arthur Koestler's *Darkness at Noon*). *'Ilm va Zindagī* 1:1 (Day 1330/1951): 78–79.

1951 (1330) "Āyā barā-yi Nawrūz Āmādah Shudah'īm?" ("Are We Ready for New Year's?"). *'Ilm va Zindagī* 1:3 (Isfand 1330/1951): 205–208, 267.

1952 (1331) "Mushkil-i Nīmā Yūshīj" ("The Difficulty with Nima Yushij"). *'Ilm va Zindagī* 1:5 (Urdībihisht 1331/1952): 393–400.

1952 (1331) "Shūrá bā Khānandigān va Nivīsandigān" ("A Consultation with Readers and Writers"). *'Ilm va Zindagī* 1:6 (Khurdād 1331/1952): 481–483.

1952 (1331) "Sukhanī Chand bā Khānandigān va Nivisandigān" ("A Few Words with Readers and Writers"). *'Ilm va Zindagī* 1:7 (Shahrīvar 1331/1952): 577–579.

1953 (1332) "Chand Kalimah az Miyān-i Gawd" ("A Few Words from the Center of the Ring"). *'Ilm va Zindagī* 2:1 (Farvardin 1332/1953): 1–3, 85.

1958 (1337) "Safarī bih Shahr-i Bādgīr'hā: Dār al-'Ibādah-'i Yazd" ("A Journey to the City of Windmills: The Temple of Yazd"). *Andīshah va Hunar* 3:1 (Shahrīvar 1337/1958): 18–30.

1958 (1337) "Chand Kalimah bā Mashhāṭah'hā" ("A few Words with the Bride Dressers"). *Andīshah va Hunar* 3:2 (Ābān 1337/1958): 92–97.

1959 (1337) "Muqaddamah'ī kih dar Khur-i Shā'ir-i Buland Nabūd" ("An Introduction That Was Not Worthy of a Great Poet"). *Andīshah va Hunar* 3:5 (Bahman/Isfand 1337/1959): 344–350. A highly critical reaction to Parviz Natil Khanlari's introduction to the first edition of Āl Aḥmad's *Zan-i Zīyādī.*

1959 (1337) "Varshikastigī-yi Maṭbū'āt" ("The Bankruptcy of the Press"). *'Ilm va Zindagī* 3 (Isfand 1337/1959): 1–18.

1959 (1338) "Kitābī dar Siyāsat va Daftar-i Shi'rī dar Ẕamm: 'Īn Kaj Ā'īn-i Qarn-i Dīvānah' " ("A Book on Politics and A Book of Poetry: This Warped Custom of an Insane Century"). *'Ilm va Zindagī* 5 (Tīr 1338/1959): 26–32.

1959 (1338) "Chand Nuktah Darbārah-'i Khaṭṭ ū Zabān-i Fārsī" ("A Few Points Concerning The Persian Language and Script"). *'Ilm va Zindagī* 6 (1338/1959): 27–42.

1959 (1338) "Chand Kalimah darbārah-'i Ālbir Kāmū" ("A Few Words about Albert Camus"). *'Ilm va Zindagī* 6 (1338/1959): 43.

1960 (1338) "Nīmā Dīgar Shi'r Nakhāhad Guft" ("Nima [Yushij] Will No Longer Write Poetry"). *Andīshah va Hunar* 4:8 (Day 1338/1960): 515–516. A eulogy for the poet Nima Yushij.

1960 (1338) "Vurūd bih Dih" ("Entering the Village"). *Andīshah va Hunar* 4:8 (Day 1338/1960): 567–586.

1960 (1339) "Bilbishū-yi Kitāb'hā-yi Darsī" ("The Confusion in Textbooks"). *'Ilm va Zindagī* 10 (1339/1960): 33–48.

1961 (1340) "Chand Yād'dāsht darbārah-'i *Guldān*" ("A Few Notes Concerning *The Flowerpot*"). *Ārash* 1:1 (Ābān 1340/1961): 93–96. A review of the play by Bahman Fursī.

1961 (1340) "Jashn-i Farkhundah" ("A Joyous Celebration"). *Ārash* 1:1 (Ābān 1340/1961): 15–29.

1961 (1340) "Pir-Mard Chashm-i Mā Būd" ("The Old Man Was Our Eyes"). *Ārash* 1:2 (Day 1340/1961): 65–75.

1962 (1341) Interview with Architect Hushang Sayḥūn. *Ārash* 1:5 (Āzar 1341/1962): 47–50.

1964 (1343) "Sag'hā va Gurg'hā" ("Dogs and Wolves"). *Andīshah va Hunar* 5:4 (Mihr 1343/1964): 374–379.

1964 (1343) "Vilāyat-i Isrā'īl" ("The State of Israel"). *Andīshah va Hunar* 5:4 (Mihr 1343/1964): 380–386.

1964 (1343) "Guftugū bā Jalāl Āl-i Aḥmad" ("A Conversation with Jalāl Āl Aḥmad"). *Andīshah va Hunar* 5:4 (Mihr 1343/1964): 387–408.

1964 (1343) "Mu'allim va Darvīsh: Faṣl-i Dīgarī az *Nifrīn-i Zamīn*" ("The Teacher and the Dervish: A New Chapter from *The Cursing of the Earth*"). *Ārash* 2:1 (Tīr 1343/1964): 2–14.

1964 (1343) "Bih Muḥaṣṣis va Barāyi Dīvār" ("To Mohasses and for the Wall"). "Guft u Shunūdī bā Muḥaṣṣis-i Naqqāsh" ("A Conversation with Mohasses the Painter"). *Ārash* 2:2 (Winter 1343/1964): 86–134.

1964 (1343) "Sitāyish-i Khujastah az *Āhan*" ("Khujastah's Praise for *Iron*"). *Ārash* 2:2 (Winter 1343/1964): 135–141. A review of the play *Āhan* [*Iron*] by Khujastah Kīyā.

1964 (1343) "Guzārishī az Khūzistān" ("A Report from Khuzistan"). *Ārash* 2:4 (Summer 1343/1964): 143–62.

1964 (1343) "Guzārishī az Kungrah-'i Bayn al-Milalī-yi Mardum'shināsī" ("A Report on the International Anthropology Conference"). *Payām-i Nuvīn* 7:1 (Āẕar, 1343/l964): 61–72.

1965 (1344) "Mudirn Bāzī dar Masjid" ("Playing with Modernity in the Mosque"). *Firdawsī* 723 (29 Tīr 1344/1965): 9, 17.

1965 (1344) "Darbārah-i Intiqād-i Kitāb" ("On the Criticism of Books"). *Firdawsī* 723 (29 Tīr 1344/1965): 12, 17.

1965 (1344) "Mihrgān dar Mashhad-i Ardihāl" ("Autumn in Mashhad's village of Ardihal"). *Andīshah va Hunar* 5:6 (Urdībihisht 1344/1965): 711–716.

1965 (1344) "Ā'īn-i Faṣl" ("The Season's Custom"). *Payām-i Nuvīn* 7:9 (1965): 37-42.

1966 (1345) "Guftugū'ī bā Yak Farangī-yi az Farang bar Gashtah va dar Justujū-yi Zabān-i Balūchī bar Āmadah" ("An Interview with a European Returned from Europe in Search of the Baluchi Language"). *Jahān-i Naw* 1:1 (1345/1966): 83–95. An interview with the Austrian physician Hans Strasser.

1966 (1345) "Kārnāmah-'i Daw Māhah-'i 'Hārvārd'" ("A Two-Month Report from Harvard"). *Jahān-i Naw* 1:2–3 (1345/1966): 12–28.

1966 (1345) "Rawshanfikr Chīst? Va Kīst?" ("What Is an Intellectual? And Who?"). *Jahān-i Naw* (Shahrīvar—Mihr 1345/September—October 1966): 15–32.

1966 (1345) "Shawhar-i Āmrīkā'ī" ("The American Husband"). *Jahān-i Naw* (Ābān—Bahman 1345/November 1966—January 1967): 3–11.

1967 (1345) "Rawshanfikr Khudī Ast yā Bī gānah?" ("Is the Intellectual a Native or an Alien?"). *Jahān-i Naw* (Ābān–Bahman 1345/1967): 89–111.

1968 (1346) "Guldastah'hā va Falak" ("The Minarets and the Sky"). *Ārash* 3:1 (Bahman 1346/1968): 9–19.

1968 (1346) "Sulūkī dar Harj u Marj" ("Random Notes"). *Ārash* 3:2 (Isfand 1346/1968): 94–106.

1968 (1347) "Bih Rāh-i Gūdū" ("On the Path of Godot"). *Ārash* 3:3 (Farvardin 1347/1968): 14–15.

1968 (1347) "Ṣamad va Afsānah-'i 'Avām" ("Ṣamad [Bihrangi] and the Folk Tale"). *Ārash* 3:5 (Āẕar 1347/1968): 5–12.

1968 (1347) "Guẕarī bih Ḥāshīyah-'i Kavīr" ("Journey to the Edge of the Kavir Desert"). *'Ulūm-i Ijtimā'ī* 1:1 (Autumn 1348/1968): 98–108. Reprinted in *Nigīn* 7:78 (Ābān 1350/1971): 19–20. A sequel [written in 1958] to his "Safarī bih Shahr-i Bādgīr'hā: Dār al-'Ibādah-'i Yazd."

1968 (1347) "Yādbūd-i Nīmā" ("In Memory of Nīmā"). *Ārash* 5:2 (Urdībihisht, 1360/1981): 136–142. The transcript of an Āl

Aḥmad speech given at the Tehran University College of Fine Arts on Jan. 31, 1968.

1969 (1348) "Masalan Sharḥ-i Aḥvālāt" ("An Autobiography of Sorts"). *Jahān-i Naw* 24:3 (1348/1969): 4–8.

1969 (1348) "Ḥarf'hā-yi Jalāl" ("Jalāl's Words"). *Firdawsī* 954 (1 Farvardīn 1349/1970): 10, 110.

1969 (1348) "Ḥarf'hā'ī az Ān Zindah Yād" ("May His Words Live On"). *Firdawsī* 1129 (10 Sep. 1973): 19–20. Selected quotes from Āl Aḥmad.

B. Books

1946 (1324) *Dīd va Bāzdīd* (*An Exchange of Visits*). Tihrān. Reissued (Tihrān: Amīr Kabīr, 1956/1334), bound with *Haft Maqālah.* A collection of 12 short stories.

1. "Dīd va Bāzdīd-i 'Īd" ("A Holiday Exchange of Visits").
2. "Ganj" ("The Treasure").
3. "Ziyārat" ("The Pilgrimage").
4. "Ifṭār-i Bīmawqi'" ("An Untimely Breaking of the Fast").
5. "Guldān-i Chīnī" ("The China Flowerpot").
6. "Tābūt" ("The Coffin").
7. "Sham'-i Qaddī" ("The Giant Candle").
8. "Tajhīz-i Millat" ("The Mobilization of a Nation").
9. "Pust'chī" ("The Postman").
10. "Ma'rikah" ("Uproar").
11. "Ay Lā Mas, sabā!" ("Oh Heathens!").
12. "Daw Murdah" ("Two Corpses").

1947 (1326) *Az Ranjī kih Mībarīm* (*Our Suffering*). Tihrān, 78 pp. Reprinted (Tihrān: Amīr Kabīr, 1978/1357). A collection of 7 short stories.

1. "Darrah-'i Khazān'zadah" ("A Valley in Autumn").
2. "Zīrābī'hā" ("The Miners").
3. "Dar Rāh-i Chāplūsī" ("On the Way of Flattery").
4. "Muḥīṭ-i Tang" ("A Tight Spot").
5. "I'tirāf" ("Confession").
6. "Ābirū-yi az Dast Raftah" ("The Lost Reputation").
7. "Rūz'hā-yi Khush" ("Happy Days").

1949 (1327) *Sih'tār* (*The Seh'tar*), Tihrān: Ravāq, 132 pp. Reissued (Tihrān: Amīr Kabīr, 1971/1349, and Tihrān: Shirkat-i Sahāmī, 1978), both with 200 pp. A collection of 13 short stories.

1. "Sih'tār" ("The Seh'tar").
2. "Bachchah-'i Mardum" ("Someone Else's Child").
3. "Vasvās" ("Evil Ideas").
4. "Lāk-i Sūratī" ("Pink Nailpolish").
5. "Vidā'" ("Farewell").
6. "Zindagī kih Gurīkht" ("The Life that Fled").
7. "Āftāb Lab-i Bām" ("The Sun Setting Behind the Roof").
8. "Gunāh" ("Sin").
9. "Nazdīk-i Marzūn'ābād" ("Near Marzun'abad").
10. "Dahan'kajī" ("Making Faces").
11. "Ārizū-yi Qudrat" ("Hoping for Power").
12. "Ikhtilāf-i Ḥisāb" ("Differing Accounts").
13. "Al-Gamārik va al-Makūs" ("Customs and Excise").

1952 (1331) *Zan-i Zīyādī* (*The Unwanted Woman*). Tihrān: 'Isá Ismā'īl Zādah, 1952/1331. Reissued (Tihrān: Maṭbū'ātī-yi Jāvīd, 1964/1342), 159 pp. (Tihrān: Intishārāt-i Tūs, 1970/1349), and (Tihrān: Intishārāt-i Ravāq, 1978/1356), 201 pp. A collection of 9 short stories.

1. Introduction by Parvīz Nātil Khānlarī (included only in first edition).
2. "Risālah-'i Pawlūs-i Rasūl bih Kātibān" ("The Apostle Paul's Letter to the Scribes," a translation of one of the apocryphal epistles of the apostle Paul [not included in 1st ed.]). Reissued separately, *Ārash*, 5:1 (Isfand, 1359/1981), 1–6.
3. "Samanū'pazān" ("The *Samanū* Makers" [not included in 1st ed.]).
4. "Khānum-i Nuzhat al-Dawlah" ("Madame Nuzhat al-Dawlah" [not included in 1st ed.]).
5. "Daftarchah-'i Bīmah" ("The Insurance Policy").
6. "'Akkās-i Bā'ma'rifat" ("The Discrete Photographer").
7. "Khudādād Khān" ("Khodadad Khan").
8. "Duzd'zadah" ("Stolen").
9. "Jā Pā" ("The Footprint").
10. "Maslūl" ("The Consumptive").
11. "Zan-i Ziyādī" ("The Unwanted Woman").

1954 (1333) *Awrāzān: Vaz'-i Maḥall, Ādāb va Rusūm, Fulklūr, Lahjah* (*Awrazan: Topography, Customs and Manners, Folklore, Dialect*). Tihrān: Dānish, 63 pp. Reissued (Tihrān: Māzyār, 1973/1352, and Tihrān: Ravāq, 1978/1357), both 98 pp. An ethno-linguistic study of the village of Awrazan, with illustrations and maps.

1954 (1333) *Sarguzasht-i Kandū'hā* (*Tale of the Beehives*). [Tehran]: [s.n.], 98 pp. Reissued (Tihrān: Jāvīdān, 1977/1356). Reissued (Mashhad: Ravāq, 1971/1350), with 88 pp. Reissued ([Tehran]: Ravāq, [1978]), with 78 pp.

1956 (1334) *Haft Maqālah* (*Seven Articles*). Tihrān: Amīr Kabīr, 144 p, bound with *Dīd va Bāzdīd*. Reissued (Tihrān: Ravāq, 1978/1357), as a separate volume with 165 pp. A collection of 7 articles.

1. "Hidāyat-i *Būf-i Kūr*" ("The Hedayat of *The Blind Owl*").
2. "Mushkil-i Nīmā Yushīj" ("The Problem of Nima Yushij").
3. "Darbārah-'i 'Ādin'" ("Concerning 'Auden'," a discussion of the work of the poet W.H. Auden).
4. "Safarnāmah'ī Az Yūnān-i Imrūz" ("A Travelogue of Greece Today").
5. "Dar Zindān'hā-yi Rākifilir" ("In Rockefeller's Prisons," a translated selection from *The Autobiography of Mother Jones*, by Mary Harris Jones).
6. "Salmānī Zanash-rā Kusht" ("The Barber Killed His Wife," translation of the short story "Le coiffeur a tué sa femme," by Albert Cossery).
7. "'Arūs va Dāmād-i Burj-i Īfil" ("The Eiffel Tower Newlyweds," translation of the one-act play *Les mariés de la Tour Eiffel*, by Jean Cocteau).

1958 (1337) *Mudīr-i Madrasah* (*The School Principal*). [Tehran]: [s.n.]. Reissued ([Tehran]: Kitāb'hā-yi Parastū, 1966), with 170 pp. Reissued ([Tehran]: Amīr Kabīr, 1350/1971), with 134 pp.

1958 (1337) *Sih Maqālah-'i Dīgar* (*Three More Articles*). [s.l.] : [s.n]. Revised, 1963. Reprinted (Tihrān: Ravāq, 1977), 109 pp. A collection of 3 articles with an introduction.

1. Muqaddamah: "Faryādī az Sar-i Chāh" (Introduction: "A Cry from the Well").
2. "Varshikastigī-yi Maṭbū'āt" ("The Bankruptcy of the Press").
3. "Chand Nuktah Darbārah-'i Khaṭṭ va Zabān-i Fārsī" ("A Few Points Concerning the Persian Language and Script").
4. "Bilbishū-yi Kitāb'hā-yi Darsī" ("The Confusion in Textbooks").

1958 (1337) *Tātnishīn'hā-yi Bulūk-i Zahrā* (*The Tati Speakers of Boluk-e Zahrā*). Tihrān: Dānish, 177 pp. Reissued (Tihrān: Amīr Kabīr, 1973/1352), 178 pp. An ethno-linguistic study of two villages near Qazvin, illustrated with photographs and drawings.

1958 (1337) *Varshikastigī-yi Maṭbū'āt* (*The Bankruptcy of the Press*). [Tehran]: 'Ilm va Zindagī, 1337/1958, 20 pp.

1960 (1339) *Durr-i Yatīm-i Khalīj: Jazirah-'i Khārg* (*Orphan Pearl of the Persian Gulf: Kharg Island*). Tihrān: Dānish, 160 pp. Reissued (Tihrān: Amīr Kabīr, 1974), 181 pp. An ethno-linguistic study of the people of Kharg Island, illustrated with photos, diagrams, and maps.

1961 (1340) *Nūn va al-Qalam* (*The Letter "N" and the Pen*). Tihrān: [s.n.]. Reissued (Tihrān: Ravāq, 1978), with 232 pp.

1962 (1341) *Gharbzadigī: Maqālah* (*Weststruckness: An Essay*). Tihrān: [s.n.], 116 pp. Revised 1964, with limited distribution. Reprinted (Tihrān: Ravāq, 1977), 227 pp.

1964 (1343), and 1968 (1356) *Yak Chāh va Daw Chālah va Masalan Sharḥ-i Aḥvālāt: Risālah* (*One Well and Two Pits and An Autobiography of Sorts: A Pamphlet*). Tihrān: Intishārāt-i Ravāq, 54 pp., [1978?].

1965 (1344) *Arzyābī-yi Shitābzadah* (*A Hasty Assessment*). Tabrīz: Ibn Sīnā, 253 pp. Reprinted (Tihrān: Ravāq, 1977), with 310 pp. A collection of 18 articles.

1. (Introduction) "Sirkah-'i Naqd yā Ḥalvā-yi Tārīkh?" ("The Bitterness of Life, or the Sweetness of History?")
2. "Muqaddamah'ī kih dar Khur-i Shā'ir-i Buland Nabūd" ("An Introduction That Was Not Worthy of a Great Poet," a highly critical reaction to Parviz Natil Khanlari's introduction to the first edition of Āl Aḥmad's *Zan-i Ziyādī*).
3. "Kitābī dar Sīyāsat va Daftar-i Shi'rī dar Zamm" ("A Book on Politics and A Book of Poetry," A comparative review of Tibor Mende's *reflexions sur l'histoire d'aujourd'hui, entre la peur et l'espoir*, and the poetry collection *Ākhar-i Shāhnāmah* by M. Umīd [Mahdī Ikhavān Sālis]).
4. "Nīmā Dīgar Shi'r Nakhāhad Guft" ("Nima Will No Longer Write Poetry," written in memory of Nima Yushij).
5. "Pīr-Mard Chashm-i Mā Būd" ("The Old Man Was Our Eyes," written in memory of Nima Yushij).
6. "Chand Nuktah Darbārah-i Mushakhkhaṣāt-i Kullī-yi Adabīyāt-i Mu'āṣir" ("Several Points Concerning the General Characteristics of Contemporary Literature").
7. "Yak Guftugū-yi Dirāz" ("A Long Talk").
8. "Dāstāyivskī va Nīhilīsm va 'Āqibatash" ("Dostoevski and Nihilism, and its Outcome").
9. "Yāddāsht Darbārah-'i Namāyish-i *Guldān*" ("A Note on the Play *The Flowerpot*" [by Bahman Fursī]).
10. "Sitāyish-i Khujastah az Daryā va Nifrīnash bih Āhan" ("Khujastah's Praise for the Sea and Her Curses Upon Iron," review of the plays *Sitāyish-i Daryā* and *Āhan* by Khujastah Kīyā).
11. "Vīnchinzū Bīyānkīnī—Ṭabīb va Naqqāsh" ("Vincent Biancini, Physician and Painter").
12. "Bih Muḥaṣṣiṣ va Barā-yi Dīvār" ("To Mohasses, and for the Wall").

13. "Safarī Bih Shahr-i Bādgīr'hā" ("A Journey to the City of Windmills [Yazd]").
14. "Guzārish-i Haftumīn Kungrah-'i Mardumshināsī" ("Report of the Seventh Anthropology Conference").
15. "Nigāhī bih 'Ṭarz-i 'Amal-i Mazhab dar Īrān'" ("A Look at 'The Function of Religion in Persian Society'"), a critique of Brian Spooner's article on this subject in *Iran: Journal of the British Institute of Persian Studies* Vol. 1, 1963.
16. "Mihrgān dar Mashhad-i Ardihāl" ("Autumn in Mashhad's village of Ardihal").
17. "Mahātmā Gāndī ("Mahatma Gandhi").
18. "Chand Kalimah Bā Mashāṭah'hā" ("A Few Words With the Bride-Dressers").
19. "Muṣāḥabah'ī Kūtāh" ("A Brief Interview").

1966 (1345) *Kārnāmah-'i Sih Sālah: Dah Maqālah* (*Three-year Report: Ten Essays*). Tihrān: Intishārāt-i Ibn-i Sīnā. Reissued (Tihrān: Intishārāt-i Zamān), with 248 pp. Reissued (Tihrān: Ravāq, 1357/1979), with 268 pp.

1. "Khordah Bar'dāsht" ("Narrow Interpretation," an introduction).
2. "Kārnāmah-'i Daw Māhah, 1" ("Two-Month Report, 1").
3. "Ā'īn-i Faṣl" ("The Season's Custom").
4. "Guftugū'ī bā Yak Farangī-yi az Farang bar Gashtah va dar Justujū-yi Zabān-i Balūchī bar Āmadah" ("An Interview with a European Returned from Europe in Search of the Baluchi Language," an interview with the Austrian physician Hans Strasser).
5. "Guzārishī az Khūzistān" ("A Report from Khuzistan").
6. "Kārnāmah-'i Daw Māhah-'i 'Hārvārd'" ("A Two-Month Report from Harvard").
7. "Bīzhan va Manīzhah 'Kunsursīyūm' va Dasātīrash" ("Bizhan and Manizhah and the Consortium, and Its Orders").
8. "Kārnāmah-'i Daw Māhah, 2" ("Two-Month Report, 2").
9. "Sulūkī dar Harj ū Marj" ("Random Notes").
10. "Guftugū'ī Dirāz bā Dānishjūyān-i Tabrīz" ("A Long Talk with the Students of Tabriz," revised and edited transcript of a question and answer session before the Tabriz University Student Art Organization held April 4, 1967. Respondents were Āl Aḥmad, Tabrīz poet Maftūn Amīnī, and Ghulām Húsayn Sā'idī).
10. "Guzarī bih Ḥāshīyah-'i Kavīr" ("Journey to the Edge of the Kavir Desert," A sequel [written in 1958] to his "Safarī bih Shahr-i Bādgīr'hā: Dār al-'Ibādah-'i Yazd").

1966 (1345) *Khasī dar Mīqāt* (*Lost in the Crowd*). Tihrān: Intishārāt-i Nīl, 181 pp. Reissued (Tihrān: Ravāq, 1357/1978), with 180 pp.

1967 (1346) *Isrā'īl: 'Āmil-i Impiriyālism* (*Israel, Agent of Imperialism*). First published in *Jung*, [Tehran]: 1346/1967. Second edition, [Tehran]: Kārvān, 1357 [1978], 32 pp.

1967 (1346) *Nifrīn-i Zamīn* (*The Cursing of the Earth*). [Tehran]: Intishārāt-i Nīl, 293 pp. Reissued (Tihrān: Ravāq, 1978), with 308 pages.

1968 (1347) *Dar Khidmat va Khiyānat-i Rawshanfikrān: Maqālah* (*On the Service and Disservice of Intellectuals: An Essay*). Tihrān: [s.n.], 432 pp. Reissued with additions ([Tehran]: Intishārāt-i Khavarizmī, 1978/1357), 2 v. This is the most complete edition presently available. It contains all the additions published in the 1978 Ravaq supplement (listed below), and the following:

1. "Zamīmah-'i Chahārum: Taṣṣavur-i 'Nukhbah-'i Ḥaqīqī' dar 'Ilm-i Ijtimā' va Tārīkh" ("Fourth Supplement: The 'True Essence' of Sociology and History," a translation of an article by Louis Masignon).
2. "Istidrāk" ("Sources").

Dar Khidmat va Khiyānat-i Rawshanfikrān: Ākharīn Zamāyim (*On the Service and Disservice of Intellectuals: Final Supplements*), a booklet containing portions left out of the 1964 edition, subtitled *Raf'-i Ishkāl-i Fannī va bā I'tiẕār* (*Correction of Technical Problems, and with Apologies*); (Tihrān: Intishārāt-i Ravāq, 1978/1357), 78 pp. Supplement includes:

1. The previously unpublished conclusion of the original edition's chapter 4.
2. "Ay Jalāl al-Dawlah," an extract from Mirzā Āqā Khān Kirmānī's *Sih Maktūb*.
3. The text of a speech by Ayatollah Khomeini on November 4, 1964.
4. "Siyāsat-i Āmrikā dar Īrān az Jang-i Jahānī-yi Duvvum bih Īn Sū" ("American Policy in Iran Since the Second World War," a translation of a talk given by T. Cuyler Young at a Harvard University seminar, attended by the author, on the contemporary problems of Iran, 17 April, 1965).
5. "Iḥsān Ṭabarī: Guftugū bā Yak Rawshanfikr-i Ma'yūs" ("Ihsan Tabari: Interview with a Disillusioned Intellectual").

1969 (1348) *Panj Dāstān* (*Five Stories*). [s.l.]: [s.n.], 96 pp. Reissued (Tihrān: Ravāq, 1976), with 87 pp. A collection of 5 stories prefaced with a brief autobiographical sketch.

1. "Maṯalan Sharḥ-i Aḥvālāt" ("An Autobiography of Sorts," not included in Ravāq edition).
2. "Guldastah'hā va Falak" ("The Minarets and the Sky").
3. "Jashn-i Farkhundah" ("The Joyous Celebration").

4. "Khāharam va 'Ankabūt" ("My Sister and the Spider").
5. "Shawhar-i Āmrīkā'ī" ("The American Husband").
6. "Khūnābah-'i Anār" ("The Blood of a Pomegranate").

1969 (1348) *Sangī bar Gūrī* (*A Stone on a Grave*). Tihrān: Intishārāt-i Ravāq, 1981/1360.

1969 (1348) *Nasl-i Jadīd* (*The New Generation*). An unpublished collection of short stories.

1969 (1348) *Nāmah'hā* (*Letters*). [s.l.] : Intishārāt-i Sīyāhkal, [s.d.]. Al Aḥmad's collected correspondence, with an introduction by 'Alī Aṣghar Ḥāj Sayyid Javādī.

C. Translations by Āl Aḥmad

Anonymous. *Chihil Ṭūṭī* (*Forty Parrots*). Tehran: Intishārāt-i Mawj, 1972/1351. A modern popularization (done with Sīmīn Dānishvar) of the medieval *Ṭūṭī Nāmah*, a work originally translated into Persian in 1330 from the Sanskrit *Çukasapatī* by Shaykh Zīyā' al-Dīn Nakhshabī.

Camus, Albert. *Bigānah* (*The Stranger*). [Tehran]: 1949/1328. A translation of the novel *L'Étranger*, done with Aṣghar Khibrahzādah.

————————. *Sū'-i Tafāhum* (*The Misunderstanding*). [Tehran]: 1950/1329. A translation of the three-act play *Le Malentendu.*

Cau, Jean. "Safar Nāmah'ī az Yūnān-i Imrūz" ("A Travelogue from Today's Greece"). *'Ilm va Zindagī*, 1:5 (Urdībihisht 1331/1952), 401-411. A translation of "Notes sur un voyage en Gréce." *Les Temps Modernes* 76 (Feb 1952): 1409–1428.

Cossery, Albert. "Salmānī Zanash-rā Kusht" ("The Barber Killed His Wife"). Published in *Haft Maqālah.* Tihrān: Amīr Kabīr, 1956/1334: 241–266. A translation of the short story "Le coiffeur a tué sa femme."

Cocteau, Jean. "'Arūs va Dāmād-i Burj-i Īfil" ("The Eiffel Tower Newlyweds"). First published in *Andīshah va Hunar* 1:4 (Tīr 1333/1954): 211–223, republished in *Haft Maqālah.* Tihrān: Amīr Kabīr, 1956/1334, 267–291. A translation of the one-act play "Les Mariés de la Tour Eiffel."

Diakonov, Michel. "Taḥqīq-i Zabān-i Fārsī dar Shuravī" ("Persian Language Research in the Soviet Union"). *Sukhan* 2:8 (Shahrīvar 1324/1945): 599–603. From an unidentified article in French.

Dostoevsky, Fyodor. *Qumārbāz* (*The Gambler*). [Tehran]: 1948/1327

Gide, André, 1869–1951. *Bāzgasht az Shuravī, bih Zamīmah-'i Tanqīḥ-i Bāzgasht az Shuravī* (*Return from Russia, and Return from Russia Revisited*). Tihrān: 'Ilm va Zindagī, 1954/1333, 140 pp. Second edition, [Tehran]: [s.n.], [1979?], 153 pp. A translation of *Retour de l'U.R.S.S., suivi de Retouches a mon retour de l'U.R.S.S.*.

————. *Mā'idah'hā-yi Zamīnī* (*The Fruits of the Earth*). [Tehran]: 1955/1334. A translation of *Les nourritures terrestres*, done with Parvīz Dāryūsh.

Ionesco, Eugene. *Kargidan* (*The Rhinocerous*). [Tehran]: 1966/1345. A translation of the three-act play *Le rhinocéros.*

————. *Tishnigī va Gurusnigī* (*Thirst and Hunger*). [Tehran]: 1972/1351. A translation of the three-act play *La soif et la faim*, done with Manuchihr Hizārkhānī.

Jones, Mary (Harris) 1830–1930. "Dar Zindān'hā-yi Rukifilir" ("In Rockefeller's Prisons"). *'Ilm va Zindagī* 1:1 (Day 1330/1951). A translation of "Dans les Prisons de Rockefeller," an extract translated by Colette Audrey and Marina Stalio from *The Autobiography of Mother Jones*, as published in *Les Temps Modernes* 69 (July, 1951): 136-141.

Jünger, Ernst. "'Ubūr az Khaṭṭ" ("Crossing the Line"). A translation of the essay "Uber die Linie," done with Maḥmūd Hūman.

Sartre, Jean Paul. *Dast-hā-yi Ālūdah* (*Dirty Hands*). [Tehran]: 'Ilm va Zindagī, 1952/1331. A translation of the seven-act play *Les mains sales.*

Tomiche, F.J. "Naẓarī bih Ta's̱īrāt-i Tilivīzīyūn dar Ingilistān" ("A Look at the Effects of Television in England"). *'Ilm va Zindagī* 7 (1339/1960): 16–28.

D. English Translations of Āl Aḥmad's Work

Āl Aḥmad, Jalāl. *Gharbzadegi [Weststruckness]*, translated by John Green and Ahmad Alizadeh. Lexington, Kentucky: Mazda Publishers, 1982.

———. "The Hedāyat of *The Blind Owl*" ("Hidāyāt-i *Būf-i Kūr*"), trans. by Ali A. Eftekhary in *Hedāyat's "The Blind Owl" Forty Years After.* Austin, Texas: Center for Middle Eastern Studies, The University of Texas at Austin, 1978, 27–42.

———. *Iranian Society: An Anthology of Writings by Jalāl Āl-e Ahmad*, ed. by Michael C. Hillmann. Lexington, Kentucky: Mazda Publishers, 1982. Sixteen selections with a preface and notes by the editor.

1. "An Autobiography of Sorts" ("Maṯalan Sharḥ-i Aḥvālāt"), trans. by Michael C. Hillmann.
2. "My Sister and the Spider" ("Khāharam va Ankabūt"), trans. by A. Reza Navabpour and Robert Wells.
3. "The Pilgrimage" ("Zīyārat"), trans. by D.G. Law, first published in *Life and Letters*, 63:148 (December, 1949), 202–209. Republished in expanded form in this volume.
4. "The China Flowerpot" ("Guldān-i Chīnī"), trans. by Michael C. Hillmann. First published in the introduction to *The School Principal.*
5. "The Untimely Breaking of the Fast" ("Iftār-i Bī mawqi'"), translated by Carter Bryant.
6. "Seh'tar" ("Sih'tār"), translated by Terence Odlin.
7. "The Sin" ("Gunāh"), translated by Raymond Cowart.
8. "The Unwanted Woman" ("Zan-i Zīyādī"), translated by Leonard Bogle.
9. "A Principal's First Day in School" (excerpted from the novel *Mudīr-i Madrasah*), translated by Karim Emami. First published in the article "Crisis in Education: *The School Principal*," in *Kayhan International*, October 19, 1984. Revised version published in this volume.
10. "The General Characteristics of Contemporary Literature" ("Chand Nuktah darbārah-'i Mushakhkhaṣāt-i Kullī-yi Adabīyāt-i Mu'āṣir"), translated by Peter Dutz.
11. "The Old Man Was Our Eyes" ("Pīr-Mard Chashm-i Mā Būd"), trans. by Thomas M. Ricks. First published in *Literary Review*, 18:1 (Fall, 1974), 115–128, reprinted in slightly revised form here.
12. "The Tale of the Shepherd Vizier" (The combined "Pīsh dar Āmad" [Prelude] and "Pas Dastak" [Epilogue] from the novel *Nūn va al-Qalam*), translated by Mohammad R. Ghanoonparvar.

13. "Iranian Education and the University" ("Farhang va Dānishgāh chah Mīkunand?"; the ninth chapter of the essay *Gharbzadigī*), translated by Michael C. Hillmann. First published as a part of the introduction to *The School Principal*, republished in *Literature East and West*, 20 (1976) as "What are the University and Education Doing," published here in revised form.
14. "First Day in Mecca" (an excerpt from the travelogue *Khasī dar Mīqāt* [*Lost in the Crowd*]), translated by John Green and Ahmad Alizadeh.
15. "Samad and the Folk Legend" ("Ṣamad va Afsānah-'i 'Avām"), translated by Leonardo P. Alishan.
16. "Epilogue" (the concluding chapter of *Gharbzadigī*), translated by Michael C. Hillmann.

———. "The Joyous Celebration" ("Jashn-i Farkhundah"), in *Modern Persian Short Stories*, edited and translated by Minoo Southgate, 19–33. Washington, D.C.: Three Continents Press, 1980.

———. "The Mobilization of Iran" ("Tajhīz-i Millat"), translated by David C. Champagne. *Literature East and West* 20 (1976): 61–70.

———. "Pink Nailpolish" ("Lāk-i Sūratī"), translated by A. Reza Navabpour and Robert Wells. *Iranian Studies* 15 (1982): 81–96.

———. *Occidentosis: A Plague from the West*, translated by R. Campbell; edited by Hamid Algar. Berkeley, California: Mizan Press, 1984.

———. *Owrazan: Iranian Village*. (*Āwrāzān: Vaz'-i Maḥall, Ādāb va Rusūm, Fulklūr, Lahjah*), trans. by I.V. Pourhadi. Tehran: 1955.

———. *Plagued by the West* (*Gharbzadigī*), translated by Paul Sprachman. Delmar, New York: Caravan Books, 1982.

———. *The School Principal* (*Mudīr-i Madrasah*), trans. by John K. Newton, with an introduction and notes by Michael C. Hillmann. Minneapolis, Minn.: Bibliotheca Islamica, 1974.

———. "Someone Else's Child" ("Bachchah-'i Mardum"), trans. by T. Gochenour. *Iranian Studies*, 1 (1968): 155–162.

II. Criticism in Western Languages

Dast'ghayb, 'Abd al-'Alī. "Jalāl Āl-e Ahmad: His Absence Has Been a Great Loss." In *Critical Perspectives on Modern Persian Literature*, edited and compiled by Thomas Ricks, 343-45. Washington, D.C.: Three Continents Press, 1984. A translation of his "Ghaybat-i Jalāl Chah Zāyi'ah'hā Kih bih Bār Nayāvard." *Firdawsi* 1079 (13 Shahrīvar 1351/1972): 17.

Ghanoonparvar, Mohammad R. "Jalāl Āl-e Ahmad's *The Cursing of the Land*: A Plot Summary." *Literature East and West* 20 (1976): 240–244.

Hanson, Brad. "The 'Westoxication' of Iran: Depictions and Reactions of Behrangi, Āl-e Ahmad, and Shari'ati." *International Journal of Middle East Studies* 15 (1983): 1–23.

Hillmann, Michael C. "Āl-e Ahmad's Fictional Legacy," *Iranian Studies* 9 (1976): 248–265. Revision reprinted in *Critical Perspectives on Modern Persian Literature*, edited and compiled by Thomas Ricks, 331–42. Washington, D.C.: Three Continents Press, 1984.

————. "The Modernist Trend in Persian Literature and its Social Impact." *Iranian Studies* 15 (1982): 7–30.

————. "Persian Prose Fiction: An Iranian Mirror and Conscience." In *Highlights of Persian Literature*, ed. Ehsan Yar-Shater. New York: Persian Heritage, 1984.

————. "Revolution, Islam, and Contemporary Persian Literature." In *Iran: Essays on a Revolution in the Making*, ed. by Ahmad Jabbari and Robert Olson. Lexington, Kentucky: Mazda Publishers, 1981: 121–142.

Jazayery, M.A. "Recent Persian Literature. Observations on Themes and Tendencies." *Review of National Literatures* 2:1 (1971): 11–28. Reprinted in *Critical Perspectives on Modern Persian Literature*, edited and compiled by Thomas Ricks, 70–87. Washington, D.C.: Three Continents Press, 1984.

————. "Review of *Modern Persian Prose Literature*." *Literature East and West* 11:2 (1967): 187–191.

Kamshad, Hassan. *Modern Persian Prose Literature*. Cambridge: Cambridge University Press, 1966.

Machalski, Franciszek. "Principaux courants de la prose persane contemporaine." *Rocznik Orientalistyczny* 25:2 (1961): 121–130.

———————. "Principaux genres et espèces de la prose persane contemporaine." *25th International Congress of Orientalists*, Moscow, 1960, v. 2 (1963): 278–280.

Monnet, G.J. "Jalāl Āl-e Ahmad, ecrivain iranien d'aujourd'hui," *Melanges de l'institut dominicain d'études orientales du Caire* 9 (1967): 221–225.

Sabri-Tabrizi, G.R. "Human Values in the Works of Two Persian Writers," *Correspondence d'Orient: Actes* 11 (1970): 411–418.

Tikku, Girdhari L. "Some Socio-religious Themes in Modern Persian Fiction," in *Islam and its Cultural Divergence*. Urbana: University of Illinois, 1971: 165–179.

de Vries, Gert J.J. "Al-i Ahmad." *Encyclopedia of Islam: New Edition Supplement* (1980): 60–61.

Yar-Shater, Ehsan. "The Modern Literary Idiom," *Iran Faces the Seventies*. New York: Praeger, 1971: 284–320. Reprinted in *Critical Perspectives on Modern Persian Literature*, edited and compiled by Thomas Ricks, 42–62. Washington, D.C.: Three Continents Press, 1984.

Zavarzadeh, Mas'ud. "The Persian Short Story Since the Second World War: An Overview." *The Muslim World* 58 (1968): 308–316. Reprinted in *Critical Perspectives on Modern Persian Literature*, edited and compiled by Thomas Ricks, 147–55. Washington, D.C.: Three Continents Press, 1984.

III. Criticism and Sources in Persian

Adamiyat, Fereydoun. *Āshuftigī dar Fikr-i Tārīkhī* . Tihrān: [s.n.], 1981. 22 pp.

Afshār, Iraj. "Sawg-i Āl-i Aḥmad." *Rāhnimā-yi Kitāb* 12 (1969/70): 331–335.

Afshīn. "Gharbzadigī yā 'Arabzadigī?" *Firdawsī* 787 (3 Ābān 1345/1966): 12–18. Sequel in *Firdawsī* 788 (10 Ābān 1345/1966): 6–8.

Āl Aḥmad, Shams. "Dast-i Sabuk va Dast-i Sangīn." *Firdawsī* 1148 (1 Bahman 1974/1353): 18–19.

"Āsār-i Jalāl." *Firdawsī* 957 (24 Farvardīn 1349/1971): 220.

"Āsār-i Jalāl Āl Aḥmad." *Firdawsī* 931 (14 Mihr 1348/1969): 26.

Āzād, M. "Pas az Hidāyat Dāstān Nivīsī-yi Mā bih Kujā Raft va Kujā Mānd?" *Firdawsī* 863 (20 Khurdād 1347/1968): 30–32.

Āzād Tihrānī, Maḥmūd. "Dāstān-i Buland va Kūtāh dar īn Sarzamīn." *Ārash* (Winter 1344/1966): 144.

Baraheni, Reza, 1935–. *Qiṣṣah'navīsī.* Tihrān: Ashrafī, 1969.

Bihnām, Jamshīd. (Review of *Tātnishīn'hā-yi Bulūk-i Zahrā*). *Rāhnamā-yi Kitāb* (Shahrīvar 1338/1959): 209–12.

Dānishvar, Sīmīn. *Ghurūb-i Jalāl.* Tihrān: Ravāq, 1981.

Dast'ghayb, 'Abd al-'Alī. "Darbārah-'i Nūn va al-Qalam, Qiṣṣah-i Jalāl Āl Aḥmad, 1340." *Firdawsī* 722 (22 Tīr 1344/1965): 8, 14, 16.

————. "Ghaybat-i Jalāl Chaḥ Zāyi'ah'hā Kih bih Bār Nayāvard." *Firdawsī* 1079 (13 Shahrīvar 1351/1972): 17.

Hillmann, Michael. "Jalāl Āl-i Aḥmad az Dīd-i Yak Gharbī." *Daw Haftigī-yi Kākh-i Javānān* 7 (1973/74): 14–15, 16–17.

Ibrāhīmī, Nādir. "Bāzdīd-i Qiṣṣah'hā-yi Imrūz." *Payām-i Nuvīn* 8 and 9 (1966/67 and 1967/68).

Jahāni, Mihrzād, ed. *Mi'ād bā Jalāl.* Tihrān: Mihrzād Jahānī, 1362/1981. A collection of 22 articles.

1. Mihrzād Jahānī, "Sarsukhan."
2. Jalāl Āl Aḥmad, "Salām-i Yak Lur-i Shahrī."
3. Mahdi Ikhavān Ṣāliṣ, "Dar Risā-yi Ān Zindah Yād."
4. Shams Āl-i Aḥmad, "Az Chashm-i Barādar."
5. ————, "Dar Marg-i Jalāl."
6. Sīmīn Dānishvar, "Jalāl az Dīdgāh-i Sīmīn Dānishvar."
7. Ḥusayn Za'farānī, "Dar Sitāyish va Sawg-i Jalāl Āl Aḥmad."
8. ————, "Chakidah'ī Pur'mafhūm az Faryād-i Qalam-i Jalāl."
9. Mihrzād Jahānī, "Bashārat-i Rūz."
10. 'Alī Aṣghar Khibrah'zādah, "Jalāl az Dīdgāh-i 'Alī Aṣghar Khibrah'zādah."
11. M. Ḥ. Nawmīd, "Bā Mā az 'Ishq Bigū."
12. ————, "Jalāl va Zamānah'ash."
13. Engineer Tavakulli, "Jalāl az Dīdgāh-i Muhandis Tavakullī ."
14. Mihrzād Jahānī, "Jalāl, Jalāl Ast."
15. Ḥ. K. Nawmīd, "Akhlāqiyat-i Khāṣ-i Rawshanfikr-i Hunarmand."
16. ————, "Jalāl, Rawshanfikrī-yi Shab Sitīz."
17. 'Abbās Baḥrī (Gīlak), "Sharm Nigāh."
18. ————, "Jalāl az Dīdgāh-i Duktur Sharī'atī."
19. Muṣṭafá Zamānī'nīyā, "Tarāsh-i Risālah-'i Rawshanfikrān."

20. Āyat Allāh [Sayyid Maḥmūd] Ṭāliqānī, "Jalāl-i Rawshanfikr-i Ṣādīq va Ḥaqīqat Ṭalab."
21. Reza Baraheni, "Taṣvīr-i Jalāl."
22. ——————, "Jalāl az Dīdgāh-i Duktur Rizā Barāhinī."

"Jalāl va Ṣamad: Daw Usṭūrah" *Iran Express* 2:18 (Urdībihisht 1357/1979): 8, 14.

Jamālzādah, Muḥammad 'Alī. (Review of *Mudīr-i Madrasah*). *Rāhnamā-yi Kitāb* (Summer 1337/1958): 168–174.

Kasmā'ī, 'Alī Akbar. *Navīsandigān-i Pīshgām dar Dāstān'navīsī-'i Imrūz-i Īrān.* Tihrān: Shirkat-i Mu'alifān va Mutarjimān-i Īrān, 1363/1984. See especially his chapter on Āl Aḥmad, pp. 113–134.

——————. "Yak Chihrah-'i 'Iṣyān Zadah." *Firdawsī* 816 (16 Khurdād 1346/1977): 9–10.

Khabīrī, Farāmarz. "Dar Iqlīm-i Nasr-i Jalāl Āl Aḥmad." *Andīshah va Hunar* 5:4 (1964): 409–419.

Khu'ī, Ismā'īl. "Dar Chashm'andāz-i Najābat va Sharaf." *Firdawsī* 1079 (13 Shahrīvar 1351/1972): 9.

Kiyānūsh, Maḥmūd. "Āl Aḥmad dar Dāstān'hā-yi Kūtāh'ash." *Andīshah va Hunar* 5, no. 4 (1964): 464–484; reprinted in *Barrasī-yi Shi'r va Nasr-i Fārsī-yi Mu'āṣir.* Tihrān: Mānī, 1972.

Maḥjūb, Muḥammad Ja'far. (Review of *Jazīrah-'i Kharg...*). *Rāhnamā-yi Kitāb* (March, 1961): 733–36.

Mallāḥ, Khusraw. "Sawgī bar Jalāl." *Jahān-i Naw* 26:3 (1348/1969): 1–8.

Mīr Ṣādiqī, Jamāl. *Qiṣṣah, Dāstān-i Kūtāh, Rūmān: Muṭāli'ah'ī dar Shinākht-i Adabīyāt-i Dāstānī va Nigāhī Kūtāh bih Dāstān Nivīsī-'i Mu'āṣir-i Īrān.* Tihrān: Intishārāt-i Āgāh, 1360/1981.

Mirahmadi, Maryam. "Ta'sīr-i Nufūẓ-i Maẕhab dar Āsār-i Jalāl Āl Aḥmad." *Sukhan* 26:10 (Āzār/Day 1357/November/December 1978): 1079.

Mu'minī, Bāqir. *Dard-i ahl-i qalam.* Tihrān: Intishārāt-i Tūkā, 1357/1978.

Nāvak, 'A. "Marāsimī bā Darīgh-i Bisyār az 'Azīzānī kih Nabūdand." *Firdawsī* 1039 (Aban 24 1350/1971): 10–12, 36.

Nuvīn, Farīd. "Kāvushī dar Dunyā-yi Hidāyat va Āl-i Aḥmad." *Nigīn* 83 (Farvardīn 1351/1972): 8–10.

Qābūsī, Farhād. "Sulūkī dar Harj u Marj." *Firdawsī* Special New Year's Issue (1352/1973): 40–43.

Raḥīmī, Muṣṭafá. "Jalāl Dīgar Nakhāhad Nivisht." *Jahān-i Naw* 26:3 (Murdād/Shahrīvar 1348/1969): 9–11.

S., Gh. "Sar Nivisht-i Kandū'hā, Qiṣṣah-i Jalāl Āl Aḥmad." *Andīshah va Hunar* 2:7 (Shahrīvar 1334/1955): 553.

Tabrīzī, Ḥamīd. *Jalāl-i Āl-i Aḥmad, Mardī dar Kishākish-i Tārīkh-i Mu'āṣir.* Tabriz: *Kāvah*, 1357/1978.

Tājūr, Bihrūz. "Bā Yād-i Jalāl." *Firdawsī* 1049 (4 Bahman 1350/1972): 10, 29.

Ṭāhbāz, Sīrūs. "Āl Aḥmad dar Dāstān'hā-yi Kūtāhash." *Andīshah va Hunar* 5:4 (1964): 485–489.

"Vaṣīyat-i Jalāl dar Mawrid-i Tarjumah-i Yak Kitāb." *Firdawsī* 1152 (29 Bahman 1353/1974): 23.

"Vizhah-'i Āl-i Aḥmad." *Andīshah va Hunar* 5:4 (1964): 344–489.

"Vīzhah'nāmah-'i Āl-i Aḥmad." ("Special Āl Āḥmad Issue"). *Iṭṭilā'āt.* Two issues: Esfand 12, 1350/1972, and Shahrīvar 2, 1351/1972.

"Vīzhah'nāmah-i Jalāl Āl Aḥmad." *Javān* 27 (Tir 1358/1979): 35-64.

Vusūqī, Nāṣir. "Tāt'nishīn'hā-yi Bulūk-i Zahrā." *Andīshah va Hunar* 3:5 (Bahman/Isfand 1337/1959): 351.

———. "Az Awrāzān tā Khārk." *Andīshah va Hunar* 5:4 (1964): 420–30.

———. "Jahānbīnī va Paymānash." *Andīshah va Hunar* 5:4 (1964): 431–48.

"Yād-i 'Azīzī kih Dīgar Nīst." *Firdawsī* 978 (16 Shahrīvar 1349/1970): 7.

"Yādnāmah-'i Jalāl." *Ārash* 31 (Shahrīvar 1360/1981): 47–98. Republished in *Hunar va Muqāvimat* 4 [s.l.]:[s.n], [s.d.]: 36, as "Yād Nāmah-'i Jalāl Āl Aḥmad."

"Yādnāmah-'i Jalāl Āl Aḥmad." *Nāmah-'i Kānūn-i Nivīsandigān-i Īrān* 1 (Spring 1358/1979): 223–253.

Yūshīj, Nīmā . "Nāmah-i Nīmā bih Jalāl Āl Aḥmad." *Andīshah va Hunar* 9:2 (Farvardin 1338/1960): 624–627.

Zamānīyā, Muṣṭafá. *Farhang-i Jalāl.* Tihrān: Intishārāt-i Mu'āṣir, 1362/1983. A two-volume compilation of quotable Āl Aḥmad passages, arranged by subject.

IV. Selected Works on the Hajj

Al-Alem, Mustafa. "A Guide to Hajj Rituals." *Muslim World League Monthly Magazine* 3:10 (Dhū al-Ḥijjah A.H. 1385—March–April 1966): 52–58.

Alexander, Grant. "The Story of the Kaba." *The Muslim World* 43 (January 1953): 43–53.

Assad, Muhammad [Leopole Weiss]. *The Road to Mecca.* New York: Simon and Schuster, 1956.

Begam, Shah Jahran. *The Story of a Pilgrimage to Hijaz.* Calcutta: Thacker, Spink and Co., 1909.

Bell, R. "The Origin of the Id al-Adha." *The Muslim World* 13 (February 1933): 117–20.

———. "Muhammad's Pilgrimage Proclamation." *Journal of the Royal Central Asian Society* 24 (April 1937): 223–24.

Burton, Richard F. *Personal Narrative of a Pilgrimage to al-Madinah and Meccah.* 2 vols. London: George Bell and Sons, 1898.

Cobbold, Lady Evelyn. *Pilgrimage to Mecca.* London: John Murray, 1934.

The Haj: A Special Issue. Aramco World Magazine 25:6 (Nov.–Dec. 1974).

Kamal, Ahmad. *The Sacred Journey: Being Pilgrimage to Makkah.* New York: Duell, Sloan and Pearce, 1961.

Khan, Hadji, and Sparroy, Wilfred. *With the Pilgrims to Mecca: The Great Pilgrimage of A.H. 1319; A.D. 1902.* London: John Lane, 1905.

Kirimly, H. "The Oldest Tour in the World: Mecca Pilgrimage." *World Health 20* (August–September 1967): 10–13.

Long, David Edwin. *The Hajj Today: A Survey of the Contemporary Makkah Pilgrimage.* Albany: State University of New York Press, 1979.

Philby, H. St. John B. *A Pilgrim in Arabia.* London: Robert Hale, 1946.

Rutter, Eldon. "The Muslim Pilgrimage." *Geographical Journal* 74:3 (September 1929): 271–73.

———. *The Holy Cities of Arabia.* 2 vols. London: P.G. Putnam's Sons, 1928.

Rutter, Owen. *Triumphant Pilgrimage: An English Muslim's Journey from Sarawak to Mecca.* Philadelphia: J.B. Lippincott Co., 1937.

Sarab ab-Din, A.B. "Pilgrimage to Mecca." *Studies in Comparative Religion* 1:4 (1976): 171–80.

Somogyi, J. "Ibn al-Jauzi's Handbook on the Makkan Pilgrimage." *Journal of the Royal Asiatic Society* 25 (1938): 541–46.

Stanton, H.U.W. and Pickens, Claude Leon. "The Muslim Pilgrimage." *The Muslim World.* 24 (July 1934): 229–35.

Wavell, A.J.B. *A Modern Pilgrim in Mecca.* Constable and Co., 1918.